THE
MOON
DWELLERS

Book One of The

Dwellers Saga

David Estes

For Adele. Just for being you.

Prologue
Adele
7 months ago

Hands grope, men shout, boots slap the rock floor.

Clay dishes and pots are smashed to bits as the Enforcers sweep recklessly through our house. There are more bodies in the tiny stone box that I call home than ever before. The walls seem to be closing in.

My mother's face is stricken with anger, her lips twisted, her eyebrows dark. I've never seen her fight like this. I've never seen her fight at all.

It takes three bulging Enforcers to subdue her kicking legs, her thrashing arms. For just a moment I am scared of her and not the men. I hate myself for it.

I realize my sister is by my side, watching, like me. I can't let her see this—can't let this be her last memory of the ones who raised us. I usher her back into the small room that we share with my parents, and close the door, shutting her inside alone.

When I turn back to the room, my mother is already gone, taken. Undigested beans from our measly supper rise in my throat.

My father is next.

The Enforcers jeer at him, taunt him, spit on him. As he backs his shoulders against the cold, stark, stone wall, five men corner him. Smart. They don't underestimate him.

He makes eye contact with me; his emerald-green eyes are hard with concentration. Despite the inherent tension in the room, his face is relaxed, calm, the exact opposite of his eyes. *Run*, he mouths.

My feet are frozen to the floor. My knees lock, stiffen, disobey me *and* my father. I am ashamed. After all that my father has done for me, when it counts the most, I fail him.

One of the men lifts an arm and a gun. I hold my breath when I hear the shot, a dull *thwap!* that doesn't sound like a normal gun. The man moves backwards slightly from the force, but his legs are planted firmly and he maintains his balance.

Father slumps to the floor. I feel my lips trembling, and my hand moves unbidden to my mouth. My frozen feet melt and I try to run to him, but a big body bars my way. I kick him hard, like my father taught me. My heel catches the Enforcer under his chin and his head snaps back. Like most people, he underestimates me.

The next Enforcer doesn't.

The Taser rips into my neck and tentacles of electricity slam my jaw shut. My teeth nearly snap off my tongue, which is flailing around in my mouth. They don't take it easy on me just because I'm a kid, or a girl—not after what I did to the first guy. Still stunned by the Taser, I barely feel the thump of their hard boots as they kick me repeatedly in the ribs. My eyes are wet, and through my blurred vision I see the arcing nightstick.

Strangely, it feels like destiny, like it was always going to happen.

I hear my sister's screams just before I black out.

Tristan
A brief history of the Tri-Realms

They say the meteor was enormous. Any life left on the surface of the earth when it hit was wiped out by either the shockwave caused by the collision, or the resulting tsunamis unleashed across the world's oceans. Humans were forced to move underground. Or so the story goes.

Secretly, government scientists expected it for years, using covert teams of miners to dig the world's largest caverns in preparation for the inevitable. But still: There wasn't room for everyone. It would've been terrible: the Lottery. Families ripped apart; friends lost; blossoming relationships cut off at the knees. Of course, key individuals, like politicians, doctors, scientists, and farmers received a free pass, but all others just got a number. The number gave them a one in a hundred chance of getting selected to move into the underground facilities.

All the rest were destroyed.

And that was just the United States. No one knows for sure what happened to the rest of the world. Perhaps they weren't so prepared. Perhaps they were all dead.

Year Zero would have been difficult for everyone. Losing relatives who didn't make the cut; eating from the rations of rice and beans and hoping it wouldn't run out before the leaders and their teams of advisors could come up with a way to grow food underground; most people becoming miners; living in darkness.

Now all of that is just a part of everyday life.

These days, time is measured from the day the meteor hit. It's 499 PM (Post-Meteor). Time before Armageddon is referred to as Before-Meteor, or BM. The funny thing about Armageddon: we survived. Well, some of us anyway.

Year Zero's first president was Stafford Hughes. Things were run much like before Armageddon, albeit in a slightly more haphazard manner. The U.S. Constitution was upheld, laws were revised as required for our new living situation, new laws were created.

But it didn't last. It couldn't last.

Things were too different. People were too scared. There was too much chaos.

More structure was required.

The first Nailin was elected to president in 126 PM. His name was Wilfred Nailin. He was my great-great (and a lot more *greats*) grandfather. At that point elections were still held regularly. Congress decided that given the state of America, elections should be held every five years instead of four, with the opportunity for reelection after the first term. But Wilfred wasn't satisfied with ten years in power, so after his first reelection he pushed a new law through Congress that allowed for a third presidential term, but only if supported by the people, of course.

There were rumors of ballot-rigging.

After his second reelection, he passed a law that allowed him to remain in power indefinitely, assuming he obtained approval from Congress every five years. At the same time he passed a law that also permitted Senators and Representatives to maintain their elected positions indefinitely, unless the president released them from service. It was a circular system, one where bribery and deep pockets ruled. Who you knew meant much more than what you knew.

The people had lost their voice.

That wasn't the end of it.

Wilfred's next move was to secure his family's future. He had one son, Edward Nailin. With the full support of Congress, Wilfred managed to pass a law that allowed positions to be handed down from generation to generation within each family, so long as Congress and the president unanimously approved it. Public elections continued to be held, but they were fixed so that no new contenders could infiltrate the inner circle of the government, which was holding all the cards.

It worked for a while. In fact, people seemed to like the more rigid and consistent structure. Soon, however, the gap started to widen between the classes. The wealthy began to take more and more liberties, much to the middle and lower classes' frustration. The complaints started pouring in from those who were being disadvantaged, but they were largely ignored. It got to the point where fights were breaking out in the streets. "Elected" officials couldn't walk down the street without being accosted by the poor and depressed. Something had to be done!

The Tri-Realms were created from 215 PM to 255 PM. First the Moon Realm was excavated, using the advancements in mining technology to create massive caverns deep beneath the original caverns, to build more cities in. Natural caves were used as a starting point, widened and heightened to the extensive size required to house thousands of people. Heavy beams of rock were used to support the caverns' roofs, which were prone to cave-ins. Middle and lower class citizens were used to do the work, having been convinced by large salaries and the opportunity to "advance our civilization for the good of humankind."

Once the caverns were complete, the workers were forced to take their families to live in them. Then the work on the Star Realm began, digging even deeper below the earth's surface. Fewer resources were allocated to excavating the Star Realm, and therefore, the caverns were smaller, more confined, more densely populated. The poorest citizens were sent to live in the deepest caverns.

The top level was given the name of the Sun Realm.

Each of the Tri-Realms was split up into eight chapters, and each chapter into between two and six subchapters depending on its size, each of which was populated by between ten and a hundred thousand people.

Over time, taxes were increased annually for the moon and Star Dwellers, as those living in the Moon and Star Realms were called, until the Sun Realm was receiving significant resources to improve their own caverns. Life was good for the Sun Dwellers. Unfortunately, it wasn't for anyone else.

The U.S. Constitution was legally abolished in 302 PM.

A Nailin has been in power for more than 350 years.

My father told my brother and me the whole story when we turned twelve. I still remember the smug smile on his face when he finished. He's proud of what Wilfred accomplished.

I'm disgusted by it. Sometimes I think about it, and it makes me sick. Like now, lying in bed and wishing my mother was still around. I don't know why I'm thinking about history right now, but I am.

One

Adele

Present day

Something's happening to my body. There's a dull ache in my skull and ripples of energy coursing down my spine. It all started when I saw him. I know I should hate him—everyone else around me does.

"Filthy mutt," I hear one guy growl. "He should've stayed above."

"Yeah," another guy says. "I'm surprised he's gettin' his shoes dirty down 'ere with the rats."

I'm sitting in the Yard. The Yard is what we call the expansive area outside the Pen's main building, although I don't know who came up with the name, because it makes no sense. There's no yard, just barren rock. Real yards—with grass, bushes, and trees—are magical places that don't exist in our world.

The high fence surrounding the prison buzzes with electricity and threatens us with barbed wire. Through the fence we can see our town, subchapter 14 of the Moon Realm. And the non-prisoners can also see us, the convicted.

Even as I stare at freedom through the fence, the feeling gets stronger, like a tingling in the back of my scalp; but it really hurts, too—achy and throbbing. I feel…I feel *drawn* to him, in the most painful of ways. Now wait just a minute before you judge me, it's not love at first sight if that's what you're thinking. It's something else entirely, but I don't have a name for it. I'd like to think it's magic, like in the illegal fantasy books my grandmother used to read me, but there's no magic in the dark, underground world we live in. Nothing but rocks and electrified fences and pain.

The parade passes the Pen, just outside the fence, so close, making all kinds of noise: people cheering, drums thumping, dogs barking.

And Tristan, smiling and waving.

All the girls in my old school are in love with Tristan. Obviously, none of them know him, but like any male celebrity, he captures the attention of young, naïve females. But I've always hated him, because of what he represents.

Now, stuck in the Pen, it seems like an awfully big waste of energy—to hate the son of the president, who I don't even know. Perhaps if I hadn't hated him in the past, none of this

13

would've happened. Perhaps my family would still be together. Maybe it was bad karma. But no matter how much I try to wish it all away, my past is the zit that you pop, watch bleed, watch heal, only to see poking from your skin again a week later.

Tristan is the polar opposite of a recurring blemish. Blond, curly hair. Seventeen but already over six feet tall. Strong, solid frame. A princely face. Big, navy blue eyes. An addictive smile, with right-sized lips and ivory teeth. My brain is telling me to stop staring at him, but for some reason I can't, like the pain coursing down my spine is only tolerable if I continue facing him. He flashes a smile.

The throbbing grows duller in my head, the buzzing down my spine sharper. My body is telling me something. The pull toward Tristan is getting stronger and more painful. But why?

There are about a thousand of his adoring fans outside the Pen, lining the streets, screaming his name and throwing flowers at his car. I even see one of them chuck her undergarments at him.

"You like him, don't you?" a voice says from behind.

I turn, unable to stop the look of surprise that blankets my face. A tall, thin girl stands before me. Her strangely white hair is long and straight, reaching all the way to the small of her back. She has porcelain features, as if her face was drawn on by an artist. I can't help wondering what a beautiful girl like her is doing in a place like this.

"Can I help you?" I say, somewhat rudely.

"I'm Tawni," the girl says, sticking out her hand.

I stare at her slender fingers like they're a nest of snakes, hesitate, and then eventually take them. I shiver at her icy touch, but her handshake feels surprisingly firm for how thin she is.

"Sorry. Poor circulation," she says.

I chew my lip, considering her. "Have a seat," I finally say with a slight wave of my arm.

Flashing a grin, she takes a seat next to me on the rock bench. "Thanks," she says.

I grin back. I can't believe it. I'm actually smiling. Well, sort of. I think it's a pathetic attempt, but at least my lips are curled up in a crooked, awkward, I-don't-know-how-to-smile-for-pictures kind of way. You know, like those kids in Year Three who always end up with the worst yearbook photos? The ones with the crazy eyes and fake smiles. That's me trying to smile at my new friend, Tawni.

"Are you going to answer my question or what?" she says.

I go back to chewing on my lip. "What question?" I say, feigning ignorance.

"C'mon," she says. "Do you like Tristan or not?"

"I don't know him," I say neutrally, internally considering whether she's one of his crazed fans, obsessive to the point of throwing underwear.

The parade passes slowly—Tristan will be out of sight in a few minutes, moving down another street, probably heading toward Moon Hall, where the local politicians gather to do whatever it is that they do. Mostly screw us over. I crane my neck, trying to get a final glimpse of his smile.

"I don't think he's a bad guy," Tawni says.

"Mmm, really?" I say, only half listening.

"No. I mean his dad's a jerk, but I don't think kids should be judged by what their stupid parents do."

My ears perk up. I glance at Tawni. Her slight grin has melted. Her lips are pursed and thin. If nothing else, her statement has piqued my interest in her. Where she comes from, who she is, what she's done to land herself in this hellhole. And why she cares about what Tristan and his father do.

Tawni ignores my look and continues watching the parade, so I turn back, too. The lead car, in which Tristan is standing, is about to turn the corner. He's waving to his fans, smiling his mesmerizing smile, and then…

…he looks at me.

Right at me, like his eyes are gun sights and I'm their target. Despite the distance, it's like they pierce my soul, sending waves of energy up my back and through my neck, slamming into my brain like a freaking sledge hammer.

"Arrr!" I cry out, flinching. I tear my eyes away from him and settle my head in my hands, massaging my pounding temples.

"What is it?" Tawni asks, putting an arm on my back.

Ignoring her, I glance up at Tristan, who's still looking my way. The pounding in my skull comes back in droves, but not quite as strong this time.

As I stare at him, his face changes. Gone is the smile. Gone are his piercing eyes. All swallowed up in a frown. At first I think I was rude, that I've stared too long, or too crazy, because of my weird spasm, but then I feel a presence approaching from the side—a dark shadow.

Not good.

Two

Tristan

It feels like something's gnawing on my spine.

Then I see her and an agonizing pang rips through me, but I manage to keep the fake smile plastered on my face. She's just a prisoner—nothing to me. A random, dark-haired prisoner. And yet I can't pull my eyes away from her. She's pretty hot, but not train-stopping hot. So why am I staring at her?

And is she staring back at me? No. Not really. Not just her. *Everyone's* staring at me.

An ache in my bones, a knife in my back.

The sensation is growing stronger by the second. My jaw clenches as I try to stifle the scream rising from the back of my throat.

She's still staring.

Something's different about the way she looks at me. The only way to describe it is intensity. I'm used to people watching me, but they usually only do so in one of three ways. First are the obsessive girls, the stalker types, who want to marry me and have my babies and wait on me hand and foot for the rest of my life. I think I saw one of their undergarments fly past my head during the parade—that would've been from one of the obsessives. I tolerate them, but unlike my brother, do not enjoy their affections. Next are the admirers. They think I can do no wrong, and are generally old, gray men who look at me with a respect usually reserved for the dead. Not that I've earned it. I haven't done anything; except be born. Last are the haters. Simply put: they hate me. Want me dead. Stare at me with steely eyes, like they think if they stare at me long enough I'll spontaneously combust. They're the ones who sit at home with voodoo dolls of me and my dad and my brother, poking and prodding and twisting with needles. Hoping we can feel what the dolls are feeling.

Is that what this pain is? Is this girl using a voodoo doll on me? I wouldn't normally believe in that sort of thing, but…

My fists clench at my sides.

Her jet-black hair cascades around her face like a funeral shroud, and I find myself mesmerized. Her skin is a natural pale, the result of living underground her entire life, not like the fake-tanned bodies that parade around the Sun Realm. What the hell? Why do I care? She's nobody to me!

And yet…yet I have this crazy urge to leap from the parade car and charge the electrified fence to get to her. It's not love, it's not lust—it's something else.

There's a flash of heat in my head, as my headache intensifies. I raise a startled hand to my scalp at the same time that she does. She's not looking anymore, her head in her hands.

The parade car starts its slow arc around a bend; soon the Pen, and the girl, will be out of sight.

A big guy approaches the girl. His footsteps are malicious. His demeanor screams violence. Her hands are still covering her face. I have to warn her!

Look up, look up, LOOK UP!

She does, her eyes returning to mine.

Although I know I should make a warning motion of some sort, I don't. Only my facial expression—a deep frown—alerts her to the impending danger.

Her eyes pull away and she sees the guy. My view is partially blocked by the edge of a building as the float turns the corner. Craning my neck, I see her twist away from the guy, say something to her friend. The guy says something to her. My view is nearly blocked. The headache rages in my skull.

She stands up and pushes him.

No! I scream in my head as subchapter 14 surrounds me. Then she's gone. Although there's nothing I can do now, my muscles are twitching, almost urging me to run to her, to save her, to do something crazy. It's like I've lost control of my own body.

I fear for her, a girl I don't even know.

19

Three

Adele

I turn my head and see a guy.

I've seen him around the Yard before. A teenager in a man's body. Six-five, about two hundred and fifty pounds, covered in tats: he's one of the local gang leaders. Not a good guy.

"Hey, beautiful," he says.

I ignore him and look at Tawni, hoping he'll pass straight by me. He doesn't. Tawni's wide eyes give away her fear.

"Hey," he says.

I keep ignoring him.

"I said 'Hey,'" he repeats.

"I heard you the first time." I still don't look at him, not wanting to inadvertently extend an invitation with eye contact. My head's killing me. I'm really not in the mood.

"You should watch your mouth," he says.

"And you should keep on walking," I say.

He doesn't. "I haven't seen you around before," he says.

"You must be blind. I'm here every day."

"Nah, I would've noticed *you* for sure," the gang leader says.

Tawni stares at me like I'm crazy. I'm looking at her, but talking to the guy. "Whatever. Doesn't matter. Leave me alone."

I finally swivel my head and make eye contact with him, giving him my iciest stare. I know he's not scared of me, but I want him to decide I'm not worth the effort.

"Not gonna happen," he says, moving in close to me.

Something inside me snaps. It probably doesn't help that I'm in a fair amount of pain, lingering in my head, neck and back. I'm sick of people ruining my life, acting like they own me. He reminds me of the Enforcers who barged into our house and abducted my parents. Arrogant. Selfish.

I stand up, gritting my teeth, my eyes on fire. My fire-eyes barely reach his chest. His gray sweat-stained tunic is right in my face and makes me nauseous. I push him as hard as I can, which doesn't do much, but moves him back a couple of steps. My hands are knotted into fists. I hold them out in front of me, ready for the guy's response.

"You're a real bitch," he says. "And you smell like filth. See you around." He slowly turns and saunters off, chuckling to himself.

21

I take a deep breath, trying to get control of my rage.

"That was amazing," Tawni whispers from behind me.

I sit back down and try to relax my face as I look at her. Her eyes are still wide and white. "He's a jerk," I say through clenched teeth.

"A scary jerk," she says. "That was awesome how you stood up for yourself."

"Wouldn't you?"

Tawny shrugs. "Honestly, I probably would've tried to run away, or yell for help or something. Not fight—that's for sure."

Tawni's eyes flick back to the fence and I follow her gaze. The parade. Tristan. I forgot all about him when the gang guy approached me.

But now Tristan is gone, the front of the parade having moved out of sight while I was dealing with the thug. With each passing second the throbbing in my head and pulsing in my spine seems to lessen. Weird.

"That was pretty weird." Tawni echoes my thoughts, still looking past the fence.

"What was?" I say, glancing at her furtively. Did she notice how it hurt me when Tristan looked at me? Did she sense what I had? Had I imagined the look of concern on his face just before the confrontation with the gang guy, or had she seen it, too?

"I didn't see many photographs being taken of Tristan during the parade. I thought the face-stealers would be out in full force."

I roll my eyes at myself. Of course Tawni didn't notice Tristan looking at me, hurting me with his stare. Probably because he didn't. He'd probably just looked in our general direction, past us. He was probably frowning at all of us—at the criminals. Disgusted by us. Clearly he wasn't warning me about the approaching gangster. And the pain? More likely a result of lack of sleep. There was another suicide last night, and the awful keening of the death toll cried out for more than two hours, keeping everyone awake.

Yeah, in reality Tristan probably didn't even look at me. I might have seen his head turn in my direction, perhaps a random glance at best; certainly not the laser-beamed, tethered gaze that I'd obviously imagined.

But still. My body reacted strangely when I saw him, when he was near. It didn't feel natural though. It's like my mind knew to stay as far away from him as possible—he's a Sun Dweller after all, one of the bad guys—but my bones, my skin quivered in his presence.

Very weird.

"Helloooo? Earth to...What's your name anyway?" Tawni waves her hand across my face—apparently I've spaced out, lost in my own random thoughts.

"Adele," I find myself saying, to my surprise. Giving my name away so easily like that—what am I thinking? Tawni is penetrating my social defenses faster than a mine cave-in swallows a trapped traveler.

"Well, Adele, it's been a true pleasure meeting you and watching you handle that guy. Truly impressive, really. Would you like to dine with me and my friend Cole tonight?"

Dine? This girl has a funny way of speaking. Like she has no clue that we're locked up in a juvenile detention center. And that we live underground. And that most of us will never get our freedom back. Certainly not me. Maybe she's just a few days from being released, which would certainly explain why she seems so cheery. I hope so. If I can't get out, at least someone I know can.

"Uh, yeah, I guess so," I say. "Thanks," I add quickly, realizing how rude I sound.

"Great! Meet us in the northwest corner—we'll reserve a table."

There she goes again: speaking as if we're going out to some fancy restaurant that accepts reservations. I shake my head and realize I'm smiling. Not my normal smile—no, I'm not ready for that yet—but slightly better than the crooked, awkward smile I attempted earlier. Maybe things are looking up for me. I've made a friend. At least, the closest thing to a friend I've had in a long time.

* * *

There are only two hours to kill before dinner, so I use the time to think. I start with the past—my happiest memories. My father coming home from a long day of work in the mines, filthy and dripping sweat, but bringing my sister and me a treat of some kind. Either a small gemstone that he'd smuggled out or a piece of candy he'd bought in town. He always seemed to have a twinkle in his eye and a bounce in his step, no matter how tired he was. Sometimes he even gave me a piggyback ride before he got cleaned up. My mother hated it when he did that, because then I'd have to take a bath before supper, too.

God, how I love my father.

I love my mother, too, but in a different way. She isn't as playful as my father, is quicker to punish, and is less rebellious toward the Sun Dwellers. She says that it isn't our place to tell the wise leaders—who'd gotten us through Year Zero, she likes

24

to remind—how to run the government. I try to see her point, but it's been nearly five hundred years since Year Zero, and all of the people from back then are long dead.

I shake my head and try to focus on the happy memories of my mom. When we'd cook radish stew together, play games of chess and checkers, watch the late-night news on our beat-up old telebox.

My mother is the most compassionate person I know. If someone in our neighborhood was sick, she was always the first to deliver a meal to them, using our already scant supplies to help out a friend. Sometimes I got mad at her, wished she wouldn't do things like that, wished she wouldn't give away our stuff. But I usually felt bad about my thoughts later on. In the deepest recesses of my soul I am always proud of her.

But as usual, my thoughts quickly do a one-eighty. Now I am thinking about all that has gone wrong, all that is bad. About the cruelty of life.

About how I've failed my parents. I don't dare to hope that they're still alive.

I think about all the waste in the world. Although we live underground now, we still require many of the same basic necessities humans have needed for decades. Toothpaste, for example, produced in a cave somewhere. The point is: we use up the toothpaste and then throw out the container. It is sent to the lava flow for destruction. Have human lives become like a tube of toothpaste? Something to be used up and thrown away? At first the tube seems so big, so full of life. But after just a few uses it becomes dented and lumpy—already life is ebbing away from it—and it's only a matter of time before the final bit is squeezed out, rendering it an empty vessel, good for nothing.

I feel myself being squeezed out every day.

I try to distract my scattered thoughts, gazing up at the dimly lit cavern ceiling rising more than twenty stories above me. It's weird being in the Pen, cut off from the town, and yet being able to see everything that the non-prisoners can see. From the Yard, I can see the same massive cavern that houses our town, the Pen, all of us. If I didn't know it so well, the 14th subchapter might be a stunning sight, with an arcing roof coated by the glossy sheen of the panel lighting that controls our days and nights. The cavern was excavated more than two hundred years ago, and covers more than five square miles. Most of the rough and jagged rocks were smoothed over, huge stone support columns built, stone roads laid, and houses and buildings erected.

There's a light commercial district, where goods can be bought, sold, and traded. Mostly they're traded, because the wages are so low that money is short. I remember well the first money I ever had. My father saved for a month so he could give it to me on my tenth birthday. A single Nailin, bright and shiny and round. Printed with the face of the President. I stared at it for hours, trying to imprint its memory in my mind, for I knew it would soon be gone, wasted, on a silly dress I'd coveted for over a year. Every time I passed by the dress shop in town, I stopped to look at the dress. It was black and long, and would sweep the floor as I walked. The sleeves were sheer and translucent, elegant in their simplicity. Simple—that's the way I like things. There were no frills, no laces, no bows— simple. I bought that dress with my first Nailin.

I outgrew it in three months. Funny the way the world works sometimes.

The pinnacle of the town, however, is the mine. All things considered, we are lucky. Many of the other subchapters in the Realm have mines, but none so valuable as ours. For ours is full of gemstones, raw and uncut—and worth a fortune to the Sun Dwellers. So you'd expect us to be a rich town. We should be, but once the taxes are taken out of the workers' wages, it's a pittance, barely enough to survive on.

When my father complained, they took him away. My mother, too, guilty by association. I was sent to the Pen and my sister to a crummy, broken-down orphanage. Yeah, life is good as a Moon Dweller.

Given my dark thoughts, I am glad when the two hours pass. I leave the Yard, weaving my way through the kids who are still lounging about. Some are clustered in groups, speaking in hushed whispers, trading pages of books for cigarettes, and cigarettes for socks, and socks for whatever else will help them forget they are prisoners, that their lives are forfeit. Others are sprawled out on the rock, sleeping their sentences away.

My headache is gone, I realize.

Inside the Pen it's like a cattle call. Kids are pushing against each other in mob-like fashion, all trying to get to the cafeteria. Feeding time is about the only time any of the kids show any kind of energy. Also when they're fighting. Interesting how both instances are a matter of survival.

I ease my way into the mash-up of bodies and manage to find a human flow that's moving swiftly in the right direction, like a strong current in one of the many underground rivers of the Tri-Realms. Soon—after only a few minor collisions—I'm in the cafeteria.

Given the crowds, one might expect that the food is to die for. Perhaps it *is* a trendy new restaurant, one where you have to make a reservation, like Tawni suggested earlier. However, one bite of the lukewarm mashed potatoes or a spoon of the mystery stew is enough to clinch the notion that the executive chef would be much better suited to some other occupation—*any* other occupation. Seriously. It's bad. Tasteless. Like eating a shoe. And not a new one. One that has been worn for years by someone who suffers from severe foot sweating.

But we have no choice. It's the only show in town, a monopoly—on our stomachs. So we add lots of salt, which by some miracle they provide in plenty.

Once in the food line, I order—by pointing at things and grunting—a gob of something covered in brown gravy, a noodle dish that looks like dead worms, and a plastic cup of brownish water. Yum.

I find Tawni right where she said she'd be—at one of the corner tables. Most every table is already full, so I'm glad she arrived early enough to get it. Usually I just take my food outside, to eat alone in silence.

There's a guy sitting across from her. He's naturally dark-skinned, which is the only way to not have pale skin when you live underground; unless, of course, you reside in the Sun Realm, where tanning beds are a staple in every household.

He's wearing a shirt with the sleeves cut off, highlighting his muscular arms. He's tall, but not as tall as Tristan. Funny how I'm already comparing other guys to Tristan, like I even know him.

Tawni spots me and motions for me to join them. I manage to squeeze through the throng of eaters and slide onto the bench next to her.

"Hi!" she says brightly, like we're just a bunch of friends going out to eat at our favorite haunt.

"Uh, yeah, hi." I still can't seem to remember how to speak like a normal human being. I glance at the black guy. He smiles.

"I'm Cole," he says, extending a hand.

When he grasps my hand it disappears, as if it's been swallowed by his enormous paw. I shake his hand firmly, trying to act tough, but to my surprise he doesn't return my iron grip. Nor does his hand crumple under the raw power of my squeeze. It's just sort of there. It's like his hand absorbs my strength, simply by the sheer solidity of his bones. His hand is also somewhat tender and gentle, smooth and well cared for. Somewhat feminine, if I'm being honest. It's a contradiction, which I'm always intrigued by. Like bittersweet chocolate, which, by the way, I've only tried once in my life when my dad gave me a square for my eighth birthday.

By just shaking Cole's hand I've started to like him. Can it be: another friend? Two in one day? It's like a Christmas miracle.

"I'm Adele," I say, feeling quite gabby all of a sudden.

"I know," he says. "Tawni told me. She said you're a real badass."

I feel my face flush slightly. "Oh. Not really. It was just some punk who's all talk."

"She told me who it was. He's not all talk. I've seen him bust some heads before. You were lucky; you don't want to mess with that dude."

"I can take care of myself," I say. I hear coldness creep into my tone. I grit my teeth and try to relax.

Cole shrugs. "If you say so. Don't say I didn't warn you. Whatcha in for anyway?" he asks.

Geez, this guy cuts right to the chase. But I tell him anyway. "Mass murder. Got burned by the shallow graves—I knew I should have dug deeper."

Cole doesn't flinch. "Oh yeah?" he says. "Me, too. Weird coincidence, huh?"

My jaw drops open.

Cole grins. "Gotcha!" he says proudly.

I realize that, like me, he's joking. The way he delivers the line, combined with his soft handshake, combined with the fact that I'm actually speaking to real humans for the first time in a long time, makes me completely miss his sarcasm. Me, the queen of sarcastic comments—self-declared—has been outsarcastified.

I grin at Cole. That's when I notice the strength of his eyes. When I say strength, I mean *strength*. Most people talk about eye color when they talk about people's eyes—I certainly do. And yes, Cole's eyes are a beautifully warm shade of milky chocolate brown. But what I notice is what's behind his eyes. It's like he's wearing steel-plated contacts. There's no trace of nervousness, or fear, or worry, or any of those other feelings I constantly have; the feelings that lead my eyes to look away, to flutter, to close. Right away I know Cole is someone you can count on in the most dangerous situations.

"Nah, I'm not sarcastic at all," Cole says. Again, I can't detect even the slightest trace of sarcasm in his voice. He's good, that's for sure. I'll have to listen closely whenever he speaks.

Despite having only just met these two people, barely spoken three sentences to either of them, I find myself opening up.

"I'm the daughter of a traitor," I blurt out. "What about you?"

Tawni looks at Cole. Cole looks at Tawni. A thousand words seem to be conveyed by their simple eye contact. Are they considering whether to trust me?

Finally, Tawni turns back to me. "Well, you've got us beat," she says. "I got caught trying to travel interdistrict without a travel card, and Cole here stole a couple of loaves of bread to feed his starving family." Something about the way she delivers the information, so matter-of-factly, almost makes it sound like a well-rehearsed line. But before I consider it further, Cole plows ahead.

"It was six loaves of bread," he says, "which, let me tell ya, are hard to carry when you don't have a bag and you're in a hurry. When my family didn't have anything to eat for three nights in a row, I came up with a plan. I was so stressed that sweat was dripping off my forehead and into my eyes. I could barely see when I smashed the bakery window. My hands were sweaty, but somehow I managed to grab the six loaves. Someone shouted at me—an Enforcer, I think—and I started running. Right away one of the loaves slipped out of my fingers. I grabbed for it, but that made another one slip, then another. Soon I was juggling the bread, batting it up in the air over my head. I did pretty well, too, keeping all six up in the air for like five seconds before one fell. My luck didn't get much better at that point. I slipped on the loaf, which, for your information, was about as slippery as a banana peel, and went down hard. They brought me here."

I almost want to laugh. Cole has a twinkle in his eyes, so I don't think he'll mind. But laughter is still coming hard for me, so I just smile lightly. "Truth," I say, starting a game that has the potential to last for a long time.

Cole grins. "Correct," he says. "As stupid a way as that was to end up in the Pen, it's all true." I'm starting to get a better read on him, noticing subtle things like the way his bottom lip pouts slightly when he's being honest. His eyes are always the same, though, like metal, so I won't be able to use them to read him, like you can with most people.

"How long you in for?" Tawni asks me.

I raise my eyebrows. "How long?" I parrot.

"Yeah, you know," Tawni says, "a year, two years, what?"

"Try forever," I say.

Cole stares at me. "Truth," he says.

"No, that can't be right," Tawni says. "Lie. She's messing with us."

With tight lips I shake my head. "Not a lie. They told me rebelliousness is passed through blood, genetically, like eye color or being able to snap your fingers. They won't ever let me out. I mean, when I turn eighteen I'll move out of this place and into an adult facility—probably the Max, in the Star Realm—but I'll never have my freedom again."

Leave it to me to put a damper on my first meal with my two new friends. But they *did* ask, and I wasn't about to lie. I expect them to shun me, to get up and leave, like just being in my presence will add years to their own sentences. They don't.

Cole says, "That's horse manure. I'll never go for that."

He says it in such a way that I know he's dead serious, as if he's already made up his mind to do something about it. Not that he can. If he tries anything he'll just end up with his own life sentence.

"There's nothing you can do," I say.

"There has to be *something*," Tawni says. The way she emphasizes the word *something*, I know she isn't talking about legal methods.

"No, there's not," I say adamantly. "You guys barely know me and you'll just screw up your own chances. When do you get out anyway?"

Cole looks at Tawni and motions with his head. She answers for them both. "I'm out in six months and Cole's out in a year."

I nod. Even their sentences seem exceptionally harsh considering their crimes, but they sound a whole lot better than mine. In a year they'll both be out of the Pen, able to make their own decisions again, even if under the increasingly intolerant oppression of the government.

I'm glad when Tawni changes the subject. She says, "Wasn't it weird today how Tristan looked at you?" My breath catches in my lungs. So she *did* notice.

I look at Cole. "Tawni told me about *that*, too," he says, "but I want to hear it from you."

"I thought it was all in my head," I say, feeling my face go slightly warm again. One negative of having highly pale skin is that a blush stands out like a hairy wart on a nose.

"No—it wasn't," Tawni says. "It was like all the crowds and everything else just disappeared, and Adele and Tristan were the only people left. I could almost see his laser eyes touching you, caressing you…"

"Tawni!" I shout, ignoring a couple of strange glances from the other eaters. "It wasn't like that at all. I didn't feel any…*touching*." I say the last word like it's something disgusting, like moldy bread, crinkling my nose and curling my lip. "But I did notice him looking at me."

"You see? I told you, Cole. But it hurt you, didn't it?" she asks. When my eyes widen, she says, "You cried out. You were holding your head."

"I don't know," I say honestly. "I just had a headache."

She shrugs, as if she's satisfied, but I get the feeling that she and I both know it was much more than just a headache.

Four

Tristan

My meetings with the leaders of the Moon Realm pass torturously slowly. Although I'm barely listening, by the end of the day I'm so annoyed with the leaders kissing my hind parts that I want to scream.

As the rough gray cavern walls flash past on either side during the train ride back to the Sun Realm, I think about when my next scheduled visit to the Moon Realm is. Not for months, I realize. All the key contracts are signed. The Moon Dwellers will slave away for another year, providing sustenance to the lazy Sun Dwellers, for a measly wage of five Nailins a day; all because of the lopsided contract my father forced their leaders to sign. You'd think that as son of the President there'd be something I could do to help. There's nothing. I'm merely a puppet, sent across the Tri-Realms to collect signatures and smile for the cameras. All the real negotiations are performed by my father, behind closed doors—and he always gets what he wants.

I have to find an excuse to go back to the Moon Realm. To find out what happened to the mysterious headache-inducing dark-haired girl. I have no choice in the matter; an unseen force drives me. I wonder if I would feel this strongly if she hadn't been in danger when I saw her. If we'd only looked at each other, would I have simply shrugged her off as just another beautiful girl? I don't know the answer to my own question, but my every instinct is urging me to find her.

But it's more than that. It's not only that she was in danger that interests me. It's the way she handled herself. With confidence, with strength. Different from the girls in the Sun Realm, who can't seem to do anything for themselves.

And I need to know why my body reacted the way it did when I saw her. Was it simply a strange seventeen-year-old hormonal response to a pretty face? Seems farfetched given how many pretty girls I see every day, each of whom try to throw themselves at me. But it's even more farfetched to think of alternative reasons for the stabbing pain in my spine, for the thundering headache in my skull. Both of which, by the way, disappeared soon after she disappeared from sight.

Another question pops into my head: Does she hate me like so many other Moon Dwellers do? Just because I'm the son of the president?

She probably does. Not that I would blame her. We call ourselves a democracy, but rule like a dictatorship. The title of President for my father should've been replaced with something else long ago. King, Master, Czar…something. If I lived in the Moon or Star Realms, I would probably rebel against my father, against the Sun Dwellers. I'm surprised there hasn't been a major rebellion, at least not in my lifetime. The last time it happened was the Uprising in 475 PM, but it was quashed by my father's troops in less than a year. Another rebellion is my father's greatest fear, and yet he takes liberties away from the moon and Star Dwellers as easily as he shakes out stones from his shoes. I hate him for it.

"Sir?" I hear someone say. It's my servant, Roc. He's staring at me strangely.

I look around and realize the train has stopped. "Oh, we're here," I say, jumping up.

Roc escorts me out of the first-class car and onto the palace grounds. Everything's brighter here, nothing like the gloominess of the Moon Realm. We're still underground, yes, but the entire roof glows brightly, illuminating the massive cave network. It's all part of the distinction between the Realms. Electricity is strictly rationed, such that the Sun Realm receives eighty percent of it, of course, with a paltry fifteen percent going to the Moon Realm, and a measly five percent to the Star Dwellers.

At least those are the published figures. In reality, I know that closer to ninety-five percent of all energy goes to the Sun Dwellers, allowing us to live like kings. Not that we are—there are no kings in a democracy.

"Your father requests your presence immediately," Roc says as we walk.

"Of course he does," I say. To any other servant, I'd probably sound smug, self-righteous, like I'm pleased my father has requested my audience. But not to Roc. He knows I'm being sarcastic. Roc's more than just a servant. He's my friend—maybe my only one. In public I'm forced to treat him as I would any servant, because to my father anything else would be a sign of weakness.

But in private we're best friends. We've grown up together, after all. Before he reached the age of accountability—eight years old—we played every day together. He loved my mother, too. Sadly, Roc's mother died giving birth to him. But my mom adopted him, treated him just as well as my brother and I. Kissing him goodnight, taking him on our adventures, giving him presents on the day of the Sun Festival: Roc was like a third son to my mom…and is like a second brother to me.

Roc grins. "We'll try to get out of there fast, sir. If we have time afterwards, can I have another lesson?"

I grin back. A few months prior, Roc requested that I teach him to fight. Swords, guns, battleaxes, knives—that sort of thing. I gladly agreed. It was just another chance to disobey my father. He doesn't want Roc and me to be friends. The servant/master code is far too important to him. Even Roc's father, who is my father's chief servant and has known my father for years, isn't a friend to him.

"Absolutely," I say. "We'll keep focusing on swords—because they're useful and awesome."

We reach the palace garden. Creating and maintaining the underground garden costs more in a month than the entire population of Star Dwellers earns in a year. It isn't possible without the sun-like technology that was invented decades earlier. Not that my father cares. Ignoring the insane cost, the

38

garden is extraordinary. Pillars of perfectly pruned green hedges frame the entrance. Hundreds of varieties of flora and fauna are meticulously maintained by the garden staff, providing splashes of color throughout the garden's boundaries. The garden looks weird inside the massive cavern.

I always loved the palace garden growing up. Running around in bare feet on the soft, lush lawns, playing hide-and-go-seek around the bushes and trees, Roc and I pretending we were palace guards as we charged through the garden, fighting off marauders with our invisible swords. Now, like most things in the Sun Realm, I hate the garden. For me the garden is just another reminder of how unfair the world that my father governs is. The world that I am meant to inherit, being the eldest son.

Perhaps it's my mother's influence, but I can never be the man my father wants me to be.

We walk quickly through the garden, like we always do.

Along the way we pass many people. Most of them are servants, who acknowledge me with a slight bow, which I ignore—another one of my father's requirements. But some of them are palace guests—Sun Dwellers. Those are the ones I most like to look at. Because they look ridiculous. The current fashion is to wear bright colors, and the Sun Dwellers take it to the extreme, wearing gaudy red and pink tunics with blue and green polka dots. But compared to the hats, the tunics are tame. There are hats of all shapes and sizes, some glittering, some sparkling, some shimmering with diamonds and pearls, or stuck with feathers like a bird. All worth laughing at. Time and time again I'm forced to hide my amusement as I'm greeted by men, women, boys, and girls, all seeking "just a moment of your time." It's a wonder we ever make it to the palace.

By the time we do, the sun is waning in the west. Or at least that's how some of the books my mom used to read to me described the sunset. In the Sun Realm, the artificial sun is just slowly dimmed, to simulate nightfall.

In reality, it's always night in the caves.

My father is waiting, keeping court in his throne room—I mean *meeting* room. He'd have to be a king to get a throne.

"You're late," he says.

He's wearing a spotless white tunic with shimmering gold embroidery along the seams. His gray goatee is groomed to perfection, no doubt trimmed twice already that day by a servant. Probably by one of the two pretty little things that stand by his side now, ready for his next command. They're both blonde and deeply tanned, wearing tight, black tunics cut off well above the knees. The V-necks reveal just how mature they are. It's all part of my father's dress code for the female servants. Roc's father excepted, all of my father's personal servants are women—as beautiful as they are sleazy. I suspect they do a lot more for him than just iron his tunics and trim his beard.

"I was delayed by some journalists who wanted some quotes for tomorrow's paper," I say flatly.

"Sir," my father says simply.

I sigh. "Sir," I repeat. Another one of my father's pet peeves.

"And everything else went according to schedule?" he says.

"Yes. Next year's contracts with the Moon Realm have been finalized under the terms you stipulated…" I pause…one beat, two. My father drums his fingers on his wooden armrest impatiently. "Sir," I say finally, enjoying my little game. I don't dare to openly rebel against my father, but I can still have a bit of fun.

"Good," my father says. "Is that everything?"

I nod.

Without waiting for his permission, I turn on my heel and march off, with Roc in tow. I hear my father say, "You may go," as I walk away. It's his lame attempt to show off his power in front of his Barbie Doll servants.

When we are out of eyesight and earshot, Roc says, "You really shouldn't push him like that."

I sigh. "I know, I know." Roc is usually right. Flashing a grin, I say, "But it was fun, wasn't it?"

"It's the little things in life," Roc says, smiling. His dark features look even darker as shadows fall upon the palace.

"Like swords?" I say.

"Yes!" Roc says, a bit too loudly. A passing servant woman glares at him. Mrs. Templeton—the palace housekeeper. She's a nasty one.

We make our way through the business end of the palace and into the residential quarters. The change in décor is like night and day. The government side is stark and official-looking, everything clean-cut, free of clutter, and stamped with the symbol of the Sun Realm—a fiery red and orange sun with wavy heat lines wafting to the sides. The living quarters still feel a bit too posh and sterile, but at least there are a few personal touches, all of which my mother added before she disappeared.

There's the family portrait on the entry room table. Normally, I wouldn't have any interest in a family photo. But this one I love, because it presents our family in such an honest light. My brother and I look bored, restless, with tousled hair and cheeky grins. My mother has her arm around the both of

41

us, pulling us into her side. About a foot away, on her other side, is my father, not looking happy at all. The cameraman snapped the photo a split-second before he was able to turn on his friendly-President face, as I like to call it. You know, the one that's so obviously fake it's painful to watch. The kind of face you just want to slap.

After that photo was taken, my father's face went all red and he looked like he was ready to slug the photographer. But my mom managed to soothe him, rubbing her hand on his back and telling him how she liked the photo, how she wanted to keep it. That was back when she still had some power over him.

Somehow she convinced him to display the photo prominently in our home. After she disappeared, I expected him to take it down. But either he'd grown to like it (which I doubt) or he'd forgotten it was even there (more likely). And so it remains, making me smile every time I pass by.

A part of me clings to the hope that my father kept the photo there because he misses her, wants to remember her, but the more grownup part of me knows better. Before my mother vanished, there was no love between them. It was purely another of my father's business relationships, using my mother for the sole purpose of demonstrating stability at the top of the government.

At some point in my parents' relationship there must have been love—at least from my mom's side—but I don't think it lasted very long. As far back as I can remember he had the young, scantily clad servant girls. As a kid I thought they were just fun little helpers who giggled and helped my dad around the office. Almost like elves. That is one fantasy I wish I hadn't outgrown. The truth is far too sickening.

Roc is saying something. "Huh?" I say.

He repeats himself. "You know it wasn't your fault."

Roc's words sound cryptic, but I know exactly what he's talking about. My mother's disappearance. Two years ago, but still as fresh in my memory as if it was yesterday.

"I wasn't thinking about that." Well, not really. But it *is* on the fringe of my thoughts; it is always there, buzzing around the edge of my consciousness, suffocating my heart.

"It doesn't matter what you were thinking," Roc says. "I know you still blame yourself."

I don't want to talk about it, don't want to dredge up the memories again—they're too painful. I'm fine to just let her memory cling to the edges of my mind where maybe, just maybe, I won't have to face them. Sometimes talking to Roc is like talking to a shrink, only without the comfy couch to lie on.

"Not now, Roc," I say.

"Then when?" he asks.

"Maybe never," I say honestly.

Roc stops, grabs my shoulders with both hands, forces me to look at him. His dark eyes are serious. "Blaming yourself is like a curse eating you from within, a rogue virus, cancerous and poisonous. It will drive you mad if you let it. You're my friend and I hate to see you like this. And your mother would hate to see her disappearance cause you to self-destruct."

I expected Roc to say something cliché like *Blaming yourself won't bring her back, Tristan*, but instead, his words are like darts embedding themselves in my chest. I don't want to let him down. Nor my mother. But I can't help it. The pain is more than I can bear. The what-ifs *are* a cancer, like Roc said. What if I was a better son? What if I'd stood up to my father? What if I'd been with her on the day she disappeared, refusing to let her out of my sight? Would everything be different then? Would we be a happy little family?

I want to believe the answer is *yes*, but in my heart I know it isn't so. Accepting that fact will set me free. But I can't...or won't.

Not that it matters. I will hang on to the what-ifs and continue to blame myself regardless of whether I truly believe I had any influence on the events that transpired.

There isn't much to believe in these days. I once believed in the love of a mother, but then she left me. I used to believe in honor, in chivalry, in the power that one person has to enact real, positive change in the world. My mother taught me all that. It vanished when she did.

Now all I believe in is pain.

Pain is the great equalizer, the cure to mental anguish, the antidote for a hopeful heart. It comes in all different forms—physical, mental, emotional, spiritual. Most days I like physical the best, choosing to throw myself into my training with unbridled aggression. I make my challenges impossible, sometimes facing twenty or more opponents simultaneously. And because I'm the President's son, they have to obey me, have to attack. At first they're timid, afraid to bruise me, but after taking a whack or two from the broadside of my steel blade they change, becoming more ferocious than attacking lions.

I still have scars from those training sessions.

The beauty of physical pain is that it wipes out the other forms of pain. Not necessarily completely or for an extended period of time, but long enough to grant a reprieve from my tortured mind and soul.

"On guard!" Roc yells, his teeth clenched together like a wild beast. He's realized I'm not going to speak to him about my mother. I'm glad he's given up for the time being. His new approach: beat it out of me.

I don't even have my weapon yet, but it doesn't matter. Roc's clumsy swings feel like they're in slow motion, coming in at awkward angles, without any attempt to hide his intentions: he's going for my head. He's probably trying to knock some sense into me.

He knows better than that—I've taught him better. Feinting is as important as the actual attack. Disguising one's intent is the key to fighting. But he's on a mission. I know it's because he cares about me—wants better for me—that he's trying to crack me across the skull.

Not today.

I spin to the left and drop to a roll, hearing Roc's wooden blade crash thunderously into the wall behind me. When I fight my senses seem to magnify. I'm looking in the other direction, reaching for my own practice blade, grasping it, but I can picture Roc's blade rebounding off the wall, him repositioning his feet like I've taught him, his next swing…

I whirl around just in time, catching the tip of his sword low on my own. *Thud!* The sound is dull and won't carry past the walls. We fight with wooden practice swords in the privacy of my room because no one can ever know I'm training my servant to fight. It's nearly as effective as using metal practice swords out in the yard—I can teach him the proper technique, the footwork, the positions—but I know at some point we'll need to find a place to practice with real swords. If he's to get any better, that is.

Instinct takes over. That and years of the highest quality training that money can buy. Without thinking, I bend my knees, straighten my back, keep my hips aligned with my shoulders. Roc attempts to do the same, but in the wall-length mirror I can see that next to me he looks amateurish, awkward.

I'm not being vain. Just realistic. Roc needs lots of work on his posture. I can help with that. But not today. Today is about passionate fighting. At least for Roc. Me, I'm calm, unemotional, businesslike. Just like I've been taught.

I easily parry Roc's next three attempts at taking my head off, and then duck the fourth, moving in close to his body and elbowing him hard in the chest. One of the most important lessons in sword fighting—especially for real, life or death, fight-like-there's-no-tomorrow sword fighting—is to use all parts of your body. Most people assume that because you have a pointy sword you should use it exclusively. Not so.

With a grunt, Roc goes down hard. Lucky for him he crashes onto my bed, ruffling the perfectly ironed red comforter. One thing Roc has going for him is his athleticism. While not trained in the art of fighting, or of swordplay, he has a natural speed and quickness that is particularly effective on the defensive side. His speed temporarily saves him from another defeat at my hands.

After crushing him with my elbow, I continue surging forward, following him onto the bed and attempting to get the point of my dull wooden blade under his chin and against his neck, which is the requisite for victory.

He recovers beautifully, executing a graceful backwards roll, and manages to maintain his grip on the sword. He lands on his feet on the other side of the bed, grinning slightly. His brown skin is shining with sweat under the soft lantern glow.

Outstretching his off-sword hand, he flicks his fingers back toward himself, as if to say, "C'mon, bring it!"

I bring it. I launch myself over the bed, pointing my sword forward like a battering ram. Roc is forced to jump backwards, which allows me to land on my feet and go on the offensive. I feint hard to the left and Roc completely buys it. When I go right he's left exposed. I connect sharply under his ribs and then whip a leg behind his knees, sweeping him off his feet. He smashes onto his back, losing his sword in the process. When he reaches for it, I step on the wooden blade.

He gives me a wry grin.

I give him my hand.

Big mistake.

He grabs my hand and pulls hard, throwing off my center of gravity and forcing me over the top of him. Although I've been trained to maintain a firm grip on my sword at all times, even to the detriment of the rest of my body, it's difficult to do in real life when every instinct is telling you to release your sword and use your hand to break your fall.

I practically throw my sword across the room. By the time I stop my fall and start moving to recover my sword, Roc's quickness gives him the advantage. He already has his own sword in one hand, and mine in the other.

"A little cheap, but a victory nonetheless," I say.

"My first one, sir," Roc says, laughing.

I hate losing, but I laugh, too. Roc knows I hate it when he calls me *sir* in private. It's his way of getting even with me for my unwillingness to talk about my feelings.

"Thanks, Roc," I say, feeling a stronger bond with him than I've felt for anyone in a long time. Without him I'm not sure where I would be. A wreck for sure. Well, at least more of a wreck than I already am.

For no reason at all, an image flashes through my mind: the black-haired girl sitting on the stone bench; her sad, sad eyes; the eternal gulf between us bridged when our eyes meet. Then her fists are out to fight the ogre. Bone-crushing pain surges in my head.

That's when I pass out.

Five

Adele

A riot breaks out as I make my way back to my cell. That's the way things work in the Pen. You're minding your own business and then you're in the middle of a brawl. Like the one I'm in now.

A fist the size of a miner's hammer bashes the side of my skull, forcing my eyes shut and sending stars dancing across my field of vision. When my sight returns, I see what hit me. Wielded by a tattooed mountain, the clenched fingers are like a wrecking ball, colliding with anything and everything in their destructive path. And I'm in the way.

I can fight the guy, but he isn't even fighting me. He's just fighting in general, swinging at anything that moves.

Each time I try to push through the human net surrounding us, claw-like hands force me into the center. Ducking under another arc of human flesh and bone, I fire back, aiming my own punch at his ribs. When I connect, tendrils of pain rip through my hand and explode up my forearm. I know how to punch, but for a moment I think I've punched the stone wall by mistake. The steroidal teenage mountain looms over me, finally focusing his violence on a single target: me. I'm in way over my head.

His fist is the size of a basketball as it cuts toward my face. There's no time to move. I close my eyes.

I hear a groan before I'm knocked to the floor by a big body, but my head doesn't hurt. When I open my eyes I'm surprised to see darkness on top of me. And then I'm pulled to my feet by Cole, who charges through the impenetrable human blockade, tossing surprised bodies to either side as he pulls me to safety.

We race down a hall and pass by guards who are striding in the other direction, their eyes sparkling with excitement, their knuckles white and gripping clubs and Tasers. They like when there are riots. It means they get to satisfy their lust for blood.

We turn a corner and nearly run into Tawni, who's galloping toward us. Her eyes start on me, but then flick to Cole and widen. "Are you okay?" she says, lifting a hand to his face.

I follow her gaze to Cole's eye, which is already swollen. I realize that the reason my head isn't hurting is because Cole's *is*. He took the hit for me, and took it well. I've been protecting myself for so long it feels weird to have someone else do something for me.

"I'm fine," Cole says, pulling Tawni's hand away from his face.

"Thanks, but—" I start to say.

"No problem."

"I wasn't finished. Thanks, but I could've handled him on my own. I know how to look after myself." I'm being a brat, but I can't seem to stop myself.

Cole half-grins, half-grimaces. "Sure," he says.

"No, really, I was fine," I say. "I know how to fight."

"If you say so," Cole replies. "It just looked like that dude was gonna make mincemeat out of your face, but next time I guess I won't bother…"

I take a deep breath, try to stop being the cold, isolated person I've become. "Sorry…I mean…thanks. Yes, thank you—that's what I meant to say."

"No problem," Cole repeats. "Now we better get into our cells before that riot spills out this way."

I know he's right because I can hear the roar of chaos growing louder. I don't know what else to say, so I leave them and head back to my lonely cell.

* * *

The sunlight retreats along the white windowsill. With each passing minute, the shadows lengthen, until the light gives way to a troubled darkness, gray and soggy. The dark clouds challenge the omniscient sun, and the clouds prevail, like a black-armored army descending upon a shining and pure city of light. Skeins of rain beat upon the panes of glass. Moisture splutters under the base of the barely opened window, leaving the painted sill slick and wet. A few drops gather and push forward to the edge, slipping off and onto the plush brown carpet.

If only.

I wish that's what I am seeing. Only I've never seen sunlight. Or sunshine, or sunbeams, or even a ray of sun. Those are just words in books—not real. Nor have I seen rain—or clouds, for that matter. Like sunlight, those are things of myth and legend. As told by my grandmother, who was told by her mother—a story passed down for generations. Not even my father has seen the sun. Or my father's father. Or my father's father's father. You get the picture.

But no, I'm not seeing rain, or clouds, or much of anything. Just the inside of my pitiful gray cell inside the Pen. The walls are made of stone. And the ceiling. And the floors. Even the bed. Shocking, I know. It seems that everything in my world is made of stone.

Weird that we're called Moon Dwellers, when none of us have even seen the moon, much less dwelt on it. We're still stuck on earth. Well, not *on* earth so much as *in* it, at least a mile below the deadly surface. I'm not sure who the idiot was who decided to call us Moon Dwellers, but I'd guess he or she was a Sun Dweller. It seems that most of the dumb ideas come from them. In school they told us that the logic behind the names is related to how bright each light source appears in the sky. For example, the sun appears the brightest—at least that's what we're told and how it looks in the pictures—and therefore, those nearest to the surface should be called Sun Dwellers. We're next and are like the moon, second brightest. At the bottom, of course, are the Star Dwellers, miles from the earth's surface. I also heard that there are some references to this kind of thing in the Bible, too, but I've never read it so I'm not sure if it is true. Bottom line: I think the names are stupid.

I'd prefer them to be called Deep, Deeper, and Deepest.

No matter how they spin things, it's a class system, one predicated on those at the top being worth more than those at the bottom. My grandmother said the distinctions between the classes are more obvious in our world, but that it had been the same when people lived above the earth, only no one talked about it as much.

I've also heard stories about how the Sun Realm has buildings made of wood, a substance that comes from the trunks of trees. I've only seen pictures of trees. Old pictures saved from up above. Or pictures my grandmother drew for me based on what her mother told her. They have all kinds of plants up there, or so people say. It's almost like they are living aboveground, with a synthetic sun, fake rain, and artificial stars that come out at night. Why they are so privileged, I may never know. I grit my teeth and try to think about something else.

My thoughts turn to my new friends, Cole and Tawni. With their sudden entrance into my life, I now have puzzles to solve. Clearly they haven't told me everything. I mean, who would? They've just met me, barely know me. I certainly haven't told them everything about my past, although I've told them a lot more than I planned to. Something about the way they looked at each other tells me there's more to their story than they've let on.

An electronic voice blares through the speaker in my ceiling. "All guests are in their rooms. Lights out in exactly five minutes."

I roll my eyes like I usually do when I hear the announcement. They're always trying to make us feel better about our situation. It's like just because we're juveniles, the so-called adults can't be honest with us. *Guests?* Really? We're locked up, our freedoms restricted beyond recognition. Everyone knows we're inmates, plain and simple.

And *rooms?* Come on. I look around my "room" as if I'm seeing it for the first time. No windows. A thin slat in the door is used to let air in and to speak through. It's a cell. Sometimes I awake from a restless sleep and find the walls closing in on me, threatening to suffocate me, crush me. Sometimes I wish they would.

I've heard they named it *the Pen* after the word playpen, like a young child's little safety enclosure, full of toys and bright-colored bobbles and trinkets. But it just makes me think of the longer version of the word it's really short for: penitentiary.

I'm not sure whether they sugarcoat everything to help us sleep at night, or to help *them* sleep at night. Either way, it's a waste of time.

The lights go out and I'm thrust into abject darkness.

I learned in school about the biological changes that humans have slowly undergone, generation after generation, since moving underground. We gained improved night vision due to long exposure to dim or no lighting. Our senses of hearing and smell have been heightened, making us less reliant on our slightly improved sight. Our skin has become paler and dustier. Human lungs are now more resistant to the constant intake of rock dust. Evidently, average life expectancies are about twenty years shorter than when humans lived aboveground, but no one really talks about it. Long story short: we've adapted, for better or worse.

Having a sudden urge, I manage to half-roll off the thin padding on my stone cot and stumble to the corner, where there's a small hole in the floor. I squat and manage to relieve myself before collapsing back into bed.

In the dark, I bend my legs and flex them at the knees a few times, trying to get some feeling back. My eyes are quickly adjusting to the dark and I can just make out the faint outline of the slot in the door. I close my eyes but sleep continues to evade me.

Finally, I fall asleep.

* * *

My body's convulsing, shaking uncontrollably, rattling my teeth as I make an unearthly, high-pitched noise. Tristan's standing nearby, just watching.

I wake up, not shaking, not screaming. Just a dream. Just a dream.

Once more, I drift off to sleep.

* * *

The lights blink on and the computer voice screeches through the speaker. "Good morning. All guests may now exit their rooms for the day,"—I hear the click of the lock on my door—"breakfast will be served in the cafeteria." *As if it would be served anywhere else.*

I lie in bed for a few minutes, blinking, trying to remember the strange dream that woke me in the middle of the night. I can't. It's like the dream has been permanently deleted from my memory. Logically, I know what the dream was about—me being in pain, Tristan watching—but I can't seem to remember the feelings from it.

I sigh, not because I remember the dream, but because I forget it. Swinging my legs over the bed, I force myself up. Some days I feel like staying in bed all day, but that's not permitted. One of the stewards—their name for prison guards—will eventually come and make me leave my cell, by force if necessary. It isn't worth the hassle.

I go through my morning routine—use the "bathroom," do a few stretches, feel sorry for myself—and then exit my "room." First stop is the washroom. To my surprise, I find myself hoping—almost wishing—that Tawni will be in there. It feels weird looking forward to seeing someone again. Especially someone in the Pen. All the people I usually want to see are on the outside, or more likely, dead. Like my sister, who I hope is still alive.

The washroom has a few toilets, but I prefer the hole in my floor, because none of the stalls have doors. There are no mirrors—no one cares about their appearance in the Pen—and a simple trough-style basin covers one whole wall.

A bunch of girls are already using the trough: washing their faces, combing their hair with their fingers, brushing their teeth. The Pen management provides loads of crappy, gritty toothpaste, but no toothbrushes, so we're forced to use our fingers. I scan the line of girls, looking for Tawni's long, white hair.

She isn't here.

I feel a bump from behind as another girl pushes past me and into the washroom. "Move it," she says. Evidently I'm standing in the doorway. Even still, a simple "Excuse me" would've done the trick.

I go to work on my teeth, rubbing hard with my index finger to clean off the stale saliva still inhabiting my mouth. I rinse my mouth out with a swish of brown water from the rusty faucet. I can never understand why all the water in the Pen is brown. It's like they purposely add dirt to it. Most of the water in the Moon Realm—or at least our subchapter—is clear, having been filtered naturally as it flows through the rocky tunnels around us. It's just another way to punish us, I guess.

I skip a shower, because I'm really not in the mood to be naked in front of a bunch of other girls—there are no private showers in this hotel. Plus, we run out of hot water in about two minutes, so unless you're the first one in, you have to shiver under the cold, drippy showerhead. Needless to say, I've reduced my standards on hygiene to about two showers a week, and quick ones at that. No one really notices the smell, though, because we all smell equally nasty. Freshly showered, smelling like soap, you'd actually stick out like a clown at a funeral.

I go to find Tawni, or Cole, or both.

I guess that they'll be hungry, like me. I find them before I make it to the cafeteria. As I push through the crowds of kids, all zigzagging in different directions, I spot Tawni's white hair next to Cole's dark skin. The contrast is stark.

They're slightly apart from the mob of bodies, against the wall, leaning in close to each other. Their heads are together and their lips are moving, like they're whispering. It seems like such a funny place to have a secret conversation, but no one seems to notice. I remember something my dad used to say about how sometimes it's best to hide in plain sight. It's like that now. If they were further away from the crowds, crouching behind some rock in the Yard, or tucked away behind a door, they probably would've drawn everyone's attention. Instead, they're invisible.

I move closer, staying behind a really big guy who's lumbering along in front of me. Next to Tawni is a janitor's closet. The door is slightly ajar and I manage to slip from behind the big guy and into the closet. Out of the crowded hallway I can hear much better and, because they're next to the wall, their voices are amplified and projected into my hiding place. I push my hair away from my ear and listen intently, trying to pick up every word.

Tawni says, "I know what I saw. He looked at her—no, it was more than that: he stared at her, right at her. You should've seen the way she screamed out in pain."

Cole's deep voice grumbles through the door. "What the hell does that even mean? That he's got some sort of mental powers? Hurts people with his mind?"

"I don't know," Tawni says.

"What difference would it make? He's a creep anyway. Just like his father. He comes down here and parades himself around, flaunts his power, allows his ugly mug to be put on every Sun Dweller magazine." My nostrils flare suddenly and I feel my face go red, heating up. It's anger. Directed at Cole for the things he's saying about Tristan. They haven't said any names but it's obvious who they're talking about. Me and Tristan. I take a deep breath, surprised at wanting to defend a random celebrity.

"He's not a creep," Tawni says. "I've heard things…"

"Yeah, right."

"How long have we known each other?" Tawni asks.

There's a pause, like Cole is trying to remember, or count the days or something. Then he says, "Five years." *Five years?*

I'm shocked. I expected him to say three months, or maybe six at the most. They've known each other since *before* the Pen. They must've met in school. That changes everything. The deepness of their relationship; what level of friendship I can have with them; what I can share with either of them.

"Yeah, five years, Cole. And how many times have I lied to you?"

"Never. At least not that I know of." Cole sniggers to himself.

"Never—that's right."

"You might've just misheard, or misunderstood something."

Tawni's voice is rising. She's getting emotional. "No. No, I didn't. I heard both my mother and father say it before I ran away. I wouldn't have left if I wasn't certain. They're spies for the freaking president. They know things. All I really needed to hear was that they were working for the Sun Dwellers, and then I was ready to leave, run away forever. But they kept talking. They said how Tristan's different from his father. How they didn't think he'd carry on the traditions if he became president. They were worried about that. I always wondered why we had so much more money than everyone else. I mean, I went to the same school as you. You couldn't afford to eat, and I was eating with a silver spoon. Kickbacks for their dirty work. They were afraid the money would stop if Tristan took over. That's how I know, Cole. That's how I know!"

She almost shrieks the last bit and I hear Cole shush her, trying to get her to calm down. "Okay, okay," he says. "I believe you. Maybe Tristan's all right, but I still don't get what that has to do with us, with Adele. Just because he looked at her funny…"

"Not *funny*. Intently, seriously, the way you look at someone you might try to track down at some point in the future. Particularly if you have the resources, which he obviously does."

"What?" I hear myself say out loud. I mean for it to be a thought, confined to the safety of my own mind, but my wayward lips betray me.

Silence. I slap a hand over my mouth, hold my breath, listen to my heartbeat crunch in my chest like a miner's axe on a slab of ore.

The door flies open and Cole's face is silhouetted against the lights in the corridor. Some of the light sneaks past his large frame and spills across my face. One of his eyes is swollen shut, his cheek marbled with black, blue, and greenish yellow.

"Are you spying on us?" he says accusingly.

"No. I mean, yes. I mean, I just saw you talking and wanted to hear what you were saying." Insert foot in mouth. Translation: Yes, I am spying. Bye-bye, new friends. Hello, loneliness.

Cole looks like he wants to hit me.

"Why didn't you just ask us?" The question comes from Tawni, who wedges her way between us.

"Ask you?" Again, the words pop from my mouth before I have a chance to stop them. They sound stupid. Like, *Duh, asking would've been far easier than sneaking into a broom closet and listening through a door.* I try to recover. "I, uh, I just thought you wouldn't, uh, tell me these kinds of things," I finish lamely.

"What kinds of *things* exactly?" Cole says.

Tawni pushes Cole back a bit with one arm. I'm surprised she can move him at all. Her arm looks like a toothpick compared to his armor-like chest. I guess she has hidden strength.

To my surprise, she says, "Cole, we need some girl time. We'll catch up with you later." Despite the evenness of her tone, her words sound like a command, and a powerful one at that.

Cole stares at me with one eye for a second, and then melts into the stream of bodies, disappearing in the mob.

When Tawni turns back to me, I say, "Thanks."

Tawni offers me a hand and I take it. Unlike the previous day in the Yard, her hand is warm. Without another word, she pulls me out of the closet and leads me against the flow of human traffic. Where I'd normally bump and knock into a dozen kids if I tried such a maneuver, Tawni is graceful, able to find the path of least resistance. I stay in her wake, protected. I haven't felt protected in a long time.

Soon the crowds thin and we are walking alone. I'm surprised to find myself still holding her hand. I feel like I should shake it free, but it feels so good—wonderful actually. I guess I need it. Human contact, that is. Having been deprived of human touch for so long, my body is craving it.

We reach a cell door. Not mine but the one next to it. Tawni's. Funny that I never knew her and the whole time she was sleeping right next to me, just a rock wall between us. Not that it matters. I've lost Cole's brief friendship and I'm about to lose Tawni's slightly longer friendship. It's time for my last-ditch effort to save it.

"Look, Tawni, I'm really sor—"

"It's okay," Tawni interrupts.

Huh? This time I manage to keep my stupid remark inside my head, but I'm sure my confusion is written all over my face.

I can feel one cheek lifted weirdly, the opposite eyebrow raised, and my mouth contorted beneath my flaring nostrils. If Tawni and I are the lead characters in a magical fairy tale, it's obvious who the ugly stepsister is. Not Tawni.

I realize Tawni's back is to me; she's facing the bed. *Thank God*, I think. Using my fingers, I manage to mold my face back into what I think is close to its normal shape. Just in time, too. She turns around.

Her eyes blaze with a sort of fire. Not real fire, but determination. It's unexpected. She just looks so thin, so frail. Although she towers above me, I feel so much bigger than her. At least normally I do. But now she looks strong, like maybe her bones are made of a tougher material than I thought. I wait for her to speak.

"Your father is alive," she says.

Six

Tristan

I like calling the Tri-Realms the *underworld*. For to me, that's what it is. At times it feels more hellish than if I were at barbecue with a bunch of demons and zombies, roasting the undead on a fiery spit.

I long to feel the wind tousle my hair, the sunlight on my face. Not the fake sun my father's engineers have created, but the real thing. There's nothing like it.

The underworld is so different. Dark, gloomy—it feels dead to me. Like it isn't natural that any form of life other than the spiders and snakes and bats should occupy it. Certainly not humans.

And if we live in the underworld, then my father is the Devil himself, shrewd, evil, self-serving. They say that blood creates an unbreakable bond. If there's a bond between my father and me—created by blood, DNA, or something else entirely—it's as brittle as talc, cracking and crumbling while I was still in my mother's womb.

I see her face again—the Moon Dweller with the shimmering black hair—so beautiful, so strong, so sad, like she's crying invisible tears. Just seeing her, the pain is back. My brain feels like it's expanding outward, pushing against my skull, trying to crack it, break it. But still, I want to help her. Reaching out, I try to touch her, to comfort her. But each time I try, she seems further away, as if some unseen force is keeping us apart. I run, pumping my arms and legs harder and harder, trying to keep up with her, but never able to close the gap. Finally, when I think my legs will collapse beneath me, she stops. I approach, my heart fluttering, my head pounding. I hear a slight whirr and feel a whoosh of air as something flies just past my ear. A flaming arrow. No! Already a spot of blood is seeping through her white tunic where the arrowhead has pierced her breast. The flames are licking at her clothes, charring them. I try to run to her, to douse the flames, to pluck the arrow from her skin and stop the bleeding, but my feet won't move. At first I think I'm in shock, that I'm simply too weak-minded to gain control of my body, but when I look at my feet, they're encased in stone. He moves past me. The archer. I can't see his face, but I'd recognize his gait anywhere. My creator. I scream at him to *Stop, please stop!* but he ignores me, instead blowing softly on the flames, fueling them until they spread. I have to turn away—God, how desperately I want to turn away—but I can't. Can't. Can't even close my eyes. I watch her burn. She's brave—doesn't even cry out, but I can hear her screams anyway. When she dies, my head stops hurting.

I wake up sweating and yelling, thrashing about in my bed. And thinking about the underworld.

Roc is by my side. As always. "Shhh," he says. "Someone will hear."

My legs stop thrashing, my arms stop flailing. I'm breathing heavily but not screaming anymore. It was just a dream. I'm on my bed; Roc must have carried me.

"What happened?" I say.

"You fainted," Roc says, his lips curling slightly.

"Does that give you some kind of pleasure?" I snap.

Roc continues grinning. "Given it was brought on by your battle with a ferocious warrior, namely me, I'd say yes, it does bring me a level of pleasure. Especially because it was in the midst of my stunning and heroic victory," he adds.

Normally I'd laugh. But I feel anything but normal. I feel like I've lost someone special to me, someone close. Like my mother—but a different kind of close, a different kind of special. I grunt.

Roc seems to recognize that something is wrong and his smile fades. "Tristan, are you okay?" he asks.

I honestly don't know. So I swing my legs over the side of the bed and tell him everything. About the girl in the Pen, the pain in my back and head, the big guy who was about to assault her, how I saw her face just before I fainted, and about my dream—what my father did to her. When I finish I look for his reaction. I think he might make fun of me. If the roles were reversed it's what I might do.

Instead, his lips are tight, his eyes narrow. He says, "I think it means something."

"You do?" I say, genuinely surprised.

"Yes. A storm is coming. I've felt it for some time now. I think you have, too. Why we've never spoken of it before, I don't know. Perhaps we were scared."

My first instinct is to contradict him. Not the stuff about the storm—whatever that means—but about being scared. He might be, but not me. I'm not scared of anything. Not even my father—not anymore—although I probably should be. But I know I've been too reactionary lately—too quick to fire back at Roc if I don't like something he says. Like a good friend, he's put up with it, shaking his head and ignoring my outbursts. So, for once, I don't say the first thing that pops into my head. I actually think about what he said.

A storm? I know he doesn't mean a physical storm, like the ones that rage on the earth's surface from time to time. Therefore, a metaphorical one. Like a conflict. A battle maybe. No, more specific than that: a rebellion. I *have* felt it, too. Have even commented on it. If not out loud, then in my head, to myself. How it's a wonder that everyone puts up with my father's tyrannical politics, his cruel and unfair treatment of the people that support his way of life. Not a wonder—a *miracle*. And miracles simply don't happen these days. Not anymore. They're a thing of the past, of legends, of stories. Which means it's bound to happen eventually. From time to time we hear whisperings of secret groups of radicals, plotting and scheming in hidden caves, using secret handshakes and passwords. My father dismisses them as casually as he swats pesky flies from his shoulder.

I *have* felt it, too. So why haven't we talked about it before? I try to open myself to the possibility that I'm scared, like Roc suggested. I know right away that isn't it. It's something else: I don't believe my own feelings. And why would I? Things have been the same my whole life. Things will never change, can never change. Can they?

I feel Roc's eyes on my face. I look at him. There's a twinkle in his eye, like he knows I've worked it out.

I say, "I'm not scared." You know, just to set the record straight.

"I know," he says.

"You what?" I say. "Then why did you—"

"Because I *am* scared, and I wanted you to think about things seriously."

I rise to my feet. "What? I do take things ser…What are you suggesting, that I'm not serious enough?" My face is starting to feel hot.

Roc puts his arms out, palms open. "No, I just think that ever since your mom…"—his eyes drift down—"…left, you've been in a funk, a haze, not really as engaged as you used to be. The only time I see light in your eyes is when we're training."

"What are you, my shrink or something?"

"There you go—not taking things seriously again."

I grit my teeth. I'm determined not to make another light comment or joke for the rest of the conversation. I hope our talk won't last too long.

"Fine," I say. "Okay, so I've been in this *haze*, hating life, no light in my eyes except when I'm beating the snot out of you with a wooden sword…" *Blast!* A joke—I've failed already.

Being serious is harder than I thought. Maybe Roc is right, but I'm certainly not going to say *that* out loud. Pausing, I try to gather my thoughts. Roc lets the joke pass without comment. "So I see this girl, this Moon Dweller. Roc, lemme tell ya, she was pretty hot. Beautiful. Even wearing her gray prisoner's tunic she was stunning. Her hair fell like a black waterfall around her shoulders. Her eyes were intensely fascinating. And her curves, my God, Roc, were they ever—"

"Get to the point, Tristan," Roc says.

Right. Serious. My point. What is my point anyway? Ahh, yes. "It's like she was metal and I was a magnet, Roc. But at the same time it felt like someone had shoved an electric wire into my skin and was frying me from the inside. It hurt like hell. No, worse than hell, man. And yet, somehow across the distance, through the fence, over the mob of people, I felt a pull to her, even though I knew it would hurt me to be closer to her. I probably would've just let it go, chalked it up to male hormones, but then when she acted so strong, pushed that guy…I don't know, since then I can't get her out of my mind."

"That's called a crush, sir."

Oh, damn you, Roc! He seems intent on making this more difficult than it has to be, even throwing a "sir" in there for good measure. I can feel the grit in my mouth as I shave the enamel off each tooth with my incessant grinding. Yeah, Roc's like a brother to me, but also like a brother, I wish he'd just go away sometimes.

When I speak again, I'm proud of how even my voice is, pretending like I haven't even heard Roc's comment. "It's weird. I know it's not just a crush because of all the pain I felt. There's something more to it. Like…like the pain was a sign. Yeah, maybe that's what it was. A sign. Like our lives are tied together. Like our destinies are intertwined. I think I have to find her, Roc, if only to know that she survived, that her strength didn't lead to her death."

"Is this Moon Dweller girl the only reason you want to go?"

I raise my eyebrows. "I, uh, I think so…" I'm so unsure of my answer that I rub my head to try to think. Yes, I want to know what happened to the Moon Dweller. Yes, I want to meet her, if only to figure out why I feel so much pain when I'm near her, what it means. It hits me. "She's only part of it," I say.

"I know," Roc says.

Of course he does. Roc always seems to be one mental step ahead of me. I sigh. "I want to get out of here, Roc. I'm tired of living like this. There's no meaning in my life. I hate my father. I hate this place. Finding her is as good a reason as any to get out of here. I just have to get out of here. I can't deal with my father anymore."

"We can't just leave."

"Why not?"

"Don't you think they'll notice?"

"Of course they'll notice, Roc. But who cares?"

"I do. I don't feel like being chased all over the Tri-Realms by a bunch of your dad's goons."

"My *father's* goons," I correct.

"Your dad, your father: What's the difference?" Roc says through clenched teeth.

I frown. "It's…different…to…me." We're on the verge of another brawl.

"Whatever. In any case, I'm not leaving with you on some half-baked journey all over the Moon Realm, just to chase the first pretty tunic you've seen in a while. She's a prisoner, for God's sake."

"Then I'll go alone. And for the record, I'm not chasing a tunic. Yeah, she was pretty, but who cares? There are lots of pretty girls. And yeah, I'll try to find her, because I want to know why she makes my head feel like it's about to explode. But this is not all about her, Roc. Like I told you, I need to do this for me. I thought you of all people would understand that."

Roc's hard stare continues for another moment and then his eyes soften. "Tristan, I…"

"What?"

"Never mind. You promise you're not just doing this to find some silly girl?"

"Yes," I say, my tone more confident than I feel.

"Okay."

"Okay?"

"Yeah. I'll come with you."

I can't hold back my smile. I'll say it again: Roc is like a brother to me; I'm not sure what I would've done if he decided not to come. I'm glad we've made it through our serious talk without killing each other.

Roc says, "I'll help you find your *crush*." I spoke too soon. I leap off the bed, tackling him to the ground, pushing his face into the soft carpet. I'm laughing, he's gasping, trying to take a breath. I release him and stand up, but I'm not done yet. As he turns over I place a foot atop his chest and raise my fists over my head, relishing my small victory.

* * *

70

We spend the rest of the day making plans. Now that the contract negotiations are finally over, I'll request a holiday. My father will insist I go to one of the finest Sun Dweller resorts, one that has the brightest fake sunlight and truckloads of synthetic sand. But I'll tell him I'm tired of those places, tired of the same old scene. It won't surprise him—he already knows how I feel about the customs of the Sun Dwellers. If I request another trip to the Moon Realm—an unofficial, off-the-books trip—I think he'll authorize it, as a sort of reward for all my work over the last few months. The first chance we have, Roc and I will ditch my security guards and go find the girl, and hopefully ourselves at the same time.

When we leave my apartment, I'm feeling good. I won't go so far as to say I'm happy—I haven't been happy in a long time—but I'm satisfied that I'm finally doing something real. Something I want to do. Cutting another one of my father's ropes away, so to speak.

* * *

We're at dinner, the three of us—me, my brother, Killen, and my father, his lordship. Dinner is funny in our palace. The table we sit at is about a mile long, with enough place settings to host the entire forty-third ghetto of the Star Realm (their population is only twenty-three). My father, his majesty (a president, not a king), sits at one end. My mother used to sit at the other head, but now her seat is vacant, like it has been for a long time. My brother and I sit across from each other, in the middle, so far from my father that we can barely see him.

When we were younger, my brother and I would get into all kinds of trouble at dinner, kicking under the table, slinging food across at each other, whispering nasty names so our parents couldn't hear what we were saying. It was great fun, and we enjoyed the challenge of trying to get away with things while our parents shouted across the length of the table in a ridiculous attempt to have a conversation.

Now it isn't worth the effort. Day by day, my brother is becoming more and more like a clone of my father. He even sits like him at the table, his back straight, his head held so high I don't think he'll be able to get his fork to his mouth without dropping his food. Killen is two years younger than me, but I know he thinks himself to be the older, wiser son. We haven't had fun together in forever, since before my mother left.

"So I hear the contract negotiations were a success, brother," Killen says. He's trying to sound smart. In reality, he's never so much as negotiated a turd from his butt.

I put on a fake voice and say, "Splendid, my dear brother. Simply splendid. We got an even better deal than last year and the people of the Tri-Realms seem to love us even more!" To my father it'll sound like we're having a mature, brotherly conversation. Killen knows better.

"That's wonderful, Tristan," he says. Under his breath, he mumbles, "Quit being a dumb arse."

"I'd never take that title away from you, Brother," I hiss. I feel his leg swing out as he tries to kick me. He misses, his toe thudding against the leg of my chair. His face turns red and he curses under his breath. It probably hurt, too, because he's wearing these absurd shoes that look like white ballet slippers and provide zero protection for the foot. They're just another Sun Dweller fashion trend that my brother has bought into. It's a hard decision, but I'm sticking with my boots.

"Father," I say loudly, maintaining my fake voice, "I'd like to take a holiday, now that the negotiations are complete."

My brother is glaring at me, but I ignore him.

President Nailin shouts, "Of course! Shall I have Lima book a few weeks at the Sandy Oasis like last year?"

Shocking how predictable my father is.

I pretend to consider it. "Hmm, maybe…" I say. "But I'm also considering doing something a little different…something a bit more exotic."

"What did you have in mind?"

I glance at my brother. His head is cocked to the side. It makes him look even younger than he is.

"I'd like to travel inter-Realm, to the Moon Realm. I think it'll be a good way to show the Moon Dwellers that we appreciate their support. You know, by having a holiday there, spending some Nailins at their shops."

"Absolutely not," my father says.

I really thought he'd go for it, that my lie was a good one, believable, sensible. So I don't have a backup plan. Killen is snickering, which doesn't help.

"Why not?" I ask, really wanting to know what has prompted my father's quick and decisive rejection.

"It's just not proper," he says simply.

I've never hated him more than I hate him now. It's the way he says it more than his words. As though such a trip would be like me sleeping with the rats—no, worse, with the cockroaches. He wants me to be all smiles and winks when I'm in the other Realms renegotiating our so-called contracts, and yet I can't even take a simple holiday there?

Killen's nodding, wagging his head up and down like a dog. "It wouldn't be proper, Brother," he parrots. Now *I* kick.

My aim is true, connecting solidly with my brother's shinbone. To his credit, he doesn't cry out, although I know it hurts, can see it all over his face. He winces and holds his breath, trying to stifle a groan of pain.

"You're right, Father, Brother. How silly of me. Have Lima book my usual." I've lost my appetite. Before standing up I take another shot at Killen under the table, and from the shade of purple his face turns, I know I've hit the same spot. It's the only thing satisfying about the meal.

Seven

Adele

"What do you know of my father?" I say. It comes out as a croak, because I stop breathing when my heart rises into my throat. I gulp the words back down, trying to clear a passage. I take a deep breath.

"Only that he's probably alive," Tawni says.

I don't think the words will come out right, so I hope she'll anticipate my next question.

"How much of our conversation did you hear?" Tawni asks.

Damn. I'm hoping for answers, not questions. I'll have to speak. I try a single word: "Enough." It comes out better this time, but still isn't my natural timbre.

"Look," Tawni says, "I'm sorry I didn't open up to you before, but we'd only just met. The things I know are dangerous…"

She glances left and right, like the walls might have ears. She's making me nervous. Although the snippets I'd heard of Tawni and Cole's whispered conversation intrigue me—particularly the stuff about Tristan—I'm not interested in that now. I only care about one thing.

"It's okay. Just tell me about my dad."

Tawni takes a deep breath. She looks stressed, her brow furrowed and eyes narrowed and intense, like something heavy is weighing on her. She says, "As you probably gathered, my parents are traitors. They live amongst the Moon Dwellers, but work for the Sun Dwellers. They're spies for the president. I heard them talking one night. They thought I was out with my friends, but I'd returned early with a stomachache. They spoke about how Tristan is different from his father, how he cares about the people from the Lower Realms, even if he enjoys the comforts of the Sun Realm."

Her words are interesting, and typically I'd be hanging on every single one, but I'm still missing the point. "What does that have to do with my father?" I blurt out.

Tawni stops abruptly, her eyebrows rising. "Sorry. Your father first—then the other stuff."

She sits on the bed and motions for me to join her. I don't feel like sitting; I'm too wired to do anything but pace around the room, but I don't want to argue as I'm afraid it'll delay the conversation further. I sit next to her, tapping my toe rapidly on the stone floor.

Tawni looks at me with sincere blue eyes and says, "My parents were the ones who recommended that your parents be taken away."

It wouldn't sting any more if she'd slapped me across the face. My parents dragged away in the middle of the night, out through the kicked-down door; Enforcers swarming through our home, smashing picture frames and tables and chairs and anything they could get their hands on; me, fighting like an animal to defend my family, who were eventually wrenched away anyway. The most disturbing image from that night: my father's eyes, intense and scared, not fearful for his own life, but for mine and Elsey's.

All because of Tawni's parents. *I don't think kids should be judged by what their stupid parents do.* Tawni's words from before suddenly make sense.

I want to walk away from her, to leave her and her evil family behind forever, but I stay. First, because I owe her for sitting down and talking to me in the first place, in the Yard; for not walking away when I was rude and acting like a nutter. Second, because she still hasn't told me everything she knows about my father—and I have to know. And third, because I want to believe in her words about kids having the potential to be different than their parents. I want to believe it for Tristan's sake. Because if he isn't different than his father, then all my thoughts and feelings over the last day have been fake, pure fantasy.

As I try to make sense of my thoughts, of my feelings, I realize Tawni's crying. Her earlier strength gives way, her body crumples, she tucks her face into her hands. I know she's been putting on a front—an attempt to be strong, to chase away her sadness with a brave face. She thinks I'm going to leave. She doesn't know I have three reasons to stay.

I feel warmth in my bones, welling up from beneath my feet, until it reaches the top of my head. The warmth is compassion for Tawni. She didn't ask for her parents to be traitors. And from what I understand, their treachery caused her to run from them, to leave home all alone, and to eventually be caught and brought to the Pen. No, she isn't like her parents at all.

The sudden compassion I feel reminds me of my mother. I always think I'm more like my dad, but now I wonder if there isn't a lot more of my mom in me than I realized. I hope so. My mom is a special soul.

Instinctively, I put my arm around Tawni and pull her close. Her eyes flick open for a moment, red and wet, and then reclose as she buries her head in the nook between my shoulder and chest. "I'm so sorry, Adele," she moans.

I say nothing—there's nothing to say. I just hold her while sobs shake her body. I rub her back, smooth her hair—even kiss her forehead. Those were the things my mother used to do to me when I was scared—usually when still stuck in the throes of a waking nightmare about drowning, my greatest fear. Slowly, Tawni's body stops shaking and her muffled sobs relent. Her choked breaths deepen and grow consistent. For a moment I think she might've fallen asleep.

But then she says, "Why are you forgiving me?"

I haven't said a word to her, certainly haven't uttered the words *I forgive you*, but I guess my actions speak louder. But I haven't forgiven her, not really, because there's no need.

"You haven't done anything wrong," I say.

Her puffy eyes look into mine as she sits up straight again. "Thank you," she says.

"My father?" I say.

Her words come out in a rush, without pause to breathe. "He's been taken to a camp set up for traitors—my parents called it Camp Blood and Stone—where the prisoners are made to work in some of the most dangerous mines in the Moon Realm. I understand it's somewhere in one of the Northern subchapters; my parents mentioned subchapter twenty-six, I think."

"What about my mother?" I say, realizing Tawni hasn't mentioned her. She was very specific: *Your father is alive.*

"I don't know," Tawni says, "they only mentioned your dad."

"How did you know they were talking about my dad?" My questions are coming rapidly now, as all of the investigative skills that my father taught me come back.

"They said that the traitors they'd turned over to the authorities had two daughters, Adele and Elsey. Your name isn't that common, so when I heard it and then later you told us about your parents, I made the connection." Tawni crinkles her nose, like she knows what my next question will be and is dreading it. But I have to ask it.

"Why didn't you tell me last night when you realized?" I ask.

"I don't know. I should have. We'd just met and I usually talk to Cole about stuff before I do anything. He's my best friend. Has been for a long time."

I'm not mad at her. She was in a tough position, not knowing how I would react when she told me, and yet she told me anyway. She could've just kept it to herself, told me to go stuff it when I eavesdropped on her, but she didn't. She did the right thing. She's not like her parents.

"What about the other stuff?" I ask.

"You mean about Tristan?" Tawni says, understanding immediately what I mean.

I nod.

Tawni says, "We should include Cole in the conversation."

My heart sinks. *Cole.* For a moment I've forgotten about him. He looked so angry at me. I've just met the guy, so I shouldn't care what he thinks about me, but to my surprise, I do. Probably because of what he did for me yesterday during the riot. Or perhaps because he's Tawni's best friend, and she seems like a good person, so that must mean he is, too. Or it might just be because I actually like him. Certainly his sarcasm works well with me.

"Will he still be pissed off at me?" I ask, frowning.

Tawni laughs. "Don't worry about him. Sometimes he has a bit of a temper, but he makes up for it by forgiving and forgetting faster than anyone I know." Wiping the tears from her cheeks, Tawni rises, offering her hand to help me up. I take it.

I allow her to pull me down the hall. Already some of the juveniles are leaving the cafeteria, looking unsatisfied by their breakfasts, heading outside for another long, boring day spent lounging in the Yard.

When we enter the crowded eatery, I notice Cole right away, sitting alone in the corner. Thankfully, he's facing away, so he doesn't stare at us as we approach. When Tawni slides onto the bench across from him and he sees her tearstained face, he nearly knocks over the table as he leaps to his feet.

"What happened? Are you okay?" he says. His eyes flit back and forth between Tawni and me, one minute showing concern for his friend and the other angry and glaring, like how he'd looked at me earlier.

"I'm fine. Please calm down, Cole," Tawni says, reaching across the table to rest a comforting hand on his shoulder. At first his body stiffens at her touch, but then he relaxes and melts back into his seat. For a second I'm jealous of the kind of relationship they have. It's a true friendship in every sense of the word. I've never had that kind of friendship—probably never will. There isn't room for it in my world.

I tense up, waiting for the next spout of anger from Cole. It doesn't come.

"I'm sorry," Cole says.

Never would I have expected those to be his next words. To be honest, I don't understand.

"What for?" I say.

The corners of Cole's mouth turn up slightly, a complete one-eighty from his tense expression a moment earlier. The steely twinkle I saw in his eyes the day before is back. "For my temper," he says. "Tawni tries to help me with it, but it usually gets the better of me. Sneaking around and spying on us wasn't right, but my reaction was even worse. I should've let you explain."

"Thanks," I say. Tawni's crying coupled with Cole's quick forgiveness makes me feel even worse about what I've done. "And I'm sorry for eavesdropping. I won't do it again."

Cole dismisses me with a wave of his hand. "Even," he says. The way he says it makes me believe my transgression is like a distant memory to him, soon to be forgotten entirely. Tawni wasn't kidding about him.

"Can I get you something to eat?" she says.

I nod, sliding out of the booth to let her past. "Anything not green, not slimy, and not still moving," I say wryly.

Cole chuckles. "Good luck with that," he says.

Tawni marches off, her hands fisted and her head firm, as if she's on a mission. Meeting my criteria *will* be a mission, I think.

When Tawni is gone, Cole says, "How are you feeling?"

"Feeling?" I say absently, trying to decide how to respond. In truth, I have no idea how I'm feeling. In the last twenty-four hours a lot has changed in my life. Two new friends, the strange pain I felt when I saw the president's eldest son, my dad being alive: it's all too much to take in, to process. I mean, I'm happy—no, make that extremely happy, ecstatic, over the moon—that my dad might be okay, but it feels weird, too. For one thing I don't know anything about my mom's whereabouts. Also, for the last six months I've been trying to come to terms with the possibility that my parents are dead, executed as traitors. Now there's hope that at least one of them is alive...I dunno, it just feels weird. Then again, I'm not sure it really matters that he's alive. It's not like I will ever get to see him again. And I'm sure that the conditions for him are awful to the point of complete misery. So that isn't much to live for either.

I almost shout at myself aloud. Thankfully, I keep it inside, opting to scream in my mind: *No, no, no! You're better than that, better than a quitter! Dad would be ashamed by such thoughts!* I know then what I have to do: rescue my father and find out whether my mother is still alive. Oh, and also take a detour to find my sister, too, if I have time. Should be easy, simple, no problemo! Or impossible. It's definitely one or the other.

I still haven't answered Cole's question. I'm not sure how long it's been since he asked it, but probably awhile, because he's looking at me strangely, like I have poo on my face. While I've been battling with myself in the comfort of my own head, I can only guess at what weird facial expressions I was making.

"I'm guessing you're not sure how you feel?" Cole says.

Bingo! Give the guy a prize. I *am* impressed by Cole's recognition of my feelings without me having said a single word. Maybe he is a mind reader. I hope not. With my muddled thoughts, having a mind reader around will be far too embarrassing.

"Yeah, I'm a bit confused right now."

"But I bet you want to go rescue your dad," Cole says.

Crap! He IS a mind reader! Or possibly just very perceptive. I'm hoping for the latter. "Yeah, and my sister and mom, too, while I'm at it. Should be easy," I say.

"Especially with us around," Cole says.

"What should be easy?" Tawni says, returning with two plates of gunk that are meant to be food. To her credit, the gunk on my plate isn't green, slimy, or moving. But it is brownish and gooey. I take a bite, swallowing quickly before my taste buds have much of a chance to linger on the flavor.

"Rescuing Adele's family," Cole says. "It shouldn't be a problem. Only small hurdles to get over, like escaping from the Pen, crossing hundreds of miles of cave networks while avoiding detection by Enforcers, breaking into at least one maximum security prison, and then breaking back out. Piece of cake."

I groan. "I was trying to be positive," I say. "In any case, I'm doing it alone, so it's not your problem."

"Wrong," Cole says.

"Right," I retort.

"Look, whether you like it or not, we're going to help you," Cole says.

I stare directly into his strong eyes, trying to get him to back down. About three seconds later I look away. What am I thinking trying to beat Mr. Power Eyes in a staring competition—I can't even beat myself in the mirror.

"Why would you do that for me?" I ask.

Cole shrugs. "You're growing on me." His bottom lip doesn't pout the way it normally does.

"Lie!" I declare, raising my arm in victory before it's even confirmed.

Cole laughs and Tawni nearly spews out the spoonful of yellow goop she has in her mouth. "You're right, Adele, you're not growing on me. That would be disgusting. Hair grows on me, foot fungus on occasion, too, due to the shameful hygiene of the guys' bathrooms, but not other people, and most definitely not you."

His eyes are twinkling even more than before. I grin. "So what's the real reason for wanting to help me?" I ask.

"I've got nothing against you, nor your magical mysterious love affair with the sun prince"—I try to interject, but Cole sees it coming and raises a finger, silencing me—"but I just don't trust Tridlan one bit."

"Tri*stan*," I say, "and there's no love—"

"What?"

"His name is Tristan. You said Tridlan."

"Did I?" Cole says, throwing his hands up and feigning ignorance. I realize he's mocking me. I want to be angry, but his mannerisms make me smile.

84

"Yes, and I was in pain when I saw him so, trust me, I'm not in any hurry to get near him again." Although I would like to know what caused it.

"Anyway," Cole says, "him being the son of the president and all, it's not easy for me to be as trusting of Triftan as you guys are."

I ignore his repeated mispronunciation of Tristan's name and try to focus. It'll be great to have friends help me—at least to get out of the Pen. But I still don't understand their motives, which bothers me. At least not Cole's. Tawni's probably trying to make up for the actions of her parents—to prove that she's better than them. Also, she seems to just be a nice person, willing to help a friend in need, even a new friend like me. But Cole's a mystery. It doesn't help that he jokes around so much, which makes it even harder to get a read on him. He has no reason to help me.

"Seriously, why do you want to help?" I repeat.

His eyes darken. "Okay, look. I'm just really tired of everyone getting screwed over by the Sun Dwellers. I've been in juvie once before, when I was eleven. I had this teacher, Mrs. Witchikata. She was really kind, really pretty, always saying nice things to me. What can I say? I fell for her—head over freakin' heels."

"You're joking," I say.

"Me? Joke? Never," Cole says. "Anyway, one day I told her I loved her. Mrs. W would never have reported it, but a nasty little Year Five kid overheard and told the principal, who told the authorities. Unauthorized flirting, they called it. I got six weeks in the Pen. Since then, I've always wanted revenge."

Tawni giggles. I look at her, then back at Cole. "La la lie," I say.

"Almost, smarty," Cole says. "It was a half lie. All the stuff about Mrs. W *was* BS—in fact she was about ninety-five years old, two hundred pounds overweight, covered in warts, with a mean streak a mile wide. I hated her guts. But I did give you the truth about why I want to help you. The Sun Dwellers are creeps, period."

From experience, I can't argue with that.

"Okay," I say. I believe him. It certainly fits with what little I know about the male species. Their motives are generally simple: fun, honor, sex, food, pride, revenge, sex. Pretty basic stuff.

"Okay?" Tawni says, confirming.

"Yeah, we'll escape together."

"And then go rescue your family," she says.

I haven't thought that far ahead, but I figure I can talk them out of it when the time comes. "Uh, yeah, whatever. So how do we pull it off?" I say, leaning in.

Cole dips his head forward conspiratorially and lowers his voice, half-covering his mouth with one of his hands. "I know a guy who can get one of the guards to turn off the electric fence for a few minutes, maybe ten if we're lucky," he says.

I gawk at him like he's an alien.

"What?" he says. "We were thinking about trying to escape once so I looked into it."

I don't have to confirm that he's telling the truth—his face is dead serious. "Okay. If we get your guy to turn off the fence at say…midnight, two hours after lights out, we can sneak out of our cells and climb the fence," I say.

"Our cells will be locked," Tawni points out.

"There's a trick for that," I say. "I've done it before. Get a small piece of cardboard or plastic from somewhere, anywhere, and when you shut your door for the last time at night, slide the plastic between the door and the frame, blocking the deadbolt. When the door automatically locks, it will still click, but you'll be able to open it."

"Nice," Cole says, nodding. I smile. I'm glad to be able to bring some level of expertise to the table.

"Right," Tawni says, "so at five minutes to midnight we leave our cells. Adele and I will be together and we'll see you"—she gestures to Cole—"at the fence. We'll meet in the shadows in the northeast wing. When the electricity goes out we start climbing."

Cole's eyes narrow and he screws up his face. "How do we tell the time?" he asks.

"We'll have to base it off of the guards' patrols," I say. "Start counting from the ten o'clock lights out. Approximately every fifteen minutes a guard will go by—watch through the slot in your doors. Once seven patrols pass we'll know it's about quarter to midnight. Then we'll just have to count in our heads for ten minutes—six hundred seconds. Then we go." I'm feeling confident—probably too confident—but it's a good feeling, one I haven't felt in a while. Anything's better than just sitting around waiting to turn eighteen and be transferred to a maximum security prison.

"When should we do it?" Tawni asks.

"How about tonight?" I say, feeling eager butterflies in my stomach.

"That's pretty tight," Cole says. "I'll have to check with my guy to see if it's possible on such short notice."

"It better be," I say. Acting in a hurry is better than taking a long time to plan our escape. That way the dirty guard won't have time to rethink his choice to help us.

"We'll need money to pay him," Cole says. "You know, the guard who helps us."

I knew it sounded too good to be true. I don't have any money and certainly no way of getting any. But I ask anyway. "How much?"

"At least fifty Nailins I expect."

My heart sinks. I haven't seen that much money in my entire life. It might as well be a million. Even if we come up with a way to raise some money, we won't be able to get that much in ten lifetimes. I close my eyes tightly and clench my teeth, trying to stifle a scream. I need a miracle.

"I can provide the money," Tawni says.

My eyes flash open and I look at the skinny, white-haired girl beside me. I glance at Cole. He doesn't seem surprised. In fact, it's like he expected her response. I realize that when he mentioned the money he wasn't talking to me. He was talking to Tawni the whole time.

I turn back to Tawni. "You have access to fifty Nailins?" I say in disbelief.

"More if we need it," she says. "When I got caught trying to go interdistrict without a travel permit my parents were all over me, asking me why, *why would I do such a thing?* So I gave them a BS story about how I really wanted to see the Lantern Caverns of the ninth subchapter and how I never thought they'd let me go." She pushes a strand of hair out of her face, grinning. "They bought it, and although they couldn't get me out of doing time in the Pen, they were able to make my stay here as easy as I want it to be. I could have had a plush room on the third floor, five-star meals, access to a telebox, pretty much anything I want."

"Then why do you sleep in a crappy cell next to me?"

Tawni's face falls. "Because if I took advantage of what my parents could do for me, then I'd be just as terrible as them. They don't know where I sleep, and the guards won't tell them. When they visit, the guards move me upstairs for a few hours. I swear to God, Adele, I'm not like them—never will be."

"Truth," I say solemnly.

Tawni nods. "In any case, I still have access to an account they set up for me with the warden...I mean with the concierge." I chuckle at her little joke. "There are more than two hundred Nailins in it."

Cole whistles. "I didn't know you had that much dough. How about sharin' some with an old friend of yours?"

Tawni smirks. "We'll need all of it if we're going to pull this off." She lowers her voice again. "First to pay off the guard and then to travel across the Moon Realm."

I nod. "Thanks, Tawni. And you too, Cole. I wouldn't stand a chance without your help." I realize then that I don't have to be alone anymore—can't be alone, can't stand it for one more second. I hit a new low the previous day and then everything started moving up again. It all started with a bit of pain. My downward spiral is finally over.

It reminds me of something my dad said one year at Christmas, when we didn't even have the money for presents, or fancy food, or anything. He said, "Sometimes, girls, you have to hit your lowest low just before you hit your highest high. It makes you appreciate the good things so much more." Right now is starting to feel like one of those times. Yeah, maybe meeting a couple of friends and coming up with a plan to escape from a juvenile delinquent facility isn't the best of times in my life, but it isn't the worst either, and for that I'm thankful.

We leave the cafeteria long after we arrived—we're the last to go. Although we aren't satisfied by the food, we're still satisfied. By other things. More important things. Life-changing things. I am going to rescue my family, and hopefully myself at the same time.

Yeah, things are looking up.

Eight
Tristan

Ahhh, a holiday at the Sandy Oasis. It has everything anyone could ever want. Soft, plush beds to sleep on. Warm, sandy beaches (they even simulate waves and paint picturesque ocean views). Half-naked girls ready to throw themselves at any celebrity who happens to make eye contact.

I throw up in my mouth when we arrive.

Roc is carrying my bags while my security detail protects me from the girls.

You're probably thinking that I'm a big wimp to let my father dictate the terms of my holiday so easily. I could've pushed back harder, tried to force him to see my point of view. But you see, the thing is, my father doesn't like being pushed around. And I could tell he was in one of his moods, more stubborn than the lovechild of an ox and a mule. So I played along.

Roc and I aren't staying in the Oasis. Not for long anyway.

We're going to the Moon Realm. The back of my head is buzzing in anticipation. I hope the girl's still alive when we get there. If she is, I'll demand that she tells me how she did it. How she caused me so much physical pain just by looking at me.

We reach my room with a record low of only three girls offering to have my babies. I guess I'm losing my touch. From the looks in their eyes, I think they were offering to have them, like, right then, immediately. I didn't make eye contact for fear that they'd rip off their clothes and throw themselves at me and my entourage.

The room isn't really a room. More like an entire wing of the hotel, comprised of ten distinct rooms, only five of which are bedrooms. The others are sitting rooms, standing rooms, massage rooms, and kitchens. I don't even count the six bathrooms as rooms. The cost for a single night would feed an entire subchapter of the Moon Realm for a year.

Luckily we aren't staying long. "Quick and unexpected action is the most effective in battle," my fighting instructor used to say. I'm about to put his advice to the test. Perhaps not in a traditional battle, but in a battle nonetheless. A battle to take back my life.

I ask my security guards to wait outside, to monitor the four doors for any fake-tanned girls trying to gain access to my suite. When they're gone, I say, "Is this going to work, Roc?"

"I'm not sure, sir," Roc says.

"Cut the sir crap, Roc, please," I say. "We're about to embark on a rogue mission and I want you to be with me as a friend, not as a servant."

"I'll try, sir," Roc says, grinning from ear to ear. I grin back, swatting at him playfully. He punches at me and for a moment there's a good chance it's going to escalate into another practice fight, but then there's a sudden knock at the door.

A guard enters: a giant with no neck and fists the size of boulders. His nose looks like it's been broken a dozen times—it's flat and wide. Although I expect to have to translate a series of grunts and hand signals, he surprises me by speaking perfect English in an unexpectedly high voice.

"You have a visitor. He says he's expected."

"Name?" I ask, already knowing the answer.

"Kruger."

"He's okay," I say.

The guard leaves, closing the door behind him, and a minute later the door reopens and another guy walks in. Compared to the guard, this guy looks tiny. He's about my size. Well, exactly my size actually, both in height, weight, and body type. Athletic build, six-two without shoes, a hundred and eighty five pounds dripping wet. It always amazes me how I can just snap my fingers and make things happen. That's something I like about being who I am, living where I live. Can I really give it all up that easily? Can I really walk away from it all? Something tells me my jaunt to the Moon Realm will only be temporary. Before long, I'll be doing my father's dirty work just like always.

I have no idea how they found someone who so closely resembles me in such a short time, but I don't really care about the details. His face even kind of looks like mine. If he wears a hat and sunglasses, the guards won't be able to tell the difference. Although each member of my security team would rank well across the entirety of the Tri-Realms when it comes to muscle, their IQs would likely sit in the bottom quartile.

"My money?" Kruger says. This guy gets right to the point, which is fine with me.

I wave Roc forward. He extracts a paper envelope from his pocket, which clinks as he hands it across. "A hundred Nailins," he says. "Count it."

The guy shakes his head and the parcel at the same time. "No need. It's all there," he says, as though he's done so many shady deals that he can count the coins just by the sound of their clinking. Maybe he can. What do I know?

Next, Roc hands him some clothes, identical to the ones I'm wearing. A gold tunic, a silver bracelet, brown moccasins. He even gives him a pair of my blue silk boxer shorts, just to be thorough. "Put those on," I say.

The guy strips right in front of us—clearly modesty is low on his priority list. I turn away, removing my own clothes and swapping them for a black tunic, black pants, and black boots. While I add a dark hat and sunglasses to my getup, Roc provides Kruger with a similar pair of sunglasses and a floppy, white beach hat. A current edition of a Sun Dweller magazine and a bottle of expensive wine from my father's personal stash complete the façade.

With a nod, Kruger slides the money into the magazine and heads for the door. Roc trails after him. We've agreed that if the fake me leaves without Roc it will raise eyebrows; Roc goes everywhere with me. I hide off to the side, behind the red velvet drapes that provide privacy at the poolside windows. They exit, and just before the door closes, I see the gaggle of guards surround them. Kruger's head is tilted slightly downward, so there will be even less likelihood he'll be recognized as anyone but me. The door closes and I hear Roc's muffled voice as he explains to the guards that my *guest* will be resting in the suite while I'm at the pool.

I'm not worried. They'll buy the story. After all, they aren't really trained to question their masters. Plus, they're trying to protect me from those who might hurt me, not from escaping. I'm not a prisoner—not technically.

I slip back around the drapes and peek through the window. A few minutes later, the dummy me and my entourage enter the pool area. Because we arrived in the early afternoon, it's already packed—finding a place to sit would be near impossible for any normal person. But I'm no normal person, at least not to these people. It's all been prepared ahead of my arrival. A carved-out section of the patio, complete with tables, chairs, a vase of flowers, trays of food. To my disgust I notice a couple of deeply tanned, fake-boobed girls standing ready to fulfill my every desire. No doubt they're a gift from my father.

I hope I never see him again.

Do I really mean that?

Roc leads the imposter to the reserved area and motions for the guards to stand in a surrounding circle, blocking "me" from view of all the rubberneckers who are already standing up and trying to catch a glimpse of the president's son. That makes me laugh.

Before leaving, I run my fingers along the hilt of my sword. Although my father insisted that my training include more advanced weaponry, including various types of guns, I've never felt fully comfortable with them. For one, the Moon Dwellers and Star Dwellers have very few guns, which is one of the reasons their rebellions have been quashed so easily in the past. Is that fair? They can never hope to fight for equality if the very weapons they have to fight are not equal.

Screw you, Father, I think, sliding my sword back into my belt.

It's time to go.

I leave the suite, taking a minute to scan the hallway for any guards who might've remained behind, or for any hotel staff who might witness my escape.

The hall is empty.

I go the opposite way down the hall from where we entered, intent on using the private exit, specially designed so celebrities can leave without being noticed. It'll be guarded by one of my men, but that won't be a problem. He'll be looking for someone trying to get in, not for someone on their way out.

I tiptoe down the stairs, cognizant that any scuff of my feet or scrape of my toes might echo to the bottom, thus alerting the guard to my presence. I have to maintain the element of surprise if I want to avoid an ugly confrontation.

I reach the bottom without so much as a tap of my feet on the stone steps. The thick security door is bolted shut; I raise the lever gently, hoping it's been oiled recently. When it doesn't creak, I breathe a sigh of relief. So far, so good.

I take a deep breath, trying to concentrate. To focus my mind. To prepare myself for swift and decisive violence. To incapacitate, not kill. I have no hatred for my guards, no desire to harm them. They aren't smart enough to think for themselves. They just follow orders. Maybe that's not a good excuse, but I let them have it.

Using my shoulder as a battering ram, I burst through the door, bobbing my head left and then right to locate the guard. He's surprised, but alert, already reaching for his gun. But I already have my sword out and am ready for combat. Before he raises his arm in defense, the point of my sword is at his throat. I'm not sure if he recognizes me beneath my sunglasses, but in a few hours it won't matter.

As soon as he drops his gun, I swing around behind him and clamp his chin between my forearm and bicep, slowly tightening the force on his neck. At first he fights it, but then his feet stop kicking, his arms stop waving, and he goes to sleep. I wait a few more seconds before releasing him, just in case he's faking it, and then lay his unconscious body to the ground, kindly propping his head up on his hip bag. Before I leave I steal his sword for Roc. I leave the gun; it's not really my style.

I slip around the edge of the resort, but no one's nearby; everyone's drinking cocktails and splashing around in the pool. In some ways, I envy them. Do I still have time to change my mind? I could go back to the guard, tell him I was testing him—that he failed. In ten minutes I could be enjoying the cool water and cold drinks. Living the life I was born to live. Would that be so wrong?

Gritting my teeth, I slip around the side of the resort.

I make my way back to the arriving and departing visitors' entrance, and stride confidently past the greeters. They're too busy welcoming some big shot Sun Dweller and don't even seem to notice me pass by. The dark clothing probably helps in that regard, too.

I wait for Roc at the mandated location, near the south end of the transporter platform. I hope we've timed it right, that Roc will have enough time to meet me. If I have to I'll leave without him, but I really don't want to. I tap my toe on the stone platform nervously.

The ground rumbles as the transporter approaches.

Still no Roc.

The transporter bursts through the end of the tunnel.

Still no Roc.

A whoosh of air hits me as the transporter rolls to a stop.

No Roc…and then—

Roc appears at the other end of the platform, running hard toward me, fear radiating from the whites of his eyes.

He crosses half the platform and I'm still wondering why he looks so scared. Yeah, the train will be leaving soon, but he's made it with plenty of time to board with me. The platform is empty; no one else in their right mind would be traveling from the hottest resort in the Sun Realm to the Moon Realm.

He's almost to me when his pursuers arrive, charging through the resort entrance and gunning straight for us. Evidently I've underestimated my guards, or Roc has done something stupid, or maybe both, but whatever the case, they know they have to stop him. It's likely they haven't worked out exactly what's happening, just that something is going down that isn't supposed to.

When Roc reaches me I grab his arm and run with him onto the transporter. To his credit, Roc smartly thinks to hit the door close button repeatedly.

"Doors closing," the speaker says. "Nonstop to subchapter six of the Moon Realm."

The doors begin closing and we peer through the tinted windows to catch a glimpse of our pursuers. When the doors are halfway closed I think we'll make it. The guards realize they're too late and intelligently veer off toward one of the front sections of the transporter, but they're still at least five long strides away.

They'll never make it.

One of them dives headfirst at the rapidly closing door, thrusting his arms in the tiny crack and using his elbows like a wedge to pry it open.

"Damn," I mutter, as they board the train. "What happened?"

Roc's eyes are wild, flitting from side to side, unable to focus on mine. "I don't know—I just freaked. I tried to sneak away, made some excuse about needing to go to the bathroom. One of your guards said he'd escort me, that he was bored anyway. When I said I'd be fine on my own, he started asking questions and I got flustered and just started running. That's when they came after me."

"Damn," I say again. I should've known Roc wasn't cut out for this type of work.

"What are we going to do?" Roc says. His face is as white as a ghost's. He's probably been under more stress in the last five minutes than in the last five years combined.

I glance through the small window in the door at the end of our car. Two cars ahead I can see the guards making their way toward us, transferring cars swiftly, methodically.

The doors close and the transporter silently leaves the station.

"Remember all that training we've been doing?" Roc's eyes don't light up the way they usually do when I mention training.

Not this time. He isn't ready for this. But he'll have to be anyway.

I put both my hands on his shoulders, look him in the eyes. "This is gonna be okay, man. I promise. We'll do this together."

I hand him the stolen sword and raise my own.

The guards enter our car.

I'm not sure whether they know who I am yet, so I can't depend on my true identity to protect me from the sharp swords they're brandishing. After all, they've just left the pool, where they think I'm wasting away the afternoon, getting drunk and looking to score with one of my desperate admirers. Not that I ever do that. But they might think there's a first time for everything. They probably think Roc has stolen something and I'm his accomplice.

They've got guns, too, but they've left them holstered for now. One of them is chuckling to himself, like this is a chance for a little fun.

Anyway, they come at us with blood in their eyes, swinging to kill, or at least maim. I know these guys are out of Roc's league, accomplished fighters, but I also know I'll need his help if we're going to survive the next five minutes—or even the next five seconds.

I block both their swords with my own, feeling their collective strength as I'm thrown back against Roc. Pushing Roc hard against the side of the car, which is moving faster and faster, already nearing its top speed of two hundred miles an hour, I spin hard to the left, ducking under another sword that wants to lop my head from my shoulders.

Roc cries out as he slams into the wall, which draws the attention of one of the guards. The distraction provides a short reprieve, as now I'm only facing one guard. I deftly slip under his attempt to gut me like a fish, simultaneously launching my own attack, slashing him hard across both legs. I avoid his chest and head—I still don't want to kill anyone.

He goes down like a sack of potatoes, dropping his sword and screaming in agony.

I turn back toward Roc, who's also crying out. The other guard has him cornered, slashing at him with short, flashing strikes. Roc's doing his best to maintain his swordfighter's stance, but each time he parries a blow, it seems even less likely he'll be able to block the next one.

I charge the guard from behind, dropping my sword and tackling him hard to the floor. His sword clatters to the ground next to Roc, who kicks it out of range of the guard's scrabbling fingers. I swing my elbow hard, crashing it into the back of his head. He slumps, unconscious.

Turning back to the other guard, who is writhing on the floor in the fetal position clutching his legs, I pick up my sword.

"No!" Roc cries, when he thinks I'm going to run him through.

But I'm not going to kill him. I spin the sword around and use the long handle to give the guard a major headache. He stops flopping about, stops yelling. Lies there, silent.

Roc's face is even whiter now, like it's powdered with chalk. "You okay?" I ask.

Roc seems unable to speak, taking short and uneven breaths, his fists balled and legs stuck firmly shoulder-width apart, slightly bent at the knees—just like I've taught him. He's going into shock. I need to snap him out of it.

"Roc, stay with me, man. It's going to be okay, we're safe now." I know I have to secure the guards—they've probably taken a lot of collective hits to the head over their lifetimes and their recovery time will be shorter than most—but I'm worried about Roc, so I take care of him first.

I put an arm around Roc's shoulder and the other on his elbow and lead him to a seat. He's trembling slightly, his body reacting to the sudden decline in stress. Once he's seated, I look him in the eyes. "All okay," I say. He's staring at his feet, refusing to meet my eyes.

I try to make casual conversation to snap him out of his funk. "Remember the last time we were in the sixth subchapter, Roc?" He continues to stare at the floor. "We were riding on that float, trumpets playing, people cheering—when it tipped over. You remember that? It was chaos, Roc. A mob of bodies, mashed up against each other, nearly getting trampled to death. But we survived it. And we just survived an attack by two highly trained guards, Roc. We're just fine. You did great."

Finally, his chin rises ever so slightly, and he manages a grin. "You're talking to me like I'm a child," he says.

I laugh. Good old Roc. "I thought you were in shock," I say.

"I think I was...or nearly was," Roc says. "Thanks," he adds.

"Hey, what are friends for?" I say lightly. I don't want him getting all emotional on me. There will be time for that later.

Luckily, in his haste, Roc didn't forget the pack that we prepared together. In it is a long coil of rope. Using my sword, I cut off four small sections and use them to bind each guard's hands and feet. I stuff the bodies under the seats at the other end of the car, as far away from Roc as I can get. Their swords and guns clatter onto the tracks beneath the transporter when I throw them out the door. Roc watches me do all this with interest.

When I come back and sit next to him, he turns to me and says, "That was my first real fight."

"You did great," I repeat.

He laughs. "How do you figure? I was screaming like a banshee and on the verge of sudden death throughout the entire thing."

"You didn't die," I say. "That's why. And *everyone* is on the verge of sudden death in a swordfight. All that matters is who doesn't die."

The guards stir halfway through the trip and start yelling. I wrap cloth around their mouths to shut them up.

Roc is better for the rest of the transporter ride, telling upbeat stories about when we were little, the trouble we used to get into. He might be overcompensating for the way he's really feeling, but I'm not about to stop him; it's better than listening to him talk about near-death experiences.

At some point along the way, the well-lit tunnel dims, as we cross over the border into the Moon Realm. Less electricity is provided to the commoners. Their leaders have signed a contract so it's okay. Yeah, right.

An hour or so later the transporter begins to slow, pulling into a dead Moon Realm station. Moon Dwellers don't travel much; they're too busy trying to survive. I'm somewhat concerned there will be a welcoming party waiting for us: either Moon Dweller soldiers acting on my father's orders, or Sun Dweller soldiers who somehow managed to get there in front of us. But there's no one waiting with guns, or swords, or handcuffs. I dare to hope that perhaps the only guards who know what is happening are tied up in the last car on the train. Despite the low traffic, they'll eventually be found. We need to be as far away from the sixth subchapter as possible when they're discovered.

We exit, our swords tucked under our clothing, and Roc carrying the pack. I scan the platform for any signs of trouble. There are only three people in sight. A cleaner scoops rubbish into a long-handled dust pan. An old woman steps onto the transporter a few cars in front of us. There's no way she is going to the Sandy Oasis. More likely the transporter is headed deeper into the Moon Realm, sending our tied-up pursuers far away from us. The third person is a platform attendant, who eyes us warily—he probably isn't used to many Sun Dwellers stepping onto his platform.

I approach him, keeping the cap of my hat low to shield my face. I'm still wearing sunglasses. Although it's unlikely he'll recognize me, I still need to take precautions. So I change the tone of my voice slightly, making it gruffer and deeper. I say, "Where can I catch the first transporter to the fourteenth subchapter?"

He looks at me like I'm crazy, like he's never heard such a request in all his life. But then he says, "Platform seven. Just around the corner." He motions in the direction we need to go. He doesn't offer any information on when the next transporter will arrive, but Roc already checked the schedule. It's due only ten minutes after our arrival.

"Thanks," I growl.

We round the corner and my eyes widen when I see the next platform. Based on the noise level—which is almost nonexistent—I expected to find another empty platform. Not so. Instead, the platform is packed with people, shoulder to shoulder, back to front, most of them staring straight ahead. No one speaks. They're like statues.

I check my watch. We've arrived eight minutes late, which means the train will arrive any second. It's early evening—quitting time. I've heard that jobs are becoming so scarce in many of the Moon Realm subchapters that some people commute to other subchapters to work, and then return home at the end of the day. That must be what these people are doing.

We join the crowd, wedging ourselves between a fat guy and an even fatter lady, trying to blend in. We get more than a few suspicious glances—it doesn't help that I'm wearing dark sunglasses.

I hear a rumble in the distance and the crowd pushes forward, anticipating the train's arrival, anxious to get home. The train arrives and the doors open. It's empty; apparently subchapter 6 has a lot more jobs than subchapter 14. By the time we push, jostle, and elbow our way onto the car, all the seats are taken. We fight our way to the wall and lean against it, trying to get some breathing space. No luck. The biggest man I've ever seen in my life stands right next to us and raises his gigantic arm so his sausage-like fingers can grasp the handrail. Out of his exposed armpit wafts the smell of dried sweat and too many days without a shower. He burps, letting out an even worse odor, one I can't easily identify, but which reminds me of rotten onions.

It should be a terrible ride, but it isn't. After all, I'm doing something for myself, making my own choices. For once in my life.

Nine

Adele

It has all been arranged. The greedy guard has been paid. Tawni has withdrawn all of the money from her account. We've broken three pieces of thin plastic off of a cheap food container that we stole from the cafeteria. We're ready.

All we have to do is wait.

Sometimes in the Pen waiting is dangerous. Although a lot of the kids are wrongly convicted—screwed by the system, like me, I guess, and probably Tawni and Cole, too—there are plenty of bad kids in here as well. Real bad kids. Kids that'll knock an old lady over on the road, steal her walker, and then break it down and sell the parts. Like the giant tattooed guys I'd been dealing with in the last couple of days.

There's also a lot of violence in the Pen. Kids form gangs, fight over turf that doesn't belong to anyone, try to control the cigarette and booze trade.

I am no stranger to violence.

I remember my first week in the Pen. I was scared, didn't know anyone—which didn't change much in six months—didn't know what to expect. I was sitting in the Yard, trying not to make eye contact with anyone, working on my *leave-me-the-hell-alone* vibe, when I saw a fight break out. I'm still not sure what it was about—one guy looked at the other guy's girlfriend maybe. Anyway, all of a sudden the punches started flying. And I don't mean like a schoolyard fistfight, where one kid gets a bloody nose and it's over. This was a no-holds-barred, savage, kick-him-when-he's-down kind of fight. And neither guy would relent. They were both twice as big as me and had clearly fought before. By the end of it they were both covered in blood, staggering around like they were drunk, probably suffering from concussions, or worse. Eventually one of them went down for good, but that didn't stop the other guy from stomping him into the ground until the guards finally came to break it up. I never saw either of the kids again. For all I know the guy on the ground is dead and the other guy is now an Enforcer for the Sun Dwellers. Bottom line: the Pen isn't a friendly place.

Early on, I had a little trouble from one of the guys. I can promise you he wasn't bothering me because of my brains. He wanted something else, something I wasn't about to give him. His legs are still broken more than four months later.

No one messed with me after that—at least not until that day with Tawni. I'm not sure if it's because of the message I sent with my fighting ability, or simply because my lack of hygiene makes me less and less attractive with each passing day, but whichever it is, I'm thankful for it.

I don't have a problem with violence. I've grown up in a violent world, where miners are killed every day by cave-ins, and Sun Dweller Enforcers roam the streets cracking the knees of anyone unwilling to cooperate with them. My dad taught me to only use violence when provoked.

Today is one of those times.

I'm sitting in the Yard by myself. We've just finished going over the plans one final time and now Cole and Tawni are walking along the perimeter of the fence, doing what Cole likes to call "his zoo thing," staring at any people passing by on the outside, growling and carrying on like a caged animal. I guess he does it for kicks.

I showered after breakfast for the first time in weeks. I did a way better job than usual, scrubbing all the nooks and crannies, even rubbing the bar of soap through my hair. The water was freezing, but I suffered through it. I smell good for the first time since entering the Pen. I want to be as clean when I leave as when I arrived. Call it a symbolic cleansing of sorts.

No one, besides Tawni and Cole (and a few obnoxious girls in the bathroom), have spoken to me in months, but now a gang guy saunters up, staring at me the whole way. It's the guy who approached me before, when I first met Tawni, when I first saw Tristan. The tatted-up gang leader with the big muscles and the small brain.

"Hey, beautiful," he says, in the exact same way he did before. Like I said, no brains. My dad used to say the definition of stupidity is doing the same thing over and over again and expecting a different result. Or maybe that's the definition of crazy. Either way, it sprang to mind when the guy spoke.

"Like I told you before, leave me alone," I say.

"Not gonna happen," he says. "Not this time. You see, you're looking even better today, and there's something I want. And when I want something, I get it." I'm trying to act tough, but inside I'm trembling, scared shitless, but I learned a long time ago that inside the Pen you can't show your fear. The others thrive on it, smell it, gravitate toward it, like bats to blood.

I could run from him, try to hide, perhaps avoid him for the rest of the day until we escape, but that's not how I was raised.

My father taught me to fight.

I stand up, finally making eye contact with him. His dark eyes are vicious and uncaring.

"You ready to play," he says, licking his lips, eyeing me from top to bottom and back up again. I don't wait for him to make the first move, which is another thing my father taught me. Especially not when your opponent is bigger than you.

I kick him hard and below the belt. Then I follow it up with a roundhouse kick to his head, which has dropped to waist level as he clutches his groin, groaning in agony.

I hear a yell, which likely comes from one of his mates, who are surely watching the exchange with interest, getting a good laugh up until the point I'd kicked him. Then I hear shoes pounding on the barren rock. Coming toward me. But I'm not worried about the footsteps, because strangely enough the Pen has a code of sorts. With the exception of multiple gang member brawls, fighting is limited to those involved in the fight. There is no jumping in, no ganging up. You can watch, but not intervene. The code won't protect me the following day or the next week, when, had I been staying in the Pen, I would most definitely have to fight the rest of the gang members in succession, but I'm relying on it now.

"Get up, boss," I hear one of them say. I almost smile. Verbal encouragement is permitted. The guy he refers to as *boss* is a tough guy, and he *would* get up despite the brutality of the wounds I've already inflicted on him, but I'm not about to let him, not about to underestimate him like he has me.

So as soon as he pushes up to his knees I kick him in the face again. He spins away from me, lifting slightly off the ground before crashing onto his back. I think his skull bounces off the rock because blood starts seeping from the back of his head where I didn't kick him. This time he isn't getting back up.

And then Cole and Tawni are at my side, grabbing a shoulder each, backing me away from the semi-circle of gawkers who have formed to watch the painfully lopsided fight. It is over before it ever really starts. *A fast fight is a good fight,* my father always used to remind me during my training.

Tawni takes my hand and pulls me over to my stoop. I close my eyes, dip my head into my hands, start trembling. My whole body is shaking, like a virulent flu has attacked my insides all of a sudden, giving me a bad case of the shakes. I don't think I'll ever get used to the rush of adrenaline that comes with extreme violence. I'm no kind of adrenaline junkie, am not addicted to it, don't crave it. Although I'm prepared to engage in violence when I'm forced to, I don't particularly like confrontation. Unfortunately, confrontation seems to like me quite a lot.

The last time I fought in the Yard—when I victimized that guy's legs and sent a message to the rest of the inmates—I'd cried afterwards, in my cell, alone. I'd never wished more to have my parents with me, to comfort me like a child, to hold me and tell me everything was going to be okay.

This time, however, I have Tawni. I'm not crying this time, but I'm distraught, exhausted, both mentally and physically. She wraps an arm around me, pulls me close, holds me. Normally it would be a bad idea to show such weakness in front of the rest of the "guests," but I don't care. We're leaving and I'll never look back.

My thoughts are interrupted by Cole. "How'd you do that?" he says.

"Preemptive strike," I say simply, my voice muffled through my hands.

"No. I mean, where'd you learn to fight like that?" he persists.

"I told you I know how to fight."

"But where'd you learn it?"

"My father taught me," I say, opening my hands and raising my head. Tawni is still holding me, and where it had felt good a second earlier, it now feels weird, I think because it's such a public place and Cole is watching. I give her an awkward look and she seems to get the message, withdrawing her arms.

Cole's looking at me with those strong eyes of his. Clearly he's perplexed by me, like I'm a puzzle. But I'm not really. It's simple: my father was taught how to fight by his father, my grandfather, and he taught me. Growing up, he never let me rest on the fact that I'm a girl. Not in the world we live in. He said everyone will need to know how to fight eventually given what's coming. I'm not sure what he meant by that.

I was a good student and loved our training sessions together. From hand-to-hand combat to shooting slingshots, to fighting with a staff, I relished every new lesson. He was hard on me, but I didn't mind. I just knew I wanted to spend time with him and it was as good a way as any to do it. I remember the day he told me I was ready. I didn't understand. He said he'd taught me everything I needed to know. I didn't feel ready.

My father is not a violent man. He told me never to use my training except to defend myself or others. "Never be the initiator, never the aggressor." Including my most recent fight in the Pen, I've only fought three times in my life, outside of training. I haven't lost yet, unless you include the skirmish with the man-giant that Cole pulled me out of. But I don't, that was hardly fair.

Although I had a good teacher in my father, he said I have a natural talent for fighting. I would tell him I got it from him, but he always countered that I inherited my talent from my mom. I never understood that. My mom is the least violent person I know. With the exception of the night she was taken, I've never seen her so much as lift a foot to squash a bug. When I asked her about it, she just shook her head and said, "Your father has a big mouth sometimes, Adele. He's the fighter, not me." I never really believed her, but that's all she'd say.

Cole looks like he's about to ask another question about my fighting, but I wave him off with a hand. "I'd really rather not talk about it right now," I say. I'm glad when he doesn't push it any further.

To his credit, he doesn't so much as mention fighting the rest of the afternoon, or the evening for that matter. The last day in the Pen seems to sprout wings and fly away. I think it's because I can't wait to get out of this dump.

Night falls. Not that it makes things look any different. Outside the Pen it's still the dull gray that it always is. Inside the Pen it's still fluorescent white, painfully bright in most areas. Tawni and I walk to our cells for what I hope will be the last time. After a quick and knowing sideways glance, we push through our respective doors. As I close the steel barrier, I insert the plastic square between the bolt and its hole.

Ten minutes later the speaker announces lights out and I hear the lock click. It sounds different than most nights—not the hollow click announcing my nightly imprisonment, but a duller *thwap!* that confirms the plastic has done its job.

The waiting is painful—each fifteen-minute interval drags on until I'm straining to hear the clap of the guard's footsteps on the gray-painted stone floor. By the third guard, it feels like an hour has passed since the last guard clipped past my cell. That's when I start worrying.

At first it is just a nagging voice in my head that says something isn't right. But soon it becomes a shout that says that the guard's patrol pattern has been altered, that someone knows about our attempted breakout, that even now they're handcuffing the wayward guard who took our money. Perhaps it's already past midnight. Perhaps the fence is still charged and ready to shock us into oblivion when we touch it. Perhaps, perhaps, perhaps.

I try to think about my family to take my mind off of my nerves. I desperately want to see them again. For the past few months I've done my best to forget them, letting their smiles fade from my memory like a hunting bat drifting into the gloom. Elsey, with her contagious optimism and proper way of speaking. My mom, with the heart of a lion and an abundance of compassion. My dad, the fighter, quick to smile, slow to anger. My rock, my hero.

The fourth guard comes. Eleven o'clock—if the patrol pattern hasn't changed. My mind is relentless, and soon my heart joins in the fun, hammering in my chest, striving to pound its way through my bones and skin. But I'm handling it. Barely.

Until my lungs decide to join the party.

My breaths start coming in ragged heaves, short and choppy, until I'm gasping for breath. It's like my whole body—all its parts, internal organs, and nerve endings—decide to mutiny at the exact same time.

That's when I lose count. I can't remember if the last guard I heard was the fourth or the fifth. I'm thinking fifth, but I can't be sure. When the seventh—or is it the sixth?—guard goes by, I know I have to play it conservatively. This is one time I can't be late.

So I block out all my kooky, mutinying body parts and start counting. I put every last ounce of concentration and brain power into keeping count, maintaining a steady rhythm, treating the act of counting like it's the most complicated math problem.

Right on six hundred, I pull my door open and step into the dim hallway. Ten seconds pass and Tawni still hasn't emerged. I think I must be too early. It's probably eleven-forty and the next guard will be coming soon—the guard that should have triggered my counting. But then I have a very bad thought. What if I'm too late? What if I missed two guards passing and it's really twelve-ten now? What if Cole and Tawni waited for me, and when I didn't come, carried on the plan without me?

Tawni's door creaks open, and, like a shadow, she emerges. I take a deep breath and approach her. "You count slow!" I hiss.

She raises her wrist, displaying the digital numbers on a wristwatch. 11:55. "Sorry, I forgot I had this," she whispers. "I guess you got excited and counted too fast."

I don't know why the twelve o'clock guard chooses to come down the hall at that moment. It's possible he's just bored, choosing to start his circuitous route through the complex a few minutes early to pass the time. Or perhaps Tawni's watch is slow, as well as my counting. Maybe he's right on-time. Whatever the case, all of a sudden he's here and we have nowhere to hide.

When he sees us standing in front of our cells, he stops, looking confused. He rubs his eyes, as if he thinks the shadows are playing tricks on him.

We run.

It doesn't take him long to realize we're real. He opens fire on us with the big gun he's hefting. Yeah, he actually shoots at the backs of two defenseless teenage girls who are inside a secure facility, presumably for the petty crime of breaking curfew. I don't know where the Pen hires these psychos from, but I make a mental note to write a letter to the government about them. The same government that abducted my parents. Yeah right, like they're going to listen to me.

At first I don't realize what's happening. As I flee, I feel a weird rush of air burst past one of my ears, and then see a spark to my right when something glances off the wall. It isn't until we reach the end of the hall and I see the bullet holes that I know for sure that we're being shot at.

Somehow we manage to get down that first hall without getting shot, but we aren't even close to being out of the mines yet. We start to turn right, to take the fastest route to the Yard, but are forced to veer left when we see three more guards charging toward us. A few more bullets whiz past, shot by the original guard. I hope he hits the other guards by mistake.

The three new guards are yelling to the other guard to "Stop freaking shooting!" which gives me hope that perhaps they aren't all so trigger happy. With a parade of slapping feet behind us, we take the long way around to the Yard.

As we round the next bend, the sweat is dripping into my face and I have to use the sleeve of my gray prisoner's tunic to wipe it away. I try to stay with Tawni, but her legs are longer than mine and her long graceful strides soon edge her several paces ahead. Just as she passes a corridor on her right, a guard steps out, facing me. He's holding a thick black nightstick and looks ready to use it.

I leap, aiming a high kick at his face and hoping he'll get the worst of whatever collision is about to occur. I catch him high, just above his left eye, but not before he's able to take a half swing with his club. Thank God he doesn't have time to wind up the entire way. *CRACK!* I feel the rod slam into my ribs, sending shivers of pain through my stomach and into my chest.

There's a cringe-worthy *crunch!* as I land on top of him, one foot on his head and the other on his chest. I think I might've broken his sternum. Somehow I manage to keep my footing and stumble off of him, using my momentum to continue moving forward.

Tawni hears the commotion and stops, waiting for me to catch up. I try to yell, "Keep running!" but it comes out as a wheeze—I'm having trouble getting air into my lungs after the hit from the nightstick. I wave Tawni on with my hand and she gets the message. She turns and continues running, but at a slower pace, until I'm able to get alongside her. We run abreast at my slower pace, cutting through the back entrance to the cafeteria, past the benches and long tables, and out the front entrance. Each step sends shockwaves through me, and my stomach heaves, threatening to toss up whatever gunk I ate for dinner.

Once out of the eatery, we cut sharply to the left and push through the outer door in tandem, crashing each of the double doors into the stone wall in the Yard. Compared to the air inside the Pen, the outside air feels fresh and quickly fills my faltering lungs.

A headache starts in my skull, maybe from the exertion or the explosions of gunfire that are still ringing in my ears. Or from something else. It's the first headache I've had since seeing Tristan. But there's no time to think about all that.

A dull light illuminates us for a moment, before we have a chance to duck against the wall. Cole is waiting just outside, in the shadows.

"Could you be a little quieter!" he hisses. "Someone's gonna hear us!"

"Too late for that," I choke out.

"They're after us," Tawni says, grabbing Cole's hand and pulling him toward the fence.

We have no idea whether Cole's guy came through for us, but by God we're going to try anyway. Cole finally seems to grasp the urgency and powers ahead, reaching the fence about five seconds before us. He uses the time to rip his prisoner's tunic over his head and chuck it against the fence.

Nothing. No crackle of electricity, no smell of burning cloth, nothing. The fence's power is off—but for how long?

We aren't about to sit around and place bets. Cole already has his tunic on and is a quarter of the way to the top when Tawni and I start climbing. As usual, she gets in front of me immediately, using her long reach to skip as many rungs as possible. I hear a shout from the Yard, but don't risk looking back. I have to keep climbing. Stretching my arms over my head makes my stomach throb and my crushed ribs grate against each other, but I push through it, even when the pain grows so bad that I start seeing stars.

We're so close I can practically smell the freedom.

So close.

And yet so far.

Cole is straddling the barbed wire at the top of the fence, trying to avoid getting poked somewhere that will have a permanent impact, when I hear the next shout. It isn't from the Yard this time, but from the street outside the fence.

This time I look. I don't even have to turn my head, just have to look down. Half a dozen guards, armed to the teeth with automatic weapons, which are pointed right at us, are shouting for us to get down.

We're trapped like rats.

My head pounds in rhythm with my heart.

Ten

Tristan

When we exit the transporter, it's getting very dark in subchapter 14, but it's only early evening, perhaps seven o'clock. The day lights on the roof of the cavern—which are already dim to begin with—are nearly extinguished, simulating twilight. I'm glad. It makes it easier to avoid being spotted.

Although most of the time the many subchapters in the Moon Realm blend together in my memory, becoming one continuous subchapter in my mind, I have a pretty good idea of the layout of subchapter 14 because we just visited it. Roc also has a map—he has a map for every place in the Tri-Realms—

and we use it, along with our memories, to navigate our way from the transporter station, through the streets past the familiar government buildings, and into the light commercial district, near where the Pen is located.

I still haven't worked out what to do when we get there.

We emerge from a crowded street, full of people bartering goods and services for their next meal, and see the intimidating fence surrounding the Pen. It's a formidable obstacle, complete with barbed wire and signs warning of "Electrified Fence—Keep Back!" It certainly makes you appreciate being on the outside of it.

I feel a strange pull toward the Pen, but I resist it, trying to be patient. It feels like someone's poking me in the back with pins. Not like the stabbing-knife pain from the last time I was here, but a lesser, more prickly pain.

The rock yard beyond the fence is empty. It's getting late and the inmates are probably in their cells. I've never visited the Pen before—never had a reason to—so I don't know their rules around prisoner visitation.

We have a choice to make. Hole up for the night and wait until morning to try to get inside the Pen, or give it a try now, at a time which will be considerably more suspicious. I manage to tear my eyes from the Pen and we head for a hotel.

The only option in near vicinity to the Pen is a ratty old building across the road. The ancient clerk at the front desk has a wispy white beard and pockmarks covering the whole of his face.

"We'd like a room for the night," I say gruffly.

The guy doesn't bother to look up from his newspaper. "Which one would ya like?" he says.

120

"Do you have anything available that overlooks the Pen?" I ask.

The man starts to chuckle, but then starts coughing—a heaving, wheezing blast of air from his mouth that reeks of disease. When he gets control of his lungs, he says, "We currently have one hundred percent availability."

I guess I should've known, considering the number of people commuting out of the city every day. There's no reason for travelers to stop in the 14th subchapter.

"Top floor, dead center view of the Pen," I say.

"Room twelve thirty-five," the man says, handing me a key. He'd slipped the key from a peg on a board without even looking at it. Roc and I make eye contact; his lips are curled into a smirk that I'm pretty sure mirrors my own.

The room is more like a closet, but is clean at least, with painted-white stone walls and slate floors. A single bed fills most of the room—we'll have to duke it out for bed rights. There's a shared bathroom in the hallway, but with no guests other than us, we'll have it all to ourselves. It's not the Sandy Oasis, that's for sure. I could be having a massage right now. Am I crazy?

I close the door.

First we check the view. For someone wanting a view of the Pen—like us—it's a good one. The Pen is dark and quiet. I can picture the girl sitting on her bed in her cell, wishing to be anywhere but there. I don't dare to picture her on a slab of rock in the morgue.

But even so, if I can somehow get her out of the Pen, no doubt she'll be pleased, willing to answer my questions about her use of voodoo dolls. That's my best theory as to why when I'm near her it feels like I'm being tortured.

I feel the familiar pull toward the Pen, my scalp tingling. No headache yet, but I know it's there, just below the surface, waiting to come out.

It's freaking weird.

"I've got to find out if she's alive tonight," I say suddenly.

Roc glances at me, raising his eyebrows. I'm ready for him to advise me that I should wait until morning, that I should do the responsible thing, be patient, but to my surprise, he says, "I know. Let's go have a look."

When we pass the front desk, the same old man is sitting in the same position, reading the same paper, like he's glued to the seat. Perhaps he has a neck problem, which explains why he again doesn't bother to look up. Or perhaps he just doesn't like guests; or more specifically, doesn't like us. It doesn't bother me—the fewer questions and looks we get the better.

The security at the front gate of the Pen is light—only a single guard with an automatic weapon mans the station. The prisons are all secured by Sun Realm employees, so they have access to more advanced weapons than most people in the Lower Realms.

I remove my shades, as they'll make me stick out even more wearing them at night. I hope the low-brimmed hat will be sufficient to hide my face. I approach the guard with my head down, but I can feel him eyeing us.

"Hoping to visit an inmate," I say casually.

"A guest?" the guard replies.

I almost say *what?* but then realize we're talking about the same thing. Funny how they call their prisoners *guests*. "Uh, yeah, a guest," I say.

"Visiting hours are over. Come back between ten and two tomorrow."

The guard doesn't sound like he'll easily change his mind, but I have to try anyway. "Is there any chance of an exception?" I say.

"No," he says simply, his voice sounding tired, like he hates having to constantly have this conversation with people. I consider playing my son-of-the-president card, but decide against it as I don't really want to give away my identity just yet. There's a good chance the press will get wind of it and then my father will send guards to bring me back. Plus, I don't want to rely on my name, or my father, for this mission. I might regret it, but for once I just want to be a random guy. Tomorrow I might change my mind, but not tonight.

"Okay, we'll be back at ten in the morning," I say.

The guard doesn't answer, just stares at us. No, it's not *at* us, more like *through* us, like we aren't even there. We leave.

I know it isn't a good idea to roam the city, especially at night, but we have to eat so we go for a walk. The subchapter has seen better days. Although the cavern it's built in is magnificent, rising hundreds of feet above our heads and extending many miles in each direction, the town itself is deteriorating. Most of the shops and restaurants are boarded up, having insufficient business to exist. When people don't have money, they can't buy things—simple as that. I expect it means the remaining restaurants will be crowded, enjoying the benefits of being the only show in town, but I'm wrong.

The buzzing in my scalp lessens with each step away from the Pen.

We pass a tavern. Through the window I can see a lone drinker propped on an elbow, sitting on a stool at the bar. Nursing a drink. And I mean *nursing*. He's sipping it like it might be the last drink he'll ever take. Maybe it is. Maybe things are so bad that he spent the last of his money on the drink, and plans to commit suicide later tonight. I don't know. Things like that don't happen in the Sun Realm.

We get to the end of the street without passing another open eatery. Turning left, I hear the distant murmur of music playing. Halfway down the block the soft glow of candlelight drifts through an open doorway. The sign above the door simply says, *Pizza*. Not seeing any other options, we make for the light.

Entering the pizzeria, I let Roc step in front of me as I see half a dozen heads turn toward us. The music playing is by some Sun Dweller rock band, The Stone Crushers, I think, and has an up-tempo beat that makes you want to get up and dance. No one is dancing tonight. They are, however, eating pizza and it smells pretty good.

There's no one to greet us so we just take a couple seats and wait for service. None of the other customers pay any attention to us. A few minutes later, a short bald man with horn-rimmed glasses pushes backwards through a set of swinging doors. He's wearing a red apron and balancing four circular trays of pizza across his outstretched arms.

"Who 'ad the cheese?" he grunts.

Every hand in the place goes up except ours. He quickly dishes out the pizzas and collects a few coins from each party. Then he turns toward us. "What'll ya have?" he says.

"Whaddya got?" I ask. When the guy's eyes narrow, I realize I should've just said *cheese pizza*, because I know he has it. Instead, my simple question instantly draws more attention to us than I want. I glance at Roc. He's chewing his nails off one by one.

"You're not from around 'ere, are you?" the guy says.

"Just visiting for a day or two," I say, hoping it will satisfy him and he'll go back to serving us.

He raises a single bushy eyebrow. "Travelers, huh?" he says. "We don't get many travelers. Where ya from?"

Now I know we're in a bit of trouble. I can tell him the truth, tell him we're Sun Dwellers, but I have no idea what effect that will have. Will he and his patrons be excited that Sun Dwellers are visiting their subchapter? Or will they be angry, ready to have a political *discussion* that involves their fists and our faces? All it takes is one Moon Dweller with a chip on his shoulder to cause us serious problems. On the other hand, if I lie, tell him we're from some other subchapter, he might ask questions that I'm not able to answer. I'll have to keep lying, spinning myself deeper and deeper into a web of deceit.

I opt for truth, for better or worse.

"We're visiting from the Sun Realm," I say.

Suddenly, it gets so quiet I can almost hear the sound of one of Roc's chewed-off nails drop to the floor. It even feels like the music stops playing, although in reality the song just happens to end at the exact same time.

"The Sun Realm, eh?" the pizza man says. I know that everyone inside is listening to our conversation now, slices of pizza dangling from fingertips, some in mid-bite. I know the man isn't going to let it go in a hurry. I'm glad the restaurant is only lit by candles—it'll be near impossible for him to identify me.

"Yeah," I say.

"Never served a Sun Dweller before," the guy says, his light tone switching to heavy right about the time he says the words *Sun Dweller*. I sense a hidden meaning behind his words: It's not that he's never had a Sun Dweller in his pizzeria, but that he will *never serve* a Sun Dweller, even if they're his only customers.

"Fair enough," I say, standing up. "We'll take that as our cue to leave."

The pizza man puts a hand on each of my shoulders and pushes me firmly back into my chair. "There's a first time for everything," he says.

I'm not sure what he means. That he's going to serve us like any other customers? Or that he's going to head back into the kitchen and cook up the most delectable, hot, gooey, *poisoned* pizza he's ever made? Whatever the case, I'm not going to take any chances. As soon as the owner barrels through the swinging doors to the kitchen, I'm back on my feet. Roc's up at the same time, knowing without asking what our next move will be.

We move toward the door.

Two big men block the exit, standing tall with their arms crossed. *Not good.* I don't even know where they've come from. I don't recall seeing them in the restaurant—and if they had been, we would've seen them moving across the room to block us. They could've come from outside, but I probably would've heard them scuffle across the threshold, unless they're professional sneaks. There's a staircase that rises up from just to the right of the entrance, however, presumably leading to sleeping quarters for the bald pizza man. Perhaps he has sons who live with him, who, upon overhearing our conversation— key words being *sun* and *dwellers*—thought it polite to pop down and say hello. Of course, these men are staring right at us and their lips aren't exactly moving; if not "hello," I would take "good evening," "welcome," or even "hiya" at this point. No words—just stares. If these guys are his sons, they're genetic freaks, more than twice the size of their dad.

"Excuse me," I say, still trying to avoid a confrontation. They don't move, just stand there staring. I try to squeeze through the middle of them, but they inch closer together, shoulder to shoulder. I attempt to skirt around them, but they move like a single organism, blocking the side. The only option left is *through* them. So be it.

I take a few steps back and charge.

The feint is as important as the attack itself.

I fake like I'm going to try and club each of them over the head with a different one of my fists. Because all of my activity is aimed high, they counter with high defenses and attacks of their own. The guy on the left covers his head with his arms and hands to block my attack. The guy on the right goes on the offensive, attempting a haymaker punch intended to end the fight quickly, possibly breaking my jaw or giving me a mild concussion.

At the last second I throw my head back and launch both feet forward like torpedoes. Each boot heel hits one of the guy's knees. I have so much forward momentum that the impact is like getting hit by a concrete block. I feel their knees buckle, crack, bend back the wrong way. And I hear their screams of pain, a harmonized "ARGHHH!" that will surely bring the pizza man running back out of the kitchen.

They tumble backwards out the open doorway and I land on them in a mess of arms and legs, at least two of which contain broken bones. Not mine.

While I attack, Roc is not idle. He's already out the door, grabbing me under my arms, hoisting me back on my feet. And then we're running.

The guys with the broken kneecaps won't be chasing us, but we don't know who else might come to their rescue. Given our first taste of subchapter 14 hospitality, we aren't about to stick around and plead our case to the locals. Apparently, all those screaming, cheering girls—the ones chucking underwear—at the parade the day before live outside the town.

We don't hear anyone pursuing us, but we don't stop running until we're back inside our hotel lobby.

The hotel guy should look up, considering the way we burst through the door, panting and sweating and out of control. But he doesn't. He isn't reading his paper anymore either. He's rolled it up and is using it as a pillow, his craggly old cheek resting upon it, smudging the print all over his face. Buzzing snores arise from his vibrating lips. *Deep sleeper*, I think. *Hear no evil, see no evil.* The perfect place for us to stay.

I never thought I'd be so happy to see the inside of that tiny shoebox room. Roc and I sit on the bed and look at each other, our eyes wide. Then we're laughing, in between taking deep, heaving breaths, happy to just be away from that terrible pizzeria.

"What was that all about?" Roc says.

"I dunno. I guess they don't like us," I say.

"More like *hate* us."

I nod. "Good thing they didn't recognize me."

"We can't stay too much longer in this place," Roc points out.

"I know. But I have to at least try to see her, to do something, to make sure she's okay."

"Then we have to do it tonight. We can't linger, Tristan." Roc's eyes are dark and serious. I value his counsel, even when I don't want to hear it.

128

"We'll go in the middle of the night," I say. "Two in the morning. Let's get some sleep." My stomach is growling, but I ignore it.

It's only nine, so we'll get five hours of sleep. I let Roc have the bed. It isn't often he gets something that I don't. Roc sets an alarm and goes straight to sleep. I linger, taking the time to brush my teeth and shower in the empty bathroom.

By the time I get back to the room, Roc's breathing heavily, twitching slightly on the bed as he dreams about getting chased by angry guards, or perhaps deranged pizza chefs.

I take my place on the floor, using the extra pillow to rest my head on. The stone is hard under my back, a terrible contrast to the plush mattress I'm used to sleeping on.

Before I drift off to sleep, I think about how I fainted when I pictured the Moon Dweller girl. Was it some weird neurological response to a stimuli of some sort? I hope I won't faint when I meet her—it'd be hard to ask her questions while unconscious.

I sleep, either dreamlessly or without memory of my dreams.

We wake up, not by Roc's alarm clock, but by the muffled sound of gunshots in the distance. Before I'm fully awake I know where the sounds emanate from: the Pen.

I leap to my feet, reaching the window at the same time as Roc. My back is aching from sleeping on the hard, stone floor. I'm not used to it.

We huddle together, gazing across the road and through the fence. The Pen is dark and quiet—like before. Gunshots ring out once more. Although the sound is stifled, both by walls and distance, neither Roc nor I have any doubt as to the origin: a semi-automatic weapon. Countless times we've heard similar sounds tremor through the walls of the palace, a result of army training exercises nearby.

I spot movement along the fence. I point it out to Roc, and we watch as a dark form creeps in the shadows, moving silently toward a door leading inside. The figure reaches the door and waits. A minute passes without gunshots or movement from the ghost.

The hollow door clangs open, ringing like a bell across the outer courtyard, through the fence, and into our ears. Two forms spill from the Pen, momentarily thrust into the glow of a single light illuminating the entranceway. They move quickly out of the light, joining the shadow in the shadows. Although they're only visible for a split-second, a mere wrinkle in time, I know without a doubt who they are—I suddenly feel dizzy.

Roc seems to recognize that something's wrong, and manages to thrust an arm behind me, catching me just before I collapse. "Tristan?" he says.

Thankfully, I don't pass out this time. My legs feel like rubber and the whole room is spinning, my head thudding like a war drum, but I hang on to consciousness. Roc holds me up until the feeling passes, my head settling into a less painful throb.

"It's her," I say. "We have to go." Although she didn't look at me, I felt the warmth of her eyes hit me, like a blast of hot air from a furnace. She's alive! Although I've been trying to convince myself that she survived the encounter with the big guy the day of the parade, in my heart I believed it had ended in tragedy, that I'd never get to ask her the questions I need to.

Before leaving, I risk a final glance out the window, hoping I won't be affected by seeing her again. There are a few stabs in my spine, but nothing serious. The threesome reaches the fence and starts to climb. "No electricity?" I say aloud.

A group of guards, at least six, I think, charge out into the courtyard. They're headed straight for her, toting guns and nightsticks.

Time to go.

Roc's already in the hall, looking back like he expects me to be right behind him. I cross the room in two long strides. We tear down the hall.

If the twelve flights of stairs have a hundred and forty-four steps, I think my feet touch about thirty-six of them. It's a wonder I don't trip and tumble all the way to the bottom, breaking every bone in my body.

We rush past the sleeping deskman and into the cool night.

We freeze on the sidewalk when we see the scene before us.

Eleven

Adele

The explosion rocks the still night air like a freight train crossing a rickety wooden bridge. I cling to the fence for dear life, as superheated air whooshes past me with the force of a stick of mining TNT.

We're lucky. Damn lucky.

The bomb blast knocks out a section of fence twenty yards to the left of us, leaving us relatively unscathed. Had we chosen that part of the fence to climb, we would've been hurtled to our deaths on the unforgiving rock slabs in the Yard.

The good news: The bomb has also taken out every last guard in the Yard behind us. Evidently they were running along the fence when it hit, trying to get to where we were climbing. Their bodies are scattered throughout the Yard, some quite a distance away from each other, tossed like ragdolls by the power of the explosion. I don't know if they're dead. Frankly, I don't care.

The bad news: The guards on the other side of the fence were as protected as we were. They're still standing under us, still aiming their guns at us. Given the stress they're under—what with all their friends out cold on the other side and the bomb going off—I'm afraid they might just open fire and ask questions later.

We're frozen in place, waiting to be torn apart by hot steel bullets. All watching the guards, waiting. It's horrible. An eternity in hell wouldn't be worse than these ten seconds. Or maybe it's only five. I don't know—all I know is it's bad.

My whole body is crackling with a sharp pain in my bones. Did I get hit by one of the bullets back in the Pen and not even realize it? Or maybe shards of shrapnel are all throughout my body, ripping and tearing. I quickly scan my tunic for blood. Nothing.

Dark shadows move along the tops of some of the buildings, running, running, and then stopping, heaving something over the side…

BOOM!

The next bomb hits a building across the street from the Pen, directly beyond our section of fence. A maelstrom of glass and rock rubble rains down upon the guards and they do what any other well-trained officers of a fine juvenile delinquent facility would do when three of their *guests* are trying to escape:

133

they run. For good measure, they even throw down their guns to allow themselves to run faster. I've never understood the expression *turned tail and ran* until now. If the guards had tails, they most definitely would've turned just before they took off.

I glance at the tops of the buildings, scanning for the shadows. There's movement somewhere in my peripheral vision, but I can't seem to pinpoint it. Who are the shadows? And why the hell are they blowing up subchapter 14 of the Moon Realm, of all places? My guesses are: 1) Sun Dweller military are attacking our subchapter because we only pay 80 percent taxes instead of 82 percent; 2) fed up, underpaid miners have gone crazy and are determined to destroy everything in sight; or 3) other Pen inmates have managed to get their hands on incendiaries and are shooting them off from the roof.

Cole swings his leg over the top and starts climbing down the other side. I'm still frozen in place, trying to process all that has happened. As I watch Cole shimmy down, I can see the hole in the building in the background. The scorching hole is about three times his size, making him look extremely fragile and exposed all alone on his side of the fence. Not that Tawni or I are any more protected.

I'm glad Tawni is there, because I'm not thinking clearly. I'm ready to continue my ascent to the top of the fence, to finish what we started, carry out the original plan, when she brushes past me, heading back down on the Pen-side of the fence.

"C'mon, this way, Adele," she says.

Duh. Why fight gravity and barbed wire (and my aching bones) when we can go through the fence? Given a full fifth of the fence has been toppled, it'll be far easier to just walk straight out.

We make it down without incident and climb over the mangled fence. We fight through a few nests of barbed wire, but it isn't too difficult. Just as we get on the street side of the fence, we see Cole waving wildly from down the road. *Hurry!* his body language screams.

Alarms begin whooping in the background, coming from the Pen. Jailbreak alarms. For us. The jailbreakers.

We run. We run because we're worried about the alarms and the guards that will surely pour from the Pen as a result.

BOOM!

Hot stone shrapnel drills me in the cheek, snapping my head to the side. I see Cole and Tawni get pelted by similar flying projectiles, but none of us so much as considers stopping to check for serious injuries. I think we all know that the only thing to do is keep running, to try to get as far away from the commercial district as possible. Whoever is blasting away—the shadows on the roofs—isn't showing any signs of stopping anytime soon.

It's weird—the way the night can be lit up so brightly and quickly and then just as quickly return to darkness, lit only by the soft glow of the streetlights. That's the way our run goes. Flash! And then dark. BOOM! And then silence. It's eerie, like we're in a war, bombs exploding all around us as we literally run for our lives.

The thundering explosions fade and the manufactured lightning grows distant as we escape the city limits, moving into the sparsely populated suburbs.

With each step another aching bone recovers, until I'm left feeling refreshed, like I just took a long nap. My body is strange these days.

None of us speak as we continue running, making our way around the huge stone columns that help support the cavern roof. I'm not sure how far or how long we run, or why we finally stop when we do. I think we all just stop at the same time, like robots, perfectly synchronized, slipping behind a high stone wall that rings one of the houses.

I'm breathing heavily—Tawni is, too. I'm out of shape. There isn't much use for exercise inside the Pen. My mind is racing; my side is hurting. I feel a twinge of pain on my cheek and I flinch. Pressing a hand to my face, I feel the sticky wetness of drying blood. I guess the rock hit me harder than I thought.

"Do you...think...we're safe?" I pant, directing the question at whoever has enough energy to listen.

Tawni hunches over, trying to catch her breath. Evidently she's as out of shape as I am. Cole, on the other hand, has apparently kept up his fitness while on the inside. He doesn't even seem winded.

"I expect we're all right," he says, glancing to his right and left, as if they might be surrounding us any second. "Especially given everything else that's happening."

Everything else. If only we knew what everything else is.

"What do you think *is* happening?" I say.

Cole laughs. "Uh, I think our subchapter is getting bombed to hell and back again." He laughs again.

"No kidding," I say. "I meant who do you think is doing it? And why? I saw people on the roofs of some of the buildings—or at least their shadows. They were the ones throwing the bombs."

"My guys," he says. "I paid a little extra to get a small diversion to ensure we'd get away."

A day earlier, before I knew him at all, I might have believed him. Not anymore. "Lie," I say. "Is now really the time for sarcasm?" Despite myself, I smile. "Are we really free?"

Tawni's breath is mostly back. She rises to her full height, once more towering over me. "For the moment we are," she says. "As long as we don't do anything stupid and get ourselves caught."

"Or killed," Cole says.

I cringe. My mind is clearing and already I'm analyzing the situation. It's like a puzzle. There are certain tasks we need to complete, in a certain order, and wrapped around them all is the requirement that we can't get caught. The first task is obvious.

"We need to get rid of these tunics," I say.

Cole smirks. "Yeah, I was thinking going naked was a good idea. They'd never expect it." He starts to raise his tunic over his head, revealing his strong dark legs and a pair of tight, black briefs.

"That's more than I wanted to see," I say, looking away.

When I look back he's lowered his tunic and is winking at me. I shake my head.

"Where are we going to get different clothes?" Tawni asks. "I mean, I've got money, but I'm not sure it's a good idea to walk into a shop wearing these."

"Yeah, plus we'll be public enemy number one after the breakout. Our faces will be plastered all over town," I say.

"Do you think so?" Tawni says, suddenly looking excited. "I would die to see my parents' faces when they see me on the news."

"I knew I should've had them retake my mug shot," Cole says. "I think I blinked during the first one."

"No amount of retakes would be able to help you," I say dryly.

Cole stares at me, his eyes widening and his mouth opening wide to form an O. "My gosh, Adele. Was that…was that a joke? Well played."

I play-punch him in the arm and am surprised when he winces. At first I think he's kidding, but then I notice the slight tear in his tunic. "Are you hurt?" I ask.

"I think we all are," he says. "But nothing serious for me. Are you guys all right?"

Tawni glances at me. "Just a few cuts on my arms. I think Adele is hurt the worst."

I raise a hand to my face, once more feeling the stickiness. "Nah," I say, "it's a scratch. Probably looks a lot worse than it is."

"That's not what I meant," Tawni says.

Damn, I was hoping not to talk about my crushed ribs—where the prison guard smashed me with his club—just yet. Evidently Tawni saw more than I thought. "It's not that bad, really," I say. "I'll deal with it once we find a better place to hide." I try to breathe evenly, despite the pain.

Cole looks at me suspiciously, and then at Tawni. I squeeze my fists tight, hoping they'll both just let it go. Thankfully, they do.

"Okay, where should we go?" Tawni asks.

"First, we need clothes," I say, bringing our strange conversation full circle.

"I can help with that," Cole says. "We'll just go shopping somewhere less visible."

Tawni frowns, clearly not understanding his meaning, but I get the message. "You want to steal them?" I confirm.

"Not steal, just borrow," Cole says. When Tawni gives him a look, he adds, "We can even leave some money for them if you want."

I'm not that comfortable with the idea of stealing from innocent people, especially because things are so tough in our subchapter at the moment, but it's not like we have much of a choice. Tawni, however, isn't such an easy sell.

"I'm not stealing from anyone," she says firmly.

"Shhh, keep your voice down," I say, glancing at the house for any signs of activity.

"Don't worry, Tawns, I'll do the stealing," Cole volunteers. "Consider the clothes a gift from me and don't worry about where I get them from."

"No," Tawni says, lowering her eyes and putting her hands on her hips. I'm not sure why she has such a big problem with it considering our situation. I guess she's just a person of principle, unwilling to budge on certain things. It's probably caused by her parents—her way of proving she isn't like them, isn't willing to cross some line in her head. I'm more of a realist.

"We don't have much of a choice," I offer.

Tawni's eyes brighten all of a sudden, like she's just thought of something. She's really pretty when she gets excited. Her blue eyes sparkle against the whiteness of her hair. If she'd been born in the Sun Realm, she probably could've been a model in one of their fashion magazines. Funny how our lives are so affected by where we're born.

"What?" I say.

"We'll get the clothes from my parents' house…my house," she says.

"I'm not so sure that's—" I start to say.

Tawni plows ahead. "My dad's a big guy, like Cole, I think his clothes will fit perfectly. I can wear my own clothes, of course, and you can wear my mom's clothes. Don't worry, she's shorter than me, about your size, so it should work. C'mon, let's go," she says, before either of us has a chance to disagree. "We should be able to make it there in less than an hour. It'll still be pitch-black when we arrive." She grabs my hand and starts pulling. She seems to like to do that, and normally it would bother me, but for some reason with Tawni it doesn't, maybe because of how willing she is to help me.

Cole just grunts and follows us. Given how long he's known Tawni, I guess he knows how hopeless it is to argue with her when she sets her mind to something.

Stopping to catch our breaths was a bad idea. At least for me. My body is completely frozen up. My thighs and calves burn from the sprint through the Pen, the frantic climb up and then back down the fence, and our distance run across the subchapter. My back is sore and pleading with me to take a break—*just rest for a minute, or even thirty seconds, please!*—and my bruised side, well, it gave up on pleading long ago and is practically screaming at me to stop. I want to look at it, but am afraid to stop, because I might not be able to start again if I do. Plus, Cole and Tawni will see it then, too, and it might be too hard to convince them I'm okay. Instead, I just ignore my body. I'm sure it will punish me later.

We try to stay off the main roads, sticking to the shadowy fringes of houses and properties. As we walk, we talk, speaking in hushed tones. We can still hear the dull boom of explosions in the distance, can see intermittent flashes of light exposed against the dark backdrop of the giant cavern, but they're neither loud enough nor bright enough to wake the sleeping Moon Dwellers. Closer to the city, I'm sure it would be pandemonium.

Tawni says, "I think it's the Sun Dwellers."

"What reason do they have for attacking?" Cole says. "They've got a sweet deal with us, and your boy Tristan"—he motions to me—"was just here shaking hands with the leaders and mugging for the cameras."

"I don't think it's the Sun Dwellers either," I say, although I'm not sure why.

"Of course not," Cole says. "Your lover boy and his people could do no wrong."

My face flushes, but in anger, not embarrassment. "I never said that!" I hiss, a bit too loudly. Tawni gives me a look and I lower my voice. "What's your problem anyway? We know nothing about Tristan—I know nothing about him. All I have to go on is that seeing him gave me a headache and that Tawni heard he's an alright guy from her parents. That's it. For all I know it's a bunch of crap. He might be a total creep. Regardless, it doesn't matter. I'll probably never see him again."

Even in the shadows I can see that Cole is shocked by my outburst. Maybe he isn't the only one with a temper. "Sorry," he mumbles.

I feel bad right away. I really don't know anything about Tristan, and he's not here anyway. Cole is. One of my two friends at the moment, willing to risk his life to help me escape. I try Cole's tactic of forgiving quickly. "It's okay," I sigh. "Look, I don't like the Sun Dwellers any more than you do— that I can promise you—and they *did* abduct my parents, but

141

seriously, I just don't think they'd start bombing us all of a sudden. Like you said, they've got the leaders in their back pocket. Why would they ruin such a good thing by beating us down even more?"

"Sorry," Cole says again, hanging his head. Suddenly I feel even worse about snapping at him.

Tawni says, "You guys are probably right. But if not the Sun Dwellers, then who?"

"If I had to guess," Cole says, "I'd say it's a Moon Dweller rebellion." When I frown, Cole explains. "You know, like a civil war. An uprising of Moon Dwellers who are sick of our leaders getting into bed with President Nailin."

"No way," I say, without really thinking about it. I don't even want to consider the possibility that we would destroy our own stuff, our own buildings, the fruits of our labors. Would my father, who's somewhat of a revolutionary himself, support such tactics? *No*, I think, more certain of the answer than I've ever been of anything in my life. "No way," I say again.

"Then who?" Cole asks. "Not the Star Dwellers. They don't even have guns, much less bombs. They've got knives and bows and slingshots, and that's about it. Not bombs."

I know he's right, which leaves the Sun Dwellers, the Realm with the greatest resources. I try to think of any other possibility. I have no idea, but something about the timing seems far too coincidental. "Do you think it was someone trying to help us?" Even as I say it, it feels stupid. No one knew we were leaving. And anyway, who would want to help us?

"Not likely," Cole says.

Eventually, everyone stops talking and we trudge along in silence. It's probably safer that way anyway. After what feels like miles, Tawni finally says, "We're here."

It is a good thing, too, because with every step my legs threaten to topple underneath me. I yearn for a soft bed, for a comfy pillow to rest upon.

"We'll have to sleep in the shed," Tawni says. Cole and I groan simultaneously. "We'll stay there at least until morning, when my parents leave for work, or wherever it is that they go every day."

I sigh. "Won't your house be under surveillance?" I say. "We did just escape from prison."

"Not this quickly," Tawni says. "With the bombings, they'll have more important things to worry about. Plus, with my parents' connections to the Sun Realm, there's no way they'd allow surveillance of their property."

I mull it over, hoping she's right. "Okay," I say. "Lead the way."

We steal across the front of the house, which is bigger than most in the Moon Realm, at least five times as big as my house. My eyes have adjusted to the dark (plus there are small night lights along the front walk), so I can make out artsy rock formations littering the landscaping. They're hand-carved and probably cost a fortune. We easily zigzag our way through them and I guess that Tawni could guide us without injury even if she was blindfolded, such is her familiarity with the landscape.

I can't see much of the house, except that it looms up like a fortress in front of us. Compared to most homes in the Moon Realm, and particularly in our humble district, it's as big as a palace. I can't wait to see it when the dim cavern daylights are illuminated.

We reach a medium-height wall separating the back from the front. Raising one of her long legs, Tawni clambers over it easily, like she's done it a thousand times. Following her lead,

143

Cole hops over the barrier swiftly and looks back at me, as if he's considering offering me a hand over. I pretend not to see him and, against my better judgment, place my hands firmly on the top of the wall and push off hard, using it to vault over the top. Although I clear the wall easily, I pay the price on the landing, feeling the jolt of my feet on the stone through my entire body, particularly around my battered ribs.

It hurts like hell, but I grit my teeth and dare myself not to show any discomfort. Cole's watching and I don't want to look weak in front of him. I don't know why. He's already seen me fight, knows I'm tough, knows I'm strong and capable. Maybe I'm just trying to prove my toughness to myself.

Regardless, I don't think it works. Cole pretends not to notice that I'm in pain, but I think I see a twinkle in his eyes and a casual smirk on his lips. I brush past him and follow Tawni around the house.

The backyard is even bigger than the front, possibly bigger than my parents' entire property. In the center of the space is an in-ground pool, probably the only one in the entire subchapter. The still waters glow an eerie blue, lit from beneath by underwater pool lights which evidently stay on all night. I try not to think about how much *that* would cost—and that it's funded by the sweat and blood of people like my father.

The shed is past the pool. It isn't what I expected. When you live in relative poverty, the word *shed* fosters an image of a tiny stone cubbyhole, crumbling around the edges and filled with rusty tools, spiders, and the occasional bat. Not a four-room building with running water, electricity, bunk beds, and shelves of food. Maybe I'm going to get a bed after all.

Tawni pushes open the door without a key and slips into the darkness. We can't risk turning on the lights, so she gives us a brief tour using the soft glow of her digital watch. Then she breaks out a can of beans, which we eat at room temperature, a box of salty crackers, and a tube of some kind of mint jelly. Although it shouldn't be, the food is amazing, and we eat frantically. It's a good thing there are no lights, because I don't even stop to wipe the crumbs or juices from my mouth.

We risk turning on the faucet and cupping our hands to drink. My throat is so dry the water burns slightly on the way down. The second gulp goes down better.

No one speaks until we finish all the food.

When the last cracker is gone, Cole says, "Will your parents come in here in the morning?"

"No," Tawni says. "Never. I've never seen either of them in here." Her voice is thick with distaste. "They think it's beneath them. These are the servants' quarters. They used to live with us, but it became too expensive, so now they just come during the day to clean and cook and maintain the place."

I'm shocked. Disgusted. The rest of us are barely scraping by and Tawni's family has *servants*. Seriously! I want to say something but I hold my tongue, because I know she's uncomfortable with the set-up, too. It isn't her fault. Like I said before, you have no control over what situation you're born into.

Cole changes the subject. "What happened to you guys in the Pen?"

I'd almost forgotten that he only saw the butt end of our escape from our cells. It feels like all three of us have lived through the entire thing together.

I give him a taste of his usual sarcasm. "See, Tawni and I were playing poker with a few of the guards, when it came time to meet you. We thought they'd let us go because, by that point, they owed us a bundle of money. Instead, one of them whipped out an Uzi and started firing away. We ran like bats out of hell, leaping bullets and fighting guards the whole way. It was crazy." Maybe not all true, but it *was* crazy.

"Mostly lies," Cole says in the dark. "But a hint of the truth, the crazy part, right? Oh, and I expect you did get shot at, too." He's good, all right, but I'm not about to tell him that.

"Okay, the true story is…"

I tell him the full story, downplaying the incident with me and the guard who stepped in front of me, but totally milking the "barrage of bullets whipping past our heads, tearing our clothes—I think I felt one trim off a lock of hair." I don't mention the mysterious aching I felt on the fence.

"Let me see where the guard hit you with the stick," Cole says when I finish.

I don't want to. Don't want the sympathy. Don't want them to worry about me. I know it's bad, but probably not as bad as it looks.

He won't leave me alone until I show him.

Even using only Tawni's watch light to see, my side looks awful when I raise my tunic. Already my skin is marbled with purple and blue at the top and green splotches at the bottom. The shape doesn't look quite right, like I'm missing a rib or two.

To my surprise, Cole laughs. If I'm expecting sympathy, I don't get it. "You'll live," he says. And then: "I've seen worse from a single punch on the schoolyard."

I thought I didn't want sympathy, but then when I don't get it, it makes me mad. It's probably just lack of sleep, the pain I'm in, the gamut of emotions I've felt this night—or I'm just a head case. Probably that, too.

Tawni is nicer, immediately tearing off strips from one of the bed sheets and wrapping them around my stomach and side to support my battered ribs. I grumble about her pampering, but afterwards I'm glad she does it, because my ribs stop hurting temporarily.

The servant's bed I sleep on is more comfortable than the one I'd slept on growing up. I practically melt into it. Although I'm too tired to be excited about having escaped the Pen, I do smile in celebration just before I fall asleep.

Twelve

Tristan

I shudder when a flash of blinding pain blurs my vision. Shaking my head and blinking, I try to regain control of my body. When my vision returns, it's not a pretty sight.

They're surrounded with no hope of escape. I don't know why of all nights they've chosen this one to attempt to gain their freedom, but I know if we don't help them they won't make it. *She* won't make it. For all I know, the guards might shoot first, rather than try to apprehend them. For all I know it might be another policy, like no visitors allowed outside of certain hours. The gunshots we heard earlier certainly point to that conclusion. I can see the new guards on the first day of training. Lesson 1: Always shoot guests attempting to escape.

Not a nice way to treat your so-called guests.

I can see her halfway up, frozen in place, eyeing the guards on the outside of the fence. Even between the tightly woven chain links, she looks fierce and strong. If she was a type of energy, she'd definitely be nuclear.

I'm coiled tighter than a snake ready to strike, my muscles tensed and flexed, my fists balled, my feet naturally assuming a runner's stance. I start to sprint toward them just as the bomb explodes. It's louder than a cannon in the quiet night, and I can feel the shockwaves from the force so strongly that they stop me dead in my tracks.

Frozen in place, I'm unsure of what just happened, or what to do. The acrid smell of smoke and dust fills the air. I can't see the guards on the inside, but presumably they're taking cover or were injured by the bomb blast. The guards on the outside are still pointing their guns at the prisoners, but they're pacing, nervous, much less sure of themselves than they were a few seconds ago.

Compared to the second bomb, the first was like getting hit by a feather. The incendiary tears through the hotel above us, maybe through the exact room we're staying in—whether by coincidence or design—sending shivering tremors through the street below our feet. I lose my footing as a crack widens in the stone beneath me. I roll hard, narrowly avoiding falling into the widening tentacle in the street. Instinctively, I cover my head, curling up in the fetal position. Heavy chunks of stone shower down, battering my defenseless body. Some of the rocks are sharp, having splintered off dangerously, piercing my skin. If one penetrates my eyes I'll be instantly blinded.

When the rubble shower ends a few minutes later, I sit up quickly, scanning my surroundings. Roc hasn't fared much better than me, although he's sitting up, too, rubbing a nasty red bump on his head. His clothes and face are covered in gray dust.

"You okay?" I say.

He coughs and gives me a thumbs-up sign. I turn my attention back to the Pen. The guards on the outside are gone, their guns scattered haphazardly on the ground. The escapees are gone, too.

She is gone.

"Tristan!" Roc shouts behind me.

I turn, and then, seeing him gazing at the hotel above us, follow his line of sight. Several columns of heavy stones are wobbling precariously, on the verge of toppling.

"Go, go, go!" I shout, running hard toward the Pen's fence line. I hear Roc's footsteps pounding behind me, and then a dull, machine-gunning clatter as the stones collapse.

I whirl around, saying the quickest prayer of my life for Roc. He's fine, having escaped the impact zone just in time. With Roc safe, my thoughts go to her. But then I remember someone else: the deskman at our motel.

Without explaining to Roc, I rush back to the building, leaping heavy stone slabs and piles of smaller rubble along the way. The doorframe is mangled, but still holding itself up amidst the pressure of the collapsing floors above it. I slip through, rapidly locating the old man. Despite his seemingly innate ability to sleep anywhere and through anything, he finally met his match when the bomb hit, or perhaps when the roof partially collapsed.

I'm not sure what happened to his desk—perhaps it's splintered beyond recognition—but it isn't there anymore. In its place: the old man—and a huge slab of stone that has him pinned to the ground. Finally, his head is up, his wild eyes looking at me, scared and helpless, begging me to save him.

The stone slab is far too big for me. Even with the adrenaline cocktail coursing through my veins, my first effort at lifting it is fruitless. It doesn't budge, not even a little. The task is like trying to lift the very earth on my shoulders, a feat only accomplished by Atlas—and I'm no god. While my mind races, I feel a hand on my shoulder. Roc pushes me gently aside and slides a thick metal pole beneath the stone. I have no idea where it came from, but I know exactly what he's doing—making a tool, a lever—and so I locate a good-sized roundish stone that I'm able to roll over. Together we push it under the pole. Overall, I'm the bigger of the two of us, so I push down hard on the end of lever, using my entire body weight to force it to the ground. The stone is massive, and even with the lever, it strains against me, trying to thwart my attempt. Eventually the lever moves down an inch, and then two, gaining speed as I gain leverage. I'm straining so hard that I have to close my eyes for fear they'll pop out of my skull.

I feel the pole drop suddenly beneath me and hear a loud crack and a thundering crash. Even with my eyes closed, I know what happened. The pole snapped in the center like a twig, releasing the stone. The man was crushed, broken beyond repair. I slowly open my eyes.

Roc is holding the man, who is not crushed, not broken— at least not beyond repair. Evidently I raised the stone a sufficient height for Roc to slide him out safely before the lever snapped. For that I thank God.

Roc is smiling, helping the man to his feet. The guy is clearly injured, so we each flop one of his arms over our shoulders and half-carry him out of the cracking building. As we pass through the doorframe, the rest of the roof collapses, kicking up a cloud of dust around us as we escape.

We're lucky. The old man is even luckier.

I've never felt so unsure of what to do next. I guess because I've never been in such an unbelievably confusing situation. We hear booms echoing around the town as more bombs hit, presumably destroying other buildings. There are shouts in the distance, both from the Pen and from other streets. Other people, probably just like us, trying to decide what to do, where to go, figure out what's going on.

"He needs medical attention," Roc says, looking at the man.

"I'm fine," he grunts.

"No...you're not," I say. "Where's the nearest hospital?"

"It'll have been bombed, too," he says gruffly.

He has a point. Nowhere feels safe at the moment. But still, out in the open I feel like we're too exposed, like at any second another bomb might land at our feet. We have to keep moving.

Roc seems to be thinking the same thing. We both start moving, forcing the injured guy to come with us. We turn the corner, but stop immediately when we see the scene in front of us. Smoke, rubble, buildings collapsed and collapsing. People running. We skip that street and head another block down. The next street is quieter, not yet hit by any explosions, perhaps not a target of the attack by...well, by whoever is attacking—I have no idea who.

We travel another half-block without event and then hear a noise as we're passing an old building on our right. "Psst," a voice says.

A woman is waving at us from down a set of stairs, from inside a doorway. "Psst," she says again.

"Yes?" I say, unsure of how to respond to such a strange greeting.

"Do you need help?" she says.

We do need help—desperately need help—so I say, "Please."

She beckons to us with one hand. We make our way down the steps awkwardly, trying not to bang the man's already battered legs on the stonework. The woman turns sideways and shepherds us through the door and onto a small landing. Below us steps descend into darkness.

Once we're all inside, the woman closes the door and says, "You'll be safe down here." She moves past us to the stairs, holding a long candle in a small ceramic bowl high above her head. We follow her down, carrying the old man between us. The stairway is wide enough for us to walk three abreast.

At the bottom is another door, which the woman opens. As she enters, she says, "I've got three more."

We poke our heads through the doorway, into a small cellar. It's crowded. Not including us and the woman, there are eight others. Four candles identical to the one carried by the woman are positioned in each corner of the space, providing spheres of light that overlap in the center.

"Make yourselves at home," the woman says, before exiting back the way we came and closing the door behind her. We gingerly lower the old man to the floor, next to a couple of kids who are staring at us with wide eyes. They can't be more than six years old.

"Thank you," the man says, his voice cracking. His demeanor has changed slightly, as if he's been softened by our persistent willingness to go out of our way to help him. I wonder what made him so hard in the first place. Perhaps it was just the cruelties of life—the faltering economy, old age, living in a cave—but I sense it was something more specific. He wears a wedding band but hasn't once mentioned his wife, out of concern or interest or anything. I guess that he's lost her already.

Roc sits down next to the man and I follow suit. My back to the rock wall, I take in my surroundings. The place is only about fifteen by fifteen feet. It reminds me of a small wine cellar—perhaps that's what it is, or used to be. No wine adorns its walls anymore. I'd be surprised if *anyone* can afford wine in this subchapter these days. Regardless of what it used to be, or could've been, it will serve well as a bomb shelter now, deep under the ground-level rock surface.

In addition to the two kids, there are three women and three men. Two of them hold hands and are younger, sitting next to the kids, probably their parents. The young wife looks fearful, maybe not for her own life but surely for her children's; her eyes dart about nervously, always returning to her young ones. The other four are older, gray around the edges, with serious faces that would fit in perfectly at a funeral. Well, at least three of them look that way. The fourth—a short, frail man with an impressive mop of gray hair—is wearing the biggest grin you could imagine. I wonder if my mother's threat from my childhood—that if you make a face for too long it will get stuck like that—has cursed this man. Perhaps in the throes of an extremely merry moment, his face was frozen in the biggest smile of his life.

"Crazy weather we're having out there," he says, somehow managing to keep his smile unchanged while he speaks. He's looking right at me so I feel obliged to answer.

"I think we're under attack, sir," I say, assuming his comment is made from senility, rather than lighthearted humor.

"Silly child, I know that, just trying to get a little laughter going in this damn dismal place."

I don't particularly like him referring to me as a child, but I'm also not going to start a fight with a crazy, big-smiled old man, not after our experience in the pizzeria. Instead I say, "Oh. Ha ha." My laugh comes out even faker than it is. And it's pretty fake.

"Geez, it's like trying to get a nun to laugh in a bar in here," the guy says, still smiling. "How'd you end up lugging around ol' Frankie here?"

The hotel deskman suddenly has a name.

"Don't call me that, Chet. It's Frank—I've told you a million times," Frankie says.

"We were staying at his hotel," Roc offers.

"*Hotel?* Ha! That dump's more like a dormitory."

Frankie glares at him, burning a hole through him with his eyes.

"I didn't think it was that bad," I say, trying to get on Frankie's good side. Instead, he just shifts his glare to me. I guess the whole saving his life thing has worn off.

"So you're travelers then? What part of the Moon Realm are ya from?" the funny guy asks.

Probably remembering how well I'd handled a similar question in the pizzeria, Roc answers this time. "Subchapter

155

six," he says. "We're just here for the night. So many of your people have come to work in our subchapter that jobs are scarce, so we thought we'd have a look around at what you have to offer."

I hold my breath, hoping he'll buy the lie.

"Ha!" the man exclaims, so loudly he makes me jump slightly. "You're Sun Dwellers if I'm an eternal optimist." I freeze, waiting for the trouble to start. As if he senses my discomfort, he adds, "Don't worry, your secret's safe with us. We won't give you any trouble. Name's Chip, ol' Frankie was just messin' with me earlier when he called me Chet. He's always purposely gettin' my name wrong, callin' me all kinds of things like Chaz, Chris, and a whole lot of other names I can't repeat in public. What did your mothers call you, anyway?"

"I'm Tristan," I blurt out. Stupid, stupid, stupid. Roc glances nervously at me. He probably thinks I've lost my mind.

I'm Roc," he adds quickly.

"Tristy and Rocky…" the man says, moving his tongue in a circle as if he is rolling the names around in his mouth to see how they taste. "They're good names, boys."

I should just let it go. But I don't. Stupid, stupid, stupid. If anything, my mother should have named me Damn Fool. "It's not Tristy, it's Tristan," I say sternly. "And we're not boys."

The man chuckles, high and mirthfully. "You've been hangin' out with ol' buzzkill over here for too long," Chip says, motioning to Frankie. "But as you wish, Tristan the Man."

"You can still call me Rocky," Roc offers unhelpfully.

I think we're out of the woods—clumsily dodging a bullet. Wrong again.

"Heyyy, wait a minute," Chip says. I know exactly what the perplexed tone in his voice means. He has another question,

156

probably a lot more questions. Because he's probably figured something out. "You say your name's Tristan, eh?"

"Uh, yeah, but you can call me Tristy if you really want to," I say, backtracking, hoping it will help, even though I know it won't.

"You've got a very famous name, young man," he says. "What's your last name?"

I go blank. Not a single real Sun Dweller last name pops into my head. All I can think of is: "Goop…and…no…I…mean…Troop."

"Tristan Goopandnoimeantroop? What kind of name is that?" Chip says, laughing again.

"Sorry, I'm just a little lightheaded from all the smoke out on the street," I say, shaking my head and trying to appear confused—not that it's that hard for me. "My last name is spelled T-R-O-O-P-E, and is pronounced True-Pay. It's French." I'm feeling clever all of a sudden.

"Tristan Troop-ay, huh? Are you lyin' to me again, young man?"

I have the perfect comeback for that. "No," I say, not even convincing myself.

I get the feeling he may have worked it out already, and is just enjoying himself, watching me flounder in my scummy old pond of lies. I cringe, waiting for him to seal the deal.

"So you're not Tristan Nailin, the son of President Nailin, the boy wonder who will one day become the most powerful man in the Tri-Realms? You're not *that* Tristan?" Chip asks, his smile growing even wider—impossibly wide—spreading from ear to ear.

"I think you have me confused with—"

157

"Ha! We've got a real treat tonight, everyone. Tristan Nailin himself, in the flesh! Well, bless my lucky stars!"

My instinct—especially after our encounter in the pizza shop—is to be ready to fight, but the man's tone sounds light, friendly even. Either he's a very good actor or he has nothing against me.

With unexpected swiftness, his tone changes. "Your father is a real piece of work, son," he says in a low voice.

"And me?" I ask, dreading the answer.

"Eh, I think you're all right, kid." I'm so overjoyed by the fact that he doesn't harbor any ill feelings toward me that I manage to ignore him calling me kid again. He continues: "I have a good sense about people, ya know? Just like I could tell you were lyin' earlier, I can tell you have a good heart. I think maybe you could be the one to make some positive change when you become president."

"I'll never be president," I say honestly.

"For heaven's sake, why not?"

I scan the room. The others in the cellar are listening to the exchange in silence. Their dark eyes feel like those of silent executioners. I hope it's just my imagination.

I know I should stop the conversation now—*for God's sake, shut your big, fat mouth!*—but I tell them anyway. "I've run away. *We've* run away." I look at my interlocked fingers in my lap. "I don't want anything to do with my father or the Sun Realm." A whirl of energy spins through my stomach as I realize: That's the first time I've said that and truly meant every word.

The guy with the smile winks at me. "You see? I told you I knew you were one of the good guys."

I change the subject, cutting my losses. "So who do you think is behind the attack?" I ask. Despite his age, the guy does seem perceptive, and I really think he might have some valuable insights. Instead, Roc jumps in.

"I think your love for that girl is so strong that it causes explosions," he says playfully.

"Roc, no," I say, but it's too late. The talker seems to enjoy clamping his mind around whatever topic is on the table.

"What girl?" he says, leaning forward.

I warn Roc off with my eyes. "Just a girl," I say. "But I don't even know her."

"A girl*friend*?" he guesses, ignoring my rebuttal.

"No, nothing like that. Just a girl," I say, hoping that will end the conversation. But Roc isn't ready to let it go. Good friend.

"Yeah, Tristy and his girlfriend just had their first date," Roc says, smiling brightly. "They almost even spoke to each other this time." I want to slug him, but I don't think a spat of violence will win me any points with the Moon Dwellers.

"A Moon Dweller?" Chip asks, a gleam in his eyes.

I wait for Roc—who's suddenly feeling talkative—to answer, but instead he puts his palm out to indicate it's my turn. I wish there was a table I could kick *him* under.

"Yes, she's a Moon Dweller," I say. "I just need to ask her a few questions."

"Well, why aren't you with her? 'Specially at a time like this."

It's a good question. Now more than ever I want to find her, to figure out why every time I see her I feel ready to pass out. I don't think the guards recaptured her, but I can't be sure, as I was a bit busy dodging flaming rubble at the time.

"I don't know where she is," I say, dropping my head.

"I might be able to help with that," Chip says. "I'm somewhat of an amateur private investigator. Where'd you last see her?"

I know I'm approaching a dangerous level of truth, but I've told them so much already—hell, they know I'm Tristan, *the* Tristan—so I decide to just go for it. I need help, and if they can provide it, then I have to accept the risks. "Okay, look. Here's the thing…" I tell them nearly everything. The sharp pain I felt the first time I saw her; our escape from the Sun Realm; how she was trying to escape from the Pen when the bombs starting blowing up all around us; and, finally, how she was gone when the smoke cleared, like a magician performing a famous disappearing act.

When I finish, I sit back and wait for a response. I'm not sure what to expect.

Everyone starts talking at once, asking questions, making comments. The young mother exclaims, "That's so romantic!" while her husband says definitively, "You've got to go after her." The older couple, who've previously been silent, speak in succession: "I bet they went north," one says, while the other says, "No, south, she must've gone south!" Even the kids get involved. The little girl says, "Tristan, do you think you're meant to find her?" The boy is more interested in the action than the romance. "Were you scared when the guards pointed their guns at her?" he asks.

When the chatter dies down somewhat, I hear a voice from my right, from the door, which is now slightly ajar. The woman who invited us in is standing there—I didn't even notice her arrival and have no idea how much she's heard. "She'll be laying low for a few days with her friends, until things die down. You might only have one chance to find her, because as soon as she makes a move, she'll run as fast and as far as she can." The woman sounds wise beyond her years, like she's experienced everything that life has to offer. "What do you reckon, Chip? She'll head for the northeastern suburbs most likely; at least at first, don't you think?"

I realize that Chip is the only one who hasn't yet reacted to my story, and I turn to him, hoping he'll have a revelation, something that will give me some kind of direction.

"Yeah, northeastern suburbs because they extend the furthest from the commercial district, where most of the bombs were hittin'. She won't stay in one place long, though, and eventually she'll have to find a way out of the subchapter. Can't use conventional means, as she don't have travel approval, unless she can find a forger in a hurry, although I don't know how she could pay for it. I reckon she'll try one of the mining tunnels on the subchapter border, up near where she's probably already hiding."

The woman adds, "You'll also want to find out more stuff about who she's with, the other two escaped prisoners, because it might change what they do."

I scan the room, looking each person in the eyes, and waiting for any more advice. When silence ensues, I say, "Thanks. Thanks for everything."

Somehow I know they'll keep my secrets. I don't know why they would. I guess maybe they're just good people. Real good people. The kind you call friend; the kind you stand up for; the kind you fight for. I don't know what's happening above me, but I vow in my heart to help these people, somehow, some way, some day. To do whatever it takes to give them a better life.

We leave, Roc and I. Explosions continue to rock the night around us, but they're less intense and less frequent. The streets are empty, everyone having taken shelter.

We run back to the Pen, where the fence is still destroyed, and the courtyard still strewn with guards' bodies. No one is around, probably hunkering down until the bombing ends. We stop at the point along the fence line where I last saw the girl. Consulting the map, we identify the best route to take out of the city.

"This way," Roc says, taking the lead as navigator.

I follow him, hoping and praying that we're doing the right thing.

Thirteen

Adele

Sometimes I wonder whether people are inherently good or inherently bad. I'd like to think good, or even neutral, like we can all make the choice for ourselves.

After a quiet morning in the servants' quarters at Tawni's parents' house, we move inside once we're sure it's safe. Although we don't plan to linger much longer, we're careful to cover our tracks so no one knows we've been here. The longer it takes them to find our trail, the colder it will become and the safer we'll be.

The whole morning I think about Elsey. She'll be our first rescue, because she's closest and I know exactly where she is. It's all I can do to stop myself from running off alone to save her. I need to be patient. One thing at a time.

Tawni's house is even more impressive than I'd imagined based on my glimpse in the dark. Standing three stories tall, it has more than a dozen rooms. The floors are marble and swirled with illustrious blue and green patterns. Winding staircases rise majestically in at least three places, providing access to the upper floors. The entire place is spotless, a testament to the quality of the servants that work here.

We've gotten lucky; it's one of the servants' two days off. And, as Tawni expected, no one from the Pen has shown up yet.

We turn on the telly, hoping to find out what's happening in subchapter 14. There are two major news stories being run over and over again. The headline story is about the bombing. We were all wrong about the culprits. I'm shocked, to be honest.

While we've all been hating the Sun Realm—for its unfair policies and outrageous taxes—the Star Realm has been hating us. The whole time I've been thinking the Star Dwellers are like a younger sibling to us, different but on the same side—but they've taken a different approach. The video from Vice President Meriweather, the leader of the Star Realm, explains things.

He blames us for the oppression by the Sun Realm, says we let them go too far, that we set a precedent that forces the Star Realm to comply with unfair contractual terms. He says our leaders are spineless, gutless—which I tend to agree with—and that until we remove them from power and agree to join their rebellion, they'll continue to bomb the living sheetrock out of us. Earlier, I assumed subchapter 14 was the first target, and it was, but it was only one of many first targets. Overnight a dozen subchapters were bombed, although none as heavily as ours.

Tawni and Cole are as shocked as I am. "If we kill each other, then where will we be?" Cole says, exasperated. He refuses to sit down while watching the broadcast, and now he's pacing, throwing his hands around as he rants.

"It will only make the Sun Realm more powerful," Tawni agrees.

"But the Star Dwellers are right, in a way," I say. When I see the looks on my friends' faces, I explain, "I don't mean in bombing us—not that. Just about our leaders. They're just puppets for President Nailin, right? He dictates the terms, and they agree to them in exchange for a bit of money on the side."

"Yeah, true," Cole says, "but why not just come and talk to us about it, rather than chucking bombs around?"

"Maybe they did," I say. "Maybe we ignored them."

I think Cole might blow up, lose his temper again—he's certainly in one of those moods—but he doesn't. He chews on the side of his mouth like he's chewing on my words, trying to understand them, and then says, "If that's true then they *should* be removed from power. As far as I'm concerned, there should be a rebellion, but not against us, against the Sun Dwellers, by both us and the Star Dwellers."

"But so many people will die," Tawni says.

"People are dying now!" Cole shouts. He lowers his voice, looking around as if the walls might have ears. "Just more slowly. The life is sucked out of us day by day, as the Sun

Dwellers take more and more from us. One day they'll take our souls."

He has a point, but I'm more interested in something else. "Where the hell did the Star Dwellers get bombs from? They have no money, no resources."

Cole raises his eyebrows. "Where indeed," he says.

"Maybe they've been planning this for a long time," Tawni says. "Maybe they've been saving for this."

"Maybe," I say. "But there were a helluva lot of bombs going off in a helluva lot of subchapters. That would require years of saving to buy or build that many bombs."

"Not if they had support by a traitor in the Sun Realm," Cole says.

Before I have a chance to respond, the second breaking news story comes on, so we turn our attention back to the telebox.

The next story is all about us, referred to as "the escaped guests from the Pen," who are deemed to be "armed and dangerous." Our photos and names are stuck to the bottom of the screen while they show footage of the destroyed fence, the downed guards, and the dropped guns. Without explicitly saying it, they imply that we're responsible for the whole mess, rather than admitting it was the Star Dweller bombs that caused the destruction.

Next they give information on who to call if we're spotted. Security checkpoints are being added to all major subchapter borders, and roadblocks are in place to search vehicles that may be hiding us. The penalty for harboring "the fugitives"— meaning us—is a life sentence in the Max.

The lead investigator, which basically means hunter of humans, is speaking live from the Sun Realm, and will be traveling to subchapter 14 to personally begin the search. His name is Rivet, and his face is what sparks my thoughts about the inherent nature of the human race.

I don't know where they found this guy, or what hole he'd been hiding in, but he's the epitome of evil. His face is cold and hard, with black eyes that are so close together they appear beady, like a snake's. Fierce black eyebrows rim them in a perpetual frown. His mouth is the snarl of an angry dog. A three-inch scar cuts one of his cheeks in half. He has a low-cut Mohawk and multiple piercings in each ear, which fits in perfectly with the dozens of tattoos that litter his muscular frame. Everything about him screams intimidation.

His words are cold, like icicles, and I almost feel like he can see us through the screen, directing his threats right at us. He keeps his comments brief: "I cannot reiterate this enough: We *must* apprehend the fugitives as quickly as possible. They're armed and extremely dangerous. Their sentences range from murder to treason, and they deserve to be locked away for the rest of their miserable lives. This office pledges to hunt them down and bring them to justice, to be tried for their new crimes under the law. Thank you for your time." Cameras flash and reporters yell out questions, but Rivet is gone, having disappeared back inside some government building.

"Murder?" I say. "I was in for treason, but they didn't even mention your crimes. We didn't kill anyone, they can't say that!" I'm angry and flustered. I knew they wouldn't be fair to us—have never been fair to us—but I don't want people to think I'm a murderer.

"There's something I should tell you," Cole says, finally sitting down on the floor.

I glance at him, but then back to the telly as the next segment begins. It's a review of each of us—our pasts, our crimes, our sentences, that kind of thing. They start with Tawni and brush past her pretty quickly, saying Cole and I are bad influences on her and that her sentence is much lighter—for the minor charge of illegal interstate traveling.

"My parents are hard at work doing damage control again," Tawni says sullenly, as if she would prefer to be depicted as a hardened criminal.

They move onto me next, turning my parents' slight rebelliousness into an act of high treason, framing it like we're a family of thieves and spies, not satisfied until we destroy everything from the Star Realm to the Sun Realm. They go into a lot of detail about how it makes sense that I'd try to escape, given my life sentence. By the time they're done with me, *I* even feel slightly ashamed of myself, although I've done nothing wrong.

The broadcast ends with Cole, touting him as the ringleader of our little gang, noting that he is "as cunning as he is dangerous." I grin at him when they say that, expecting him to take it as a compliment, but he looks away, his lips a straight line, unreadable.

I wait for them to tell Cole's story about the bakery, his attempted theft of six loaves of bread, his apprehension and short juvie sentence.

I find out the truth.

There was no bakery, no bread, no mild sentence. Cole duped me. The way his eyes sparkled when he told the story, his attention to detail, his effortless laugh: it all made me believe without a doubt that he was telling the truth. The true story paints a much grimmer tale.

According to the reporter, Cole attacked an Enforcer without provocation. The Enforcer was conducting a routine search of Cole's neighborhood, looking for anything suspicious—they do that from time to time. They don't need search warrants; just a badge and a uniform authorizes them to go wherever they want, whenever they want. Cole jumped the guy and killed him, broke his neck cleanly. They say it was instant death and that Cole is a murderer. Cole was sentenced to life in prison, just like me.

The segment ends and Tawni clicks off the telebox.

I stare into space in silence. I'm upset that Cole didn't tell me the truth, but even more upset with the information in the broadcast. Although I haven't known Cole for long, I know enough about him to realize that he wouldn't kill someone without a damn good reason. I want to ask, want to know the real story, but also know that Cole has to *want* to tell me. I don't want to force something out of him that he prefers to remain buried. So I just wait. A few minutes go by in silence, each of us lost in our own thoughts. Cole still won't make eye contact with me—his face turned away—although I look at him a few times.

Tawni's the first to speak. "Cole, she's one of us. She should know."

Cole finally turns his head, and I see what he's been doing in silence. Crying. His cheeks are slick with moisture and his eyelashes beaded with tears. It scares the hell out of me. In the short time I've known Cole, I've found there to be a strength in him that's beyond anything I've seen in someone before. It makes me want to be his friend, to depend on him, to count on him. But now he looks broken, destroyed, *devastated*. The pain on his face is utterly complete, cracking his cheeks with jagged lines.

He starts slowly, building momentum as he unloads his pain. "There were three of them," he says, "but I thought there was only one."

"Enforcers?" I ask.

He nods. "When I came home from school he was in the house. My younger sister, Liza, had stayed home sick. My parents were both out, working, like always." He pauses and takes a deep breath. Before he starts again, a fresh stream of tears dribbles from each eye.

"He was on top of her," he continues, "trying to take everything from her. God, Adele, she was only eleven." I feel my own batch of tears well up and I fiercely blink them back. If Cole can't be strong, I need to be strong for him.

"I was like a raging bull, full of anger, and I felt stronger than ten bulls. I was on him before he even knew I was there. Liza's tunic was half-ripped and he was trying to pull it off of her. She was incredible, Adele, not giving an inch, kicking and clawing and fighting to the bitter end. Eventually he would've subdued her, but not before taking a bit of a beating. My sister was strong, like me." Although his face remains mournful, I detect a hint of pride in his voice. But as much as I want to, I can't ignore his use of the word *was*. It's there in the back of my mind, tormenting me.

"I pulled him off of her with two hands, threw him against the wall. He wasn't prepared for a fight. His hands and voice were pleading, begging for me to let him go. I wonder if I should've."

"No, Cole," Tawni says. "If you'd let him go he would've just made up a story about you attacking him and the end result would've been the same."

Cole hangs his head and bobs it up and down, like he wants to believe her but knows he never will. He says, "I was in a rage, not to be reasoned with—you know my temper. I grabbed him and slung him into the wall headfirst. I spun him around, cradled his head, and wrenched it hard to the side. I didn't even know how to do it properly, but I guess brute strength was enough. I can still hear the bones in his neck cracking. I know I should be sickened by it, but I'm not; I relish the memory."

I relish that part of his memory, too. The Enforcer was pure evil, inherently bad for sure. If anyone was deserving of death, it was him. I want Cole to stop his story there, but I know he can't.

"The other two Enforcers were upstairs when it happened," he says. "They were looting our few measly possessions of value. My mother's gold wedding band. My father's steel-toed boots. Taking our stuff while their buddy took my sister." Cole's face remains tearstained, but there are no new flows. His eyes are strong again, flashing anger. I would've pitied any Enforcer who walked into the room at that moment.

"I guess they heard the commotion, because they came down quietly, their guns out and ready to shoot. But I wasn't ready to fight anymore. I was holding Liza, helping her cover herself with a blanket. She was bawling, kissing my face, begging me to take her far away from that place. Our home, the place where we'd had so many happy memories, grown up

171

together, had become dirty to her, a prison of filthy nightmares. She would've cast it off forever, Adele."

I'm crying. I don't know when I started, but once the taps are turned on I can't seem to stop them. I feel ashamed, like I've let my friend down in his moment of need. But he doesn't seem to notice, like crying is the natural thing for me to do.

"They pointed their damn guns at us, screamed for us to 'Stand up! Stand up!'" He wipes his face with his sleeve. "One of them checked the other Enforcer, realized he was dead. They separated us, moved us apart, kept screaming at us. I didn't understand what was happening until they shot her, my Liza, oh, my poor sweet Liza!" Cole's head is tucked in his hands, his entire body shaking with sobs. I'm bawling. Tawni's crying, too, but more constrained. She moves to Cole's side and rubs a hand on his back.

I think the story is over, but a few minutes later Cole looks up, dripping tears from his chin. "They waited for my parents to get home. I was in shock, sitting there numbly, waiting to wake up from the horrible nightmare. I almost charged them, daring them to shoot me—preferring if they would—but I didn't because I knew I had to explain to my parents why their little girl was dead on the floor. They hadn't even bothered to cover her body with the blanket."

The only thing I can do for Cole now is to listen, although God knows I don't want to—don't want to know the truth—not anymore. Desperately want to believe the comedic story about him juggling the loaves of bread.

"My parents walked through the door like they always did, holding hands, laughing, as happy as anyone in the Moon Realm ever was in those days. I screamed out, tried to tell them everything in a single breath, but I was denied even that. They shot them before they'd even registered what was happening." *No, no, no, no, no!* I can't take any more of the story. I bury my head in my shoulder, sob uncontrollably, like he's telling me the tale of my own parents' deaths.

In a strange reversal of roles, he waits patiently for me to get control of my emotions. When I force my head back up, he continues. "I fought like a wild animal, trying to force them to kill me, too. I really thought they would, especially when I started throwing anything I could get my hands on at them. But no. They ran around, dodging the things and laughing, mocking me, *enjoying* themselves."

"Cole, I'm…I'm…" I can't get the right words out—there are no right words.

"I know," Cole says. "So now maybe you can see why I just can't trust that Tristan is good, not when he comes from up there." He motions to the ceiling, like he's pointing to the heavens.

"I thought…I thought you were jealous or something," I say, right away wishing I hadn't.

Thankfully, Cole laughs it off. "Jealous? I mean, you're not a bad-looking girl, Adele, very pretty actually, but I'm not really into…how do I put this delicately…*you*."

Now I laugh, too; it sounds hollow and foreign to me, like it's something I haven't experienced in a long time. "Sorry, I realize it was stupid now," I say.

He waves me off. "So that's my story. I'm the murderer in the group, I suppose." His eyes are steely again, but I can still feel a weakness behind them, a vulnerability. I've only just met him, but he already feels like a lifelong friend, like I've known him forever. Instinctively, I move over and hug him, squeezing so tightly that if he wasn't as thick as a bear he might pop. It

173

feels so good to be hugged by someone again, even under such awful circumstances. Earlier, I'd gotten a taste of it when Tawni held me close after my fight with the gang leader, and now I'm suddenly addicted to human contact, like I need it to survive. I don't want to let go, but after a few seconds I do, not wanting to make things awkward between us, or to give him the wrong impression.

He's smiling. I feel we've made a major breakthrough in our relationship, which has seemed somewhat strained at times. Tawni's smiling, too. She already feels like my sister, after all we've been through together in such a short time.

My real sister's face pops into my mind once more. "It's time to rescue Elsey," I say.

"Where did you say she is?" Tawni asks.

"She's in an orphanage not far from here. It's just across the border into the slums."

"We should be leaving soon anyway," she says. "It's not safe to linger here."

"I thought you said they wouldn't look for us here," I say, frowning.

"Of course they will," Tawni says, a twinkle in her eyes. "Just not right away."

Before leaving, we make sure that everything is put back to how we found it. We "borrow" a couple of old packs that Tawni says her parents will never miss, and fill them with nonperishable food from the storeroom. Unlike most residents of subchapter 14, Tawni's family has enough supplies to last them for months, if not years. We only take items that are available in plenty, to ensure no one will notice they're missing. Although we expect to be able to find plenty of water along the way, we fill a couple of jugs from the servants' quarters with fresh water from the well. Then we nab a few waterproof flashlights before tying our packs shut.

Lastly, Cole and I raid Tawni's parents' closets for things to wear. Tawni points out the items that her mom and dad never wear, so they'll be less likely to realize they're gone. We stuff our gray prisoner uniforms under a mattress in the shed. Tawni grabs a few old tunics from her own closet and we head out the back door.

Daylight is more dangerous for us. We don't necessarily expect that if someone spots us that they'll call the hotline and report us to Rivet, but we also can't count on silence amongst our people—Tawni's parents proved that.

The one thing we have going for us is that even during the daytime, so little electricity is provided to our subchapter that the overhead lights don't provide enough light for someone to recognize us unless they're practically right next to us.

Still, we stick to the shadows, pausing to look all around before moving across open spaces. Block by block we make our way out of Tawni's neighborhood. When the houses change from solid stone to crumbling bricks, we know we've reached the slums. I think we all feel safer now.

The slums are exactly as you'd expect. All the houses, if you can call them that (they're more like tiny sheds), are in major disrepair. Kids run barefoot in the streets, playing knights and barbarians with rocks and cardboard swords. Dead, staring faces sit at windows, as if waiting for someone to come save them. No one is coming. Except us, and we aren't there to save them.

Unfortunately, the orphanage is in the dead center of the slums. Because there's so much more activity in the slums than in most neighborhoods—none of the people seem to work and none of the kids seem to go to school—we're especially careful. Despite only covering about ten blocks, it takes us nearly two hours to reach the orphanage. I'm ready to scream when we finally arrive.

The orphanage is probably the best-maintained structure in the slums, but it still isn't fit to live in. Certainly not for children. I feel my hands squeeze into fists so tight that my knuckles start to ache. Things were bad for me, but they might be worse for Elsey.

The dilapidated door hangs precariously by a single hinge, unable to fully close. At least half the windows are broken, either by old age or a few well-aimed rocks from the neighborhood monsters. There are holes in the roof and cracks in the steps.

We can't see any activity through the windows in the front. The orphanage is ringed by a crumbling stone wall, high enough to block our view of the rear yard.

When it appears the coast is clear, we take turns climbing the wall while the others cover us—not with guns but with eyes, ready to whisper a warning if someone is coming. We all make it into the side yard safely. We creep toward the back.

As we approach the corner of the building, we can hear voices. Children laughing, children shouting, nursery rhymes: that sort of thing.

I'm leading and am about to peek around the corner when I feel something whiz past my head. I duck and throw myself flat on the ground, suddenly believing that we've been discovered and that someone is shooting at us.

Cole chuckles, somewhat loudly. A cloth ball rolls away from us into the side alley—the cause of the whizzing. Just as I regain my feet, a young girl, no more than seven, rounds the corner, nearly colliding with me. She stops like she hit a wall, and prepares to scream, opening her mouth wide and leaning her head back.

Cole grabs her, covering her mouth with his big hand just in time. Her muffled scream sounds no louder than the distant echolocation squeal made by a hunting bat. She starts kicking, so I run to her and start talking in a low, soothing voice, trying to comfort her.

"It's okay, little one. We're not going to hurt you," I promise her. "We're just looking for someone—my sister." She still looks scared, her eyes wide and her breathing strained and ragged through her nose, but she's calmer, no longer struggling so much. "Do you promise not to scream or run away if my friend lets you go?" I ask.

She thinks about it for a minute and then nods slowly. I hope she isn't lying.

"Let her go, Cole," I say.

He raises an eyebrow, but complies, releasing the girl and stepping back. She doesn't run, doesn't scream, just stands there staring at us. Then she says, "They're going to wonder where I've gone," she says in a tiny voice, more fit for a butterfly princess than a little girl.

"Okay," I say. "You can go back. But first, do you know a girl named Elsey?"

The girl's eyes light up at my sister's name, and I know we've gotten lucky.

"Oh, yes!" she says, twirling her brown curls with one of her fingers. "Elsey and I are the bestest of friends. She's older than me, but she says I'm old for my age anyways."

It sounds like something Elsey would say. She's always liked playing with younger kids, making them feel grown up, special. I used to think she might become a schoolteacher. But that was before my parents were abducted.

"Can you tell her Adele is here to see her?" I say. "And help her find an excuse to come around this corner?"

The girl is even more excited now, flapping her arms as if she's ready to fly off to find my sister. "You're her sister! You're her sister!" she exclaims.

"Yes, now please go tell her."

The girl starts to race off, but then stops, whirling around to retrieve the ball before scampering back behind the orphanage. Smart girl.

We wait against the wall, expecting an Enforcer to appear at any second, having been ratted on by the sweet little clever girl.

Instead, like a mirage, my sister appears, running so fast her legs are a blur, her jet-black hair swishing around behind her. My day is a rollercoaster of emotions. The demon drop of Cole's story has given way to a higher high, practically bursting through the cavern roof. My heart is literally soaring, rising out of my body and smiling upon me from above.

Elsey slams into me with such force that she nearly topples me over. Although we've only been apart for six months, a mere blip in our lives, it feels like we haven't seen each other in years. She seems to have grown, both physically and in maturity. Only ten, her pale face looks wizened, young but worn.

"Oh Elsey," I sigh, holding her tight against my chest, her legs wrapped around my hips. She's still a child, above all. Forced to endure far more than a child should have to endure. Far more than anyone should.

I want to hold onto her forever, but time is short.

"Let me have a look at you," I say, gently lowering her to the stone slab alley. My breath catches as I gaze on her face. She's breathtaking, has always been, with doll-like features that are so perfect they must have been carved by a master sculptor. She's always been more beautiful than me, but I don't mind, for she is a pure spirit. I can tell by the way her jaw sticks out now that six months in this place has hardened her, but in her violet eyes I can see the same pure energy she's always had.

"You're a sight for sore eyes, Elsey," I say, tearing up slightly.

"I've missed you so much, Adele," Elsey says earnestly. "I couldn't believe it when Ranna said you were here. I ran as fast as I could." She scrunches up her face, like she's making a wish. "Are you here to get me out?" she says hopefully.

I nod. "Yeah, but we're not exactly allowed, so we're going to have to do it sneakily."

"I knew you'd come!" Elsey exclaims. "Big John kept telling me I was crazy, that you were stuck in the Pen forever, but I always said he was wrong, even when he called me names. I was right, wasn't I?"

"Of course, but there'll be time to talk about all that later. We've got to go."

"But I've got to say bye to Ranna!"

"There's not time, El, I'm sor—"

I'm cut off when Ranna tears around the corner, hissing, "Miss Death is coming!"

Elsey seems to understand the urgency of the situation. With a conviction that has been her trademark for all ten years of her short life, she hugs Ranna, pulling her friend's head into her heart. "I'll never forget you, Ranna," she says. "Our hearts are one." If you don't know Elsey you'd think she was crazy.

But that's just Elsey. Everything is dramatic, although in this case it's probably warranted.

"I'll never forget you either," Ranna parrots, like a miniature version of El.

I grab El's hand and we run back down the alley. Tawni is already over the wall and Cole is waiting to give Elsey a boost. We follow closely, hearing a cry from behind just as we slip over to the other side. *Miss Doom, or Death, or whatever*, I think.

"Quick, I know a shortcut," Elsey says, running in the opposite direction we're planning on going, simply assuming that we'll follow her. We do.

And it's a good thing, because at that moment I hear a yell from far back, out on the street where we'd been heading. I half-turn, curious as to who is pursuing us.

I'd recognize that demented face anywhere: Rivet.

Fourteen

Tristan

Roc and I have been walking for over an hour, making our way to a spot on the map. We hope it will give us a shot at finding her.

It's the middle of the night. We're tired. Neither of us speaks as we force ourselves to put one foot in front of the other, time and time again, trudging onwards.

Through the first part of the suburbs, people are out of their houses, wearing sleeping tunics or just undergarments, watching the fireworks in the distance, speaking in hushed voices. They're so transfixed by the scene before them that they barely pay us any attention. We're just a couple of wandering nomads.

After a while we see fewer and fewer people, as the explosions dull to a distant rumble, not loud enough to wake the sleeping. We march on, passing through a ritzy neighborhood—at least by Moon Dweller standards—with bigger houses and well-kept streets. Whoever lives in this neighborhood has done something to please my father, that's for sure.

We transition into a lonely slum, littered with garbage in the streets and cracked sidewalks. It's a bit scary, to be honest. Even when I visit the Star Realm, I stay in the finest they have to offer, not really witnessing the true living conditions. Without speaking, Roc and I pick up the pace, moving swiftly through the downtrodden neighborhood.

We pass a lonely orphanage, named *The Forgotten Kids*. True, but a bit pessimistic, especially for the kids. It's weird to think how different my own childhood was. In a way, I was forgotten, too. Growing up, I was always the last of my father's priorities. He always had *something very important to attend to*. I guess no matter what conditions you live in, you always have complaints—your bar is just set at a different height.

We make it through the slums without event. The map shows at least twenty miles of sparsely populated terrain. Within it is a network of caves called the Lonely Caverns. But we're far too tired to attempt it tonight. We find a couple of large boulders and seek shelter behind them, rolling out our bedrolls and hoping for sleep.

I doze fitfully, having alternating nightmares of explosions rocking the night and the girl's sad face. Both send shards of glass through my back and head. Even my dreams have become a series of pain and mystery.

I awake to find Roc sitting up, studying the map.

"Morning," he says, noticing my movement in his peripheral vision.

I notice that he doesn't add *good* to the beginning of his greeting. I guess compared to our normal breakfast routine—Roc bringing me fine meats and fruits in bed, and then me sharing it with him—there isn't much good about this morning. All we have to eat are dried fruits and nuts, and a few blocks of thick wafers, which we managed to steal from the army storehouse before we left. And the change from our soft palace beds—*ugh*. Splinters of pain shoot through my back, the consequence of the dozens of sharp rocks beneath my bedroll. I shrug it off and focus on the positive.

"*Good* morning," I reply cheerfully. For, despite our modest breakfast and sleeping situation, I'm ecstatic. In fact, I've never been happier. For the first time in my life I've woken up without the weight of my father on my shoulders. And I'm doing something *I* want to do. I know it's selfish, but my whole life I've been doing whatever my father asks of me, and I desperately need a chance to live my own life. Even if it's only to find out about...

"A girl?" Roc says into his map.

My head snaps up from our pack, where I'm rummaging through for food. *How does he do that?* I think. *How does he always seem to know exactly what I'm thinking?* "Huh?" I say, trying to hide my amazement.

"Are we seriously risking our lives all for a girl? One who you've never met?"

Roc's tone sounds angry. "I'm sorry, Roc. I just have to know why I faint every time I see her. I know it's a lot to ask of you, but—"

"No, it's fine, Tristan," Roc says, finally making eye contact with me. "I volunteered, remember? I'm just a little tense, that's all—not used to all this dangerous stuff. I agree there's something to it all, I just don't know what. It's worth exploring. I just wish she'd stop and let us catch her." He grins and the tension melts away, but I'm not sure if the discussion is really resolved.

"Thanks," I say. "Think of it as part of your training. A very *real* part of your training. How about we practice with the real swords for a while? It might help you to relax."

"Sure."

For the next hour I show him the subtleties of using a real sword. By the end, he seems more confident, performing the various maneuvers with ease. It's just the basics, but it's a start.

"What time is it?" I ask when there's a break in the action.

I don't bother to look at my watch. Usually Roc is responsible for dragging me to anywhere I need to be.

Roc says, "Early afternoon. Why?"

"We should get moving," I say, worried that we've tarried in our hideaway for too long.

"First we need to find out more about our quarry," Roc says. "Remember Chip's and Coral's advice?"

"Who's Coral?" I ask.

"The lady who led us down to that cellar. Well, I don't really know her name—she never told us—but I thought she was deserving of a name anyway, so we don't forget her."

Funny Roc. But he's right, of course. We have no idea where she might be headed—we're just guessing at this point.

"Okay, let's move along the edge of the caverns. Maybe there will be a shop or something where we can find a telebox."

We travel for more than two hours before we come to a large cave mouth, near the southern entrance to the Lonely Caverns. Sure enough, there's a small stone shack with a stand, set up just outside the caves. A middle-aged man with a long, salt-and-pepper beard dozes in a hammock, an unlit pipe dangling from his chapped lips.

All around him are piles of goods, some used, some new. All for sale. It seems a bit out of the way for a shop, but he has plenty of inventory, so I assume he gets *some* business. There's also a decent selection of preserved food, like dried meats and fruits.

As we slalom through the piles of stuff, I hear the low murmur of a voice. I head toward the sound. At the very back of the area, sitting on a table, is a small telebox. It's hard to believe the man has sufficient electricity to operate a telebox, and yet, there it is, broadcasting the news.

I move closer, tilting my ear to pick up the low volume, when I hear a booming voice from behind. "What can I do for ya?"

I spin around to find the man standing close to us, much smaller than his voice suggests. He eyes us warily, as if he thinks we're thieves looking to capitalize on his midday slumber.

"I'm very sorry, sir," I say. "We didn't want to wake you. We were hoping to watch your telebox for a few minutes, if that's okay? We've heard lots of rumors about the bombings, but we wanted to hear it for ourselves."

"Customers only," he says, pointing to a sign above the telebox that I hadn't noticed.

"Of course, of course," I say. "We have Nailins." I motion to Roc, who promptly unzips the pack and extracts a handful of gold coins.

The man's eyes widen. "You look familiar. Who the hell are you?" he asks.

"Customers," I say simply. "Now, we'll take ten packs of those dried meats and twenty of the fruit. What will that cost?"

"Usually my customers just barter," the man says, almost to himself, "but I guess that would be about five Nailins."

"Give him ten," I instruct Roc. "For the exemplary service and use of the telebox."

I turn my attention back to the screen. I massage a knob to raise the volume, not worried about the man's reaction. He'll probably let me to do anything I want after the tip he just received.

We've already missed the latest report on the bombing, which, not surprisingly, is the lead story. But a close second is the report on the guests who escaped from the Pen. First they show a guy, Cole something, large and dark-skinned. In his mug shot he appears angry, which isn't that surprising considering he was convicted of murder and sentenced to life in prison. The thought of the Moon Dweller girl traveling with him scares me. The report notes that the Cole character has no family left and therefore, he'll probably try to get out of the subchapter.

Next they show a girl named Tawni, with stark-white hair and long, thin features. I recognize her immediately as the girl who was sitting next to the dark-haired girl the first time I saw her. Tawni is painted by the media as a good kid who made some bad choices, the latest being her choice of companions in the escape from the Pen. Her parents are prominent, wealthy figures in the subchapter 14 community. They show a photo of her house.

"Oh my gosh," Roc says, watching over my shoulder, "we passed by there last night!"

I glance at him. "You think they might've been hiding out with her parents?"

"Possibly," Roc says.

"We'll check it out before we go into the caves."

Finally they show *her*. Her sad, green eyes suddenly fill the screen, and then the rest of her features follow as they pan out of the strange choice of close-up.

She's even prettier than I thought. Her face is flawless. Her lips are in a tight line, but behind them I can feel the warmth of a smile that hasn't been used in a long time. Her cheeks are pale, but well-constructed. Her hair is radiant black, cascading down from her head and in front of her shoulders. Not only beautiful, she looks capable, a more important trait in the world she lives in. But her beauty is meaningless to me. I need answers. Seeing her on the screen, I don't feel the pain I did when I twice saw her in person. Curious.

At least now she has a name. For the few days since I'd first seen her, she's just been a face, an idea, but now the name *Adele Rose* shivers through my mind and body like the wings on a moth.

She was in the Pen for treason, although the report doesn't provide any details on what she had done specifically. Her parents are noted as traitors, too, but no information is given on their whereabouts, and one can only assume that they've been executed in accordance with the law. But I know differently.

She has a sister, too, ten years old and living out her childhood in an orphanage in a rough part of town. A slum. *The slums.*

Roc and I look at each other at the same time. "She's headed for the orphanage," I say as Roc nods vigorously. "Maybe already there and gone."

"You don't know that. We have to check," Roc says.

"Let's go."

Roc settles up with the shop owner and shoves the food into our pack. I'm already halfway down the path, back the way we came. The lights above the majestic cavern are dimming, simulating the impending darker gray of dusk. I feel warmth in my skin, although there's a chill in the air. I think it's the warmth of determination. Although I was determined before, now that I know her name, it's like she's finally become real to me, more than just a bearer of pain or wielder of psychic power.

Roc catches up with me at a slight jog and I immediately match my pace to his. We make our way back to where we camped, hoping we'll be able to find safe passage into the slums. The news story motivates us, and we make it back in half the time. Just as the large boulders we'd camped behind appear in the distance, we hear the scurry of frantic footsteps approaching from the path that leads to the slums.

"Down!" I cry, not that either of us need to hear it. We're both already diving for the rocks, flattening ourselves and crawling behind the biggest stones we can find on the barren landscape.

Just as we hide, a form bursts from behind a large boulder, racing along the track dangerously fast. He's big, man-size, dark. A second shape emerges, with white, flowing hair and long strides. Big, dark-skinned guy, white-haired girl: it doesn't take a mining engineer to figure out who they are.

I hold my breath, watching the entrance to the slums, hoping and praying she will emerge. No, not *she*—Adele. I'm shocked when the third figure scrapes from the path, short legs pumping wildly, dark hair pulled into a ponytail. My first thought is: she's much shorter in person. But then I realize my mistake when a fourth figure appears.

There's no mistaking her this time. Athletic strides, fiercely determined expression, piercing green eyes—it's Adele. Icy tentacles stab at my back, but not as fiercely as the last time.

My mind is a black hole; my heart is a stallion. The stallion in me wants to jump up, say, "Adele, we have to talk," but thankfully my mind's black hole implodes upon itself, evaporating and returning clarity of thought.

The orphanage. Her sister. A small girl who resembles Adele. It's clear what has happened. They've broken her out. And the way they're running—like the wolves of hell have been unchained behind them—means that someone is chasing them. Enforcers perhaps. Or orphanage security, if there even is such thing.

Wrong and wrong.

The Devil himself emerges behind her, running with purpose, perfectly balanced and efficiently functioning, like a machine. A very evil machine. I know that face, that form, all too well. Rivet. The best of my father's special purpose unit. And the most evil. The most like my father. He's chasing Adele and her friends.

Behind him is the rest of his unit: half a dozen special purpose personnel with big guns and sharp swords. Death on twelve feet.

Adele and her friends look like they might turn toward us, but then they veer left, up a slight rock hill, heading for the mouth of one of the Lonely Caves.

Rivet is gaining.

Without thinking, I stand up and run hard, cutting the distance between them like a knife, willing my legs to fly. I ignore a blast of thunder in my skull as the headache returns. My hand draws my sword instinctually, using small movements to conserve strength. My heart is pounding, not from the urgency of the run, but because I know Adele is so close, and yet she might never know I'm even here. I hear footsteps behind me and know right away that Roc has my back. He and I both know he'll be no match for the highly trained soldiers, but he's my friend—a true friend—and he'll go down fighting, whether to the grave or to a prison cell. Just like me.

Rivet is like a heat-seeking missile: Such is the intensity in his venomous eyes and the way his stare is locked on Adele that he doesn't even see me coming. One of his men shouts something as I approach, but he ignores it, thinking it's just a standard war cry, an adrenaline-induced *whoop!* of the chase.

When a collision grows imminent, I lower my shoulder and target his chest. The timing is perfect.

I hit Rivet just before he starts up the hill, ensuring his momentum hasn't lessened whatsoever, creating a human shockwave that sends tremors through both our bones. But I'm the aggressor in the collision, and I'm ready for it, so he takes the worst of it by far. He's knocked off course, his feet momentarily leaving the rock and his body contorting awkwardly in midflight until he thuds onto a hard slab of rock more than fifteen feet away.

There are people who, if hit that hard, at that speed, might die. Unfortunately, Rivet isn't one of them. Not even close. He is pure strength, sporting more muscle around his fingers and toes than most people have in their biceps, back, or abdomen. Okay, maybe a slight exaggeration, but not too far from the truth. Plus, he's wearing a thin layer of moldable body armor. The hit would've hurt, but to Rivet, pain is pleasure, all part of the game.

I glance up the slope to see if she's gotten away okay. To my surprise she's at the top gazing down, watching my fight with Rivet. I want to run to her, to grab her and shake her, demand answers. But that is madness. Rivet will just kill us both. I need to give her time. It's the hardest thing in the world to push her away when I'm so close to discovering the truth.

"Adele!" I scream. "Run!" I don't have a chance to see if she listens to me, because I sense movement to my left.

The sick puppy is on his feet and drawing his sword before I even have a chance to say *Bring it!* which is probably good because it would just make him even angrier.

As it is, he's angry enough, charging me like a steamroller. *Clang!* The impact of his blade on mine jars my teeth, threatening to dislodge each and every one of them. His next swipe nearly takes off my head, but I manage to duck at the last minute.

Roc reaches my side, and I use one of my arms to thrust him behind me, out of danger. He has improved steadily during our training sessions, but he isn't ready for the big leagues.

Rivet's men surround us, jeering and taunting as their boss and I circle each other. Roc is like my unattached tail, hovering behind my butt. I look into Rivet's eyes, hoping for some indication of mercy. I see only death. I'm a good fighter, but it's

191

too much. There are just too many of them. We're both going to die, and I haven't even spoken to Adele, haven't had a chance to ask her a damn thing. The only satisfaction I have is that I've given her a slim chance to escape, although I'm not sure why it's so important that she goes free.

But I reserve my final thoughts for Roc: how I let him down, how I led him from the safety of the Sun Realm to the dangers of the Lower Realms, how his death is my fault, too.

Ziiiip! Something whirrs through the air, sounding odd next to the raucous cries of Rivet's men. *"ARGH!"* one of the men roars. Rivet and I both risk a glance away from each other to see what's happening. A large guy with a patch over one eye is slumped to his knees and clutching his heart. A sixteen-inch shaft protrudes from his left breast, finned at the end. Blood dribbles from his mouth as he dies.

A chorus of *zips* and *whirrs* fills the air as arrows rain down on us. Realizing we're under attack by a seemingly deadlier foe than Rivet, I grab Roc and thrust him down, falling next to him flat. Cries of pain echo through the cavern as each of Rivet's guards is taken out by precision targeting. Not one arrow so much as grazes our skin. They aren't shooting at us—at least not yet.

I hunt for Rivet, but he's gone, either having lurked off or dove for cover somewhere. It's too much to hope that he's been killed along with his men. I scan the bodies anyway, looking for their leader. He isn't amongst the dead. I finally spot him by pure luck, as a stray beam of dome light catches the tip of his sword as he skulks off, escaping over a rock embankment and back toward the slums.

I stay down, preferring not to be mistaken for one of Rivet's men.

Our saviors approach, their faces cloaked in shadow by dark-brimmed hats. Most of them clutch bows, cocked and ready to kill, while others have swords, like us.

The leader stands over me, his sword pointed close to my chin.

"I'll be damned," he says. "If it ain't Prince Nailin himself. If I hadn't heard the news this mornin', I'd never have believed it. You'll make a pretty prize for the Star Dwellers indeed."

Fifteen

Adele

No beast of reality, or creature of imagination, is as terrible as mankind. Or as loving. It's a contradiction. I've always liked contradictions. Today I see both sides of the coin unveiled in gruesome and beautiful imagery, captured by my eyes and filed away in my mind, like still shots taken by a world-renowned photographer.

First the terrible: Rivet. I can see the bloodthirsty gleam in his eyes at the end of the alley. He shouts something, to his men most likely, and then comes after us.

I'm surprised when I catch up to Elsey first. She was in the lead, but is now falling behind as Cole's powerful legs and Tawni's long strides outdistance her. I urge her forward with a soft nudge on her back. I have no idea where her shortcut leads, but I hope it will be to a place we can hide.

Hiding is our only option. Fighting will be futile, as Rivet will have a horde of men with him, armed to the teeth and ready for action.

In the distance I see Cole and Tawni drop out of sight, presumably cresting a rise and banking down a slope. Glancing back, I can see Rivet gaining on us, flanked by his men. They look like robots, rigidly pumping their arms opposite their strides, programmed to obey only one command: kill.

"Go, Elsey, go!" I urge, trying to use my mind to magically lengthen her short legs.

We reach the spot where the others dropped away and feel gravity pull us forward, down a steep slope. Dusk is falling upon us rapidly—the overhead cavern lights dimming—and it's getting hard to see our feet on the gray stone. A sprained ankle or a slight stumble could cost us our lives.

Thankfully, our steps are true and we reach the bottom of the slope, veering left to where another trail leads up to a cave mouth. Cole and Tawni are waiting for us at the top.

I shouldn't look back, but I do. Rivet is already halfway down the hill, having silently sped up, moving inhumanly fast, as if sensing that an end to the chase is near.

Elsey and I try to find an extra gear to allow us to reach the top of our slope before Rivet reaches the bottom of his, although I know in my heart the feat is impossible. We're caught and I know it, but I wasn't raised to be a quitter. We push on. My thighs burn and my calves ache. My head throbs from the physical and mental stress of the chase.

I glance up to see how close we are to the top. I'll never forget the look on my friends' faces. They're staring past me, toward our pursuers. But their faces aren't those of helpless prey about to be captured; rather, they look astonished, their eyebrows raised and mouths open.

We reach the top and I look back, blood pumping in my forehead.

I involuntarily imitate their expressions, raising my own eyebrows and opening my own mouth. I'm genuinely shocked by what I see.

Rivet is on the ground, rolling to a stop. Has he fallen? I don't think so. A simple misstep wouldn't capture Cole's and Tawni's attention so completely.

That's when I see him.

Despite the dim lighting, I recognize him instantly, both because he's one of the most famous faces in the Tri-Realms and because my headache is back. He's carrying a long sword, standing stoically, waiting to fight Rivet. His blond, wavy hair is ruffled although there's no air moving through the cavern. He looks strong, confident, heroic. Clearly, he's saved us. So he *is* a hero of sorts.

He looks at me, locking eyes, like before. Also like before, the pain reaches a fever pitch, so intense it almost brings me to my knees. He screams my name: "*Adele!*" At first I think he's beckoning me to him, but his second word clears up any confusion: "*Run!*"

Despite the urgency in his tone I remain frozen, my heart and head pounding, watching what will happen next.

Rivet attacks, launching himself with an animal frenzy at Tristan. In a manner I can only describe as *professional*, Tristan blocks the attack and jumps back. I notice someone behind him, also carrying a sword. A friend of Tristan's most likely, or so I hope.

Protectively, Tristan holds the other guy back with one arm while parrying and dodging Rivet's strokes. The rest of Rivet's men arrive, surrounding them. *No!* I think.

We have to do something. He's saved us and now he's going to die for us.

I take a step forward, but a strong arm holds me back. "No," Cole says firmly. "We have to go. It's suicide."

I try to struggle free, but Cole's grip is iron. Tears spring up as I try to wriggle away. "Let go!" I yell. "Please, they're going to kill him!"

Tawni's face appears in front of me. She pulls Elsey beside her. "Think of your sister," she says.

My body collapses, all fight gone from it. As much as I'm willing to throw my life away in an effort to save Tristan, the causer of pain, I know I can't abandon Elsey. Not after all she's been through. Not after all *we* have been through. I am all she has. And she is all I have.

I let myself get half-dragged, half-carried into the absolute darkness of the cave. I feel numb. Tears continue to well up and stream down my face, but they feel cold, emotionless, a neurological response to a stimulus, nothing more.

I barely notice as we cut a random path through the cave network. In the back of my mind I know we're in the Lonely Caverns. Although we haven't necessarily meant to come this way, it is the perfect place to hide from Rivet. I remember the kids at school telling stories of the Lonely Caves, how kids are always getting lost in them, dying of starvation, or falling down bottomless pits. I used to fear the caves, but now they feel like a sanctuary.

I can hear Cole and Tawni whispering, making quick decisions about which side tunnel to take next. They're taking the most convoluted route possible, almost trying to get us lost in an effort to lose Rivet, who will surely be pursuing us again soon, if not already. But with each twist and turn, they recite the full list of the directional changes we've made so far out loud, trying desperately to remember the way back. I try to memorize what they're saying, as a backup, but get confused halfway through. I'm still not thinking clearly, am still a bit of a mess.

But listening to the sounds of their voices also helps.

Eventually I get control of my body and am able to save Cole a lot of effort by walking on my own again. When I do, Elsey appears by my side, illuminated by the flashlight she's carrying. I notice that I have one as well—we all do. Funny how I can't remember them being turned on or even someone giving one to me. We fall back from the others right away.

"Adele," she says, her violet eyes radiating compassion. "Are you okay?"

I put my arm around her as we walk. What can I say? Actually, Elsey, I'm a complete wreck because a guy I've never met, a guy whose very presence brings me immense physical pain, a guy whose father abducted our parents, is dead, all because of me.

Instead, I say, "I'm okay now, Elsey, sorry to scare you like that."

"I wasn't scared," she says. The matter-of-fact way in which she says it makes me believe her. Perhaps my sister is made of a tougher substance than I am. Or maybe she's just too young to understand the true horror of what has just happened, is just happy to have her big sister back.

"You're very brave," I say.

"What happened back there? Who was the guy that saved us? He knew your name, Adele."

My face tightens and I try to get control of my emotions—take a deep breath. "It was no one," I say.

"Tell me," Elsey says. "I'm not a child anymore."

There's so much truth in her eyes that I know she's right. Although she's only been at the orphanage for six months, she's changed, matured. Ten years might've passed in her mind. I can't always protect her anymore.

I decide on the truth. "This might sound impossible…in fact, I'm not sure I believe it myself…I might've been seeing things…I was probably mistaken, but—"

"Adele, please, just tell me," Elsey says, interrupting my ramblings.

I take another deep breath. Why is this so hard? Just say it. Say it. *Say it!* "I think it was Tristan Nailin," I blurt out, feeling dread wash over me, as if by speaking his name I've cemented his fate.

I expect Elsey to giggle, to look at me with knowing eyes, to say *Sure it was, Adele, I believe you*, using the sarcasm that I taught her. She surprises me by saying, "I thought so."

"You what?" I say, unable to hide my surprise.

"He looked like Tristan," she says with a slight nod of her head. "I mean, not as good looking as in the magazines, but…"

"I thought he looked even better," I say, surprised at my own words.

Elsey eyes me curiously. "Since when did you think Tristan was handsome?" she says, sounding more grown up than ever.

"I don't. It's just...never mind."

Elsey smirks at me. "You can tell me the whole story later."

It dawns on me. Why was Elsey so easily convinced that it was Tristan? She doesn't seem to find it strange at all that he appeared out of nowhere in a remote part of the Moon Realm. "Elsey....why'd you think it was Tristan? Was it just because he looked like him?"

Now she giggles, finally sounding her own age. "Because of the news, of course."

My heart flutters and I know she's about to tell me something important, so I stop and call to Cole and Tawni, who come jogging back, their eyebrows V'd in concern. "What's wrong?" Cole says.

I motion to Elsey to speak. "Tell them what you were about to tell me," I instruct.

Elsey's eyes widen. "You mean, you don't *know*?" she says incredulously.

"We've been kind of...*busy*," I say.

"Right," she says, changing her tone to that of a lecturer. "Well, all the kids gathered in the big room to watch the telebox this morning, like we always do. This kid we call Wiz suggested we watch the news, like he always does. He always gets voted down and we watch something else, but this morning he put it on before anyone could say anything. You guys were all on the screen." She waves her hand across us.

"We saw that," I say, hoping that isn't her big news.

She changes course, her voice softening as she says, "I just knew you would come for me, Adele." Finally, she fully sounds

200

like a little girl again, the little sister I remember, before life's challenges forced her to grow up before anyone should have to.

I put an arm around her. "I'll always come for you. Now, what else did you hear on the news?"

Elsey's eyes light up. "That Tristan ran away from home!" she exclaims.

"What? He…*ran away*?" I look at Tawni and Cole, who are staring at me.

"Yep. And apparently he was headed for the Moon Realm, subchapter six I think they said."

"That's only a single train ride from here," I say, finally connecting the dots.

"He was coming to find you," Tawni says.

Cole shakes his head. "C'mon, seriously. These strange feelings and headaches and all that crap again? Coincidence I reckon. If he really was trying to get away for a while, he probably just picked a place where no one would think to look for him."

Elsey touches my arm. "Why would Tristan have been coming to find you? And what does he mean by headaches?" she asks.

I tell her everything. Cole stalks off and pretends not to listen, but Tawni stays by me, even holds my hand for part of it.

Elsey is ecstatic when I finish. "He *did* come for you," she says positively. Under her breath, she says, "No matter what that other guy says."

It's then that I realize we haven't had time for introductions. "Elsey," I say. "This is Tawni. My friend," I add.

"It's very nice to meet you, Elsey," Tawni says. "Adele's told us so many nice things about you."

At that, Elsey beams.

"Cole," I say, a bit louder to get his attention, "come meet Elsey."

He saunters over, his dark skin glowing a strange orange color under the illumination of the flashlights. "Hi, Elsey," he says. "I'm Cole."

My sis sticks out her hand and shakes Cole's big paw. "Tristan *was* looking for my sister," she says definitively.

"Oh, great. Now it's *three* against one," Cole says, grinning. At least he doesn't seem frustrated anymore.

"He wasn't looking for me, El," I say. And if he was, it means he likes causing me pain, almost like it's his purpose in life. Although now that he saved us, that doesn't make sense either.

"Good," Cole says. "The sooner everyone gets that through their heads the better. We need to keep moving. I think we've probably done a good enough job of losing ourselves in here, but they'll keep searching until they find us."

We walk for hours. Time seems to stand still inside the caverns. Cole and Tawni give up on trying to remember which route we've taken. I think they realize we aren't going to be going out the way we came in.

The caverns are ominous and scary, and yet beautiful at the same time. Around every bend is another stalactite or stalagmite, some impossibly big, some carved by nature into complex patterns, more intricate than a master carver could ever hope to emulate on a museum statue. We pass under giant stone archways, and cross natural rock bridges, some so thin that we have to crawl across on our stomachs, trying not to look down at the never-ending drops into darkness on either side. The color of the stones darken as the miles pass under our

202

feet, changing from the reddish brown of subchapter 14 to the dark grey of whatever subchapter we're moving toward.

Much of the time we are able to walk upright, the jagged ceiling rising well above us. But at other times we're forced to stoop, or even crawl.

I'm beat, so I know Elsey must be tired, too. At first she keeps up a constant chatter, talking about anything and everything. She talks about her time in the orphanage, asks a million questions about the Pen, and tries to get us all to agree that we're on a fantastic adventure. Eventually, she ceases talking completely, so I know she's getting tired. We need to stop, but none of us seems to want to make the call. I think we all feel that every additional footstep gives us a greater chance of survival.

As we walk, I notice Elsey's tunic sagging in the back. "El," I say, "is there something in your back pocket?"

Not stopping, she reaches behind her and extracts a gleaming metal slingshot, fitted with a thick rubber band. She holds it behind her. "Ranna gave it to me," she says by way of explanation.

I take it from her, examining the handle. Cut into the wide hilt is a slot, which I flip open with my thumb, holding my breath. Inside is a compartment full of round metal pellets—ammunition. Maybe she's changed even more than I thought. She's never been the type to shoot slingshots before. Play with dolls, yeah, but not weapons.

"Take care of this, El. It's a really nice weapon," I say, handing it back. She pockets it and we continue trudging along.

Cole, who is leading, finally stops and sits on a flat stone rock that looks like someone has put there as a bench. He says,

"I think we've gone far enough. It must be the middle of the night. Even Rivet will have to stop for sleep."

Tawni checks her watch. "It's after three," she says.

We're all too tired to disagree. Or even to eat. Instead, we go straight to bed, four ducks in a row, pressed up close to each other for warmth. Cole and then Tawni and then Elsey and then me.

"He's not dead, you know," Elsey whispers.

"Who?" I say, although I know the answer.

"Tristan."

"Oh."

"If something's pulling you together, then he couldn't have died. He might be captured, tortured even, but somehow he'll find you." I can't tell if her words are wise beyond her years, or simply the vivid imagination of an innocent child. Either way, they comfort me. I don't remind her that whatever force is at play, it's more likely pushing us apart.

"G'night, Elsey," I say

"Love you, Adele."

"Love you, too."

Although I'm sure it's hours later, it feels like I start dreaming the second my eyes close. My dream isn't of Tristan, for which I'm strangely relieved. It's like I know that if I dream of him I will only see death. His, not mine. Thankfully, my mind gives me a reprieve from all my questions about him. Of course, the alternative isn't much better, full of a different pain.

I dream of war. The Star Dweller army is destroying all of the Moon Realm, running rampant across the subchapters. It's like I'm on the outside of a looking glass, watching the horror unfold before my eyes. For some reason I'm not angry at them.

I know they're just tired of being the scum of the earth, treated like rats by the Sun Dwellers. Used, abused, stepped on.

The Sun Dweller army is coming, their legions of troops marching forward, their red armor polished and gleaming. I can see them, but the Star Dwellers can't. I scream, try to warn them, but no one can hear me through the mirror. No one except Rivet, that is, who is leading the Sun Dweller army. His black eyes look right at me, challenging me to come down. I don't want to, but I know I have to.

I swim through the mirror, pushing it to the side and behind me, like it's made of a strange viscous liquid. Gravity grabs me and pulls me to the ground. Rivet smiles as he tightens his grip on his gun. He pulls the trigger and shoots me through the heart.

You know how they say you can't die in your dreams? I do. The pain is so intense, so *real*, that I cry out in my sleep. But still I don't wake up, clinging to life in my dream by reaching for a sky I have never seen, as life ebbs from my broken body.

I die tonight.

When I do wake, I'm surprised to find myself very much alive with three familiar faces hovering anxiously over me. "We're here, Adele," Tawni coos. "It was just a dream."

"So real," I murmur. "I died."

Elsey's face is clouded with concern. "You'll never die," she says.

"You got that right," I say, trying to put on a strong face for my sister although I feel weak from the nightmare.

"We need to eat something and then keep moving," Cole says. For all the emotion that Cole displayed when we were at Tawni's house, he seems equally emotion-free now. Rigid, soldier-like. It doesn't bother me.

We eat quickly, swallowing the tasteless canned beans in gulps, like it's a race.

Because of Tawni's watch, we know we've only slept three hours and that it's still early in the morning. Cole suspects that Rivet and his men have slept even less, so we need to keep moving. When we start out, I'm already dreading the day's hike. My ribs are sore and tender, but by gritting my teeth and breathing through them, I can control the pain.

Elsey seems to have slept better than me, bouncing along beside me and chattering away. "I'm so glad to be out of that orphanage," she says. "Some of the kids were nice, and I'll miss Ranna for all of eternity, but the rest of it was dreadful. We all slept in the same room and ate the same porridge every day. They only let us go outside once a day, and the rest of the time we had to do chores around the place. Once a month they let us take a bath. How was the Pen?"

"About the same," I say. "Maybe a bit better, to be honest."

"Where are we going?"

"To find Mum and Dad."

"Really? You think they're alive?"

"Tawni thinks that Dad is. And I bet if he is then Mom is, too."

Elsey's eyes light up. "We'll rescue them, won't we, Adele?"

"Of course," I say, not sure at all.

It feels good knowing where my father is, even though getting him out will be the equivalent of a suicide mission. Between knowing about my dad and having Elsey around, I feel like I'm at least half a person again, a significant improvement over the empty shell I had become. But there is

206

still a huge part of me missing, because I haven't saved my dad yet and don't even know where my mom is. I wonder where she is, what condition she's in. Despite my assurances to Elsey, I know there's a good chance she's dead. I try not to think about it.

Chatting with Elsey makes the day go by so much faster. She's like our little motivator, constantly saying positive things in her very proper-sounding way. Once she's done grilling me about what I've been doing while we were apart, she focuses on Tawni and Cole, asking them even more questions. They tiptoe around some of the serious things we've already discussed, and focus on telling funny stories from their childhoods.

All in all, it isn't a bad day, and before I know it, we're stopping again for the evening. We haven't eaten since the morning, so we're all famished. We devour our canned food again, except this time I actually enjoy it. I don't think it's the taste of the food, though; I think it's just that being free of the Pen and back with my sister makes the bland food taste better—it's the taste of freedom, I guess.

When we finish eating, Cole brings up the topic we've all been ignoring. "How the hell are we going to get out of these caves?" he says.

"Are we lost?" I say, making a bad joke.

Tawni laughs anyway—snorts actually, because she's taking a sip of water when I speak. That gets us all laughing, with Elsey's infectious giggle keeping it going for a long time. Even Mr. Serious joins in, smirking at first, then chuckling, and finally full out laughing. We all need it.

"If we just keep going, we'll come out somewhere eventually, right?" I say.

"How much do you know about the Lonely Caverns?" Cole asks.

"Not much. They connect three or four subchapters, don't they?"

"Yeah," Cole says. "For each grouping of subchapters there's a cavern that acts as a hub to connect them all. The Lonely Caverns are the hub for subchapters fourteen to seventeen. They're used by miners to travel from mine to mine. The miners stick to the main tunnels, which we left almost immediately. According to the maps I've seen, the caverns are a hundred square miles."

Tawni adds, "And we've made so many turns that we don't have the first clue as to which direction we're headed. We may have been traveling in circles all day, or we may have cut a path straight across—impossible to say for sure."

"Best guess?" I ask.

Cole says, "I think we're going to end up somewhere in subchapter sixteen. We headed straight east when we first entered, and I'm pretty damn sure we haven't cut back across any of the main tunnels, so that means we're still headed east, unless we got completely turned around and are now headed south and west again, back the way we came. We should know soon enough, because we'd end up rejoining the main tunnel."

"Okay," I say. "So we just keep walking?"

Cole shrugs. "No other choice."

Sixteen

Tristan

These days not many people believe in God anymore. I'm not sure I do sometimes. Those above, in the Sun Realm, are enjoying themselves too much to stop to think about whether they're blessed. And those below, in the Moon and Star Realms, are too jaded. My mom did, though. She believed with all her heart that there's a greater power out there, one that cares about us, watches over us. She said bad things still have to happen, because they help us learn and grow, but that in the end we'll be saved.

I could use a little saving.

I wake up with a nasty bump on my head. I don't even remember getting hit. It throbs like hell.

I try to sit up, but it's difficult with my arms and legs tied.

It's dark. Not like a cloudy night with the moon and stars blocked, like I've seen in books; dark like the sun, moon, and stars don't exist, which they don't in our world. Plus there are no overhead cavern lights, no streetlights, no houselights. I work out that we're in a cave pretty quickly.

It all comes flashing back. The girl—no, *Adele*—running, being chased by my father's demons. My intervention. Rivet's gleaming eyes. Our salvation by the same men who surely now hold us captive.

You'll make a pretty prize for the Star Dwellers indeed.

From the man's words, it doesn't sound like they're Star Dwellers, unless he's talking about them in the third person. I don't think so.

A light flashes in the dark. It moves closer.

The man holds the torch in front of my face. It burns my eyes while they try to adjust. I shut my eyelids tight, and then slowly open them, squinting for at least a minute. The whole time the man waits patiently for me to get my eyes fully open.

When I do, I gasp. I know he's the man who spoke to me earlier, the one who killed Rivet's men. He isn't wearing his hat this time, and I can see his face, which is what makes me gasp. Half his face is swollen red and bubbling with blisters. Whether a lifelong disease or a fresh scar, I do not know.

"My face got damn near blown off by the heavy artillery," he growls. "Pretty sight, ain't it?"

"What do you want?" I ask.

"From you?" he says. "Nothin'. All you gotta do is come with us. I hope I'm not makin' it sound like you've got a choice.

'Cuz ya don't. Yer comin'. As sure as the sun ain't shinin', yer comin'."

"Who are you?"

"Doesn't matter. Just a guy. A guy fed up with bein' crapped on by yer kind. For once the damn Star Dwellers got the right idear. Fight back."

"But they're killing your own people."

"Eh. So they've got their target a bit mixed up. But it's workin', ain't it? We're goin' to join 'em, and others will, too. So the plan worked, eh?"

My head is spinning, half because of what this guy is saying to me, and half because of the blow I took to the head, probably from the butt of this guy's gun. "Look, man, I'm not the one you want. I'm not like them. I hate my father. I've left the Sun Realm and I'm not going back." The words sound true off the tip of my tongue, but are they? Could I really give up everything? For what? What if Adele's dead already? What if she's not, but I never find her? Or what if I find her and she doesn't have any answers and tells me to leave her the hell alone? It's not out of the realm of possibility. Would I go back?

I blink away the answer to the last question because it makes me feel weak and pathetic. Spineless.

Yes.

I take a deep breath and continue. "Just let me go and I'll stay out of the whole thing. Please." I feel like I'm begging, my voice higher pitched than usual, all toughness stripped from it, leaving just a child's voice.

"Okay," the man says.

"Really?"

211

"Nah, just messing with you. Ha ha ha!" The guy's laugh is as rough as the chipped stones around us. "Yer my prize, kid. We can use ya. Yer one hell of a bargainin' chip."

He leaves the torch nearby and moves off into the darkness. Using my elbows as levers, and by twisting and balancing on one shoulder, I manage to get into a seated position so I can take in my surroundings—or at least what I can see of them.

Roc is sleeping nearby, his forehead marked by a puffy, red welt. They haven't bothered to give us blankets or pillows or anything, so my body is sore and cold from lying on the hard cavern floor all night.

There are several other men sleeping nearby. I'm sure there are more, at least a dozen, but the light from the torch only extends in a small sphere. I assume we're somewhere in the Lonely Caverns, most likely not very far in, as the men won't have wanted to carry our limp bodies for very long.

I have no idea how long we've been out, but I hope it wasn't long, for with each passing minute Adele is traveling further and further away from me.

How twisted is fate? Pretty twisted, I'd say. Mangled and knobby; old and decrepit. Every time you're granted a stroke of good fortune, it's offset by a calamity. Like Adele escaping from prison right when the Star Dwellers attacked. Sometimes good luck is even caused by something bad. Like when Adele's path crossed ours at that exact fateful moment. Had Rivet not been chasing her, perhaps she would have arrived later, and I wouldn't have seen her. We might've missed each other by taking different routes, like two companies of miners passing in the night, unknown to each other.

My father doesn't believe in fate. He says we make our own fate. So far, he's been right about that. I sort of believed him until now. But after everything that's happened, I know there are other forces at play. Forces that want Adele and me to meet, for some reason that I can't yet grasp.

Roc stirs in his sleep and then opens one eye, clamping it shut again immediately when the light hits it. He raises a hand to his temple, gingerly feeling around the red bump, cringing each time he touches a raw nerve.

"You okay, man?" I whisper, trying not to wake the other guys.

"I think so. You?"

"About the same. Just a knock on the head. I think it was done gently enough to avoid any permanent damage. I think they want us alive to use as hostages."

"Hostages for what?"

"They're taking us to the Star Dwellers, who will then try to get to my father through me."

"What're we gonna do?"

"Not much we can do. Go along for the ride, I suppose."

A familiar voice echoes through the cave. "That's right! There's nothin' you can do!" Each of the men around us awakes with a start, some of them jumping up and grabbing weapons, looking for someone to fight.

"It's just me, you idiots," the voice says, as a figure steps into the light. It is the guy with the burnt face. "Time to move," he says.

"Move where?" I ask.

"None of yer damn business," he says.

With impressive speed, the men get packed and move out. I ask for water but am denied. They do, however, unbind our

213

feet so we can walk easily. Our hands remain tied in the front. I smile when they don't bother to retie them behind our backs. In the front allows us lots more room to maneuver in the event that an opportunity arises.

But no chances for action come up today. Our march feels endless, especially with no water to quench my burning throat. Roc and I are separated—sandwiched in between two guys each—so we aren't able to talk to each other. When I do risk a question to one of my guards—a simple *Can I stop to go to the bathroom?*—it's answered with a rough jab to the abdomen with the end of his rifle.

Not a good day.

Twice we hear echoing voices bouncing off the walls from somewhere in the cavern. We stop suddenly and everyone strains to listen for more sounds, trying to discern who it might be or what direction it's coming from, but all we get is silence, and it's near impossible to determine where the sound originates from. I wonder if it's Adele and her friends, somewhere in front of us in the caverns, moving by some *twist of fate* in the exact same direction. Or it might be Rivet with a new troop, replacing the men who were killed by our captors. Whoever it is, they stay out of our way and we out of theirs.

I don't know the Lonely Caverns well, but from studying Roc's map I know enough to realize we're sticking to one of the four main tunnels, which intersect at a hub near the middle. We're essentially using the cavern as a conduit to move to another subchapter.

At the end of the day's march, my legs are on fire and my wrists rubbed raw by the constant chafing of the tight ropes that bind them together. My mouth and esophagus are so dry I can't swallow. My head started pounding halfway through the day, and it's all I can do to ignore the urge to collapse and curl up into a ball. I'm sure Roc's day hasn't been much better than mine.

Thankfully, they sit us down together while they prepare the evening meal, probably because we're easier to guard if we're in one place. Roc looks like hell, his face pale and his eyes barely open, and I wonder if I look any better. One of the guards finally shows mercy and gives us two gulps each of some kind of liquid that tastes like dirt. It's the best dirt I've ever tasted, and I'd drink the whole bottle if they let me.

Speaking is difficult, but I don't know whether we'll get another chance, so I use my recently moistened tongue to lick my chapped lips and attempt a few sentences. "You gonna be all right, Roc?" I say.

Roc manages a tight smile and says, "It's nothin' compared to all the chores you make me do around the palace."

I grin. I know Roc will be all right as long as he keeps cracking jokes. "Speaking of which, I've got a few for you this evening if you don't mind?" I say.

"As long as it involves knocking a guard or two on the head and getting the hell out of here, I'm game." I've never heard Roc say anything that violent before and for some reason I find it really funny. It appears that our little trip away from the Sun Realm is changing him already.

"If you take six, I'll take the other six," I say.

"How 'bout I take three and you take nine," Roc counters.

"Seven and five—that's my final offer."

"Deal," Roc says.

We should probably take the time more seriously, try to come up with a real plan, but I think the little bit of joking helps more than anything else would.

We don't knock any guards on the head tonight. We're just too tired. Plus, they keep two watchmen awake at all times, who are charged with guarding us and the camp at the same time.

Despite not having a pillow or blanket for the second night in a row, I sleep like a dead man, nestling my head in the crook between my forearm and bicep.

When I awake, the pain in my head is gone. I struggle to a seated position and look around. Roc smirks at me. "How's your head?" he says.

"Never felt better," I say honestly.

"Mine, too. I think there was some kind of medicine in the drink they gave us last night."

"Probably a slow-acting poison that will kill us in a few days."

"Probably," Roc says.

One of the guards is watching our exchange with interest. He's a stocky guy with a shiny bald head and graying beard. He says, "My daughter thinks she's in love with you."

Roc says, "Me?"

I laugh.

Baldy says, "No, you,"—motioning to me—"the one with the good head of hair and pretty-boy smile. She's got a poster of you up in her bedroom. Cost me a whole week's pay. She'll never forgive me if I don't get an autograph when I have the chance."

I've had some strange requests in my life, but this one takes the cake (if we had any cake, that is). The whole world is exploding, we've been captured by a gang of misfits, and one of my captors wants an autograph?

Of course, after he unbinds my hands, I give him one. It's not like I have a choice. I sign his canteen and he even lets me have a drink from it in exchange. "Thanks. Might be worth somethin' someday," he says. Unfortunately he doesn't repay the favor by leaving my hands untied.

No one else speaks to us this morning. But they do let us walk together this time. I guess they're feeling more comfortable that we aren't going to try anything, probably because they can tell we're getting weaker from the lack of food and water.

I hope we can make them pay for that mistake.

It's another grueling march, although it's broken up when we stop for a break upon reaching the hub, a huge cavern that was carved out decades ago. Four gaping tunnels branch off on each side. We sit on manmade stone benches that were erected for travelers. The men seem less serious, joking and laughing as they eat. They give us small chunks of the dried meat we'd bought a couple of days earlier and a swig of water. The food and water, along with whatever medicine they'd given us the previous night, leaves me feeling somewhat refreshed. If we're going to try something, now is the time.

When no one's looking, I silently draw Roc's attention with a quick flick of one of my fingers. Right away I can see the fear in his eyes. He's right to be scared: the next few minutes could kill us.

I wait patiently for the perfect moment to launch the plan I have in my head. Half the men have wandered off and are doing a bit of sightseeing, checking out the multitude of intricate carvings etched by travelers into the rock walls. They're spread out, which is bad, but no one is covering the entrance to the tunnel we've just come through. That's good, because I'm hoping to go back the way we've come anyway. It'll make them less likely to pursue us.

Four of the others, including the leader with the deep voice, are engaged in a heated discussion about Tri-Realm politics. That leaves two guys who are sort of paying attention to us, although more and more they're distracted by their friends—I can see their eyes flicking back and forth between us and them.

One of them turns his back to add a comment to the conversation.

Only one guard now.

His eyes are on me, but it's a blank stare, like he's looking without really seeing. I can tell his mind is on the conversation behind him. I rise silently, trusting it will take a few moments for his brain to register what his eyes are seeing. Before he knows what hit him, I…well, I hit him. Club him over the head with my tied-together fists. I hit him hard enough that he won't be getting up anytime soon. He doesn't cry out and the others are too distracted to notice.

There's a knife hanging from his belt and I manage to extract it by the hilt, the blade naturally gravitating toward my wrist ropes. I caress the blade back and forth, keeping one eye on the group of debaters. I saw through one rope and it falls away. I pull my wrists apart sharply, separating the weakened strands of rope.

The knife slips from my fingers.

I'm in a time warp, where seconds tick by like hours. I can see every turn of the knife as it flips end over end to the ground, moving in slow motion. It clatters loudly on the stone floor.

For a second everyone is confused, so I take advantage of the situation, grabbing the guard's gun—which is conveniently located on the ground between his feet. I point it in the general direction of the cluster of debaters.

I pull the trigger.

The automatic spray of bullets fires wildly above the men, but it has the desired effect. Some drop flat on their stomachs, while others take off running in the opposite direction. Relying on the distraction, I spin and take off the other way. I expect to have to herd Roc in the right direction, but I'm pleasantly surprised to see him halfway to the tunnel entrance, carrying our pack and both swords awkwardly with his bound hands. It's a good thing, too, because by the time I reach the halfway mark, the bullets and arrows start flying all around me.

Luckily, as perfect as their aim was when they rescued us from Rivet's men, their aim is equally off the mark this time, probably a result of the frantic nature of the shots coupled with my erratic movement away from them. Plus, I'm firing haphazard bursts of bullets over my shoulder, which surely distracts them. The closest shot is an arrow that catches a loose bit of my tunic, tearing off a tatter of cloth.

A few more bullets rip bits of rock from the ground at my sides, but nothing gets close enough to worry me. I charge into the tunnel, practically knocking Roc, who is waiting just inside, flat on his buttocks. The next problem: it's freaking dark in the tunnel and I don't have time to stop and pull a torch from our pack. Even if I did I wouldn't use it, as it would only draw more attention to our whereabouts.

I loop the gun strap over my shoulder to free up my hands and help Roc sling the pack around his neck. I tuck my sword into its scabbard and use Roc's sword to cut his hands free. I'm wasting too much time, but it will be easier with neither of us bound. I grab Roc's hand to ensure we can stay together.

Although I was quite observant as we approached the hub—looking for side passages, dangerous obstacles, etc.—I'm still worried that at any moment we might slam directly into a rock wall or boulder, ending our smooth escape and breaking our Sun Dweller noses.

I count the strides as we run, trying to estimate where the first side tunnel is. I know we're getting close. "Slow up, Roc," I say. I pull him to the left until I brush against the tunnel wall. "Stay along the wall."

I release his hand and feel along the wall, moving more quickly now that I have something to guide me. We hear a cry from behind, as one of our pursuers enters the tunnel. They can't see us, but we can see them—a half-dozen torches glow behind us.

Suddenly the wall gives way to my left. "This way," I hiss, turning the corner and continuing to use the wall as a guide. I know our only hope is to make enough turns that they'll have to continuously split up to ensure they don't miss us.

"Faster," I whisper. I pick up the pace, moving rapidly along the wall. Roc is awesome, obeying my commands to perfection and moving noiselessly behind me.

"Switch sides," I say, pushing off from the wall and wandering blindly until I find the wall on the opposite side.

I hear voices behind us. They aren't cries from the chase anymore—more like a discussion. Deciding what to do at the side tunnel. Who will search it versus who will continue down the main tunnel. I ignore them and keep feeling for the next gap.

It comes soon, leading off diagonally to the right. "Bear right," I say, moving into a new tunnel. If the men do what I expect them to do—continue cutting their numbers at each fork in the road—it will mean that six will follow us down the side tunnel, and now only three will pursue us into the angled tunnel tributary.

I move even faster, running now, praying it's not a dead end. It's freaking scary running in complete darkness, especially when you have no idea what's up ahead. At any moment we could fall into a deep pit, crashing onto jagged rock spikes at the bottom. Or we might plunge into the depths of an icy underwater river with a fierce current, sucking us deeper underground where we'll drown.

Because of fate, or the blessings of a higher power, or just plain old dumb luck, none of those things happen. In fact, the best possible thing happens: we reach a small tunnel hub. The rock wall gives way to my right, but I can tell it isn't a new tunnel because of the arc of the wall. Typically a tunnel hub links between four and eight other tunnels. I have no idea how many this hub will have, but it doesn't really matter. As long as the guys behind us don't guess right.

"Hub," I say for Roc's benefit. "Count with me. We'll take the third side tunnel on the right."

"Yes, *sir*," Roc says, managing to mock me even in the worst situation.

I pass a gap in the hub wall. "One," I say.

"One," Roc parrots.

The next gap is almost immediately after the first. "Two."

"Two."

The third gap is a bit further, but only by a yard or two. "Three," I say, cutting sharply to the right.

I barely hear Roc's muffled, "Three," as the floor drops away beneath me.

Seventeen

Adele

Elsey is saying something beside me, but I'm not listening, lost in my thoughts. Then I realize her head is cocked to the side and she's staring at me as we walk. She's asked me a question.

"Wha…what?" I say. She gives me a look. "Sorry, I'm just a little…distracted."

"Have you met Tristan before?"

"No," I say.

"Then how'd he know your name?"

"From the news I s'pose."

"Do you think he's de—"

223

"No!" I exclaim, louder than I'd planned. My voice echoes dangerously through the caverns. Ahead of us, Cole and Tawni stop and look back—Cole glares at me while Tawni stands with her hands on her hips.

"Sorry," I whisper. "No more talking for now, El."

We walk for the next three hours in silence. We don't take any side tunnels, afraid that we'll get turned around and end up going in circles. The tunnel gradually gets thinner and the ceiling lower, until we're forced to march in single file, slightly stooped, Cole then Tawni then Elsey then me. It's claustrophobic.

When my back begins to ache so badly from the awkward posture that I think I can't go any further, I hear an elated cry ahead of me. I hasten my steps, realizing I've fallen quite far behind. A minute or so later, the tunnel emerges into a small alcove. By small I mean the four of us are barely able to fit. But that's not what made someone—Tawni, I think—cry out.

I gasp at the wall of water before us. Our path is completely blocked by a waterfall, streaming so effortlessly from above that it appears as smooth as a mirror, the surface marred only by Tawni's hand, which is stuck into the flow.

"It's cold," she announces, cupping her hand and taking a small sip. "And clean, too, I think."

After our long day of marching, we don't need further invitation. We line up along the waterfall, drinking until the water is dribbling down our chins, soaking our clothes. It feels wonderful. After we satisfy our thirst, we wash our arms, legs and faces, feeling refreshed for the first since escaping the Pen.

The waterfall alcove is as good a place as any to stop, so we do, rationing the food in our packs, which are feeling lighter and lighter.

"What should we do?" Tawni asks. I dread backtracking, trying to find another tunnel to go down, more of the same rough rock walls and single file marching.

"I'm going to see what's behind that waterfall," I say, standing up.

"Be careful," Tawni cautions, "it might drop into a pit."

"Cole, hold me back," I say.

Cole joins me at the waterfall and holds my left arm with two hands, lowering himself into a well-leveraged crouch.

I push my hand into the streaming water. It tickles my skin and splashes me in the face, so I turn my head to avoid getting water in my eyes. I force my arm further in, until the water is hitting my elbow, and then my shoulder. Still my hand hasn't made it through.

"You got me?" I say.

"Yeah," Cole grunts, straining a bit. "Not too much further though."

With a deep breath, I duck my head into the icy stream, gasping slightly when the water hits me. All of my weight is being held by Cole now, as I lean over the edge of whatever abyss the falls empty into.

And then I'm through. Although the water is all around me, I can tell that my fingers aren't being pelted anymore. Mission accomplished. I try to lean back, but gravity's hold is too strong. In fact, I feel like I'm being pulled downwards. Behind me I can feel Cole's fingers slipping off my arm as water pours down my head and shoulder.

I'm going forward, not back, that much I know. If I simply let myself slip from Cole's grasp, I'll fall awkwardly, potentially hitting my head on a rock, and will most definitely end up taking a dive to wherever all the water's going. I have no other choice.

I wrench my arm free from Cole and leap.

The water pummels me from above as I fly through the air, as if the liquid has suddenly grown arms and is grabbing at me, trying to pull me down. For all I know, there might be nothing behind the waterfall, just a big dark void, spiraling downward all the way to the earth's molten core.

My foot lands on something hard and twists to the side. I let out a slight cry and tumble over, skinning an arm on the unforgiving tunnel floor. Complete darkness surrounds me. I don't have a light. I lie on the ground for a moment, panting, my heart beating faster than a miner's in a rock cart race. I can hear water rushing all around me. Not just behind, but in front, too. At first I think it's just the echo of the waterfall I jumped through, but when I crawl forward a few feet, I find that another waterfall blocks my way.

Suddenly, I have a desire to leap through the next waterfall. And then the one after that, if there is one. Hesitating for a moment, I come to my senses and feel my way back to the original waterfall. Through the tinkling water, I can hear faint voices yelling. I jump back through.

Slam!

I crash into Cole, who's just on the other side. His reflexes are quick and he manages to half catch me in his big arms, dragging me to the ground with him as I bowl him over.

Cole is on his feet in a second, his face darkening even more than it already is. "Of all the stupid, childish things to do!" he roars, looming over me.

Of course, being me, I'm shocked by the reaction and just stare at him.

I look around slowly and see that Tawni is hugging Elsey, who is crying, tears rolling over her lips. Then it dawns on me. *They thought I was dead*. I jumped through a mysterious waterfall, let out a scream, and then they didn't hear anything from me. I hadn't even thought to—or bothered to—yell back to them that I was okay.

"I was going to fall," I say dumbly.

"Tawni was about to help me pull you back when you jumped."

"Oh."

"You scared your sister half to death. All of us, Adele."

"Sorry," I say weakly.

"Not good enough," Cole says.

"*Really* sorry?" I say it like a question, which also is *not good enough*. "Look," I continue quickly, "I'm so sorry, I wasn't thinking. It was really, really stupid. Please forgive me. El?"

Elsey pulls herself away from Tawni and runs to me, throwing her arms around me and holding me so tightly I can barely breathe. By the time she releases me she's almost as wet as I am. "Of course I forgive you," she says. "I thought you were gone."

"I'll never leave you," I say.

"You will if you keep doing stupid things like that," Cole grumbles.

His forgiveness will take longer to earn.

Tawni comes over and puts an arm around me. "Try to be more careful. We're like family now."

A wave of emotion wells up unexpectedly. I get choked up, literally trying to swallow her words down as they seem to get stuck a dozen times in my throat. I'm teary-eyed, but not to the point of overflowing. It's been so long since I've had any real friends and now I've grown closer to these two in just a couple of days. Wild, thrilling, scary, emotional days, yeah, but still only days.

I realize I love them both. Tawni for her good heart, logical mind, and overflowing compassion for others. Cole for his quiet strength, fierce loyalty, and righteous anger—I don't even mind his temper.

I wave Cole over, and after a few seconds' pause, he joins us in a group hug. I've never felt more loved in my life.

It only lasts about a minute—a glorious, beautiful minute—before Cole gets embarrassed. He releases us and says, "Uh, what was behind the water anyway?"

"A landing and then another waterfall," I say.

"This has the makings of a comedy sketch," he says, managing a slight grin. His face has returned to its normal dark color.

Note to self: group hugs diffuse tempers, I think.

I grin back. "Why don't you and I go check it out?" When Cole gives me an *I-don't-think-so* look, I quickly add, "No more insane leaps of faith, I promise. I just have a good feeling about where this might lead." And I do. Something about it just feels right. Or at least more right than going back. Plus this tunnel will be safe for us. No one who actually knows their way around the Lonely Caverns would ever think to go down this particular tunnel.

"Fine," Cole says grudgingly. "How far is the jump?"

"Maybe five feet," I say.

Cole nods. "Ladies first. When you get across, move back and I'll jump five seconds after you."

Elsey looks worried so I give her an extra hug. "It'll be okay. We'll be back in just a couple of minutes."

"I'll never forget you," she says dramatically.

"Yeah, you, too, El."

I grab two of the waterproof flashlights that we stole from Tawni's parents, hand one to Cole, and then easily leap through the waterfall onto the landing. I flick on the flashlight and move back. A few seconds later Cole splashes through the liquid wall.

The light doesn't reveal anything unexpected. We're in a tiny section of nondescript cave that, except for the waterfalls at either end, could have been anywhere in the caverns.

"How are we going to test the next waterfall?" Cole says.

"Simple—we jump through," I say.

"You said you'd be careful. That doesn't sound careful."

"I *am* going to be careful," I say, smirking. "You're going to try it first this time."

Cole's reaction confirms that he bought it. His eyes narrow, he looks at the ceiling, and he throws his hands over his head. It's good to know he's gullible sometimes. "I'm just kidding, Cole. Temper, temper."

His face softens and he even manages a smile. "Good one," he admits. "So what's the real plan?"

"Chuck a rock and listen for the sound." Maybe it isn't a *much* better plan, but it's still better.

Cole shrugs and pokes around along the side of the tunnel with his flashlight until he finds a decent-sized rock. "Should make plenty of noise," he comments.

"Do it."

Hefting it over his shoulder like a miner, he gets a running start and launches it into the waterfall. We both put our ears close to the streaming water, and are rewarded a second later when we hear the rock crack against something hard. The sound comes so quickly that it's unlikely the rock fell very far.

"It might've hit a sheer wall and dropped straight down," Cole points out.

"It sounded like it bounced."

Cole nods. "Ladies first," he says.

"Wuss."

Cole suddenly scoops me up and makes like he's going to throw me through the fall. Yeah—I scream. "No, no, no!"

He puts me down. "You looked really scared," he says.

"Good one."

Turning back to the waterfall, I get a running start and plow through it, leading with the waterproof flashlight. I emerge on the other side amidst a spray of water. Surprise, surprise. It's another mini-tunnel, with yet another waterfall at the end.

"C'mon through!" I yell.

Cole arrives and laughs when he sees the wall of water cascading down from the roof. "How much you wanna bet when we try to go back there's always another waterfall?" he says.

The thought of being stuck in an endless cycle of waterfalls and sections of cave, coupled with the fact that I'm soaked to the skin, makes me shiver. "No bet, but I hope you're wrong."

The rock Cole threw is lying in front of us, slightly chipped but large enough to be effective again. The stone is heavy, but I manage to heft it with both hands, swinging it from side to side once and releasing it through the waterfall. A second later we hear the same telltale clatter.

"Same time?" Cole says, extending his hand.

Corny? Absolutely. But I've always wanted to do something like that, so I nod and grab his hand. We mouth a count to three and then jump through simultaneously. This time we're in for a surprise.

First of all, we don't need our flashlights anymore. Dull light slides into the tunnel beyond us. There's another waterfall, but not like before. It isn't a wall of water blocking our path. Instead, the tunnel ends in a small pool of water, which is fed from underground rivers pouring in on either bank. The pool overflows at the far side, dropping off into the cave where the light is coming from.

I glance at Cole and then we walk forward, perfectly synchronized. Without talking about it, we wade straight into the water. It rises above my waist to my belly button, whereas for Cole it only gets to his hips.

We reach the end of the pool, where the water tumbles over the edge. My heart stops and I gasp. *Spectacular!* is the word that comes to mind when I see the view. We're on the edge of a cliff, looking out upon a Moon Dweller city. Like most man-made Moon Dweller cities, thick stone beams rise high above the buildings, from floor to roof, protecting against major cave-ins.

Around the edge of the cliff, numerous waterfalls pour out into a massive reservoir that runs along the edge of the cavern. Each waterfall is different, but equally magnificent. Some are thin, high streams, skimming the edge of the cliff and cascading down in an unpredictable liquid spray, while others are thick, powerful falls, exploding in a thunderous display of power and beauty. And there is everything in between, too.

Our particular waterfall is of average height compared to the others, but still rises at least fifty feet in the air. By peering over the edge we can see that we're on a rock overhang, which allows the water to pour into the reservoir unobstructed. Although I'm not really afraid of heights, I pull back from the edge, feeling slightly lightheaded.

"Damn," Cole says. "The good news: we've made it to the sixteenth subchapter, also known as Waterfall Cave. The bad news: there's no way down."

"Except to jump," I say.

"If you're crazy."

I'm not any keener to launch myself down a waterfall than Cole is, but it does make sense, in a twisted logic sort of way. "We've got to get into the sixteenth subchapter, right?" Cole nods, biting back a response. "So, if we find another tunnel that leads there, an easier one, it will likely end at a travel checkpoint and we'll have to show our papers. We don't have any papers, Cole. Plus, our faces are all over the news. We'll be recognized and apprehended immediately. Our only choice is to do something crazy."

Cole looks over the edge again, biting on his lip as he considers my proposal.

The dull light is coming from the city's overhead cavern lights. The brightness is about normal for daytime in the Moon Realm, so it might be anytime between ten in the morning and four in the afternoon. "We'll wait until it starts to get dark so we won't be seen. It's a reservoir, I'm sure it's deep enough."

At that moment Tawni and Elsey splash into the tunnel, panic written all over their faces.

232

Eighteen
Tristan

We awake to a piercing shriek that echoes through the caves. I have no idea where I am or how I got here. It's becoming a bit of a bad habit for me.

"What…was…that?" Roc says from beside me.

"I don't know, but I'm not sticking around to find out," I say. I try to sit up but find it's impossible. My arms are tied to my sides, my feet together. It feels like I'm in a straitjacket.

"Oh God," Roc says. "What now?"

We hear another piercing scream and then high-pitched frantic cackling. The cackling continues for a bit, sometimes rising in volume and other times lessening. It makes it hard to tell where and how far away it's coming from.

"What do we do?" Roc says.

"Wait," I say. We don't have much of a choice. We're lying in the dark, bound as tight as a caterpillar in a cocoon, with no idea where we are. Waiting seems like the only option. "Do you remember what happened?" I ask.

"All I remember is the ground dropping away and then sliding a bit. Then everything went black."

"Yeah. Me, too." This is not good. We've successfully managed to escape one captor, only to find ourselves at the mercy of another. One that might be much less likely to give us food and water.

"Let us go!" Roc screams suddenly, scaring the bejesus out of me.

"Bloody hell, Roc. What was that?"

"Sorry. I've been awake for a while, trying to get you to wake up, too. I guess I'm going a little stir crazy."

"Ya think?"

"Are my delectable delights ready for tasting?" a shaky woman's voice calls from somewhere. More cackling.

Now I know we're in real trouble. Whoever this lady is, she's madder than a wingless bat. "Roll," I hiss, turning over and forcing my body to move toward Roc's voice. I bang into him before he has a chance to get going. He finally gets the hint. Two revolutions, three. Four, five, six. As I come out of my sixth spin, I'm blinded by a light shining directly in my eyes.

"Hee hee hee! Are my scrumptious scamperers scampering again?" the woman's voice says from right next to me.

When she shifts the light into Roc's eyes I get a glimpse of her face. I cringe. Her head is mostly bald, with only a few wisps of gray hair protruding from her scalp. She has no eyebrows and a bit of dark stubble on her chin. Her nose is long, overhanging and casting a shadow on her thin white lips. Her blue eyes might be pretty were they not on *her* face and filled with madness.

"My palettable pretties are awake!" she exclaims, showing off a mouth with only a handful of teeth, perhaps seven or eight total. Her red tongue looks abnormally long, like a serpent's, glossing over her teeth and lips.

Ignoring us once again, the woman busies herself with something that we can't see.

"We shouldn't even be here," Roc says, a bit of anger entering his voice. It's unexpected. I'd expect him to sound scared, or at least worried, but no, he sounds angry.

"If you have something to say, Roc, just say it," I say. Now isn't the time to pick a fight, but I want to know what's on Roc's mind.

"We're chasing after a girl you've never even said two words to," he spits out.

"Wrong, Roc. I've said *exactly* two words to her," I snap back, my temperature level rising.

"I don't think saying *Adele!* and *Run!* counts as having spoken to her," Roc says bitterly, imitating my voice, but making it sound nasally and girly.

"I didn't make you come!" I growl.

He doesn't have a response to that, so we both lie in silence, which is worse than arguing, because the old woman is talking to herself. In between speaking to us, she's saying things like, "A finger for breakfast, a hand for lunch, an ear for dinner, munch, munch, munch!"

235

That's when I realize what she's doing: preparing a fire. And above it is a spit, constructed with a pile of rocks on both ends and a metal bar across them. *It's about the length of a human,* I realize.

Roc and I figure it out at the same time. "She's going to freakin' eat us, Tristan!" Roc hisses, temporarily forgetting his beef with me.

We can see the flames from the fire casting shadows on the cave walls, and smell the smoke as it blusters off the growing fire.

Suddenly, anger courses through my veins, pumping fresh blood to my extremities. We've worked so hard to get this far, taken so many risks, and this woman is going to end our journey before, as Roc pointed out, I've had the chance to say more than two words to Adele?

Screw. That.

Pure determination floods my body for the first time in my pampered life. It's out of my control, my actions those of my body, not my mind.

I spin hard, rolling right at the woman, whose back is still to us. I collide hard with her ankles, tripping her backwards over me. I keep rolling…right into the fire. Like I said: it's my body doing the thinking, not my mind. It isn't a great plan, but it's all I have.

I feel the heat from the flames licking at my torso, trying to penetrate the thick nest of ropes around me, tear through my clothes, scorch my skin. The fire is a cannibal, too. Luckily, the fire is still small enough that my head and legs are outside of its range, although the smoke is choking me. I hold my breath and wait two seconds, three.

When the heat becomes unbearable and I'm sure the ropes must be on fire, I spin backwards and out of the fire. The old woman has staggered to her feet and I collide with her again, once more knocking her over. This time she falls in a heap on top of me, her face coming to rest right in front of my own. Her breath stinks and I can feel her bony knees and elbows poking into my ribs and legs.

"You filthy brat!" she screams, nearly bursting my eardrums and sending a splattering of spit into my eyes.

I can still feel the heat of the flames as they bite at my ropes. I hope the tethers are sufficiently weakened by the fire. They have to be.

I head-butt the woman right between the eyes, causing her to let loose a shriek that should only belong to dark demons from the realm from which nightmares are born. She flops to the side and away from me.

Using every last ounce of strength I can muster, I strain at the bindings, trying to break them. Evidently I lingered in the fire longer than I thought—longer than I probably should have. The ropes break away easily, black and brittle from the flames, which are finally dying.

Scrambling to my feet, I pull away the remaining strands and search for my sword. The old woman is writhing on the cave floor, shrieking and shouting obscenities, clutching at her face. I find the swords crossed on the ground near Roc, next to our pack.

It's as if I've never used my hands before—I'm unable to control them. They're trembling badly and it takes me more than a minute just to get a grip on my sword. Under normal conditions, cutting the ropes away from Roc would be a simple task, but I feel so shaky I'm afraid I might accidentally amputate an arm or leg.

"Deep breaths," Roc says, making me realize that I'm breathing in short, ragged huffs. I'm sure my face is wild, probably more crazy-looking than the old woman trying to cook us alive.

I take a deep breath. Then another. It helps. My hands stop shaking, my breathing returns to normal. "Thanks," I say.

After cutting Roc's hands free, I hand him the sword, letting him finish the job. The woman has grown surprisingly silent, lying motionless in a heap. When Roc is free, he hands me my sword, which I sheath, retrieves his own sword, and then shoulders the pack.

We're about to leave when the woman suddenly screams, leaps to her feet with speed and quickness that's almost supernatural, and charges us, her hands outstretched and curled into clawed hooks.

I scream, and Roc screams even louder. I'm getting pretty sick of the old woman's antics, and am too tired to consider that she might still be dangerous, which is probably a good thing.

I push her. Hard. Right at the fire. She stumbles and falls into the flames, wailing the whole time. We don't wait to see what will happen to her.

We run into the darkness, which becomes deeper as we get further from the fire. The space narrows and forms a tunnel, and soon we're running blind, yet again. Roc manages to get a light out of our pack and flick it on.

We should've kept running in the dark. The images that flash into view will forever haunt me, burned into my memory till the day I die.

Skeletons: some fully intact and leaning against the wall; others broken and mangled, scattered on the floor; yet others mounted on the walls like trophies—here a skull, there a foot. It doesn't take a genius to know they didn't die from natural causes, that their flesh was bitten off by ragged teeth.

If I hadn't had so little to eat in the last couple of days I'd throw up all over myself. Instead, I dry heave, as my stomach pulses repeatedly in an attempt to upchuck anything that's left in it. Roc's doing the same, bent over his knees, convulsing.

I spit out the little bile that has forced its way into my mouth, steal the light from Roc, and shine it further down the tunnel. The trail of skulls ends just a few feet down the path; nothing blocks our escape.

"C'mon, man," I say, flicking off the light and tugging at Roc's elbow. Huddled together, we shuffle through the dark, until I'm sure we're far enough away from the…the *stuff*.

I turn the light on just in time to see that the tunnel is curving tight to the left. Roc seems to be recovering, so I release him and let him walk on his own.

It isn't until we've walked for a couple of hours that I feel safe again. Neither of us has spoken, lost in dark thoughts, reliving the horrors we've just experienced.

Finally, Roc says, "All those people…" His voice sounds numb, like he still doesn't really understand what we've seen.

"Nothing we can do for them now."

A few more minutes of silence, and then Roc says, "Tristan, I'm sorry about what I said. I was just scared, that's all."

I grit my teeth. As angry as I was when he questioned our pursuit of Adele, I have to admit that there is some truth to it, which makes me even angrier. I feel foolish. Stupid! "No, Roc.

You're right. I dragged you into this mess. And for what? To find some ridiculous Moon Dweller girl who causes me pain every time I get near her. What the *hell* are we doing out here?"

Roc sighs. "I have thought that at times," he says. "But then I think how noble it is that you're taking a risk, defying your father. I don't know how it's all going to end, but if we don't go, we might regret it for the rest of our lives. I feel like maybe we're *meant* to be doing this."

Roc sounds so solemn as he speaks, as if our trek across the Moon Realm is a sacred quest and not just me chasing after some random girl, who happens to be an escaped convict and possibly dangerous. He also makes it sound like we're in it together. It isn't my quest, but his, too, and he's in it to the end. Given the argument we had just before we were about to be roasted on a spit, it's a complete one-eighty for him.

"So we keep going?" I say.

"I was just trying to make you feel better," Roc says with a smirk. "It's not like we have another choice—can't go back."

He's trying to downplay the wisdom in his words, but I know better. He isn't just trying to make me feel better. He truly believes—like me—that we're meant to be on the path we're on, for better or worse. Better would be finding Adele; worse would be falling into the evil clutches of a mad cannibal woman with super strength. My guess: we might end up somewhere in between.

But Roc's words have more than just cemented my belief that we're doing the right thing. They also make me think about what we're doing and why. To this point, it's been all about finding Adele, keeping her safe, and potentially, if the fake suns and moons and stars of the Sun Realm align, questioning her about why being near her causes me such agony. But now it feels like there's some deeper purpose to it all, one I want to explore.

"What did you mean when you said you thought we were *meant* to be doing this?" I ask as we continue walking.

Roc wrinkles up his face, squints his eyes. "I don't know, it's probably nothing, but…"

"What?"

"I just feel like we have a chance to make things better. You know, for everyone. I mean, the secrets your father is keeping from the moon and Star Dwellers, people should know that stuff."

It's been a while since Roc and I have spoken about my father's secrets. Well, one particular secret really. I'm one of only a handful of people that know, but I told Roc anyway. At first I was stunned, but later I realized it wasn't that surprising. It *is* my father, after all. I don't see the connection to our current situation, though.

"What's that got to do with us?" I say.

"I don't know. It popped into my head just now. It feels like we're in the middle of something big, or at least something bigger than what we thought."

"You think Adele's involved in something?"

"No…I mean, I don't know, maybe. In any case, that's not important. What's important is what we do at the end of all of this, or maybe at the same time, whichever makes more sense. I think we need to tell people about what your father is doing."

I think about it. I guess I'm not as big a thinker as Roc. I'm so focused on my own little world, my own feelings, that I don't really consider whether we could—or whether we should—do anything to help other people, particularly the moon and Star Dwellers. I remember during the bombing when the Moon Dwellers helped us, took us in, guided us. People like that deserve a better life.

Despite the plethora of thoughts running through my head, all I reply is, "Maybe you're right."

"As usual," Roc says.

We have no idea where we are, so we just keep walking in a straight line, hoping to emerge from the Lonely Caverns soon. We still have plenty of food in the pack—our Moon Dweller captors hadn't even bothered to empty it out. Still, if we don't find our way out soon we'll have little chance of tracking down Adele.

Thus, I'm ecstatic when we run into one of the main tunnels through the caverns. I'm cautious, too, because I have no idea where our captors were headed—for all I know they might be just in front of or behind us, waiting to pounce. We move swiftly through the main tunnel without incident, meeting no other travelers.

It's late at night when we reach the entrance to subchapter 16, the land of the waterfall caves. Although we've received no authorization to travel within the Moon Realm, we purchased some fake papers before leaving the Sun Realm. As we use them at the border, I keep my head lowered and my hat on to ensure I'm not recognized.

"Mr...Garber...from the Sun Realm," the border guard says. "It's a pleasure to have a Sun Dweller in our humble city." He says something similar to Roc, and lets us both pass straight through. A man wearing miner gear behind us is being patted down for weapons. They're asking him question after question about his reason for entering subchapter sixteen, whether he's carrying any weapons, whether he's received proper authorization to travel intra-Realm, and on and on. Even in his own Realm, being a Moon Dweller hurts this man.

Anger courses through me but I don't turn around, try to forget about it. Now's not the time.

At long last we're back to civilization. Or at least the closest to civilization that my father's ridiculous taxes allow the Moon Dwellers to be. The subchapter is dark, but has a decent number of street lights. I can't speak for Roc, but I'm desperate for a real bed.

We head for the commercial district. I can vaguely remember the city zoning—a domed, circular cave with a reservoir around the outside and the city built outwards from the center—from my previous visits, but Roc remembers far better, so I let him lead.

Although we feel relatively safe, we stick to the shadows, avoiding passing directly by any late-night strollers, and choose a deserted street from which to select a hotel. And it's a good thing we're careful. We've just taken a shortcut through a seedy alley, and are about to turn onto a main street, when we hear a chorus of footsteps moving toward us.

We shrink back into the alley, deep into the shadows, and peer to the street beyond. A group of Sun Dweller troops—at least eight—run past us, moving toward the city center. I only see the leader for a moment as he flashes by, but I'd recognize him anywhere.

Rivet is back in the game.

Nineteen

Adele

"They're here!" Tawni exclaims.

"Who?" I ask, above the roar of the waterfall.

Tawni and Elsey splash into the water to join us. They're breathing hard, already soaked from head to toe like us, a result of jumping through the series of waterfalls.

"Rivet, I think," Tawni says. "We heard them coming down the tunnel. A man was talking—I think I recognized his voice from the telebox." Tawni's eyes are wide and white.

"We don't know that they'll come through the waterfalls," Cole says.

"Yes, they will," I say. "They'll have maps. They wouldn't have wandered down this tunnel by mistake. It's probably a shortcut."

"But how will they get down?" Elsey asks. Her eyebrows are raised and her head cocked to the side. She looks more like a child than she has since we rescued her, innocent and naïve.

"They might have ropes," I say. "But we don't."

Finally, Cole agrees with the opinion I'd already voiced. "We've got to jump."

"And it's got to be fast," I second. "They could come through any moment." I glance at the waterfall, expecting Rivet's scarred face to emerge from the water in slow motion, his teeth replaced with fangs, his fingers sporting daggers for nails.

The waterfall remains untouched.

I feel like the hourglass on our lives is all but empty. We don't have time to sit around sipping tea and eating muffins and discussing the pros and cons of jumping off a cliff into untested waters. Plus we don't have any muffins. Or tea.

"Me first, then El, Tawni, and Cole," I bark. I don't have time to wait for agreement from the others. Waiting means death.

I step up and jump, not allowing myself any time to chicken out.

I should've at least thought about *how* I would jump. In my mind I'd pictured a perfect swan dive, floating through the air with grace and elegance. But my body instinctively tries to go straight down, feet first. Because of my uncertainty, I end up halfway in between, my body horizontal, chest facing down.

Belly flop time.

My heart is in my throat, and I'm feeling something between utter fear and complete elation. There's no time to think, but at the last minute I try to turn my body to improve my landing. It doesn't help.

When my shoulder hits the water I think I might've jumped too far and landed on the stone—that's how hard the impact is. Rather than a splash, I make more of a vicious *thwap!* when I enter the water. Pain shoots through the nerves in my shoulder, running quickly down my arm and into my hand. When I feel myself sinking, however, I realize it's the water that has literally put the smack on me.

The water closes in around me and I'm transported into the belly of my childhood nightmares. Falling down the well; thrashing in the water; sinking into oblivion; no way out. It's been a long time since I've felt scared of water. Growing up, my dad forced me to conquer my fear, taught me to swim. Slowly, I grew to love the feeling of water rushing around my body. *No!* There's no well—not this time. I can escape this nightmare.

Ignoring the pain and bad memories, I kick upwards. Once, twice, thrice: finally breaking the surface. I want to scream with pain, but I hold it inside me, trying to get through it by punching the water with my uninjured arm.

I look up and realize I'm still directly below the tunnel entrance. By kicking hard, I manage to get far enough away from the landing zone that I won't accidentally break someone's fall with my head.

I see Elsey jump. Her launch is more timid than mine was, but far more effective. She drops feet first in a perfect pencil dive, barely making a splash as she cuts through the water. Although I watch closely in case she needs help, I'm not worried about her; like me, El is a strong swimmer, and clearly a better jumper. A few seconds later she bobs up, smiling, like it's just a normal day down at the swimming hole.

"That was glorious, wasn't it?" Elsey says, swimming over.

"Not the word I would choose," I mumble, rubbing my shoulder while treading water using only my feet.

Seconds later, Tawni's white hair whooshes from above as she executes the perfect swan dive that I'd imagined for myself. "Just great," I say, my shoulder hurting worse than ever. Or perhaps it's my pride. It's definitely one or the other.

At least I did better than Cole, whose big dark body flails down from above like he's being attacked by an angry horde of flapping bats. In the meantime Tawni has resurfaced, so we all have a good laugh when Cole creates a liquid mountain upon smacking into the water.

My laughter doesn't last long, however, as twenty seconds pass and Cole has yet to reach the surface. Even under the dim glow provided by the overhead cavern lights, the water looks as black as oil.

I squeal as something grabs me, pulling me under. I kick away from my attacker and come up spluttering. Tawni and Elsey are laughing.

"What the hell was that?" I say.

A deep voice from behind me says, "That was for laughing at me." It's Cole.

"How'd you even know I was laughing? You were underwater."

"I just knew," Cole says, a twinkle in his dark eyes.

"Well, what about them?" I say, motioning at the other two. "They laughed, too."

"You were laughing harder," Cole says, his face as serious as stone.

I shake my head. "Rivet could be right behind us, we shouldn't be messing around. We'd better keep moving."

If Rivet and his new gang of men are in the tunnel above us, we never see them, which suits me just fine. I hope I never see his evil mug ever again.

It feels strange being in a Moon Dweller city again. Although we've only been out of subchapter 14 for a few days, it's the longest I've ever been away from the place. I know I shouldn't be nostalgic but I am. Maybe subchapter 14 hasn't been particularly kind to me as of late, but I still have a ton of happy memories there, before everything got so messed up.

The other weird thing is that we're just passing through. It feels like after such a long, hard journey through the Lonely Caverns, we should stay awhile, see the sights, try the local fare—I don't know, something. But that's not an option. We're wanted criminals, our faces known across all the Tri-Realms. There are probably plenty of Moon Dwellers who would be willing to help us, but we have no idea who we can trust. Someone pretending to be our friend could turn us in a second later, seeking a reward.

We're dripping wet, traveling on the outskirts of town, trying to decide what to do next, when Cole says, "I don't think this city has been bombed, has it? Just normal Moon Realm deterioration."

We can't see much from where we are, so I stop, trying to remember the view from above the waterfall. The city had looked pretty amazing, and definitely intact, a far cry from the smoldering wreckage of our subchapter.

"I don't think so," I say.

"I hope they stop that dreadful bombing soon," Elsey says.

"Me, too, El. Me, too."

"I'm simply famished," Elsey says.

I've been ignoring my hunger for three days now, but suddenly at the thought of food, my stomach constricts, groans, twists up.

"I could eat," Cole says, opening his pack. It seems like he's always hungry.

"Not that stuff again," Elsey says. Despite her overdramatic description of the food in the orphanage, she's already growing tired of our canned beans.

"We could all use some real food," Tawni notes.

"Sure, let's just waltz into town, looking like we crawled out of a sewer, pop into a café, shove a fistful of Nailins at the owner, and walk out with a bunch of food," I say.

"For your information, I was thinking of something a bit more discreet," Tawni says.

I sense the slightest hint of anger in Tawni's voice, which is unlike her. If she starts getting mad at my misplaced, ill-timed sarcasm, this is going to turn into a long trip. Perhaps it *is* time to take a risk—for all our benefit.

"I could go steal some loaves of bread," Cole offers. "I'm good at that."

To be honest, I'm shocked. Now that I know the true story—that there was no bread, only heartache and pain—I can't believe he can still make such a joke. To me it's more proof of his strength. That he can be such a happy, funny, good person, after all he's been through, is simply incredible. I even manage to laugh at his joke—because I know he wants me to.

Tawni smirks, quickly snapping out of her rare bad mood. "I was thinking more like we wait until nightfall, sneak into the city, and have Elsey pay someone to get us some food."

"Why Elsey?" I ask.

"Because her face will be less likely to be recognized," Tawni says, shrugging. "I'm sure she's been on the news, too, but she's not a wanted criminal."

"I don't know…" I say.

"I'll do it," Elsey says. When I frown, she says, "I can do this, Adele. I know I can. Please let me help."

I take a deep breath. It makes sense and I'm tired of beans, too. "Okay. On one condition: that we stay close by in case you have any trouble."

"Yes, yes, of course," Elsey says, waving me off as if my suggestion is the most obvious thing in the world.

The cavern returns to its natural shade of black as night falls and the lights are extinguished. The street lights remain on, but barely cast enough light to highlight the roads. We wait patiently in the dark, slowly drying out, until we're sure it's safe. Although I'm anxious to keep moving, I actually enjoy the break, and use it as a chance to speak to Elsey.

"Are you okay, El?" I ask. Cole and Tawni have walked away, on a mission to find the least conspicuous way into the city.

"I am now," Elsey says.

"But before?"

"I tried to be optimistic, like Father always taught us," she says, wrinkling her button nose. "But I was depressed sometimes. If it wasn't for Ranna I would have felt so alone, I don't know what I would have done."

"Tried to run away?"

"Maybe." Elsey looks at me with a seriousness that is far older than her age. "Do you miss Mother and Father?"

"Of course, El."

"Oh, so do I. So much I can hardly breathe sometimes."

"We'll find them," I say, making a promise I intend to keep.

"I'm so glad you made friends, Adele. How long have you known Cole and Tawni?"

After hearing how tough things were for her, the last thing I want to do is depress her with my sad story in the Pen, and how, until a few days ago, I'd felt even more alone than her. But I also can't lie to my sister—never could. "I've known them a little while."

"And Tristan? I know you told me the story, but have you really only been *interested* in him for a few days?"

"I'm not interested in him, El. Not really. I just want to know why I get a headache whenever he's around, that's all."

"Mmm," she says.

I don't have a chance to ask her what she means by that because the others return, excited.

"We found a route that's pretty dark the whole way to the center," Cole says, smiling.

They're still thinking about getting real food, but I'm thinking about what to do afterwards. We can't stay in subchapter 16—not with Rivet and his gang roaming somewhere nearby. We need a plan to get to the Northern subchapters, specifically subchapter 26, where my dad might be a prisoner. *Camp Blood and Stone.*

"Okay, food first," I concede. "Then what?" I hate asking the question without having some brilliant suggestion, but I can't seem to think. Sometimes I feel like I've only got two

251

brain cells, and even when I rub both of them together nothing seems to happen. This is one of those times.

"We've been talking about that, too," Tawni says. "And I think we've got it figured out. Why do we need to keep trekking through the dangerous inter-Realm caverns, being chased by a gang of bloodthirsty men with a license to kill us, when we could ride all the way north?"

"Ride?" I say. "You mean, like on a train?"

"Of course a train, what else? They have night express trains, direct from subchapter to subchapter. We could disguise ourselves as nomads, cover our faces, and buy a ticket. Even if they recognize us, we'll be long gone before anyone has a chance to do anything about it."

The thought of saving us hundreds of miles of walking and getting to my dad faster at the same time is tantalizing, but it also screams suicide. "I don't know..." I say. "Seems a bit risky."

Cole says, "This whole thing is risky. All I know is we've got to do something unexpected or we're gonna get caught. Let's give it a try, and if we get caught, I promise to let you say 'I told you so.'"

"I'll relish the opportunity," I say, not mentioning the fact that if we get caught we'll be dead.

The city is beckoning to us, and the thought of food is making my mouth water. As planned, we pick our way through the city via alleys and small side streets, staying out of sight like ghosts in the night.

Eventually we find a small café that seems to be open and still taking customers.

"Showtime," Cole says, gesturing to Elsey.

I scowl, still not completely comfortable with my sister's role in our operation, but I bite my tongue and manage to keep my thoughts to myself. Before I can even consider changing my mind, Elsey gives me a quick hug and sneaks away, sticking to the shadows, moving toward the café, which is conveniently located on the corner of our alley and the main street.

I watch as she spots a Dumpster and moves behind it, peeking out at the road.

A family of four passes her: a mom, a dad, two girls. They remind me of my own family in the old days. The girls look happy, holding hands with their parents and skipping along. It's good to know that even in the Moon Realm some people are still happy. Of course it helps that their parents haven't been abducted and their city bombed, but still, happy is happy.

Elsey wisely ignores the family, waits for a better target. An old man with a bad limp and a rickety old cane hobbles past. *Perfect.* Elsey evidently thinks he's a perfect candidate, too, because she sticks her head out a bit further and must make a noise, because the man stops and peers into the gloom.

He changes direction and moves toward her, taking ages to reach her behind the Dumpster. I tense slightly, ready to spring into action if needed. I'm not sure what I expect; I guess that maybe the old man is faking his injury and will suddenly smack her over the head with the cane and carry her away. Not surprisingly, he doesn't.

Apparently, Elsey is able to convince him to help, because he hobbles off a minute later, and Elsey gives us the okay sign using her index finger and thumb. I reply with a thumbs-up.

Waiting for the man is as boring as watching rocks being eroded by the flow of an underground stream. He takes so long. I swear he must be in there negotiating a peace treaty, not just ordering some food. In any event, I manage to keep my eyes open until he reemerges holding big cloth bags. He struggles under the weight of the bags, readjusting his grip and switching arms several times before finally reaching my sister. I see her hand him the pouch of Nailins as payment. As we'd instructed her, she waits until the man limps onto the street and out of sight before tiptoeing back to where we're hiding.

Her eyes are wide with excitement and her smile gleeful. "How'd I do?" she asks.

"You were perfect," I say, meaning it.

"You did really well," Tawni adds.

"Your first solo mission was a complete success," Cole says.

Elsey beams. By the way she looks at him I think Cole's compliment makes her the happiest.

It's amazing what a little money can buy these days. The spread of food is impressive, even with four of us eating. We each get a sourdough roll, two pieces of bacon, a sizable hunk of some kind of cheese we never could've afforded growing up, a sort of root we call hyro, a cinnamony potato dish, and a small flask of warm tea. The icing on the cake is literally the icing on the cake. We split two pieces of dark chocolate cake with chocolate icing. Down in the Moon Realm—at least in our subchapter—chocolate is scarce, and very expensive, so the fact that the café had it, that we could afford it, and that the old man thought to ask for it, is a small miracle. My only mistake: eating way too much too fast. By the time I finish eating I've crossed the line between pleasantly full and disgustingly stuffed.

"Uhhh," I groan.

Elsey is nibbling daintily at the corner of her cake. "You okay, sis?"

"Other than being on the verge of throwing up, I'm fine."

"Here, a little extra cake might help wash it down," Cole suggests, pushing the chocolate toward my face. I don't even have a chance to tell him how obnoxious he is, because the food is coming back up.

I barely have time to turn my head before I throw up. Although it's disgusting and unpleasant, I feel better afterwards. I even let Cole's antics go without revenge.

When we finish eating, we pack the leftover food (which isn't much), and begin the second phase of our plan: operation night train.

I'm still not very comfortable with the idea, but I've committed to it, which means I'm going to do everything in my power to help us be successful. It's just the way I am. For me it's all in or all out—no middle ground, no wishy-washy, no excuses.

Continuing to use back streets, we manage to get pretty close to the rail station. We hide in the shadows, performing reconnaissance, waiting for the right time to make a move. The area around the station looks pretty deserted, although every once and a while someone passes by and goes inside. In the entire subchapter, the lighting is the best in this area, which is good for most travelers. Unfortunately, we aren't most travelers, and would prefer utter darkness.

After twenty minutes or so of no one passing us, Cole hisses, "We can't wait here all night."

"Now or never," I agree. We each don the hoods attached to our tunics. It's a cool night, so the hoods are unlikely to draw any special attention to us.

We leave the safety of the dark and stride out into the light. We walk side by side, at a normal but purposeful pace, eyes ahead, ears listening for any signs of discovery. With every footstep I expect to hear a shout, a whistle, alarm bells, something. Something saying *We gotcha!*

We make it inside the terminal without drama.

The ticket window is straight ahead. As we previously agreed, I take the lead on buying the tickets. I walk up, trying to appear confident, like I buy train tickets all the time, like I belong here. At the same time I keep my head lowered slightly, trying to cast a shadow across at least part of my face.

"Three adults and one child for the next train to subchapter twenty-six," I say, attempting to keep my voice steady. I lock my knees to stop them from shaking.

At first the guy behind the counter—a short, grumpy-looking fellow with gray stubble and more nose hairs protruding from his nostrils than most people have in their nose—is indifferent to me, his voice monotone, like a robot.

"Three and one to twenty-six," he repeats. "Next train available…"—he pauses, consults a timetable—"…departs in six minutes. Express train."

He's just going through the motions, which is fine by me, but I know the hard part is still to come.

It comes. "I need travel vouchers for all adults," he says, finally glancing up over his glasses at my face. His boring, emotionless expression changes in an instance. It's just a slight twitch, a flash of recognition in his eyes, but I can see that he knows who I am. Smartly, he pretends not to. I wonder if he's got a big red security button somewhere underneath his desk. I can see both his hands, but he might be able to press it with his knees.

"Look, buddy, we don't have travel vouchers, but you probably already guessed that. But we do have this." I spill the pouch of shiny gold Nailins out onto his desk. "If you keep quiet you can have them all."

At the sight of the money, the guy's eyes light up and his fat lips twist into a greedy grin. "Done deal," he says without hesitation. He stamps four tickets and hands them to me in a stack.

I know we aren't out of the woods yet. Because the guy is willing to accept a bribe, he's also probably prone to dishonesty, like accepting said bribe while still planning to turn us in to the authorities. At least we have tickets.

With only a few minutes until the train's departure, we don't have time to bet on whether the guy will stick to our deal. Instead, we hurry through the automatic ticket turnstiles, praying he's given us real tickets. With each swipe of one of the tickets, the gates open and allow one of us through.

The train has just pulled into the station, its doors open and waiting for us to board. A few passengers straggle off, but they are so haggard from the long journey that they don't even look up as we pass.

"Last car," I say, leading the group into a light jog. The last car will ensure we're away from any other passengers who happen to jump on the train just before it leaves.

We're halfway to the rear car when an alarm goes off, blaring through the silent station. Red lights flash. There's maybe a minute before the train departs.

We run.

I hear a shout from behind us and twist my head to see men jumping over the turnstiles. They aren't looking for a free ride—that's for sure. They're after us. And leading the pack: Rivet.

We run harder. Thirty seconds to departure.

We reach the last car and board. I try the manual door levers but they're jammed. Just in case I'm not strong enough, Cole tries them, too, but reaches the same conclusion. We're at the mercy of the train being on time.

Pressing our faces against the glass, we watch as Rivet's group splits into two. One group, led by a big black guy with a wicked barbed-wire tattoo around his exposed bicep, heads straight for us, trying to beat the doors. The other group, led by the demon—also known as Rivet—veers left and boards the train about three cars in front of us, thus ensuring they're at worst traveling with us.

I'm not worried about the second group at the moment. The first group is closing in, running full speed, their eyes heavy with violence.

The doors start to close.

The guys are so close I think they'll make it. My instinct is to shrink back toward the back of the car, away from the doors. Cole has a better idea.

"C'mon," he says, urging me to move up to the closing doors. We inch forward until we've created a human barricade. The big guy in the front tries to charge straight through us. Without planning it, Cole and I kick at the same time. I catch him hard in the knee and hear a crunch as it bends backwards the wrong way. Simultaneously, Cole lays into him with a boot in the face, using his foot like a sledgehammer.

"Argh!" the dude roars, falling backwards into his friends.

The doors close.

* * *

I can see them through the glass, several cars back, pacing around, punching the walls, acting like they're on drugs. Maybe they are. Something to make them even more violent—as if they need that.

At first I think there might be a way for them to get to us while the train is still moving, but now I don't think so. We're seemingly safe for the moment. I know it won't last.

We haven't spoken since the train started moving. I don't think any of us has the words, or knows what to say. Even Elsey seems to be lost in her thoughts, perhaps mulling over the flash of violence she witnessed by me at the train doors. Tawni is standing in the corner, leaning against the wall, staring out the window as the rocky tunnel flashes by. Cole is seated, his head down, one foot tapping rapidly on the floor.

According to Cole, who seems to have a pretty good handle on these sorts of matters, the train ride will only take two hours, being an express. Although I know we're traveling at hundreds of miles per hour, the ride is so smooth it barely feels like we're moving.

An hour goes by in silence. Typically I'd be comfortable with the quiet, as I grew used to it during the endless hours I spent alone in the Pen, but for some reason I can't stand it now. With every second that goes by, the screaming in my head gets worse, until I can't take it anymore.

"Urrrrr!" I grunt, making a weird growling, gurgling noise from the back of my throat.

Everyone looks at me. Elsey grins nervously. Tawni raises an eyebrow. Cole laughs, of course. "Are we there yet?" he asks, purposely sounding as whiny as possible.

I take a deep breath. I need to calm down, try to get a grip on the anxiety I'm feeling. I feel like I'm about to have a heart attack.

"I hope so," I say, trying to sound tough. I'm secretly dreading our arrival, afraid of not being able to protect my friends, my sister. Afraid of what Rivet will do. Afraid of what Rivet will tell me about Tristan if I get the chance to ask him. At the same time, the waiting might be worse. It's like pulling a splinter of rock from your foot. Although the pain is minor with it in your skin, over time it becomes more and more uncomfortable, until it's unbearable, leaving you making weird grunting-gurgling noises like some sick animal. Left untreated, the splinter pushes deeper into the skin, becoming a part of you. The only treatment is to pull it out, swiftly and painfully. When the doors open at the end of the line, we'll have no choice but to remove our own rock splinter.

"What are they going to do to us?" Elsey says, sounding like a normal kid, instead of my older-than-her-years sister.

I want to reassure her, but I also don't want to lie to her. I hesitate for a moment, trying to formulate the right words, but Cole answers for me. "Nothing," he says. "They're not gonna touch any of you. I'll make sure of that."

Coming from Cole, it isn't just talk. As he cracks his knuckles, I can see a level of determination in his face that exceeds even his normal level of strength. As much as it comforts me, it also scares me, not because of what he might do to Rivet and his gang, but because of what they might do to him. Although I don't voice it, I vow at that moment to do whatever it takes to protect my friends, even if it costs me my life. There are some things more important than your own life. Like friendship, and love, and trust, and goodness.

We speak very little during the final hour, but for some reason it doesn't bother me anymore. I've made my vow, as has Cole, so there's nothing else to talk about. We have no strategy, except to run from Rivet until we're forced to stand and fight. Then we will fight.

I feel the train slowing and my heart skips a beat.

Twenty

Tristan

"It's Rivet!" I hiss. "What do you make of it?"

"Exercise," Roc says.

"Exercise?"

"Yeah. They're just out for a midnight run. You know, to keep in shape."

"No chance they're in pursuit of Adele?" I say sarcastically.

"Nah."

I'm glad to have the old Roc back, the one who jokes in even the most serious situations. "I think we should join them, I'm feeling a bit out of shape, too."

Roc nods, grinning.

We steal from the alley and jog along the street, moving silently on only our toes. We probably don't even need to be as careful as we are, as Rivet and his men are making so much noise they wouldn't hear the grind of a drilling machine following them.

Our quarry reaches the city center and enters the train terminal. We follow as close as we dare. The moment we enter the station, the emergency sirens go off. I whirl around, half-expecting a squadron of troops to surround us, but there's no one.

"Hurry," Roc says, "we're going to lose 'em."

I spin around and start chasing Rivet again, who's doubled his speed, heading straight for the turnstiles to a waiting train. Ticketless, his men hop the barrier. Finally, I can see why they're in such a hurry.

Four figures are running along the platform, evidently aiming to board the last car. They're all wearing hoods, so it's difficult to distinguish individual features, other than height. But still I know. There are four of them, one much shorter than the others. Plus Rivet is chasing them. It's her. Adele. Her sister. The other two fugitives.

Following Rivet's lead, we launch ourselves over the ticket machines. There's no way we're going to catch Rivet's men, much less Adele and her friends. I extend an arm to stop Roc.

"Wait, let's see what happens," I say.

We watch as Rivet's men split up, half boarding a car in the middle of the train and the other half zeroing in on the last car. We're flush with the doors of the first car, which start to close. One of Rivet's men tries to jump on the rear car but is met by at least two feet, which knock him back.

I slip through the crack in the doors and pull Roc in after me.

My mind is racing. We're on the train. Rivet and his men are on train. Adele, her sister, her friends. We couldn't have coordinated it any better if we'd tried.

"It's like fate," Roc says, reading my mind. Maybe my father was wrong about fate after all.

"Where are we going?"

As if in response to my question, the train starts moving and the speaker drones. "Nonstop to subchapter twenty-six."

"Subchapter twenty-six? But that's where—"

"Camp Blood and Stone," Roc finishes. It's another classified thing I've told him.

"But why would Adele go there?" I say, thinking aloud. It hits me like a sucker punch from a one-armed man. "Her parents!" I exclaim.

Roc's eyes widen. "Yes," he says. "It has to be. The reporter said they were traitors. There's nowhere else they would've been taken."

"She's trying to get her family back. First her sister and now her mom and dad."

Just then I have a flashback from the last thrilling train ride we had. *Waiting in the car. Watching as the two guards switched cars, moving along the train toward us. Slipping onto our train. The fight.*

I rush down the car, not bothering to explain to Roc. Reaching the end I tug at the door. It's either stuck, locked, or not a real door, because it won't budge. I peer through the glass window, looking into the next car. It's empty. So is the one after that. I'm not sure how many cars are empty before I spot movement. I can barely make out moving black blobs several cars in front of us.

"It's an express night train," Roc says, approaching from behind. "There's no car-to-car access. The train won't stop because of the security alarms either. They're fully automated."

"How do you now so much about Moon Realm trains?"

"That's what they pay me the big money for."

When I turn around, Roc's grinning. "What's so funny?" I say.

"Well, besides my witty sense of humor, the fact that we're on this crazy train headed for sure death brings a bit of a smile to my face."

"You're an odd one," I say.

"That coming from Mr. Pain-at-first-sight-chase-the-girl-who's-causing-it-all-over-the-Tri-Realms-getting-kidnapped-by-rebels-and-cannibals."

"Hey, there was only one cannibal, not plural."

"True," he says.

With at least a couple of hours of travel ahead of us, I settle into a booth. Roc selects a seat opposite mine. I think about Adele. Why the hell is she causing me so much pain? Is she even aware she's doing it? I think about what I'll say to her if I ever catch up to her, how I'll demand answers, threaten her if necessary. Although I'm not sure threats will work with her. She's so different than the girls I'm used to. So much stronger, there's no doubt about that. The proof: escaping prison, navigating through the Lonely Caverns, fighting off Rivet's men, attempting a suicide mission to rescue her parents from one of my father's traitor camps. All pretty gutsy.

But I can also tell there's a tenderness to her. I felt it when she looked back at me when I was fighting Rivet. Like she felt sad that I should have to struggle for her sake. But still:

The pain.

"Tristan?"

I look at Roc. I've been staring into space, but that isn't unusual for me these days. Roc's staring at my hands. I look down and realize they're clasped tightly and I'm running them over and over each other, fiercely massaging them. I stop, separate them, place them on my thighs.

"You okay?" Roc says.

"Uh, yeah. Just a little nervous, I guess."

"About what to do when the train stops?"

"Not what to do," I say. "How to do it."

"You'll do it," Roc says. "We're here for a reason. I sense it."

I search Roc's brown eyes for the truth. For a moment I sense it, too, try to snatch it out, but then it fades away, disappearing, just like all the good things in my life always seem to do. Sometimes Roc seems so confident and serious, like now, and other times so helpless, like in the midst of a fight, or when we were captured.

I try to turn my philosophical thoughts off and focus on the task at hand. "Right, I'll need your help, Roc, there are just too many of them for me to handle on my own."

Roc's wise eyes turn fearful in an instant.

"We'll get through it together. I won't let anything happen to you," I say, knowing we might both be dead by day's end.

Roc nods, purses his lips, seems to resign himself to the certain violence that's headed our way, like a meteor on a collision course with Earth.

"We'll have the element of surprise," I continue, "but that will only help us at the very beginning, so we have to take advantage of it. Rivet will head straight for Adele and we'll just have to hope she and her friends can hold him off until we get there. We'll pick off his other men from behind, one at a time. We'll each take a different one until they're all gone. Yell if you're in trouble and I'll do whatever it takes to get to you. Understood?"

"Yes, sire," he drones, but I can tell he appreciates the direction.

"Once we've downed all the men, I'll head for Rivet while you try to find a safe place for Adele to hide. They may think we're foes, so you'll have to convince them otherwise."

"I'll convince them," Roc promises.

* * *

The train slows and I stand. Roc follows suit, looking rather sick. He tries to pull his sword from his sheath, but it gets stuck three times before he can get it out. I know now is the time for a big speech, something to energize him for the battle ahead. My mouth feels sticky and dry, so I take a sip of water. I don't know what I plan to say, so I just start speaking, hoping my heart will do the rest.

"Roc," I say, "you're my brother. Always will be."

Short, concise, simple; but I mean every word, more than anything I've ever said before. And it seems to do the job. Roc's hand stops trembling and tightens on his sword, his eyes change to a steely brown, his jaw firms up.

"I'm with you, Tristan. I'd die for you."

Tears fill my eyes but I blink them away. Now is not the time for tears. "And I you," I say.

The train rolls to a stop. A heavy mist roils outside the window. Subchapter 26 is dark, but not completely. Something is lighting the sky. We're standing flush against the doors, trying to be the first off—every second will be important in the deadly game we're playing. The doors open and we step out into the mist.

I feel a thud in my head. She's near.

It turns out the mist is not mist, but smoke. The air is filled with the suffocating acrid stench of war. The platform trembles as a bomb explodes in the distance. The bombing has reached the northernmost subchapter.

I can't see through the thick smoke, but I run along the train anyway, hoping that Adele is still alive when I reach the end.

When I see Rivet his back is to me. His men are so focused on what he's telling them that they don't see me. I fade backwards into the fog and bump into Roc.

"What is it?" he whispers.

"They seem confused as to what to do. Rivet's giving them orders, but they're not rushing the end car like they probably wanted to. The war's distracted them, I think."

"Can we get around them?" Roc coughs. His eyes are already red from the smoke. We need to get away from the noxious fumes. They aren't thick enough to kill us right away, but prolonged exposure surely won't be good.

"I don't know, but we have to try."

We drift right, moving further into the smoke, trying to carve a wide arc around Rivet. Already the smoke is clearing, however, and it won't be long before we're able to see them and them us. The bombing hasn't stopped—we can still hear the rumble of explosions in the distance and intermittent flashes of light—but it's moving away; hence, the clearing smoke.

Ahead and to the left I see dark figures huddled together. Not Rivet and his men. We're past them. Adele and her friends—has to be.

As we move toward them something stabs me in the back.

I cringe and almost cry out, but no...I haven't been stabbed—not exactly. It's her. Adele.

My head pounds, my back aches.

* * *

Adele

"Something's not right," Cole says, gazing out the window as the train pulls into the station.

"There's so much smoke," Tawni says.

I try to speak but my voice catches. There's a lump in my throat. The Star Dwellers are bombing subchapter 26. My father is out there somewhere, unprotected, maybe already a victim.

Older-than-her-age Elsey grabs my hand, squeezes, and says, "He'll be okay."

Although I know she doesn't have any proof for her statement, it's comforting. The doors open and I feel a shockwave of pain flower in my head.

He's here. The realization comes as a shock, but I know it's true. Somehow, someway, Tristan has found us again. Why? I guess I'll have to ask him if I ever get a chance.

I expected us to race from the train the second the doors opened, but the situation has changed. We can hear booming explosions in the distance. It's so smoky that we can barely see anything outside.

Cole says, "Elsey should hide in the train. They'll think we've all left."

I like the idea of hiding Elsey away somewhere, but not leaving her all alone. She isn't too happy with the idea either. "No! I'm coming with you," she says.

Cole looks at me, hoping I'll back him up. "We can't just leave her here," I say. My mind is racing. Rivet might already be running down the train line, headed for us, and we're still in the car, like sitting ducks.

"Move!" I say, pacing to the door and pulling Elsey, who's still holding my hand, with me.

I step out, turn to face the other end of the train. The smoke—thick and puffy when we pulled into the station—is dissipating already. Likely a bomb exploded near the train station just before we arrived. Although it's getting easier to see, I don't see our hunters. I can only see maybe two cars down, and Rivet's gang is at least three away. Maybe even four or five—it's hard to tell.

Cole and Tawni step out next to us. "Where the hell are they?" Cole says, thinking out loud.

I feel someone approaching from the left, out of the mist. I quarter-turn to see two dark shapes moving toward us. Rivet—has to be.

"Run!" I hiss.

We take off away from the platform, staying in a group, although Cole and Tawni could easily outdistance Elsey and me anytime they want to. I hear thumping footsteps on the stone behind us, someone chasing us. I don't look back, don't want to see Rivet's bloodthirsty eyes.

As we move away from the platform, the smoke disappears completely. It's strange how it's clustered around the train. The bomb must've hit really close to the tracks.

Ahead I can see the twinkling lights of subchapter 26. It seems everyone has their lights on, probably because of the bombing, although being able to see won't protect them from death by explosion.

I hear the footsteps getting closer, hear a shout, but can't make out what the voice says. It doesn't sound like Rivet's snarl, but it might be one of his men. It's weird. I felt scared when I first started running, but everything changed at some point. It's like a magic trick, where a magician turns a rock into a bat or something; except it's my fear turning into anger, to the point where I feel capable of great violence. Even when I fought in the Pen, I never felt capable of anything. I just did what I had to do and hoped for the best. But now I feel strong, like I *can* fight Rivet, even though he's a highly trained soldier.

Enough is enough.

I whirl around, my head full of explosions, ready to face him.

They're right on top of us, having closed most of the distance. I just react, swinging a high kick in self-defense. I catch my pursuer under the chin, knock him off his feet. He rolls onto his stomach. His companion stops dead in his tracks and just stares at me.

He doesn't look like a trained killer. He's holding a sword, but it doesn't look natural; it looks more like he's holding a bread knife. Brown-skinned with brown eyes, he appears more shocked than anything.

"Who are you?" I say, wondering if I'm making a big mistake.

The guy opens his mouth but no words come out. The other guy, the one I leveled, groans and rolls over, showing his face.

I gasp.

It's Tristan.

My vision goes black but then returns. Black and then back. It cycles for a few seconds, until my mind seems to make sense of him being so close to me. My vision returns, steady, consistent. But the headache doesn't fade, keeps ham-ham-hammering away.

At this point it would probably make sense to run to him and apologize profusely for having practically knocked his head off. Like I said earlier: I don't always do the right thing in social situations.

"Why are you chasing us?" I demand. It's time for questions and answers. I ask, he answers. Simple.

"Trying…to…help," Tristan murmurs. Weird. He's massaging his head although I know for a fact I kicked him in the jaw.

"Oh," I say. I guess I should've guessed that.

"What happened?" Cole says, appearing with Elsey and Tawni beside me. They must've stopped when they realized I wasn't with them.

"It's him," Elsey whispers. "Tristan."

"I know," I say.

"Why'd you hit him? I thought you wanted to talk to him," Cole says.

"I didn't hit him, I kicked him,"—I elbow Cole hard in the stomach—"and shut up about the other thing." I'm mortified. How could Cole say something so stupid? Tristan's going to think I'm just another school girl with a crush on the president's son. Yeah, I want to talk to him, but not like one of his fans. Like a real person with real questions.

"You should probably help him up," Tawni suggests.

"You help him up," I retort. My social skills are falling apart at the seams. I'm just shocked, is all. I didn't expect to see him. Truth be told, I thought he was dead. Thankfully, his friend helps him up.

Tristan approaches me. His midnight blue eyes are hard, like steel. Each time they meet mine I feel a jarring thud of pain and I have to look away. What is he doing? Why is he here? It makes no sense. I'm nobody, and he's the prince of the Tri-Realms. Why is he causing me such pain? I want to shout at him, shake him, tell him to leave me alone, but my mouth doesn't seem to work.

He extends his hand and takes mine, which still hangs loosely at my side. When our skin touches daggers slice through my back. "Oww!" I yelp, arching my back and pulling away. I look at him sharply, but I see he's in a similar position, cringing at some unseen pain. What the hell? Is he feeling what I'm feeling?

He shakes his head, looks at me narrowly. "I'm Tristan," he says.

Before I have a chance to respond, Cole yells, "Get down!" and tackles us both to the hard ground.

* * *

Tristan

I can't believe she kicked me! And with a wicked roundhouse no less, powerful and precise. Although I'm in pain—both from the kick and from her very presence—I try to hide it as I reach out to shake her hand. When she doesn't raise her arm, I reach down and take her hand, lifting it for her. As my fingertips contact her skin, she burns through me, ripping me apart one chunk at a time. I jump back, almost cry out but swallow it down. When I look through suspicious eyes, I see she's hurting too. Did I do that to her?

I swallow hard, say, "I'm Tristan."

When the big dark guy yells *Get down!* and smashes us both to the ground, I think it might just be some kind of a joke. Like maybe that's how Moon Dweller teenagers have fun; a kick in the jaw to show affection, a hard tackle for a laugh. Of course, my thoughts make no sense considering we're in a warzone *and* being tracked by one of my father's psycho thugs.

Our bodies are so close together and she grabs my arm as we fall. On the ground, she clings to me, her hands warm on my skin. I'm in a trance, unable to tear my gaze from her sparkling, emerald eyes. The pain is there, all around me, but it's not as strong as before, as if our single touch—our hands brushing against each other—broke the curse. But no, that's not right either, because the pain *is* still there.

I hear a yell and Adele looks away from me. I wince, feeling physical pain when our eyes unlock. She pushes off of me, gets up.

Something flashes past my field of vision.

I follow her to a standing position and see why she pushed away so suddenly. Her big friend, the one who tackled us, is charging toward Rivet, who is further down the platform, fitting an arrow into his bow. An arrow—that's what flew past my head. He has all the resources of the Tri-Realms at his disposal, and he's shooting arrows. He's enjoying this, doesn't want it to be over quickly.

Adele lets out a yell and chases after her friend. "Take El somewhere safe!" she calls over her shoulder to her white-haired friend.

This can't be happening. I can't let it happen. Regardless of whether she's trying to hurt me with her weird stares and fire-hot touch, I have to save her. Rivet will rip them both to shreds. I don't doubt their fighting ability, but am just being realistic. Rivet is a pro and a sadist. A deadly combination.

I start after her.

* * *

Adele

Why did he touch my hand, hurt me like that? And why did Cole knock us over? Is the whole world going crazy? Something moves behind Tristan. Glancing past him, I see Rivet let loose an arrow. Cole lets out a roar as it pierces his shoulder, the sharp tip exiting through his back. Blood spatters from the wound. His entire body torques hard to the left, forcing his head around toward me.

Those eyes. Dark, serious, *strong*. I know what he's going to do.

Despite the excruciating pain he must be in, Cole turns and charges Rivet. This is it. All his pent-up emotions: first and foremost, sadness; then anger; misery, loneliness, and desperation follow; all sprinkled with a lust for revenge, hidden well by sarcasm and joviality in stressful situations.

It's suicide—I have to stop him.

I push away from Tristan and race after Cole. Rivet's next arrow zips past us, narrowly missing Cole's legs, my stomach, and Tristan's sprawled-out form.

I brush past Tristan's friend, whose mouth is opening and closing like a fish out of water. He looks shocked by the whole situation, unable to cope with what's happening. I'm probably in shock, too, but I don't have time to think about it.

So I won't slip, I avoid stepping directly on the trail of blood that Cole leaves in his wake. Cole's faster than me, reaching Rivet twenty feet ahead. Lifting his bow, Rivet tries to get off another shot, but Cole plows into him, sending the arrow twanging end over end into the air. The bow flies out of Rivet's hands and clatters harmlessly to the stone.

On top of Rivet, Cole is in a rage, pummeling him with iron fists. Five other men charge out of the thinning smoke, aiming to help their leader. I'm ten feet away when I hear Rivet yell, "Get the girl!" in between taking punches from Cole.

His men stop just short of him, hesitate, and then follow his order, rushing past him and toward me. I'm running so hard it's difficult to stop, but I manage to plant one of my feet, only skidding slightly on the stone before stopping.

They're already right on top of me. The first one has a sword and a gun in his belt, but leaves both hanging, probably in the mood for some hand-to-hand fun against a helpless girl.

Not so helpless.

I duck under his haymaker punch, kneeing him in the groin and then cracking him in the back of the head with my elbow as he flies past. He crumples to the ground. Seeing what

I did to the first guy, the other four decide against the idea of fighting fair, and whip out their swords. Still no guns. Are they trying to take us alive?

They're too close for me to run. I have to dodge their swords and somehow manage to win. I have to do it for Elsey, for my father in Camp Blood and Stone. For my mother wherever she is. For myself, too.

One of the guys swipes at my arm and I dance away. He wasn't really going for me, though. It was a fake, a feint, a trick maneuver to get me moving in the direction he really wants. A highly trained swordfighter's move. Mid-swing, he reverses his blade and sends it slicing in the opposite direction, right into where I'm moving. There's no way he can miss.

I close my eyes.

* * *

Tristan

I'm impressed by the big guy. He's manhandling Rivet like a rock cutting machine on a boulder. Then the other guys show up and go straight for Adele. I sprint so hard that I don't really see how she takes the first guy down, but it looks quick...and impressive. The others pull out their swords.

Adrenaline is a weird thing. I've heard of miners who are able to lift massive boulders off of their friends who've been trapped by a cave-in. Boulders they have no business lifting and which, after the fact, they can't budge even an inch. Well, the adrenaline makes me run faster than I've ever run before. There are a few steps where I swear I don't feel my feet touch the ground, as if I'm running on air alone.

One of the guys fakes a move and then attacks in the other direction. It's a professional move, but he's so focused on her that he doesn't see me coming. *Clang!* I barely get my sword in front of the stroke before it cuts Adele in half.

I shove her out of the way and jam my sword into my surprised opponent, whose eyes roll back into his head before he topples to the ground. The other three swing at me simultaneously, two getting in each other's way and missing completely. I parry the third's stroke and slip my sword between two of his ribs, thrusting upwards for good measure. As he falls, blood bubbles from his lips.

The other two improve their communication in a hurry, circling to opposite sides of me and closing in. One goes for my head while the other aims for my legs. I hop over one sword while blocking the headshot with my blade. Using my off hand, I backhand the guy that tried to cut off my legs, stunning him and knocking him backwards.

The guy that wants my head on a platter continues taking aggressive strokes at my neck, but I block them all, and manage to slash his hand, causing him to drop his sword. He throws his hands up in a request for mercy, but I'm not in the mood so I stab him in the heart.

Searing pain rips through my body as the final guy slashes me across the back. A cheap shot but this is a fight for life or death. I'm rooting for both life and death. Life for me; death for Rivet's guys.

I spin around and block his next attack—a jab at my midsection. My back is on fire and starting to spasm, making it hard to hold myself up. I need to end the fight or I'm toast. I swing desperately for the guy's head, but I'm not as fast as before, my energy waning as the adrenaline burst expires.

He easily ducks my attempt and slashes at my leg, splitting my thigh open and forcing me to the ground. He looms over me, his sword black and ominous under the night sky. Raising the hilt above his head, he prepares to thrust the point through my chest.

Goodbye, Adele, I think, *I hope my death isn't what you wanted all along.*

* * *

Adele

My death is painless. For that I'm thankful. The sword makes a weird clanging sound when it contacts my body, like I'm made of metal. Weird. I feel myself being shoved back, tripping, falling to the ground.

I feel fine.

I open my eyes, wanting to see what really happens when you die.

I hear the shriek of metal on metal so I turn my head to see what's happening. *Tristan!* I'm not dead. He saved me and is battling my attackers, cutting them down, defeating them one by one. I watch in awe until there's only one left, who takes a cheap shot at Tristan's back. It looks bad, but Tristan reacts well, getting back in the fight.

Then suddenly he's down, on the verge of death, a fish about to be shot in a barrel. "No!" I manage to scream.

Out of nowhere his friend appears, holding a sword in front of himself awkwardly, like a jouster with a long spear. Although the maneuver appears amateurish, it gets the job done. His sword pierces the guy through the back, causing him to drop his sword, which is pointed tip down, right over Tristan's fallen body.

The sword falls like a guillotine. At the last second Tristan roars and rolls sharply to the side, the sword thudding dully on the stone. His friend kneels beside him, his face pale, despite his naturally brownish skin.

I scramble to my feet and head for Tristan, but stop when I see movement out of the corner of my eye.

Amidst my own battle, I forgot about Cole, who was winning against Rivet when I last saw him. I don't know what happened since then, but the tables have turned, and Cole is on his back, getting smacked around by Rivet pretty badly. With a roar, Cole pushes Rivet off of him and staggers to his feet. Rivet snaps to a standing position with a karate move, and launches himself fearlessly at Cole, whose nose is bleeding profusely over his lips.

Cole hits him in midair, but Rivet's forward motion is too powerful, knocking him to the ground.

I want to help—*have* to help; to freaking do something, anything—but I'm frozen in place, shocked by what's happening.

In one swift motion, Rivet swings around Cole's back, clamps his arms around his head, and jerks it violently to the side.

I'll never forget the image, never forget the *crunch* of breaking bones. Precious, life-giving bones.

"Oh God, please no," I whisper, my eyes filling with tears. *Not him. Please not him. Take me. He doesn't deserve this. He's had enough. Oh, Cole. Not Cole. Beautiful Cole. Please come back.*

I hear a wailing, an eerie, awful pealing, that sounds more animal than human. I realize it's me. The sound is coming from my throat, unrequested, but appropriate.

I know I'll never get over this moment, will never cope with the loss I'm feeling, but that doesn't mean I can't do something about it. For him. For Cole.

No plan, tears streaming down my cheeks, I stride toward Rivet, whose bloodied face is filled with satisfaction, his eyes gleaming, his lips twisted into a deranged smile. With both arms outstretched, he flicks his fingers back to himself, as if to say *C'mon!* It's unnecessary. I'm coming.

He could use one of the weapons hanging from his belt: his sword, his gun, his razor-sharp dagger. But that isn't Rivet. He lives for the challenge. He stands with his fists clenched, snarling as I approach.

The few times I've fought before, I've used fast, powerful strikes, ending the fight as quickly as possible. This time I try the same tactic.

I aim a kick at Rivet's groin, but he dodges it with unexpected speed, catching my leg in midair and swinging a kick of his own toward my head. I try to duck, but it's difficult with him holding my leg. Adjusting the arc of his attack in mid-kick, Rivet's foot slams into my ear. Fierce pain shoots through my skull as Rivet releases my leg and lets me tumble to the ground. My head is ringing and I'm seeing stars.

I look up, and between the flashes of light that disturb my vision, I see Rivet standing over me.

Now he has his knife out.

* * *

Tristan

My attacker is a strange creature, growing a sword from his stomach. At least that's what my mixed up mind thinks. That is, until I see the spot of blood widening around the blade. He drops his sword.

It's headed straight for my head—my eye, to be more specific—but I'm so shocked I just watch it fall. In my distorted mind it looks beautiful, like a falling star, sprinkling magical stardust on everything in its path. Subconsciously, I know it's a deadly sword, and the stardust is just the reflection of distant lights on the broad side of its steely blade.

Awe battles reason.

At the last second, reason makes a surge and I spin away, narrowly avoiding being impaled by the star, which, of course, is really a sword.

A rough hand pushes my attacker to the side and he falls away. A face appears. My friend—my beautiful friend. Although he looks as white as a ghost, Roc is grinning.

"You look injured," he says, kneeling down and inspecting the gash on my leg.

"A minor wound. Not deep," I say. "Where is she?"

Roc cranes his neck and then moves aside, points at a fleeing figure, moving quickly away from us. Adele, her long, black hair billowing behind her, runs like the hounds of Hell pursue her. With my eyes, I follow her path to its likely destination and see Rivet watching Adele charge right at him, goading her with his hands, standing overtop a fallen figure. The big, dark guy. Adele's friend. *Oh no.*

Based on the crumpled body, the sneer on Rivet's face, and Adele's mad dash toward Rivet, I suspect her friend is dead. She isn't running away from Hell, she's streaking toward it, without regard for her own life.

I hope her friend isn't dead, but if he is, I certainly don't want to add Adele to the list of casualties piling up. Ignoring the intense pain that courses through my leg and back, I push to my feet and chase after her, limping badly.

Adele is like a raging beast, attacking Rivet immediately with a kick similar to the one she used to knock me down. He's more ready for it than I was and easily catches her leg and punishes her with a vicious kick to the head. Dread fills my heart as I see Rivet remove a knife from his belt.

I swat away the dread like a pesky mosquito. Nothing can stop me. No amount of pain, no distance, no obstacle can prevent me from getting to her, killing Rivet, saving her.

Or so I think.

My brother appears from the side, seemingly arriving out of thin air, traveling through some crack between dimensions. He's flanked by a dozen men. There isn't time to ask questions. The whys and whos and whats can come later. I lower my head and charge between two of the men, but they're big and strong. It's like hitting a stone block. My feet keep moving, churning, trying to push them out of my way. I'm screaming something— I have no idea what—but they won't move, won't relinquish their grip.

One of the guys twists around behind me and locks my arms behind my back.

Adele is already dead. Too much time has passed since Rivet pulled out the blade.

It's over, all over. All is lost. My mother. Adele. Roc will be imprisoned—maybe worse. My life is over.

Killen's in front of me, saying something. I can't hear, don't care to hear. Nothing he can say will matter to me. All of our childish kicks under the table, our childhood fights, were nothing compared to this. He's no longer my brother in any sense of the word, blood included.

Adele is already dead.

I lunge forward and head-butt his moving lips.

He goes down hard, but is on his feet in seconds, kicking me in the ribs, punching me in the face, spitting and snarling at me. Screaming at me. I still can't hear him and don't react to his physical abuse, which makes him even angrier. There's no physical pain that can eclipse the emotional anguish I feel. The only antidote to how I'm feeling is death. I hope Killen will finish me off.

Although I'm sure Killen wants to kill me, he doesn't. But only because he fears my father more than anyone. Bringing home a dead brother won't sit well with my father, not because he values my life, but because of what I know. He needs to know who, if anyone, I've told his secrets to. I could've told half the Moon Realm by now. Yeah, me dying will create far too much damage control, which is a headache the president won't want.

Eventually he stops beating me. Through my bloody, swollen eyes, I see them drag Roc forward. He's badly beaten, too. They sit us next to each other, back to back so that we stay up.

My hearing finally returns in a blast of noise. Bombs are still thundering around the subchapter. Roc is groaning. My brother is speaking. "Why, my dear brother, were you following this filthy *traitor* all over the Moon Realm? Answer me, or she dies."

Huh? My head is throbbing so badly and my mind is so muddled that I don't really understand what's happening. My brother is asking me about Adele, I think, but he's threatening me with her life, which is meaningless. He can't take something away that's already gone. "Already dead," I manage to whisper.

"No, brother—not dead. You can add Rivet's murder to her list of offenses."

Twenty-One

Adele

I'm not going to die until Rivet does. If we both die, that will still be a victory. A way for me to honor Cole.

Using my legs like scissors, I clamp them around one of Rivet's legs and roll, forcing his knee to buckle to the side. He lets out a cry of pain as his cartilage twists. I move faster than I've ever moved, kicking to my feet in one swift motion, a move my dad showed me countless times, but which I'd never been able to master.

Rivet's knife falls out of his hand and to the side. I scoop it up and attack, plunging the blade deep into his chest before he has a chance to react. His eyes widen and his lips let out a strange groan, a ghoulish gurgle usually reserved for the damned. Which he is. Or is about to be. Blood trickles from his lips and his life ebbs away. Justice is served.

I'd hoped my revenge would lessen the pain of the loss, but it doesn't. Now that Rivet is dead, the pain resurfaces, flowing out of my eyes in rivers of tears. My breaths shorten and I find myself gasping and sobbing. The urge to wrench the knife from Rivet's chest and stab it into my own is so strong I see my hands clench around the hilt.

An image of my sister fills my mind. Then my father. My mother. Tawni, my only friend. Tristan. Tristan is last, his very presence so full of questions.

At the moment my grip loosens on the knife, strong hands pull me up and away from Rivet. I don't know what is happening, but am powerless to stop it. On both sides of me are gargantuans, guys so big they could've only been manufactured by a steroidal experiment. They drag me to a cluster of similar-sized giants.

As they pull me into the circle of bodies, I gasp when I see who's in the center. First I see Tristan's friend, the scared one, the hero. He's beaten to a pulp, his face puffy and red. Next to him is Tristan, equally battered.

A young boy, no older than fifteen, is talking to Tristan. "…answer me or she dies," he says.

I hear Tristan mumble, "Already dead," through bloodied teeth and swollen lips.

"No, brother—not dead. You can add Rivet's murder to her list of offenses."

They dump me in front of him. Although his eyes are too puffy to widen, I see a spark of recognition flash across the blue orbs. *He really believed I was dead.* He must've seen Rivet hovering over me with the knife, just before he was captured by these goons. He didn't see me kill him.

The teenager called him *brother*. Then that must mean... I pry my eyes from Tristan to take another look at the brat. From the different angle I can see the family resemblance immediately. To Tristan; to the president. Tristan's brother—his name is Killen, I remember. Clearly not the same type of guy as Tristan. Or at least I hope they're different. Very different. Opposites would be good.

The fierce sound of bombs detonating resonates all around us. It's a full-scale attack on the city.

Tristan is still staring at me, almost smiling—if that's possible in his current state.

"ANSWER MY QUESTION!" Killen roars, kicking Tristan in the stomach with the heel of his boot.

Tristan grunts, drops his head to his knees, spits out a chunk of blood. Lifts his head and speaks through gritted teeth: "I'll tell you everything once Adele is safe."

Even in his condition, the way he says it sends pulses along my skin. He's trying to save me again. The *Why?* question again. Does he want to hurt me or help me? He needs to make up his mind.

The bomb explodes so close that the shrapnel should rip us apart. Only it doesn't because of the wall of burly Sun Dwellers ringing us.

They take the worst of it.

The men who aren't killed by the sharp blades of metal spinning in every direction are knocked off their feet by the shockwave that follows. I am, too, getting blasted into Tristan, landing on him hard, kneeing him in the chest and elbowing

288

him in the head. I feel so bad when I see the look of pain flash across his face.

But there isn't time for sympathy. We might only have one chance to get away. I start to pull him to his feet, when suddenly another set of arms is helping me.

"Tawni!" I practically shriek when I see my friend next to me. "Where's—" I start to say.

"Elsey's safe. We have to move."

Tawni helps me get Tristan to his feet, and I'm about to rope one of his arms around my shoulders when I hear a shout. "You're not going anywhere!" Killen roars, striding toward me. He probably thinks I'm just a normal, weak girl.

I forearm him in the face and use a sweep kick to trip him up. Still full of rage because of everything that's happened, I add a couple of kicks to the skull for good measure and to ensure he doesn't come after us.

I turn my attention back to Tristan, who's swaying and looks like he might collapse, or vomit, or both, at any second. Tawni is helping Tristan's friend get to his feet.

The guards that weren't killed by the bomb are pushing to their knees, trying to regain their feet. I have the urge to pick up one of their dropped weapons, blast them to pieces.

I take a deep breath and the urge passes. I settle on kicking each of them in the ribs so they collapse back on their stomachs.

We hobble away in tandem, just a couple of four-legged, four-armed, two-headed beasts. Me and Tristan. Tawni and Tristan's friend. As Tawni leads, I remember. "What about Cole?" I say, my eyes welling up once more. I choke, trying to get the words out. "I mean—his body."

"Adele, we can't," Tawni says, her eyes full of compassion. Unlike me, she isn't crying, isn't emotional. I don't understand how she can be so strong when her best friend has been brutally murdered right in front of us.

"But how are you—"

"I'm not okay, Adele. Not even close. I just can't think about it right now. Please."

I understand. Somehow she's blocking out the pain, the anguish, everything. I wish I could do the same.

We get to the stairs and descend from the train platform. Thick, chemically smoke stings my eyes and the smell of fire burns my nose. The station is on the edge of the city, so we're able to slip down a deserted street and get lost in the maze of intersections. Well, I'm lost. Tawni seems to know exactly where we're going.

Thankfully, it's a short trip, because Tristan and his friend are moving painfully slow and getting slower by the minute. We reach a nondescript building with a black door. Bodies are strewn on the street outside. The stone road is all torn up in chunks.

Tawni stops.

"What is this place?" I ask, eyeing the bodies, my stomach threatening to heave.

Tawni shrugs. "Don't know. The door was wide open. No one was inside. I think…" She doesn't have to say the rest. *They're all dead.* They must've been outside when the bombing started, got caught with nothing to protect them. Why are the Star Dwellers doing this?

She helps Tristan's friend limp up to the door, and knocks firmly three times. A second later the door opens.

"Adele!" Elsey wails, seeing my disheveled appearance and bruised skull. It probably doesn't help that I'm covered in blood from the cuts on Tristan's head, which is slumped on my shoulder. I'm a mess.

"I'm fine, El, but these guys need medical attention."

"I found supplies," Elsey says, holding the door and letting us pass. When we're all in, she says, "There's a basement. We should be safe from the bombing there. Follow me."

We follow my stalwart sister down a hall to a landing, where crumbling steps lead downwards. She lights a thick candle, which is good, because otherwise we'll surely break our necks on the crooked, uneven staircase.

The room at the bottom is like a tomb, surrounded by heavy stone block walls. Another candle sits in the corner, shedding soft yellow light on the room.

I'm not sure how she did it all so fast, but Elsey has managed to prepare for our arrival. She has almost everything we need: towels, a bowl of water, some kind of paint-on antiseptic in a black jar, long, thick bandages, crispy wafers for eating, more jugs of water. She's even managed to find a couple of pillows and two thin mattresses to make things more comfortable for the wounded.

I help Tristan lie on his back and Tawni does the same for his friend. They both groan as they settle in. I know nothing about first aid, but Tawni seems to have it covered.

Inspecting their wounds, she says, "You're going to be just fine."

She begins working with what Elsey has provided, wetting a couple of towels and handing one to me. I try to mimic her gentle cleaning motions. Tristan's friend almost seems soothed by the wet towel, but when I touch Tristan he stiffens. My arm stiffens, too, as pressure builds in my head. It's different now, though, less intense, as if my body is adjusting to whatever force Tristan is using against me.

I go about cleaning his face first. He has a deep cut above his right eye, which has bled all down his face. Although I'm cleaning all around his eyes, he keeps them open, watching me. His gaze is electric, powerful, and although I try to focus on what I'm doing, my gaze keeps flitting back to his royal blue eyes. Each time they do, I feel more and more drawn to him. It's the weirdest thing: although neither of us says a word, it feels like we're getting to know each other, getting comfortable together.

Every time I touch him, even through the wet cloth, bursts and zings of pain shoot up my spine.

The swelling in his face is getting worse, his cheeks puffy, his eyes half-closed. Nothing I can do about that. Time will have to heal his wounds.

I finish with his face and move on to his leg. I'm not sure how to go about it. He's wearing filthy black pants that look like they've been through a war. There's a long slice in the fabric from his upper thigh to his knee. Between the shredded flaps of cloth I can see a wicked red gash. If I clean the wound through the hole in his pants, it will be too hard to bandage it. There's really no choice. My face warms as I feel Tristan watching me examine him. I can sense that he's reading my mind, coming to the same conclusion as me.

I don't say anything, continuing to "get to know him" without words. I tug at his pants, but they won't budge because he's lying on them. Kindly, he lifts his hips, grimacing slightly, and I'm able to pull them off. Thankfully, his dark tunic is reasonably long, covering his undergarments. His legs are long and strong—sinewy muscles run down them. I'm no expert, but I'd say he has really good legs.

Ignoring the flush I feel in my cheeks, and hoping Tristan can't see it in the dim lighting, I focus on cleaning out the wound. Fresh red blood wells from his skin as I wipe away the dark blood that has congealed on the surface, but I manage to stop the bleeding by applying pressure for a few minutes.

"I'll do your back after we bandage everything on the front," I say.

He dips his head in a slight nod, still staring at me. "Thank you," he murmurs.

Tawni is already finished with Tristan's friend, whose face is as bad as Tristan's, but who doesn't have the added leg and back wounds. She shows me how to apply the antiseptic and helps me bandage his leg. I might've felt somewhat jealous when she touches him, but her movements are so professional that it doesn't bother me at all.

Time for more embarrassment.

"Sit up," Tawni says, putting an arm behind Tristan's back. I follow suit, helping to push him forward from the other side. "Arms over your head."

Obediently, Tristan raises both arms. Robotically, she pulls his shirt off.

I do everything in my power to maintain an indifferent expression when I see his body. Inside I'm thinking *wowowowow!* His chest and shoulders are sculpted from years of training, his stomach flat and hard—his back looks as if it's been chiseled from stone, but is mottled with scars—from training I guess. A vicious slash runs diagonally across it, from his right shoulder to his left hip. It's deeper than the cut on his leg, but not bleeding as much.

He flips over onto his stomach with a grunt, and we get to work cleaning the wound. After applying a generous coating of antiseptic, we bandage his skin, wrapping the cloth around his entire chest to provide support as it heals.

I notice a thumb-size, crescent scar toward the top of his back, directly on his spine. It looks different than the others, more fresh, more interesting. I want to ask how he got it, but my mouth won't open.

Finished, Tawni says, "You'll need to change these every couple of days."

Finally, Tristan's friend speaks. "Oh, I don't think he'll mind that at all," he says with a wink. Or at least I think it's a wink—it's hard to tell on his battered face.

"Shut it, Roc!" Tristan hisses. Beneath the purple and black of his deeply bruised face, I think I detect a hint of pink added to the palette of colors. I wonder what the son of the president has to be embarrassed about. Not much, I expect.

"Roc—is that your name?" Tawni asks.

"It's what my mother called me," Tristan's friend replies. "I'm Tristan's best friend, I mean, servant, I mean, *only* friend." Roc half-laughs and then cringes from the pain.

"Thank you for your input, Roc," Tristan says.

"My pleasure, your majesty."

I find their banter enjoyable, especially after the events of the day being so dark and heavy. It's a welcome break from it all. But it can't last.

"Where's Cole?" Elsey says suddenly.

Everything flashes back into my mind. Rivet's snarl; the violent way in which he broke Cole's neck; the sickening crunch of bones; leaving our friend's body out there, not giving him the respectful burial he deserves. Tears well up again. I'm really getting tired of all the crying.

My reaction is nothing compared to Tawni's, though. She bursts into tears, throws herself on the floor, weeps into her hands, her body shuddering and shaking. I want to cry, too, to let it all out—or whatever is left of it—one more time. But I know I have to be strong for my friend, like she was for me earlier. It's her turn to grieve.

I crawl over to her side, sit by her, rub her back tenderly, stroke my hand through her hair. "Shhh. It'll be okay, Tawni. He's in a better place now—with his family again." I don't know why I say it—I'm not even sure I believe it—but I guess I want to believe it. It's what Cole deserves: relief from all his subearthly pain.

I glance at Elsey, whose face is stricken, her mouth contorted and her eyes sharp, and say, "El, I'm sorry, but he didn't make it."

She looks like she wants to cry but she doesn't, not so much as a single tear. Even growing up, she was never much of a crier. If she got hurt or disappointed she'd always just go silent, preferring to keep her emotions on the inside. That's what she does now, shifting to the corner, hugging her knees, staring into empty space.

"Thank you for your help, and I'm so sorry about your friend," Tristan says. "If we hadn't chased after you, maybe he would have survived. I feel responsible."

"No!" I say fiercely. Tristan isn't going to take the blame for this. Rivet's the one to blame, and whoever sent him after us—the president, or his advisors, or whoever. "It wasn't your fault. You tried to help us."

"We just got in the way," Tristan says softly, lowering his head.

I shake my head. "This is our life," I say. "As Moon Dwellers it doesn't seem to matter who does what, it always ends in tragedy." Even I am surprised by my words. They sound so defeatist. Perhaps because I feel defeated.

"Maybe we can change things," Roc says.

"How?" I say blankly. Change is so far from my mind I can barely even focus on it; I'm just trying to survive.

Tristan says, "Use my reach. I might not act like my father, but I'm well known across the Tri-Realms. If I can convince others to join the cause, maybe we can change things."

"The cause?" I say. "What cause? All I see are Star Dwellers blowing up Moon Dwellers, Moon Dwellers acting like sheep, Sun Dwellers ruling over all. There is no cause." I am starting to annoy even myself with my pessimism. *Snap out of it!* I scream in my head.

"We *are* the cause," Tristan says. "That is, if we want to be."

"We?" I say. My mind is racing. My sister is in a faraway place, Tawni is a mess, and I'm talking to two guys, who've been beaten to a pulp, about a revolution. This is not at all how I expected things to go with Tristan. I haven't even had a chance to ask him about why I've got a headache again—a headache caused by *him*.

"Well, I don't know, we haven't really thought much about it yet," Tristan says.

Great, I think. I'm joining an ill-planned revolution now.

"Look, guys, I appreciate what you want to do, but I'm just trying to find my parents."

"In Camp Blood and Stone?" Tristan asks.

296

I freeze. "Yes, how do you know that?"

"I know a lot of things. You know, because I'm the president's son and all."

"Well, we're going to be leaving soon to rescue my dad, so…"

"We're coming with you," Tristan says.

Coming with me? Why would he do that? Why would he even offer? Here he is talking about revolutions and changing the world, and he's willing to risk his life to help a random Moon Dweller, who happens to be an escaped convict, rescue her father from a secure prison where he's being held on charges of treason? I just don't understand.

"Why would you do that?"

"Because…because…"

"Because he's been chasing you all over the Moon Realm—of course he's gonna do it!" Roc exclaims.

"Chasing me? But…but…" I'm about to ask why, but I already know the answer. I've known it the whole time, but chose to ignore it.

He feels pain when he's near me, too.

Twenty-Two
Tristan

Things get pretty awkward after that. No one really speaks, and I barely make eye contact with anyone. Adele's friend, Tawni, eventually stops crying and we all agree that we need to sleep. Adele and her sister go and find a few more thin pads to sleep on.

My leg and back are throbbing, but their pain is nothing compared to the endless thudding in my head. I can't help wondering whether it's from the beating my brother's goons gave me, or from being near Adele.

When Adele and Elsey return with the sleeping pads, her embarrassment is clear and red on her face. There isn't much space to stretch out, so we'll have to cram tightly together.

Does she want to sleep next to me? I hope so. Don't get the wrong idea, I'm not thinking about trying anything with her—I'm not that kind of guy, plus the room is like a sardine can and I'm in no condition to do more than lie in one place. Consider it more of an experiment. I want to see if my body can handle being near her for an extended period of time.

Tawni seems to know it, too, which only seems to redden Adele's face further, as Tawni lays her mat near the edge of the room, against the wall. Roc seems to sense the unspoken plan, too, pulling his mattress to the opposing wall, leaving plenty of space. The bastard smirks the whole time he's doing it.

That leaves Adele, me, and Elsey. Adele could position Elsey in the middle, between Adele and I.

She doesn't.

"Here you go, El," she says, helping her sister lay out her pad next to Tawni. She places hers next to mine, while I fill the gap between Roc and her. She leaves the candle to burn itself out.

She sits down slowly and cautiously, as if taking significant care not to accidentally brush past me. She stretches out stiffly, lowering her knees and head to the floor in jerky motions. I lie like a dead person, staring at the ceiling. I'm acutely aware when Adele sprawls out next to me, mere inches from my body. The pain builds in my head and I rub at my temples absently.

Everyone else seems to fall asleep immediately, exhausted from one of the longest days of our lives. I can hear heavy breathing on all sides. I can't sleep, though. Not with her so close to me. I can't manage to deepen my breaths, or relax my body, or even close my eyes: all the standard requirements for sleep. The throbbing is still too intense for sleep. So I just lie as still as a stone, my eyes glued to the ceiling, which is getting dimmer by the minute as the candle's wax melts away.

After an hour I'm getting worried I'll be up the whole night. A lot of good that will do me when my body's trying to recover so we can break Adele's father out of jail. So I try to sleep, try to forget who's sleeping next to me, try to blink away the pain in my skull. Close my eyes. The headache starts to subside, fading into the night. It's replaced by a buzzing in my scalp, not painful, but not pleasing either. Just there. Something tingles in my spine. Not the icy stabs from before, but a constant shiver. Again, not bad, not good. Just present.

My eyes snap open when I feel something touch my hand, shooting pins and needles up my arm. I jerk my head to the right and stare through the deepening gloom at my hand, which is resting lightly on my hip. I hold my breath when I see what touched it.

Adele's hand.

Her hand is resting gently on top of mine, her fingers sitting in the cracks between my fingers. It hurts, but like with my head and back, the longer we touch, the more the pain lessens. It's like our nearness is the antidote to our nearness. Does that make any sense?

I glance over at her. Her eyes are closed, her breathing slow and even. She appears to be sleeping. Is she faking it? Or did she simply move in her sleep, her hand randomly slipping onto mine, a mere fluke of nature?

I feel her fingers push their way between mine, curling inside so they're touching my palm. My heart leaps to the ceiling and tries to rip out of my chest. It settles back into place and demonstrates its enthusiasm by beating rapidly, sending shivers through my nervous system.

She's awake, I can sense it. It's no mistake that her hand found mine. She's doing exactly what I wanted to do. Experiment.

My instinct is confirmed when I feel her thumb, the only finger not nestled under my palm, start to stroke the top of my hand. Gently sliding back and forth across it, sometimes making circles. Each motion sends shards, then slivers, then pinpricks of pain into my hand. Lessening pain. After a few minutes it starts to feel okay, then kind of good.

It's weird how good it feels. It's such a simple thing, the mere sliding of a finger across skin, but it sends tingles through my whole body. I close my eyes, like Adele, and begin slowly running my own fingers across hers. We carry on like that for a long time, at least an hour—maybe hours, I'm not sure; I lose track of time.

Is she expressing her feelings for me, her attraction? Or is she just experimenting, like me? I'm lying to myself again. As much as I want to believe we're just experimenting with the pain, I know that's not true. I'm *enjoying* this.

This is not what was supposed to happen. I was supposed to ask her questions and have her answer them. And then once I was satisfied, I would leave, maybe even go back to the Sun Realm, where I actually feel comfortable. Story over.

Why did I shoot my mouth off earlier, start talking about "a cause" and insinuating I could do anything to help the people of the Lower Realms? Can I really just walk away now? Is that really what I want? Already my brother will be telling my father what happened, what I did. There's no going back. I'll be

301

shunned, maybe even thrown in prison, even if only a minimum security one in the Sun Realm, where I could live out the rest of my days in luxurious conditions.

But what if my father forgave me, said I was welcome back? Would that change anything?

I blink in the dark, try to answer at least one of the dozens of questions spinning through my mind.

I can't answer any of them.

Eventually I fall asleep, still holding hands with Adele.

Twenty-Three

Adele

I wake up when Tawni says, "Hey, sleepyhead."

I yawn and rub my eyes, opening them to look at my friend. She looks like her normal, perky self—not the devastated girl from the day before. I wish I could cope with things the way she can.

That's when I remember the *position* I was in when I fell asleep: holding hands with Tristan. I sneak a glance down at my hand. It's alone—safe. *Whew*, I think. It isn't like I'm embarrassed that Tristan seems to have feelings for me—*ecstatic* would be a better word—but I'm not keen to have everyone know about it just yet. Am I getting ahead of myself? Did he really hold my hand because he *wanted to* or because he felt he *had to*?

I turn my head to see what Tristan looks like when he's sleeping, but he isn't there. Roc is gone, too.

"Gone with Elsey to do some recon," Tawni says, guessing my question.

"Elsey?" I say, suddenly worried.

"It'll be okay," Tawni says. "They promised to be very careful and look after her."

I nod, still worried.

I hear quick feet on the steps and then Elsey bounds through the doorway, practically crashing into me. "The bombing finally stopped!" she says excitedly. "We can go rescue Father." Her smile is a mile wide. I'm amazed at her ability to bounce back from the horrific events of the previous day.

Slower steps thud down the stairs. I raise my head in anticipation of seeing him, hoping it won't be awkward after our night together.

Roc's head pops out. He's wearing a wide smile, too, grinning like a banshee through the cover of his bruised face. I'm not sure what everyone's been smoking, but I want some—clearly it's good stuff.

Tristan follows behind him and my breath catches in my lungs. Despite his injuries—although the swelling has lessened, his face is varying shades of black, blue, and purple—he's a sight, right out of the magazines. My vision blurs as a headache forms. Not a bad one though. They're getting better each time I see him.

Really, really, freaking weird.

He looks at Elsey. "Did you tell them?"

Elsey grins at him. "Mission complete," she says, standing at attention, her hand perpendicular to her forehead in a rigid salute. "Ready for your next order."

"At ease, soldier," Tristan says, laughing. "She really likes this role-playing stuff," he says, explaining to me.

"She always has," I say, "but she's no soldier and you're not a general."

"I'm sorry, I didn't mean to—"

"I'm just kidding—lighten up," I say, grinning.

"Oh, sorry," he says again.

"And enough of the apologies," I say. I'm trying to act normal, but I'm not sure if I'm succeeding. I'm also trying to avoid making direct eye contact with him, for fear of worse pain coming back.

"Fair enough," he says. "If I'm not the general, then who is?"

"I nominate myself," Roc says.

"I second it," Elsey says.

"Hey, don't I get any votes?" I say.

"Nah, Tristan and Roc are really fun," Elsey says.

"And I'm not?"

"Not as fun as them," she says, grinning.

"Thanks a lot!" I exclaim, grabbing her and whirling her around.

"As general," Roc says, "our first order of business is to eat breakfast. Then we'll head over to the Camp of Death and Skulls and Crossbones and all that."

"Camp Blood and Stone," I correct.

"I think that's what I said," Roc says, chuckling.

Tawni hands each of us one of the wafers Elsey found the night before. It isn't a very appetizing breakfast, but it's better than going hungry. And it's quick, which I like. I'm anxious to find my dad. He's done so much for me in my life and now I have the chance to do something for him. I can't fail him.

I also need the distraction. Although I try to keep up my side of the constant bantering that has begun ever since Tristan and Roc joined us, inside I'm still a wreck. I can't block my emotions out like the rest of them seem to do. I feel bad that my heart ballooned the night before, when Tristan held my hand, feeling more alive than it has in months. I feel bad because Cole is dead, and yet I'm experimenting with my weird feelings. My heart feels as shriveled as a raisin one minute and then as big as a balloon the next.

We leave our little hideaway without seeing anyone. People are staying indoors after the previous night's bombing. The smoke has cleared, revealing the extent of the destruction. It's bad, but not irreparable, if only the Star Dwellers will let us rebuild.

Although the dusty streets are deserted, we walk single file, sticking to the edges of buildings, ready to dive for cover if any Sun Dwellers appear. Or any Star Dwellers. Probably any Moon Dwellers, too. We don't know who we can trust.

Tristan is just in front of me, which I would know even if my eyes were closed. It's like an invisible tether connects us now whenever we're close. Not just the pain, which is still there; duller maybe, but there. The tether has low-voltage electricity surging through it, leaving me tingling. His strides look awkward, ginger, like he's walking on eggshells, trying not to crack them. Each step is likely sending splinters of pain through his injured leg and back.

We speak in hushed voices.

"Where did your brother come from?" I ask.

"Although I'd like to say he was adopted, I'm pretty sure he came from my mom's stomach, same as me," Tristan says, grinning.

I shake my head and grin back. "No, I mean yesterday. How'd he know we were here?"

"I've been wondering that, too," Tristan says, his smile fading. "If I had to guess, I'd say my father sent him as soon as Rivet reported that you were headed here on the train."

I nod slowly. "But why'd he attack you like that?" I ask.

Tristan glances back and says, "We haven't been getting along lately."

That doesn't really answer my question. "But why—"

"He's not like me, Adele. He's different—like my father. Not good."

"So you mean bad, right?"

"Yeah, bad."

"Which makes you good then?"

He sighs. "I don't know. I don't believe what my father believes, does that make me good? Or maybe I'm not good, because it doesn't seem like anyone is these days. I'd rather classify myself as *not bad*." He turns his head and manages a sideways grin, but I can tell that talking about his family is hard for him.

But I plow ahead anyway. Questions and answers, just like I planned.

"So you're not like your dad or brother..."

"My *father* or brother," he clarifies. It seems the distinction between dad and father is important to him. I wonder if it's a sign of respect for the president or a lack of closeness with the man who helped create him.

"Okay—father. So if you're not like them, does that mean you *are* like your mother?"

"I hope I'm like my mom was," he says, once more changing my word slightly.

"Was?" I say, hoping I'm not probing too much.

Tristan goes silent for a moment and I worry I've offended him. We tiptoe across an empty intersection and duck behind another building. Roc is leading—he said he knows the way.

Finally, Tristan says, "My mom disappeared a while ago." Although he says it calmly, evenly, I can feel a weight behind his words. The same kind of weight I feel in my own voice when I speak about my parents.

"I'm sorry," I say. "I heard about that on the news."

"It's okay," he says. "It was better that she went. For her. I'll find her someday," he adds.

"I'll help you," I find myself saying.

He glances back. "I'd like that."

The tingling in my body, which I've started to get used to, increases suddenly, like a surge of electricity, and I find myself giddy with excitement. I have the urge to rush to his side, grab his hand and walk with him. I restrain myself.

"Why is this happening?" It's a cryptic question, but when he turns and I see his eyes I know he understands what I mean.

"I was hoping you'd know," he says. He faces forwards once more. "I came after you hoping you'd know. That I'd be able to get answers out of you."

I could be saying the same thing to him. *Crap.* Something is happening that's outside of both our control.

Roc says, "Sorry to interrupt, but we're approaching the boundary to the camp."

I look around—all I can see are buildings. For a second I think Roc might've gotten confused, but when we turn the next corner, the buildings suddenly disappear and are replaced by a high stone wall. The wall is gray and sheer and would've appeared ominous, an impossible barrier between me and my dad, except there's a gaping hole in it.

Scorch marks are burned along the edges of the breach, the result of a force so powerful it could've only been from an incendiary. *Three times*, I think. Three times we've been effectively saved by the Star Dweller bombs. At some point I'm really going to have to write the Star Dweller leaders a letter thanking them.

I chuckle under my breath at my own joke.

"What?" Tristan says.

"Nothing. I was just thinking how strange it is that I'd still be stuck in the Pen if not for the Star Dweller bombs. Or worse, I might be dead. They always seem to explode when and where I need them the most, like a guardian angel is helping me."

"You think there's something to it?"

"I don't know. Probably not. More likely it's just a coincidence. They seem to be bombing everything," I say. Despite my nonchalant response, something tells me there *is* more to it. But it doesn't make sense—can't make sense. Why would the Star Dwellers be trying to help me do anything? They don't even know who I am. They have much bigger problems to deal with now. Like how to win a war.

"I'm wondering where they're getting all the weapons," Tristan says.

My eyes jerk to his. We'd discussed the same thing, when the bombing first started. "You agree that it would be hard for them to get their hands on such advanced weaponry?" I ask.

"Yeah. Near impossible. At least, without help."

My mind is whirling. Someone *is* helping them. And it would have to be someone from the Sun Realm. Could there really be traitors in the president's midst?

I shrug off my thoughts and try to focus on our present situation.

We have a way in now, but I'm afraid to take it, afraid that the entire camp is destroyed, the prisoners left to die while the guards evacuated.

"It'll be okay," Tristan says, as if reading my mind.

"I know," I lie.

The first bomb hits just as we're creeping through the hole. Another day of bombing has begun. If we weren't so used the sound of distant bombs, we might have mistaken it for something else, a piece of machinery firing up maybe, but by now we can identify the roar of thunder as not a fluke underground storm, but as the mirthful cry of pointless destruction.

Elsey cries out, but I manage to quickly slap a hand over her mouth, silencing her. We huddle together, hoping there isn't a guard just inside the wall, close enough to hear the noise. Warmth and shivers flow through my skin as my arm brushes against Tristan's.

He looks at me, his eyes serious. "Wait here," he says.

I start to object, but he's already gone, slipping inside the wall and around the corner. I see the hilt of his drawn sword flash before he moves out of sight. He moves remarkably fast considering his wounds. He's still not moving normally, but his limp has lessened.

Roc must see the concern on my face, because he says, "Don't worry, he'll be fine. I taught him everything he knows."

I laugh. It's high pitched and nervous, but a laugh nonetheless. It helps to calm my nerves.

We hear a quick yell and then a groan, followed by a thud. I've had enough of waiting and rush through the hole, expecting violence of some sort.

Instead, there's only Tristan, grinning, standing over his fallen adversary.

I approach him, feeling my heart beat faster as the distance between us lessens. "Is he...dead?" I ask.

"Just unconscious," Tristan says. His grin fades and he raises a finger in the air. "We have to hurry."

I can hear a dull commotion further into the camp. Something's happening. Something big, by the sound of it. Inside the wall we can see all the way to the main buildings, where the prisoners are probably kept. But the sound arises from further to the left, past a cluster of massive stone blocks stacked in a pyramidal structure.

I don't know how I know, but I do: my father is here. Admittedly, being this close after not seeing him for so long makes me go a bit crazy. Okay, *really* crazy. I take off, leaving my friends behind, envisioning a joyous reunion with him, jumping into his arms, holding him to me.

It's a long run, and my initial burst of speed wanes, forcing me to drop into well-measured, paced strides. Tristan catches up halfway to the pyramids, pulling alongside me, galloping in a strange limp-run, his breathing heavy, but not as heavy as mine. To his credit, he doesn't try to stop me, to reason with me, like

311

so many other guys would do. He seems to understand that I have to do what I'm about to do.

Whatever that is.

"What's the plan?" he says as we run together.

Plan? Huh? The word sounds as meaningless to me as a phrase uttered in an ancient language by someone who forms words by clicking their tongue against the roof of their mouth. "I…uh…well…" I stammer. Finally, I say, "Get my dad?" What a plan! I even say it like a question, as if I'm not sure that's why we're sprinting across a barren prison camp. *Good one, Adele.*

Tristan deserves a medal for patience. "So go and kick some butt then?" he says. He tries to grin, but the pain of running with his injuries turns it into a grimace.

"Exactly," I say. His assured tone gives me strength, and I feel like we have a plan, even though we don't. "Are you okay?" I ask.

"Never felt better," he says.

"Liar."

The pyramids loom closer. They're a lot bigger now that we're close to them, rising hundreds of feet into the air. I veer right, heading for the outer edge of the first one in the line of three. Tristan follows, keeping pace and sticking close to my side. As we pass the corner, my eyes widen at the sight before me.

Dozens of other giant, gray pyramids dot the landscape, rising majestically above us.

The commotion we heard from a distance is getting louder and soon we can make out individuals yells. It sounds like a battle.

I continue to steer us in the direction of the sound, but we still can't see anything except the pyramids, which are staggered in such a way that they block the view in every direction once you're in their midst.

"We're close," Tristan says. "Get ready."

Ready for what? I have no idea, but I nod anyway. We pass a final pyramid and abruptly our vision opens to a wide open rock slab plain. A half-constructed pyramid stands a ways off. In front of the pyramid: chaos—the source of the noise.

A mob of prisoners are fighting the guards, who are using long whips and Tasers to hold them off. None of them have guns. Clearly the intention is to hurt, not to kill.

But the guards aren't doing so well. We pull to a stop, and as we watch, one of the guards is bashed over the head by a shirtless guy wielding a rock. A prisoner. His body is covered in scars, some dark and ancient, and others fresh—some even ooze bright red blood.

There are hundreds of prisoners, all of whom are in a similar condition. None of the men wear shirts and they all have various injuries, likely caused by the sting of the guards' whips. The women wear ratty tank tops and sport similar welts and gashes. But they've had enough.

The revolt is ultraviolent and for a few minutes we watch in awe as the prisoners start to gain an advantage. Although the inmates are taking a beating, the guards are dropping fast, being pelted with stones or bludgeoned by bare fists, a result of the overwhelming force that's gathered to defy them.

The camp name suddenly makes sense. The Stones: the massive stone blocks used to construct the pyramids—they were likely constructed off the backs of the prisoners, a pointless exercise that appears to have no purpose other than

313

to inflict pain. The Blood: the prisoners provide that when abused by the guards.

Now the guards' blood is mixed with the prisoners.

Our timing is remarkable. That we arrive during such an event is incredible, to say the least. The timing is no mistake: the Star Dwellers' rebellion has encouraged the prisoners to revolt, too.

"Do you see him?" Tristan asks.

"Who?" I say, watching the brutality with morbid curiosity.

"I don't know, your dad maybe?"

Duh. The whole purpose of our being here. I scan the mob, hoping to see his dark mop of hair and neatly trimmed mustache amongst the prisoners. I don't think about what it might mean if he's not amongst the fighters.

I think my eyes sweep past him three or four times before I recognize him. Subconsciously, I know it's him, because my gaze keeps returning to one spot, but my mind fails to believe what my brain registers. His black hair is long and disheveled, down to his shoulders; his mustache is accompanied by a thick, black beard, covering the better half of his face; his uncovered body, always strong from his work in the mines, glistens with sweat and blood and is as hard as the stones he's forced to work with.

But there's no mistaking his eyes. Emerald green and piercing, like mine. Exactly like mine. Looking into them has always been like looking into a mirror for me.

When he happens to turn toward me, searching for a guard to fight, he spots me and our eyes lock. I don't know if he thinks I'm a mirage, a misfire of one of the thousands of synapses in his brain, but he just stands there staring at me. His

314

shoulders slump as if even seeing a mirage of me is too painful for him to bear.

I wave at him.

His head perks up and his head cocks to the side. I guess maybe he doesn't think a mirage can wave. Whatever the case, he takes off running to me. I charge toward him, wild with excitement. My legs feel as light as air. I'm giddy, gleefully childlike. A few of the guards see him break away and race after him, one of them snapping a whip at his heels.

Ignoring the crackle of the whip, my dad thunders toward me with reckless abandon. The gap between us disappears. Forty feet. Thirty. Twenty.

Crack! The guard slings the whip with practiced precision and this time it connects, wrapping around my father's legs and tripping him up. He manages to brace his fall with his arms and skids to a stop ten feet from me, his arms immediately sheening with fresh blood from new scrapes.

We go for the guards. One for me; one for Tristan.

I choose the one with the whip. I'm not sure where this sudden need for revenge comes from, but I can't seem to control it. First Rivet, because of Cole. Now the whip-carrying guard, because of my father.

The guard pulls the strap back and snaps it at me. I see it coming, ducking so low I'm forced into a roll, clunky and painful on the stone. I emerge from the roll on my feet and still moving at full force. I'm not sure a train could stop me at this point. It's like I'm possessed by a demon, only observing my crazed self from afar.

When the guard sees the look on my face, his own face flashes fear, cheeks turning white and mouth contorting. I lead with an elbow, spearing him in the mouth with it and likely jarring a few teeth loose. Maintaining my momentum, I follow through with a shoulder to his sternum, flattening him onto his back and trampling overtop his chest.

I screech to a stop and look back. Tristan has the other guard at sword point, but then switches the blade to his left hand and punches the guy hard in the head twice. His head lolls to the side like he's unconscious.

The guard I battered is groaning and writhing in pain. I don't think he's going to be a threat anytime soon, so I leave him and run to my dad, who's pulling himself to his feet. Despite his aches and pains, he's smiling, his arms outstretched.

Although it isn't exactly as I planned in my mind, I jump on him, wrap my arms and legs around him, hugging him harder than I ever have before, not caring that he's covered in a mixture of dirt and blood. "Dad…oh, Dad," I murmur into his chest.

"My precious daughter," he says, rubbing my back.

I hear Tristan say, "Not trying to spoil the reunion here, but we've got to go." Reluctantly, I release my dad and turn to Tristan, who's watching us with one black eye; the other is trained on the continuing battle between the guards and prisoners. I see what he's worried about. A few of the guards have broken away from the fray and are gesturing at us wildly.

"C'mon," I say, grabbing my dad's hand and pulling him toward the closest pyramid. "I'll take you to Elsey."

"El's here?" my dad says, following me.

"Yeah, I figured I'd pick her up on the way over. You know, right after we broke out of prison."

"What!?"

"It's a long story."

316

Tristan limp-runs past us. I can tell he's fighting through the pain.

"Follow me," he says.

I'm not sure why I do it. I guess because I want to show my dad that I'm tough, that I've survived, that I'm the strong girl he raised. In any case, it's probably just childish. "No, follow me!" I exclaim. I take off, sprinting past Tristan and around the first pyramid.

I glance back and see Tristan half-grinning, half-cringing, trying to catch up. My dad isn't far behind him, looking lean and fast. Further back still is the group of guards, who have started chasing us. Great. Can't they just leave us alone? Haven't we been through enough?

To make it more difficult for the guards to follow us, I weave through the pyramids, cutting a random path toward the open flats that lead to the outer wall. I emerge from between two pyramids and into the open. Adrenaline is rushing through my veins, pushing me to *fly, fly!* I don't sprout wings and take off, but I do run pretty fast—so fast that Tristan doesn't catch me until we're halfway across the empty space.

I look back to see where my dad is. He's fallen behind a bit, unable to keep up with our younger legs. Or it might not be age that hinders him. It might be the weight of the abuse he's been subjected to in the camp, rendering his body tired and weakened. Whatever the case, the guards are gaining on him— five of them, closing in like a net.

"My dad," I say, pulling to a stop. Tristan stops, too, and we reverse our course. My dad sees us coming and slows up. He isn't about to let us do all the fighting for him.

He turns just as we reach him. The guards are upon us. Five on three. Tasers and whips again fists and feet and spirit— oh, and Tristan's sword, too.

A Taser lances out toward my father's legs, but is blocked by a quick thrust of Tristan's sword. A whip snaps at my head, but I duck and charge. I'm not full of rage anymore, but I do feel confident. Next to my father I feel invincible. He's my teacher. The best fighter I've ever known. Although I've never seen him fight anyone for real, I've always believed he's unbeatable.

I leap at the guard who missed me with the whip, kick him in the head, knock him over. Glance to my right.

My dad clotheslines two of the other guards, his heavy arms catching them in the neck and forcing them to the stone. Flopping on the ground, they gasp for air. Tristan has another one at sword point. Rather than finishing him off, he uses his forearm to send a shiver through the guy's skull, knocking him senseless.

There's only one guard on his feet. The new odds: three on one. He runs, dropping his whip and Taser and pride in a heap on the stone.

We run in the other direction. I let Tristan lead this time. I want to keep an eye on my dad. I can't believe it was that easy—almost too easy.

A barrage of bullets keens past us and, instinctively, I duck and throw my arms over my head, as if mere flesh and bone will stop the hot metal pellets from hurting me. In front, Tristan yells out sharply and stumbles, clutching at his leg, which is slick and red. He's been hit. The rest of us will be soon. It must not be bad, because Tristan manages to keep running, albeit less gracefully, with us in tow.

We reach the gap in the wall. The air is thick and heavy and smells of war. The bullets have stopped temporarily, presumably as our pursuers reload.

Tawni, Roc, and Elsey are waiting for us. We've led the danger right to them.

I look back, expecting a dozen guards armed to the teeth. One guy is running toward us, frantically trying to release an expired clip from his automatic weapon. It's the guy who ran away before. He had time to get his gun but not the rest of his friends.

"Anyonegotanythingwecanshoot?" I ask in one breath. The guy's gun will be loaded soon and we'll be dead.

Tristan, cringing in pain, says, "Roc, did we pack anything other than swords?"

"Sorry, no," Roc says. "You specifically said no guns." He glances warily at the guy with the gun. He's getting closer. The old clip falls away behind him and he pulls a new one from his pocket.

Then I remember: "Your slingshot, El," I say.

Without hesitation, she extracts it and I reach for it.

"No," she says. "I can do it."

My instinct is to grab it from her, to whirl and shoot the guard. To take care of my family and end his pursuit. But there's no time to argue. "Do it, El. Hurry," I say.

My sister, who never trained with me and our father before, grasps the slingshot handle firmly. Surely, she's never shot a human before, but it won't be any different than a tin can or a rock post or whatever else she's practiced on. In one swift motion she extends her arm, loads a pellet, and stretches the band back toward her chin. Rotating her torso, she locates our pursuer in the sights.

Despite all his bumbling, he's finally managed to snap the new clip into his gun, and he's just bringing the nozzle up to a firing position. El has maybe two seconds to get him before he gets us. Even as I stop breathing, she makes an incremental adjustment to her aim, as if she wants to hit him higher, in the head. A smaller target. *No*, I think.

The guard stops and aims his gun right at us. One second.

El fires, releasing the band with a dull *thwap!* To the human eye, the pellet moves as fast as any bullet, disappearing into the empty air as if it never existed at all. The only evidence of my sister's shot is the groan from the guy as his head snaps back and he crumples to the ground, his gun landing on top of him, having not been fired.

"Yes!" I shout. "Well done." Elsey's face is hard and strong, and I couldn't be prouder of her in that moment.

In a flash, her easy grin is back. Stoic Elsey is a little girl again, running toward my dad. "Oh, Father!" she exclaims, jumping into his arms, not unlike the way I did earlier.

"Are you okay?" Tawni says, directing the question at all of us.

"Fine," I say quickly. "But Tristan's been hit."

"It's nothing," he says. "It grazed me—looks worse than it is." The red blood is swarming over his leg and we'll have to stop the bleeding, but not here, not now.

"We've got to keep moving," I say.

"The bombs are hitting everywhere," Tawni says. "They're very close."

"We have no choice. We'll be caught if we stay here."

My dad puts Elsey down, but she continues to cling to his waist. "Adele's right," he says. "Reinforcements will be sent to subdue the prisoners. Believe me, they will. Then they'll search for us—plenty of guards witnessed our escape."

"We'll make it," Tristan says. "We *have* to make it." There's a strange confidence in his voice. Not cockiness—he doesn't seem like that kind of guy. Nor is it a statement made by someone who's gotten everything he ever wanted since the day he was born—although he has. It sounds almost like a prediction. Sort of philosophical; sort of mystical. And the way Tristan glances at Roc—intense, knowing—it's like there's something they know, or think they know, that they aren't telling us. Something important. Something life changing.

When I became a mind reader, I don't know. I'm probably just imagining things.

My dad pulls away from Elsey's grip and holds her hand, pulls her toward the exit. "Let's go," he says.

We creep through the rubble together. An explosion erupts somewhere nearby, sending dust and chunks of stone into the air. Another bomb hits further down the street, blasting the middle of a tall building. Weakened, the upper half teeters, leans, and then tumbles away, crashing across the road and into the next building, which crumbles under the weight. Beneath the buildings, people run out, frantically trying to escape the world that's caving in on them.

None of them make it. Not a single one. There are at least ten souls destroyed—five crushed under the weight of the massive hunks of rock falling from above, the other five killed by a second missile landing in the center of their escape route. Like so many others from the last few days, the memory of our horrific flight through the subchapter 26 warzone is being tattooed into my brain.

321

We flee down a street that hasn't been hit yet. Bombs are going off all around us. The smell of death is in the air. The smoke chokes my lungs and burns my eyes. Elsey is screaming so much that my dad eventually picks her up and carries her in his strong arms.

We pass through a deserted intersection filled with rubble. My mouth is dry from running and shouting and fighting. My legs are burning. I stumble on a broken stone, feel myself falling. And then a strong arm is there, grabbing me, keeping me on my feet. An electric touch: Tristan. Not grinning anymore. Lips pursed, serious. But also determined. I feel safe with him. He's badly injured, but still strong.

Roc, who seems to have a good idea of the city layout, leads us to the left, down a side street that's relatively unscathed. In fact, all the streets in this direction haven't been bombed.

We soon find out why.

Twenty-Four
Tristan

Abruptly, Roc ducks into an alley. We follow him, mimicking his movements, flattening ourselves against the wall. I want to ask what we're doing, but Roc's finger is on his lips—for some reason, complete silence is important now.

Roc has good hearing, because I don't hear anything for at least another minute. But then I hear it: the sound of marching feet. Hundreds of them, maybe more. It sounds like a parade. If the thumping feet are the beat of the snare drums, the periodic bomb blasts are the bass drums. The feet are getting closer.

Thump, thump. Thump, thump. Directly in sync with the beating of my heart.

When the first line of troops passes us I hold my breath. When I realize the soldiers are so focused straight ahead that they aren't going to see us, I slowly release the air in my lungs.

At least a thousand soldiers march by, each wearing a star patch on their shoulders. Star Dweller troops. Although their sky-blue uniforms are old and frayed, they seem to be professionals, well-organized and confident. And they're carrying shiny new guns, just another piece of evidence that someone from the Sun Realm is helping them. They look a little ragtag, yes, but deadly. Pissed off to the point of killing anyone who gets in their way.

When the last line of soldiers tramps past us and the drumbeat fades into the distance, we finally relax. Shoulders slump, deep breaths are taken, hearts slow.

"What's going on?" Adele's father asks. Other than hearing the bombs and listening to prisoner gossip, he wouldn't have any idea what's been happening while he's been stuck in prison.

"Soon," Adele says. "Let's make for the reservoir."

Once more, Roc leads the way. Although the bombing has finally stopped, I don't feel safe. At any moment another contingent of rebels could happen upon us. They'll shoot first, ask questions later.

Despite my fears, we reach the stream safely. Out of the city it's darker, but much less scary. There won't be soldiers or bombs here.

"We need to talk," Adele's father says.

"I know," Adele replies. "But first his leg." She motions to my gunshot wound.

"I'm fine," I say.

"All over it," Tawni says, removing a spare tunic from her bag. "You talk while I do this."

"As quickly as you can, tell me everything," Adele's father says.

While Tawni tears off strips of cloth and bandages my leg, Adele tells her father her story. Some of it I know, some I don't, which I listen to with wide eyes. Meeting Tawni and Cole. Their escape amidst the bombing. The news stories. Rivet. Their flight through the caves. The train ride. Cole's death. By the end her hands are shaking so hard she has to clasp them together behind her back.

Her father folds her into his arms and I expect her to weaken, to cry. She doesn't. She looks numb, like she's in shock from everything that happened. To some degree, we all must be. There are so many emotions inside me that I don't know which to focus on, which is the most important.

"Adele, it's okay now. You've done so well," her father says. He releases her, holds her out so he can look at her. "You said something about how the three bombings didn't make sense to you?"

"Yeah," she says, nodding. "The timing was too perfect. Without those bombs we might not have made it, none of us."

He nods back at her, stroking a thoughtful hand across his chin. "Things aren't always what they seem," he says cryptically.

"What do you mean?" I ask.

Adele's dad looks up, as if he forgot the rest of us were here. I noticed that when Adele told her story, she left out me and Roc, didn't mention our injuries, which are written all over our faces. Was she trying to protect us in some way? I wonder how her father will react to having Sun Dwellers in their midst.

"Why are you here, Tristan?" he asks.

He recognizes me. I wasn't sure if he did. In some ways I hoped he wouldn't. When he asks the question, his voice is even, unreadable, but I sense he's asking the question only because he thinks he has to.

Adele half-turns, still in her father's arms, making eye contact with me. Electricity crackles down my spine. I take a deep breath, trying to figure out what the hell to say, how to explain something that has no explanation—at least none that I'm aware of.

"Something drew me to Adele," I say. A breath whooshes out of Adele's lungs. And is that a...a smile?

Adele's father doesn't look surprised. "She's always been as beautiful as her mother," he says.

"No, not that," I say, flushing. Adele's smile fades. "I mean, I'm not saying she's not...I mean, she is...but that's not what I meant."

"What do you mean, Tristan," her father asks, scowling slightly.

I take a deep breath, start again. "When I saw her—Adele—In the Moon Realm, it was as if just being close to her caused me pain." I shake my head, wishing I had a more plausible story to tell. "I'm not talking emotional, mental, or spiritual pain, nothing so vague. It was real physical pain. And now I think Adele felt it too. Is that right?" I look at her.

She nods. "I did."

Hearing her say it out loud sends anxious bats through my stomach. I don't know what else to say. This is all too crazy.

Adele's father's frown deepens and he raises a hand to his beard, strokes it gently, as if thinking. "I wonder..." he says.

"Wonder what?" Adele asks.

He looks at his daughter, startled, as if he'd forgotten she was there. "Nothing," he says. "Look, I don't know why we're all here, or about all this pain stuff, but we have to make some decisions. Tristan, are you only here because you felt drawn to my daughter in the strange way you say?"

Before I can answer, Roc looks at Tawni. "Tell 'em," he says.

Twenty-Five
Adele

I stare at Tawni. Why does she know something I don't? Tristan is looking at Roc the same way—evidently he isn't in the loop either.

"Roc and I talked while you were rescuing your dad," Tawni says. "Elsey, too," she adds, which makes Elsey smile. "Although Tristan and Roc ran away to find you, Adele, to ask you questions, there's more to it. They're different from other Sun Dwellers."

"We've had enough of it all," Roc says. Tristan nods in agreement.

"They don't want to be a part of it anymore. They've decided to help do something about it."

"We have?" Tristan says, smirking.

"Yes, we have," Roc says, grinning back. "I just haven't told you yet. Tristan's going to use whatever influence he has to convince the Moon Dwellers to join the Star Dwellers, not fight them."

Mine and Tristan's eyebrows rise at the same time. Roc plows on. "Everything is such a mess. The Moon and Star Realms are going to destroy each other, making the Sun Realm even more powerful. We have to do this. It's the only option."

I look at Tristan. He looks at me. "Okay," he says.

"Okay?" I ask.

"Yeah. I want to make a difference. Do the right thing. Stop my father."

"What about me?" I say.

"You'll come, too. We could use a bit of muscle on our side," he says, smiling.

I smile back, excited about something for the first time in a long time. Traveling with Tristan, figuring out what the hell it all means, by his side, fighting for good—

But wait. "What about Mother?" I ask. "What if she's alive?"

My father's eyes are dark, and not because of the dim lighting. "I don't want to get your hopes up…" he says, his statement as wispy as smoke, trailing away into the dark.

"You know where she is," I say. It's not a question.

"The Star Realm."

"But how…?"

"Typically all convicted traitors are sent to Camp Blood and Stone, but they wanted to separate us, so they took her below," he says, pointing down at the ground. "There's only one place they would've taken her."

"The Max," I say, understanding now. The maximum security prison in the Star Realm. The same Max that I would've been transferred to on my eighteenth birthday had we not escaped. Unbelievable to think how different things could have gone. That I would have found my mom had I just left things alone. But then my dad would still be in prison. And Elsey still in that awful orphanage.

I'm so tired. Emotionally, physically, mentally. All I want is to go with Tristan, to help him, to maybe get to know him, possibly hold his hand some more, learn more about our almost preternatural connection. And yet I say, "I'll do it."

"Do what?" Father asks.

"Go to the Star Realm. Find her," I say. The words stick in my throat, but I push them out.

"No," Father says. And again. "No. We'll get you and Elsey to safety, and then I'll go after her."

"I can do this," I say. "I'm not the girl I was a year ago. Or even a month ago."

"I know you're not," Father says, "but it's too dangerous. You've done enough." He places a hand on my shoulder. "You've only just brought us together again."

I lean into the warmth of his arms and he wraps himself around me. But I'm not giving in. While he thinks he's comforting me, I'm comforting him. "I have to do this," I whisper into his chest.

He pulls back sharply, his face paling. "Adele, I can't let—"

"You trained me," I say. "I always thought it was just for fun. I enjoyed it. But it was more, wasn't it? You were

330

preparing me. *This* is what you were training me for. In case our family ever needed help. So I wouldn't be help*less*."

I hold his gaze, daring him to lie to me. He doesn't. "Yes," he says, his eyes cloudy.

I continue before he can pull his thoughts into a cohesive argument. "You have to protect Elsey. And you have to help mend the wounds between the Lower Realms. And I have to find Mother."

"Then I'm coming with you," Tristan says immediately.

"Me too," Elsey chimes in.

"No," I say, not wanting to say it. "Elsey, you need to stay with Dad. He needs you now." She scrunches up her face, but then nods firmly and grabs Dad's hand.

"And you…" I say, turning to Tristan.

He cuts me off. "We'll find your mother first, then we can talk to the Moon Dwellers."

"There isn't time," I say. "Plus, the Star Dwellers will kill you if they catch you down there."

"They'll kill…you, too," Tristan says, his words catching in his throat slightly as he says *kill*.

"No, they won't. Not if I tell them I'm joining their rebellion. That's what they want, isn't it? For all the Moon Dwellers to join them? But they won't accept that a Sun Dweller wants to betray his own people. Especially not you." My words are firm, my logic sound. Inside, my stomach is in knots, my heart crumbling beneath the power of my brain's logic. Why are you saying this? Let him come with you! Someone else can talk to the Moon Dwellers.

Tristan is shaking his head, his mouth tight and grim. His eyes look misty. When he looks away from me I feel tears well up. I barely know him, and yet…my soul aches for him. I blink away the tears.

"Adele…" my dad says slowly, his eyes tired and apologetic, "you've been through so much, I can't even imagine…"

"It's okay," I say, feeling a surge of strength in the very marrow of my bones.

My dad leans in close to me again. His voice is hoarse, merely a whisper, so the others can't hear it. "I'm so sorry, honey. I want to come with you, want to protect you, but I…"

I already know he can't. Elsey needs a father now more than ever. Plus, he can help open up lines of communication between the Moon Dweller leaders and Tristan.

Selfishly, I want him to come with me. I've been on my own for so long now, I just want my dad to be there, to tell me what to do, to protect me, to be my rock, like he's always been. I've come so far. So far.

I see my dad's face. I've never seen such pain in his eyes before. They're wet and red and tired. I have to be strong for him.

I hug him again. "I'm strong, Dad," I find myself saying. At first I think I'm just trying to act tough again. Then I realize it isn't an act. The last six months, though hard, have chiseled me into a different person. I'm the same, but different. I'm no longer reliant on my father to protect me. I'm tough. A survivor. "I'll be fine," I say firmly.

My dad tilts my chin to look at me. His eyes are blurry. "I know you will, Adele. You're an incredible young woman, courageous and strong. I'm so proud of you. Be safe."

"Do you have any advice?" I ask, hoping for some of my dad's usual pearls of wisdom.

"Remember the three bombings when you're down there. Look for answers. You have good instincts and I think you're right. Someone's looking out for you and I have a feeling you'll find out who while you're in the Star Realm. Do what's in your heart. And please, come back to me." He kisses my forehead, holds his lips to my skin for a moment, his dark and tangled beard blocking my vision.

After all the crying I've done lately, I expect to be bawling now. But I'm not. Other than the few tears I blinked away, I feel strong and resilient. The fighter my father raised me to be. I'm about to turn away from him when, almost as an afterthought, he reaches into his shoe and extracts a slip of paper, shoving it into my hand.

"Dad, what—"

"Don't read it now. Your mom asked me to give it to you if I ever saw you again. She said it's important. I've pondered its meaning many times, but never got anywhere. Maybe it will mean more to you."

"Thank you," I say, my voice catching slightly. A message from my mother. I want nothing more than to unfold it and read it right now, but I listen to my dad and hold it tight in my hand.

I release my dad and turn to Elsey. "You were so incredible back there," I say. "You saved us. Take care of Dad for me, okay?"

Elsey's eyes widen. "I will," she says solemnly. "Thank you for rescuing me." She rushes to me and throws her arms around me. She's not being overly dramatic this time—the situation warrants it. I hold her fiercely.

"I will never forget you, Elsey," I say, speaking her language.

"Nor I you," she replies. I kiss both her cheeks and then turn to Tawni.

Although I desperately want to, I can't ask her to come with me. She's done too much already, and the road ahead will be too dangerous. "Goodb—"

"I'm coming with you," she says, interrupting my farewell speech before it ever really gets started. I burst into a huge smile, hug her. I don't argue. Like before, I know she won't take no for an answer, and I don't want her to.

I go to shake Roc's hand, but he gives me a hug instead. I don't know him that well, but he seems like a good person. "Take care," I say.

"Till we meet again," he says.

Finally, I turn toward Tristan. He's still frowning, his lips still tight.

"I'm going with you," he says. "Unless you don't want me to."

I bite my lip, and realize my head is throbbing. "Tristan, believe me, I want you to. It's just…"

"I'm going with you," he repeats.

"They need you up here. The world needs you," I say.

"You make me feel important," he says wryly, allowing himself a tight smile.

It's the funniest thing in the world for him to say, and I have to hold back a laugh. *I* make the son of the president feel important? "You are," I say. "I mean, you could be. You have that kind of potential."

"Potential…" he says wistfully, "that's what my father always said."

"Not like that," I say. "You know what I mean."

I can see the tension in the hard lines of his arms, the same arms that have saved me more than once, that have fought beside me for no reason other than that he feels pain when he's near me. "We'll meet again," I say, wishing it was a promise I knew I could keep.

"You don't know that," he says.

Thud, thud, thud. My heart, not my head, although both are pounding away. "Father?" I say, looking at my dad in hopes of something…an answer to an unspoken question perhaps. *Can Tristan come with us?*

"I won't tell either of you what to do," Father says. "You've both proven you're more than capable of making your own decisions…"

"I'm sensing a 'but'," Tristan says, quirking the corner of his mouth.

Father laughs and I love the sound, even if I don't like what it means. "You have good senses too," he says. "But we could really use Tristan here. If we have any hope of steering the Star Dweller violence away from the Moon Realm, that is."

Tristan's face twitches slightly. He knows what that means. He can't walk away when people are dying. It's not in him. "There are so many unanswered questions," he says, moving a step closer to me. The pain in my head rises, but I don't care, almost want it to. It's worth it.

I take half-step forward, thinking about what he said. He's right. I want to explore those questions with him, but I have to be strong, have to stand on my own two feet. He's close enough to touch now. My body shivering slightly, I circle my arms around him, hug him. *Something drew me to Adele.* If he's right, then we'll be drawn together again, in time, won't we?

And then, as I hold him, I realize I don't feel any pain: just warmth, a faint buzzing in my scalp, a tingling in my spine.

I raise my chin and look up at him. A single tear creeps from his eye and meanders down his cheek. I wipe it away with the edge of my hand. Emotions are running through me, but I don't trust them, not under the circumstances. I have the urge to kiss him. I grit my teeth and ignore the feeling, pull him close for a final squeeze.

He stops me, entwines his fingers in mine, like the night before, a magical moment of soft touches and finger grazes and so many feelings. The gray of the caves and the smell of smoke and the fierce, fierce weariness from fighting and running and running—they fade away.

And Tristan leans in, dipping his chin, so close, so close…and his lips find mine.

A shockwave of pain surges through me and I almost cry out, but then it's gone. It's gone and all I feel is the tenderness and moisture of Tristan's lips, lingering on my mouth even as he pulls away far too soon.

I release Tristan and immediately feel the electricity leave my body. I feel numb again, unfeeling. I might be mistaken, but I notice a slight twitch on Tristan's face when we pull apart, as if it hurt him.

My father clears his throat and my face reddens, but the embarrassment was worth it. Roc chuckles, says, "That was unexpected," while Tawni and Elsey just beam at me. My gaze settles on my feet.

"Uh, where will you go?" Tristan says, also avoiding eye contact with my dad.

Honestly, I don't know, can barely think. I've never been to the Star Realm, have no idea how to get there. I bore a hole through the dirt on my shoes with my stare, before finally looking up at Tawni, who only shrugs, a big smile still plastered across her face. A good team we're going to be.

Roc chuckles again as he unzips his pack. "Here, take these," he says, handing me a packet of maps. "Your complete guide to the Star Realm. I recommend following the reservoir around the city to the north"—he points in the direction we should take—"and then hang a right through the inter-realm tunnel. Typically you'd need clearance to get through it, but I expect no one is manning it because of everything that's happening."

I nod. "Thank you. For everything."

I can't bear to drag out the goodbyes any longer. I've just kissed Tristan—like really, really kissed him—and yet now we have to part ways. And I've just brought three-quarters of my family back together, and yet I have to leave them, too, to find my mom. The last quarter.

If she's alive, I will find her—of that I'm certain.

Twenty-Six

Tristan

She's gone. I watch her long, black hair fade into obscurity, becoming one with the dark cavern walls. With each step further from me, I feel the pull toward her lessen, the energy leaving my neck and spine. When I turn away, I find her father looking at me seriously.

"She's my little girl," he says. I sense a protective undercurrent to his words, no doubt brought on by him witnessing our first kiss. Did I really just do that?

"I'm not like my father."

"You already told me that," he says. "Now you have to *show* me."

"I will," I promise. I stride to him, extend my hand. "I'm Tristan. Tristan Nailin."

He takes my hand, squeezes hard, crushes my fingers. A test, maybe. Although it hurts like hell, I control my face, don't cry out. "I'm Adele's father," he says sternly. I raise my eyebrows, intimidated by the serious man before me. My judge. My jury. Without his approval, I surely won't get Adele's.

He surprises me by breaking into a huge smile, chuckling under his beard. "Just kidding," he says. "I'm not really that tough. Unless you do something to hurt my daughter, of course. Then I'm your worst nightmare. Name's Ben. Ben Rose."

"Nice to meet you, Mr. Rose," I say.

"Just Ben is fine."

"Thanks. And I won't do anything to hurt your daughter—that's a promise."

"I'll hold you to that," he says, leaving me and going to Roc and Elsey, who are dangling their feet in the reservoir.

I crouch down, put a hand on the stone. I imagine that I can feel small vibrations through the ground, the soft patter of her footsteps in the distance. I close my eyes and picture her green eyes looking up at me, her soft lips slightly parted. It had felt like she was about to kiss me, but then when she didn't, I couldn't stop myself, like I didn't have a choice. Was it because of the pain? Did I subconsciously know it would relieve it? And why did it help?

I hope I'll get the chance to ask her what she thinks.

I fear for her. The caverns are a dangerous place, and they get more dangerous the deeper you go. Cannibals, marauding gangs of thieves, and now legions of Star Dweller troops roam the depths, preying on the weak. Adele is not weak—she's proved that every step of the way with her fighting, with the slingshot—but she's also not invincible. Like when I started this adventure, I hope I'll see her again.

I still don't know what our feelings are for each other, or why they're so strong, or even why they started with so much pain, but I want to find out. She's like no one I've ever met before. So strong and capable—but tender and compassionate, too. At least that's my first impression.

My only regret: I didn't tell her what I know; about the Dwellers living on the surface of the Earth, the first of our people in almost five-hundred years to leave the Tri-Realms. It just never felt like the right time, and it's not something you just blurt out, like a confession. I vow to tell her the next chance I get. Until then, she'll live in my dreams, like my mom.

I gulp down a deep breath as I realize it's true. I have no regrets about leaving the Sun Realm, even though now I know it's probably for good. No regrets at all. I've changed. I'm no longer reliant on a soft mattress and a fluffy pillow and servants waiting on me hand and foot. I'm not addicted to the wealth and the power like my father. I'm the person my mother wanted me to be, the person I hope Adele needs me to be.

I kiss the tips of my fingers, touch them to the ground. "Farewell, Adele Rose," I whisper.

Twenty-Seven

Adele

The tunnel is right where Roc said it would be. He's wrong about there not being any guards, though, but they're both dead, lying awkwardly at the bottom of the stone staircase leading to the tunnel entrance. They've been shot and thrown down the stairs. I try not to look at their faces as we step over them.

We reach the top of the steps and I pause, looking back over the city. Thick smoke roils over the crumbling rooftops. A cheer rises up in the distance. The Star Dwellers have taken subchapter 26.

"My father gave me a note from my mom," I say, my hand clenched tightly around the paper, crumpling it slightly.

"You should read it."

"I'm afraid it will hurt too much."

"Sometimes a little pain is good," she says.

She's right. After all, it was a little pain—okay, a lot of pain—that started everything with Tristan. I untighten my fingers, watching as red splotches replace the whiteness of my knuckles. I fold back the note, one corner at a time.

My mom's faded handwriting is smudged in the center of the half-page.

You'll know him when you see him, it says. *And together you can save us all.*

My heart sinks. I show it to Tawni. "A riddle," I say. "I guess I was hoping for something more personal."

Tawni scans the single line, says, "Maybe it *is* personal."

I look at her. Think hard. "You mean…"

"Yeah," she says. "Maybe she's talking about Tristan."

It can't be. My mom doesn't know Tristan any more than I do. She doesn't know about the pain his presence caused me, how he saved me, how the pain is mostly gone now. She knows none of it. And yet, something tells me Tawni's right. The note is about Tristan. And me. But who are we meant to be saving, and how? My family? We're almost there—all that's left is to find her, but now Tristan's not coming with us, so does that screw everything up? Although I can't even begin to understand what she means, it gives me a small measure of comfort knowing that there's someone out there who gets what I'm going through and why. My mother.

I fold the note and tuck it in my pack. "Thanks for coming with me," I say to Tawni.

"I didn't have anything better to do," she says.

I laugh. "You know, you're not like your parents at all."

Her face lights up, her gray eyes shining slightly under the glow of the overhead cavern lights. "That means a lot," she says, tearing up. "Cole said the same..." She can't get the rest of the words out as she stifles a sob with the back of her hand.

"I know," I say. "Cole said the same thing. Because it's true. He would've come with us, too. I know it."

Tawni hugs me once, still afraid to speak, and turns to the cave mouth. A year ago it would've looked ominous, like the mouth of a monster, the stalactites hanging from above its teeth, ready to eat us alive. But now it just looks like a cave. Another challenge.

And I am ready.

Keep reading for a peek into the exciting sequel, *The Star Dwellers*, now available everywhere ebooks are sold!

A personal note from David...

If you enjoyed this book, please, please, please (don't make me get down on my knees and beg!) considering leaving a positive review on **Amazon.com**. Without reviews on **Amazon.com**, I wouldn't be able to write for a living, which is what I love to do! Thanks for all your incredible support and I look forward to reading your reviews.

Acknowledgements

Oh wow, where do I start? Unlike The Evolution Trilogy where I mostly did things on my own, The Moon Dwellers was a team effort. First, I'd like to thank my wife, Adele, for letting me use her name and for always supporting me and saving me from myself. You're the best thing in my life and you always will be. Also, I'd like to thank my parents, of course, who read everything I send them (which is A LOT).

Thanks to my editor, Christine LePorte, for helping me turn my rough-cut gemstone into something sparkling and beautiful, and for your patience in my many technical shortcomings.

To my literary agent, Andrea Hurst, a million thank yous for finding me, for taking a chance on me and my books, and for being such an awesome person to work with. Your experience has helped my career so much in such a short time. Also, to Laura Whittenburg at Andrea Hurst & Associates, thank you for your insightful, honest, and thought-provoking developmental feedback. The Moon Dwellers is SO MUCH better because of you. You have an incredible career ahead of you. And to Rebecca Berus, also at Andrea Hurst & Associates, I can't thank you enough for your efforts in helping to pull together a rock star marketing strategy for the series.

Thanks to my incredible team of beta readers who gave me so much positive feedback to keep me optimistic, while slipping in those precious nuggets of constructive criticism that allowed *The Moon Dwellers* to transform into something beyond what I was capable of on my own. So thank you Laurie Love, Alexandria Nicole, Christina Maness, Christie Rich, Danielle

Dundas, Kayleigh-Marie Gore, Nicole Marie Passante, Kerri Hughes, Terri Thomas, Krystle Jones, Lynne Chattaway, and Tamika Dartnell-Moore.

Next up are my incredible cover artists/designers at Winkipop Designs. Thank you for all your hard work and for giving my story the absolute best first impression I could ever ask for. I can't wait to see what you come up with for the second book!

To all my friends on Goodreads, I'm a better person and writer from having met you. You make me laugh, blush, dance, sing, read, and write. I will never forget any of you.

And most importantly I'd like to thank all my readers who took a chance on me with this book or with Fire Country. Without you, my work would just be words on a page. You are the reason I write.

Discover other books by David Estes available through the author's official website:

http://davidestesbooks.blogspot.com or through select online retailers including Amazon.

<u>Young-Adult Books by David Estes</u>

The Dwellers Saga:
Book One—The Moon Dwellers
Book Two—The Star Dwellers
Book Three—The Sun Dwellers
Book Four—The Earth Dwellers

The Country Saga (A Dwellers Saga sister series):
Book One—Fire Country
Book Two—Ice Country
Book Three—Water & Storm Country
Book Four—The Earth Dwellers

The Witching Hour:
Book One—Brew (Coming January 16, 2014!)

The Evolution Trilogy:
Book One—Angel Evolution
Book Two—Demon Evolution
Book Three—Archangel Evolution

<u>Children's Books by David Estes</u>

The Nikki Powergloves Adventures:

Nikki Powergloves- A Hero is Born
Nikki Powergloves and the Power Council
Nikki Powergloves and the Power Trappers
Nikki Powergloves and the Great Adventure
Nikki Powergloves vs. the Power Outlaws (Coming soon!)

Connect with David Estes Online

Goodreads Fan Group:
http://www.goodreads.com/group/show/70863-david-estes-fans-and-ya-book-lovers-unite

Facebook:
http://www.facebook.com/pages/David-Estes/130852990343920

Author's blog:
http://davidestesbooks.blogspot.com

Goodreads author page:
http://www.goodreads.com/davidestesbooks

Twitter:
https://twitter.com/#!/davidestesbooks

About the Author

David Estes was born in El Paso, Texas but moved to Pittsburgh, Pennsylvania when he was very young. He grew up in Pittsburgh and then went to Penn State for college. Eventually he moved to Sydney, Australia where he met his wife and soul mate, Adele, who he's now been happily married to for more than two years.

A reader all his life, David began writing novels for the children's and YA markets in 2010, and has completed 16 novels, 14 of which have been published. In June of 2012, David became a fulltime writer and is now travelling the world with Adele while he writes books, and she writes and takes photographs.

David gleans inspiration from all sorts of crazy places, like watching random people do entertaining things, dreams (which he jots copious notes about immediately after waking up), and even from thin air sometimes!

David's a writer with OCD, a love of dancing and singing (but only when no one is looking or listening), a mad-skilled ping-pong player, an obsessive Goodreads group member, and prefers writing at the swimming pool to writing at a table. He loves responding to e-mails, Facebook messages, Tweets, blog comments, and Goodreads comments from his readers, all of whom he considers to be his friends.

A SNEAK PEEK
THE STAR DWELLERS
BOOK 2 OF THE DWELLERS SAGA
Available anywhere e-books are sold!

Prologue

Tristan

Two years ago

My mom didn't show up for dinner tonight.

Come to think of it, I haven't seen her all day. Although my schedule was jam-packed—sword training all morning, an interview for a silly telebox show in the early afternoon, a painful two hours of "life lessons" from my father in the late afternoon (where the President "his highness" imparted his unending wisdom upon my brother and me), and barely a half hour to myself to clean up and get ready for dinner—I would still usually cross paths with my mom at some point. But not today. And now she isn't at dinner, which is very unusual, her designated spot at the foot of the table empty save for the untouched place setting.

"Where's Mom?" I ask from the center of our mile-long table.

From the head, my father looks up from his juicy prime beef. "She's gone," he says so matter-of-factly I think it's a joke.

"Gone?" I snort. "What's that supposed to mean?"

There's no compassion in my father's dark stare. "Are you dumb, boy? Gone means gone. Vanished, disappeared. She left you." He wears a smirk, like the joke's on me.

"She wouldn't do that," I say firmly. I know she wouldn't. She loves me. My brother, Killen, too, who sits across from me watching our exchange with unreadable eyes.

"She would and she did," the President says. "Her handmaiden found her cupboard empty this morning. She packed up as if she's never coming back. If you're ever going to be a man, Tristan, you have to face the truth. She's abandoned you."

But that's not a truth I can face. Not now—not ever. She didn't leave. She was driven away.

"You did this," I growl. For a second my father's face is vulnerable, his eyebrows raised, as if I've struck a nerve. A moment later, he's himself again, unflappable.

"Watch your tone, son," he says back, his voice simmering with hot coals.

I know not to push him too far, but tonight I can't stop myself. "I hate you," I say through clenched teeth. Pushing back my chair, I add, "I'm going to find her."

Before I can get to my feet, he's up and moving, barreling around the table, his face a swirling mixture of wrath and fire and his idea of discipline. I've seen him bad, but never this bad, and it takes me by surprise, so much so that I'm frozen for a split-second, just enough time for him to reach me.

There's no hesitation in him as he towers over me; despite my recent growth spurt, he's still taller by a head. And his frame is that of a man, chiseled from his daily personal training sessions, while I, though athletic, still sport the body of a boy. The strike comes so fast I have no time to react.

CRACK!

My head snaps back as the vicious uppercut lands just beneath my chin. Still half on the plush red velvet cushion of my cast-iron chair, I feel my feet tangle with the chair legs as I go down in a heap, unwittingly pulling the heavy seat on top of me. Pain is shooting through my jaw but I don't even have time to massage my chin before my father's vise-like hands are clutching the top of my tunic, pulling me to my feet, and then further, lifting me in the air, my legs dangling helplessly beneath me.

I'm looking down at my father, and I feel the warm trickle of blood from my mouth. I must've bitten my tongue when he hit me. Out of the corner of my eye I see Killen watching, his face that of a ghost, white and powdery. I look back at my father when he shakes me, once, twice, thrice, a reminder of the power he holds over me.

"You will NOT speak to me like that!" he spits out. "If anyone's to blame for your mother's disappearance"—another shake—"it's you."

He drops me, and although I land on my feet, my legs are weak and rubbery, unable to sustain my weight as my knees crumble beneath me. His shadow looms over me and I shudder. Why won't he just let me be, leave me to my own grief? Because that's not who he is. I suspect that his cold, uncaring shell of a heart stopped beating years ago.

"You will not leave this house again until I say so," he commands, and despite the rebellion in my heart, I know I'll obey him. But someday, when I'm stronger, I won't.

I never saw my mother again.

One
Adele

The thunder of marching boots sends shivers through the rock and through my bones.

When I was young my parents used to tell me stories about monsters that roam the underground world we live in. Serpents with glowing eyes the size of dinner plates, longer than ten houses, slithering and slipping through the underground rivers and lakes. Faceless boogeymen, walking the caves, searching, searching…for a child to snack on. I now know my parents were just trying to scare me into not going out alone at night, to trick me into not wandering the outskirts of the subchapter.

These days there are worse things than monsters in the Tri-Realms.

Tawni and I hold our breath as the convoy of sun dweller troops pass us. When we heard them, we managed to extinguish our lights, pull back into our tunnel, and duck behind a finger of rock jutting out from the wall. We're lucky— they're not in our tunnel. Instead, they're passing perpendicular to us, through a tunnel that intersects ours, shooting off to the left and right, the first crossroads we've seen since leaving the Moon Realm. Thankfully, they don't seem to understand the concept of stealth, or they might have seen us before we even knew they were there.

It's weird: even though he's nothing like them, the sun dweller soldiers remind me of Tristan. I guess because they're from the same place. The Sun Realm. A place I've only seen on the telebox. A place I will probably never go.

Compared to the ragtag legion of star dwellers we saw back in the Moon Realm, the sun dwellers are polished and professional, with pristine red uniforms adorned with medals and ribbons and the symbol of the Sun Realm on the shoulder—a fiery sun with scorching heat marks extending from the edges. Their weapons are shiny and new, their swords gleaming in their scabbards, their guns black and unmarked. They have bright flashlights and headlamps, which make it easy for us to see them. If one of them aims a light in our direction, they will spot us.

My muscles are tense, as line after line of soldiers march past. Without counting, I know there are more of them than the star dwellers in subchapter 26. If they were to fight, it would be a massacre. But they don't turn at our tunnel, don't head for subchapter 26. They pass straight through the crossroads, moving somewhere else—I don't know where.

Some of them speak. "Damn endless tunnel," one of them says.

"Damn the star dwellers for their rebellion," another replies.

"I've got to take a piss," the first one says, breaking off from the pack. He heads right for us, the light on his helmet bobbing and bouncing off the rock walls.

"Well, turn your damn light off," a guy says. "We don't want to see you doing it."

"Shut your pie-hole!" the small-bladdered soldier says, but reaches up and switches off his light, thrusting him into shadow.

I feel Tawni grab my hand as the guy's boots scrape closer. We can hear his breathing, heavy and loud from his long march. I am coiled as tight as a spring, ready to shove my foot

354

into his groin, or my finger into his eye, if he stumbles on our bent legs.

He stops, and I know he is close, practically right on top of us. Cloth scuffles as he gets his thing out. We hear the soft *shhhhh* of moisture as he pees right next to us. It splatters on the rocks, spraying tiny droplets of liquid waste on my leg. Tawni is even closer so she gets the worst of it.

He is so exposed I could hurt him badly in an instant. As much as I want to, it would be suicide. The rest of the soldiers would be on us before I could say *Pee somewhere else, sucker!*

I resist the temptation, trying not to throw up as the tangy scent of urine fills my nostrils.

He finishes, scuffles his clothing some more, scrapes his boots away. I breathe out slowly, and I hear Tawni do the same. The guy flicks his light on and reunites with the other men just as the last line passes through the intersection. Darkness is restored as the torches disappear into the outgoing tunnel. The thunder fades away.

We don't speak for a half hour, barely move, barely breathe. It could be the first of a dozen convoys for all we know. I feel that if we stumble into the crossroads, a bunch of lights will come on, a net will be thrown over us, and we'll be dragged away.

My legs are aching from lack of movement. I feel like screaming. I am trying to outlast Tawni, but what she lacks in toughness, she makes up for in patience. I can't take it anymore.

"You smell nasty," I whisper.

"Speak for yourself," she hisses.

"That was really gross."

"It was worse for me."

"True." Silence for another minute. Then I say, "Do you think it's safe?"

"No."

"Neither do I, but I don't think I can sit in a puddle of urine any longer."

"Okay."

"I mean, I'm sure there's some spa in the Sun Realm that claims urine has healing powers, or is good for the skin, or something, and offers urine baths and urine scrubs, but I just don't buy it."

Tawni snorts. "You're nuts," she says. "Thank God for the modesty of the sun dwellers."

"Yeah, we were lucky. If they were like the guys in the Moon Realm I know, the whole platoon would've peed against the wall, lights blazing full force."

I pull myself to my feet and help Tawni to hers. We don't turn our lights on, opting to feel our way along the wall to the intersection. When the rough rock gives way to empty air, we know we've reached the crossroads. Tawni holds my hand and pulls me across the mouth of the intersecting tunnel. A bead of sweat leaves a salty trail on my forehead as my anxiety reaches a fever pitch.

No lights come on. No net falls on us. No one drags us away. Not yet.

We make it to the other side safely, and then walk another five minutes to put a safe distance between us and the intersection, before turning our lights back on.

Tawni's white tunic is yellowed with filth. I don't look at mine.

"I don't know if I can go any farther wearing this," Tawni says, motioning to her soiled garb.

"I'd prefer a hot shower before changing clothes. Check the map and see if there's a five-star hotel nearby."

Tawni smirks, but pulls out the map anyway, one of the ones that Tristan's friend, Roc, gave us before we left them. I shine the light for her while she locates the 26th subchapter in the Moon Realm. She finds it and nods when she identifies the inter-Realm tunnel we are in. Using her finger, she traces our path along the tunnel. The line ends at the edge of the map.

"We need to switch to a Star Realm map," she says. Fumbling through her pack, she selects a new map and unfolds it. She turns the map clockwise until she sees an edge with a tunnel going off the page that reads *To Moon Realm, subchapter 26*. When she pushes the new map against the old one, they match perfectly. "I guess we're done with this one for now," she says, folding the Moon Realm map and returning it to the pack.

I've officially left the Moon Realm for the first time. It feels weird, like I'm in a foreign land, not on earth anymore. As a little girl, I always dreamed of traveling the Tri-Realms as part of my job as a famous novelist, seeking inspiration for my books. Now I just wish I was at home, with my family.

Turning her attention back to the new map, Tawni continues tracing her finger along the straight blue line, until she reaches a red intersecting line. She taps the key in the bottom right-hand corner of the map. "Blue is for inter-Realm, red is for intra-Realm."

"Those sun dwellers were traveling within the Moon Realm," I say.

"Doing what?"

"Helping to squash the rebellion," I guess.

Tawni nods, goes back to the map. "So if we're here..."—she places her finger on the blue line just past the red one—"...then we are at least two days' march from the first subchapter in the Star Realm—subchapter 30."

"And the nearest hotel?" I joke.

"Probably an hour away," she replies, "but it pretty much looks exactly the same as where we're standing right now."

I groan. I guess the builders of this tunnel didn't really consider comfort to be a top priority.

"Wait a minute," Tawni murmurs, peering at the map and once more consulting the key.

"What?"

"Eureka! There's a blue dot not that far away!"

"Thank god!" I exclaim. "That's amazing, wonderful! Uh...what's a blue dot mean?"

Tawni laughs. "Watering hole."

Yes! Now I really am excited. Our canteens are dry. We are filthy. A watering hole is just what we need. "Perfect," I say.

Tawni and I are both smiling when we start walking again, our legs no longer sore, our steps bouncy and light. Funny how a little good news can have a physical impact.

We float along for an hour, expecting any second to hear the gentle slap of moving water against a rocky shore. When the second hour passes, I am getting antsy. Perhaps the map is wrong and there is no watering hole. Or maybe the underground lake has dried up, no longer fed by one of the many life-giving tributaries that flow in between and through the Tri-Realms.

"Where is it?" I say when a few more minutes pass without any change in the dull gray scenery.

"I'm not sure," Tawni says.

"You said it was close."

"It's hard to judge distance on this map. Everything looks so close when there are really miles between."

"We've walked for at least eight miles," I point out.

Tawni shrugs and keeps walking. Having no other choice, I do the same. That's when I hear it.

At first a soft tinkle, the noise becomes louder, a swishing—and then a gurgle. Water, has to be. Tawni looks at me and we both smile. The map was right!

For only the second time since we entered this godforsaken tunnel, the monotony is broken as the passage opens up to our left. The right wall remains straight and solid, but to the left there is an empty darkness. I feel cool air waft against my face, ruffling my hair. At our feet is water, lapping against the edge of the tunnel floor.

We go a little crazy. Or maybe just I do. Letting out a *Whoop!* I sling down my pack and thrust my cupped hands into the cool liquid. First I throw a handful into my face. My breath catches as the icy water splashes over my skin. But I don't shiver—it feels wonderful. It's like the water is healing me, rejuvenating more than just my skin: refreshing my soul. The wet drips off my chin and dribbles down my neck and beneath the neckline of my tunic. It feels so good I can't help myself.

With no room in my mind left for embarrassment, or modesty, I pull my tunic over my head and toss it aside, leaving just my undergarments. Oh, and my shoes, too, which I pull off, along with my socks. I leave my flashlight angled on a rock so I can see.

I splash into the knee-deep water, relishing the soft caress of the cooling elixir. The lake bed is covered with long, smooth rocks that massage my sore feet. As I scoop water onto my arms, stomach, and legs, I remember a story my grandmother used to tell me about the Fountain of Youth, a pool of water with life-extending power. The cool touch of this pool feels equally potent, and I half-expect to see myself growing shorter, shrinking to reveal a younger me, the size of my half-pint sister perhaps.

I don't shrink, but I am cleansed. When I turn around, Tawni is grinning. She tosses me a sliver of soap, which I manage to juggle and then catch. As I use it to wash my body, she methodically uncaps each canteen and fills them. She is the responsible one.

Seeing her with the canteens reminds me of the hungry thirst in my throat. I finish with the soap and hand it to Tawni to use. She is already undressed and daintily steps into the pool, looking as graceful as a dancer, particularly when compared to my own clumsy entrance.

I turn around and splash some more water on my face.

"Where'd you get that scar on your back?" Tawni asks.

Looking over my shoulder, trying to gaze at my back, I say, "What scar?"

She moves closer, places a hand on my back, and I shiver, suddenly feeling cold. Her fingers linger somewhere near the center of my back, where I can't possibly see, just below my undergarments. "Curious," she says absently.

"What is it?"

"It's a crescent-shaped scar, small, but slightly raised off your skin. It looks like a recent scar..."

"Maybe I got it in the tunnels somewhere—or from Rivet," I say, but I know that's not right—there would have been blood, and someone would have noticed the wound seeping through my tunic.

"No, it's not *that* fresh. Just looks like it's from something that happened in the last few years. If I didn't know better, I'd say it looks just like…"

I turn to face my friend, taking in her quizzical expression in an instant. "Like what?" I ask when she doesn't finish her statement.

"Nothing, I don't know what I was thinking," she says unconvincingly.

"You were going to say 'Tristan's scar', weren't you?" I laugh. "You're nuts, you know that?"

She laughs, high and musical. "And you're not?"

I grin at her and cup my hands, once more using them as a scoop to lift a portion of water to my face. As I open my mouth to receive the glorious liquid, I see Tawni's face change from mirthful to one of confusion. It looks like she's playing with something in her mouth, moving her tongue around, side to side. Her eyebrows are lowered. I plunge the water into my mouth, delighting in the slick feel as it slips over my tongue, down my gullet.

"Ahh," I murmur softly, just before Tawni grabs my arm. Her eyes are wide—she is scared. "What?" I say.

"Spit it out!" Tawni shrieks. Now I am the confused one. "Spit it out!" she says again, reaching around and thumping me on the back.

"I can't," I say over her shoulder. "I've already swallowed it."

Tawni releases me and says, "No, no, no, no…this is not good."

That's when I taste it. Something's not right about the water. Like Tawni, I make a face, swish some spit around in my mouth. Overall, the water was refreshing, delicious even, but the aftertaste is not good. The water is…. "Contaminated?" I say.

Tawni nods slowly. "I think so."

Not good.

As kids, all moon dwellers are taught to look for the signs of contaminated water. Strange coloring, frothy film on the top, a unique odor, strange taste: All are possible clues that the water is not good to drink. At home we used a testing agent every four hours to check our water. If the water turns blue when combined with the agent, it is okay. If it turns green or brown, your water is bad. Even if we had the stuff we needed to test the water, it is too late. We've drunk it.

I peer into the water. It looks okay. No film, no discoloring, no malodor. The nasty aftertaste might just be a result of trace metals in the water, picked up somewhere along its winding path through the depths. I doubt we're that lucky.

"What do you think it is?" I ask. There are a lot of dangers associated with drinking bad water. In mild cases, you might just get a bad case of diarrhea or perhaps light vomiting, but there are many worse diseases and viruses that can be picked up, too. Like…

"Bat Flu," Tawni says.

"What? No. I doubt it. Can't be. Why do you think that?" Bat Flu is the worst of the worst. Infected bats release their infected droppings into a water source, which then becomes infected. The symptoms of Bat Flu are numerous and awful: severe stomach cramps; cold sweats and hot flashes in conjunction with high fever; mind-numbing headaches; relentless muscle aches; hallucinations; and in many cases, death. There was a mild outbreak at my school in Year Three.

Four kids, a dog, and one of their parents got the Flu. The only one that survived was the dog.

Tawni steps out of the water, leaving a trail of drips behind her. She picks up the flashlight and shines it across the pool. I follow the yellow light until it stops on the far wall, which is pockmarked with dozens of small caves. Bat caves. "That's why," she says.

I feel a surge of bile in my throat as I see piles of dark bat poo littered at the tunnel mouths. Each time the bats emerge from the caves, they will knock the piles into the water with the flap of their wings. Evidently, they're sleeping now—the caves are silent.

I choke down the bitter, acidic taste in my mouth and say, "But this is a key watering hole for an inter-Realm thoroughfare. It's even on the map." My words don't change anything. The water is likely contaminated. I don't want to be in denial. I just need to deal with what has happened as best I can. My mother always told me to "face the truth with grim determination and a smile on your face." I'm not sure about the smile. "Okay, let's assume it's contaminated. We need to vomit it out, Tawni. Now!"

Without watching to see what Tawni does, I stick two fingers down my throat, gagging immediately, the stomach fire rising so fast I can barely get my hand out of my mouth before I spew all over myself. I retch, gag, cough twice, spit as much of the vile liquid from my mouth as possible. At my feet, my own vomit is floating around my ankles. At my side, Tawni is throwing up, too.

Clenching my abs, I say, "We're both going to get very sick. But we'll get through it together."

"What do we do?" Tawni asks, her voice rising precariously high. Her lips are tight. I'm afraid she might lose it. Since I met her, Tawni has always been strong, even when her best friend was viciously murdered. But now she looks seriously freaked out. She must've seen firsthand what the Bat Flu can do to someone.

"Who do you know that had the Flu?" I ask, stepping out of the bile-choked water, Tawni flitting out next to me. We are still filthy, but there's not much we can do about it now.

Tawni's eyes flick to mine and then back to the water, to the bat droppings. "My cousin," she says.

"What happened?"

"She passed."

"That's not going to happen to us."

"It was awful."

"Tawni."

Her eyes dart back to mine and stick this time.

"We're going to be fine," I say. "Stay with me."

Tawni's steel-blue eyes get steelier, and then, after reaching a hardness level I'd never seen in them before, soften, returning to their soft blue. "Right. We'll be okay," she says, almost to herself.

I take the soap from Tawni and chuck it, along with the two canteens, across the pool. They clatter off the far wall and plunk beneath the surface.

"We should dry off with our dirty tunics and then chuck them away, too," I say.

Although it's kind of gross soaking up the water with our filthy old clothes, we both do it because we have to. It's the nature of things in our world. Out of necessity you have to do a

364

lot of things you don't want to do. I wonder if it was the same in the old world, before Armageddon, before Year Zero.

When we are dry and our old clothes have been thrown into the foul water, we each don one of the fresh tunics from our packs. It feels good—the simple act of putting on clean clothes. It's like a rebirth, a second chance, a new beginning. At least usually. This time neither of us wants to turn the page on our story. But like so many things in life, we have no choice.

"How far to the Star Realm?" I ask.

"We're in the Star Realm now, technically."

"But how far to the first subchapter? Subchapter 30, right?"

Tawni consults the map. "Yeah, first we'll hit subchapter 30. I'd say at least a twelve-hour hike if we move fast."

"We've got to make it in eight," I say. "Just in case we have the Flu. First symptoms will come fast, perhaps in three hours or so. Worse symptoms after six hours. The very worst at around eight hours. So we have to move fast."

"What about water?" Tawni asks. Water will be a problem. We had to get rid of our contaminated canteens. We are already dehydrated.

"Any more blue dots on that map of yours?"

Tawni scans the page. "None in this section of the tunnel. There are blue dots all over the place in subchapter 30, but nothing between here and there."

"We're just going to have to suck it up. Can you make it?" I don't know if I can, but I will do everything in my power. I don't want to die without at least trying to find my mom.

"I don't know," Tawni answers honestly. I nod absently. "If I don't make it, leave me and find your mom."

"I won't leave you," I say.

Tawni opens her mouth, presumably to argue, but then snaps it shut and nods. She remembers who she's dealing with. I'm not known for changing my mind.

"Let's go," I say, shouldering my pack.

Made in the USA
Lexington, KY
08 May 2014